ONE STEP
TOO FAR

ALSO BY LISA GARDNER

NOVELS

The Perfect Husband

The Other Daughter

The Third Victim

The Next Accident

The Survivors Club

The Killing Hour

Alone

Gone

Hide

Say Goodbye

The Neighbor

Live to Tell

Love You More

Catch Me

Touch & Go

Fear Nothing

Crash & Burn

Find Her

Right Behind You

Look for Me

Never Tell

When You See Me

Before She Disappeared

SHORT WORKS

The 7th Month

3 Truths and a Lie

The 4th Man

The Guy Who Died Twice

LISA GARDNER

ONE STEP TOO FAR

A NOVEL

DUTTON

DUTTON

an imprint of Penguin Random House LLC
penguinrandomhouse.com

Copyright © 2022 by Lisa Gardner, Inc.
Penguin supports copyright. Copyright fuels creativity, encourages diverse voices, promotes free speech, and creates a vibrant culture. Thank you for buying an authorized edition of this book and for complying with copyright laws by not reproducing, scanning, or distributing any part of it in any form without permission. You are supporting writers and allowing Penguin to continue to publish books for every reader.

DUTTON is a registered trademark and the D colophon is a trademark of Penguin Random House LLC.

LIBRARY OF CONGRESS CATALOGING-IN-PUBLICATION DATA
Names: Gardner, Lisa, author.
Title: One step too far : a novel / Lisa Gardner.
Description: [New York] : Dutton, [2022]
Identifiers: LCCN 2021050019 (print) | LCCN 2021050020 (ebook) |
ISBN 9780593185414 (hardcover) | ISBN 9780593185421 (ebook) |
ISBN 9780593471661 (export)
Subjects: LCGFT: Novels.
Classification: LCC PS3557.A7132 O54 2022 (print) |
LCC PS3557.A7132 (ebook) | DDC 813/.54—dc23/eng/20211015
LC record available at https://lccn.loc.gov/2021050019
LC ebook record available at https://lccn.loc.gov/2021050020

Printed in the United States of America
1st Printing

*In loving memory of Pierre O'Rourke,
talented writer and amazing friend to authors
everywhere. Somewhere in the great beyond,
I picture you finally locating your car in the airport
parking lot, and yes, I'm totally laughing with you.*

*Also, to Ruby. Beloved adopted dog, best friend,
and writing companion. Each day, you greeted
me with a little lick on the hand to say hello. And at
the end, you turned and gave me that same little
lick to say goodbye. Thank you, love, for saving me
when I needed it the most.*

ONE STEP
TOO FAR

CHAPTER 1

THE FIRST THREE MEN CAME stumbling into town shortly after ten
A.M., babbling of dark shapes and eerie screams and their missing buddy Scott and their other buddy Tim, who set out from their
campsite before dawn to get help.

"Bear, bear, bear," first guy moaned.

"Mountain lion!" second guy insisted.

Third guy vomited.

Maybe, maybe not, Marge Santi thought as she sidestepped the
spew of liquid. Marge situated the young men in a corner booth of
her diner, then got on the phone and summoned Nemeth. To be
polite, Marge also contacted Sheriff Jim Kelley, likeable guy, respected by the locals, but an officer with a whole county to tend and
the drive to prove it. For immediate action, Nemeth it was.

Nemeth, former Shoshone National Forest district ranger, now
local guide, knew what he was doing. First, he plied the three men
with coffee. To judge by the rank odor of fear and booze leaking out

of their pores, they didn't need anything else. Two cups later, he had most of the story.

Five guys set out into the woods for a bachelor party weekend. All friends since college, all with some experience camping, though the trio agreed future groom Tim was The Man. Had been back-country hiking with his father since he was six. He was the reason they were camping. The other four wouldn't have minded a golf weekend or quality time at a casino/resort. But for Tim, the woods were his happy place, so into the mountains they'd gone. Fully equipped, packs, tents, sleeping bags, two-burner propane camp stove, cans of beans and franks, and yeah, as much beer and Maker's Mark as five fit young men could carry. Which was to say, a lot. But they weren't total idiots. Again, Tim knew his shit and oversaw their packing himself.

They'd hiked in seven miles yesterday, looking for the perfect camping spot in one of the deep canyons, near a broad river. Once they found it, they unloaded packs, pitched tents, and popped open the first six-pack, leaving the other four to chill in the ice-cold water.

Dusk came fast this time of year. But all was good. They built up a fire, roasted hot dogs, and ate baked beans straight out of the can. Many fart jokes ensued.

More beer, followed by whiskey chasers. How much booze can five young healthy men drink? Plenty. But no place to be, no cars to drive, no nagging cell phones to answer given the lack of reception.

Just them and the starlit sky. They killed off the first bottle of Maker's Mark, started in on the second. Tim sat next to the fire and scratched away on a piece of paper. Working on his wedding vows, writing a letter to his beloved? They teased, but he refused to fess up.

Hour grew late. How late, no one knew and it hardly mattered. They finally turned in for the night, two men each in two tents, Tim, the future groom, in a single shell all by himself. One of his last nights on earth sleeping alone. Should enjoy it while he could, they teased.

Then . . .

A sharp keening wail. Crashing in the trees around them.

"Grizzly," Neil said now, sitting in the diner.

"Mountain lion," Josh insisted.

Miggy, short for Miguel, crawled out of the booth and vomited some more.

Maybe, maybe not, Nemeth thought. Marge got a mop.

At the camp, the men had burst from their tents, flashlights bobbing, nerves strung tight, trying to pinpoint the source of the disturbance. Build up the fire, Tim demanded. Make noise of their own. Double-check the food stash they'd strung up in the trees away from their campsite.

Which is why it took a few minutes, maybe as long as five or ten, before they realized their party of five had become four. Where the hell was Scott?

Miggy had been sharing his tent and Miggy had no idea.

"No . . . fucking idea," Miggy clarified for Nemeth, in between bouts of dry heaving.

Tim, future groom, got serious. Scott could've wandered off to pee. Scott could've just plain wandered off, drunk and disoriented. But given the cold temps, dangerous terrain, and carnivorous local wildlife, they needed to find him.

Arranging their group into two pairs, Tim directed the first duo to start searching north of the campfire, while the other would cover the woods to the south. Whoever found Scott first would blow their emergency signal whistle.

Except they didn't find him. Up and down the water, bush-whacking deeper and deeper into the forest. No Scott. But they did find trampled brush. Broken tree limbs. Possibly blood.

"Grizzly bear," Neil moaned.

"Mountain lion," Josh ventured.

"Fuck me," Miggy whispered.

That, Nemeth agreed with.

Four A.M., the fall air brutally crisp, the clear night relentlessly dark, Tim made the decision: They needed help, and given the total lack of cell reception, hiking back out was the only way to get it. As the most experienced—and sober—member of their party, he grabbed his pack, clicked on his trusty headlamp, and set out for civilization.

Neil, Josh, and Miggy huddled around the fire for another three hours, pounding water and working themselves into a terrified frenzy. First glimpse of daylight, they refilled their canteens and hit the trail. Left everything behind. Tents, sleeping bags, food. Young men, fit and now semi-sober, they were on a mission to get the hell out of there as fast as humanly possible.

Still tough going. They half ran, half stumbled their way up and down steep terrain, clambering over boulders, careening through brush, splashing across streams. Till they came to the trailhead and their rented ATVs. All five of them. Shouldn't there be only four?

Which is when they started to get worried about Tim.

ATVs to town. Town to diner. And now . . . help. Nemeth. Sheriff. Cavalry. Hunters with big guns. Any kind of assistance, all kinds of assistance. Help.

Nemeth unfolded a topographical map, had the men walk him through their journey. They knew their initial path, which, like a lot of backcountry trails, started out marked before hitting rugged, less traversed terrain. Definitely not for the faint of heart. But the men could guess where along the river they'd camped. From there, Nemeth ran his finger along various geological features, thinking, thinking, thinking. Marge worked the phone, brewed more coffee.

Being a mountain town, they had a local team of fifteen volunteer search and rescuers. Given the circumstances, however, this would be all hands on deck. Neighbors contacted neighbors, people started pouring in, and Nemeth did what he did best: organized the efforts.

First up, hasty team. He wanted his best searchers dispersed along key perimeter areas encircling the PLS—point last seen—of their two missing hikers. Taking into account the average distance a person could travel an hour in that terrain, Nemeth drew a massive ring around the site, identifying their prime search area. Hasty teams would hike, ATV, or horseback into various points along this ring, conducting a down-and-dirty search of the trail and surrounding areas as they swept toward the center. They'd look for the men, but also look for signs of human passage, which might provide additional data on where Tim the experienced hiker and Scott the drunk buddy could've gone.

Ramsey, a town of four thousand situated at the edge of the Popo Agie Wilderness, was filled with experienced outdoorspeople. The mountains were both a lifestyle and a professional calling. Nemeth was a veteran general working with expert foot soldiers.

Which made it very hard for the family to accept what happened next. The first eight hours of the search, when Scott turned up wandering blindly along the rocky banks of the river. Still clad in his long underwear, face covered in scratches, fingernails caked with dirt. Clearly disoriented and shell-shocked.

"Grizzly," Neil whispered.

"Mountain lion," Josh repeated.

"Shit . . ." Miggy moaned.

Even sobered up, Scott couldn't provide any details about where he'd been or what he'd done. He remembered drinking with his buddies around the campfire and teasing Tim for working on his wedding vows. Scott went to bed and . . . Daylight. Cold. So cold. Wandering in nothing but his stocking feet, till he found his way back to the river and followed it. Eventually, people appeared and a shrill whistle blew and now he was here and hey, where was Tim, anyway?

Timothy O'Day. Thirty-three years old, first member of his family to go to college, graduating from Oregon State University with a degree in mechanical engineering. Described by his family and friends as a regular MacGyver. Engaged to be married to Latisha Gibbons, whom he'd met three years ago through his college buddy Neil. Latisha hailed from Atlanta, worked in marketing, and spent her weekends in a state of perpetual motion, hiking, biking, skiing, every bit as crazy as her future husband.

Everyone said they looked beautiful together. The ultimate, modern-day L.L.Bean couple. They'd buy a house, adopt a Lab, and produce 2.2 gorgeous children to chase along trails, down mountains, across streams.

Theirs was to be a wonderful, magnificent life lived out loud.

Until hours stretched into days stretched into weeks.

Tim's parents arrived on-site. His father, Martin, driving from Oregon to Wyoming with his mountaineering equipment piled in the back. Marty was a lean, nut-brown professional carpenter and experienced outdoorsman ready to take up the charge. In contrast, Tim's mother, Patrice, appeared nearly translucent. Cancer survivor, the locals learned. Fifteen years ago, multiple bouts, barely made it.

Marge made it her mission to serve the woman coffee aboveboard and administer a little medicinal assistance on the down low.

Martin conferred with Nemeth and Sheriff Kelley, who'd taken charge of the search efforts. In the beginning, Martin would nod, approve, express his gratitude. By day five, he questioned and stewed. Day seven he headed into the woods himself, snarling under his breath when both Nemeth and Sheriff Kelley tried to hold him back.

The hasty teams stopped being hasty. Search efforts slowed, grew more methodical, no longer hoping for an easy victory, but now settling in to scour the wilderness foot by foot, trail by trail, grid by grid. Choppers scanned with infrared. Air-scenting dogs tracked areas of interest. Couple of psychics called in with hot tips, most involving flowing rivers or dark caves.

More volunteers showed up. The National Guard arrived to assist. Until twenty-three long, arduous, exhausting days later, as the temperatures plummeted and snow blanketed the upper elevations . . .

The searchers faded back to their real lives. The canine teams went home. The choppers were redirected to new missions. And only family and friends remained.

Martin O'Day fought the good fight the longest. He had a lifetime of experience and the advantage of being the one who'd trained his son. He headed back into the mountains, expedition after expedition, while Patrice held press conferences with her future daughter-in-law by her side. Twin advertisements for grief and desperation. The college friends, Neil, Josh, Miggy, and Scott, did their best to assist while having to accommodate the demands of jobs, family, obligations of their own.

Martin O'Day searched for his son. Then he searched for signs of his son. And then he searched for his son's body.

"Grizzly bear," Neil whispered.

"Mountain lion," Josh argued.

"Goddammit," Miggy said.

As for the real answer, the woods never said. Seasons turned into years and Timothy O'Day became one more missing hiker, vanished without a trace.

HERE ARE THINGS most folks don't know: At least sixteen hundred people, if not many more times that number, remain missing on national public lands. Hikers, day-trippers, children on family camping trips. One moment they were with us, the next they're gone.

There's no national database to track such cases. No centralized training for search and rescue or, in many cases, even clear jurisdictional lines to identify who's in charge of such operations. There's also little in the way of designated funding. A large-scale search effort can cost upwards of three hundred thousand dollars a day. For many county sheriffs, that's their annual budget.

Meaning when the volunteers go away, so do rescue efforts. Leaving behind a family with little hope and no closure. Most will continue on their own for as long as they can. Some, such as Martin O'Day, continue the hunt every year, assisted by friends, funded by online campaigns, and advised by various experts.

According to the article I'm reading in a small, local paper, Martin's been at it for five years. This August will be his final attempt. His wife, Patrice, is now dying from the same cancer that tried to kill her before. She wants to see her son one last time. She wants her body to be buried next to his.

I sit in a diner not so dissimilar to the one Tim O'Day's hiking buddies must've rushed into the morning after. I've spent the past twelve hours on a bus and am now catching my breath, somewhere west of Cheyenne and south of Jackson, Wyoming. I don't particularly know, and I'm enjoying a sense of freedom—life on the road—as I read the article again, then again. Something about the story has sunk into my skin, refusing to let go.

My name is Frankie Elkin and finding missing people is what I do. When the police have given up, when the public no longer remembers, when the media has never bothered to care, I start looking. For no money, no recognition, and most of the time, with no help.

I have no professional training. I'm not a former detective or registered PI or ex-anything special. I'm only me. An average, middle-aged white woman, short on belongings, long on regret. I tried real life once. There was a house, a job, even a man who loved me enough to hold my hand as I fought my way to sober.

In the end, the walls closed in; the relentless sameness drowned me. And the man who loved me . . .

One day, a woman in my AA meeting talked about her daughter who'd disappeared and the police's lack of interest in finding a young woman with a troubled past. I became intrigued, started asking questions, and the next thing I knew, I'd found the daughter. Unfortunately, the daughter's fucked-up boyfriend had chosen to blow off her head and abandon her body in a crack house rather than let her go. But despite the case not having a happy ending, or maybe because of that, one search became another, which became another.

Ten years later, this is now my life. I travel from place to place, armed with only my good intentions. Currently, I've been traveling by bus to Idaho to take up the case of Eugene Santiago, an eight-year-old boy now missing sixteen months. I read about Eugene's disappearance in one of the various online cold case forums I frequent. Something about his soulful dark eyes, his very serious smile. I don't always know why I choose the cases I do. There are so many of them out there. But I spot a headline, I read an article, and then I just know.

Kind of like now, I think, setting down the local paper. I haven't done a woodland search in forever. Mostly I work small rural communities or dense urban neighborhoods. I gravitate more toward kids than adults, minorities more than Caucasians. But my mission is to help the underserved, and as the families of those sixteen hundred people vanished in public parks will tell you, they are so underserved.

Mostly, I keep thinking of Timothy O'Day's mother, who just wants to be buried next to her son.

Eugene Santiago has been missing for nearly a year and a half. A few more weeks won't matter. And while there may be no chance of finding Timothy O'Day alive, I know from experience that finally bringing home a body still makes a difference.

I pick up the bus schedule and plot my new destination.

CHAPTER 2

BEING POOR REQUIRES PATIENCE. I don't own a car or have the kind of bank account that can allow me a rental to get to the small town of Ramsey, Wyoming. Which means taking a bus from point A to B to C. Bus stops are more varied than many people realize. As in, there might be a beautiful mass transit station complete with restrooms and fast food. Or there can be this: a gas station mini-mart sitting completely alone off the side of the road.

The bus moves on and I stay behind, trying to get my bearings. It's early afternoon. Above me, the sky is a shade of rich blue I associate with postcards and other people's lives. This rural route is a dark gray strip rippling between the distant towering mountains behind me and the incredibly close towering mountains ahead of me.

I've never been to Wyoming, so far I love everything about it. The smell of warm earth and sun-dried grass. The sound of country music pouring out of the store's speakers. The number of trucks and cattle haulers rumbling by.

I feel simultaneously excited by the vast unknown and terrified. Just because I don't like to be tied down doesn't mean I enjoy feeling untethered.

I wander into the small, dusty mini-mart. An older man with a faded red ball cap and bushy brown whiskers looks up from behind the register. He gives me a short nod followed by a hard stare, clearly recognizing a stranger when he sees one. I'm used to it by now. I'm never the local, always just an outsider, passing through.

I splurge on a candy bar and a bottle of water, then plant myself in front of a rack of brochures advertising local attractions. The man goes back to his magazine. Nothing to see here.

Normally, I plan my targets well in advance. Research the area while skimming the classifieds for local employment and potential housing options. But now my last-minute impulse has me flying blind. I can't decide if this is incredibly daring or unbelievably stupid. Many of my decisions feel that way.

Most people would pull out their smartphones and Google away. Unfortunately, my job—obsessively locating missing people—doesn't pay at all, while my side hustle—bartending part-time at the location of the moment—doesn't pay well. The result is that my "smart" phone is an old flip phone with a limited data plan. On a good day, it might receive a text. Google would mostly reduce it to a lump of melted microchips.

Likewise, I don't own a computer or even a tablet. I'd love the luxury, but I don't just lead a nomadic lifestyle, I lead a high-risk one. As in, many of the places I frequent are known for their high crime rates and opposition to outsiders. I've had rental units broken into, property vandalized; I've had good-ol'-boy cops confront me with shotguns and grieving relatives attack me with broken beer bottles.

I originally walked away from material possessions because I felt the weight of them dragging me down. Now I don't own anything I can't afford to lose because I don't want to die one day trying to protect something I never should've cared about in the first place.

If I were near a major town, I'd utilize an internet café or public library to do my homework. But given that I'm currently stranded at a gas station in the middle of Wyoming, travel brochures it is.

I see pictures of bighorn sheep, craggy mountains, and deep blue lakes. I can attempt horseback riding, scale rock formations, and take up hunting and fishing. There are warnings about bears— *Be Bear Aware!*—maps of local trails, and orders not to pick wildflowers. After the past ten months, which I spent in an inner-city neighborhood in Boston, followed by a sad housing project near Memphis, the photos of the great outdoors make me giddy.

Though once again, that faint fissure of alarm. I've done wildland searches, but never in any place as rugged as these mountains. I've walked the woods, but I don't know anything about grizzly bears. While too many of my searches have led to sad discoveries, I've never set out explicitly to find a corpse.

I think of Patrice O'Day, who just wants to be buried next to her son.

"Why do everyone's problems have to be your problem?" Paul had griped at me. "What will it take before you realize that you're the one who matters. You, Frankie. I love *you*."

I don't talk to Paul anymore. But on occasion, I still call his widow.

I've just finished my deep dive into local intel when a beat-up Chevy truck pulls up to a gas pump. The back is piled high with straw bales, the lower sides sprayed liberally with mud. A woman in worn jeans, a sleeveless T-shirt, and a fawn-colored cowboy hat climbs out.

Perfect.

I give a parting nod to the silent store attendant, then step outside to negotiate my next mode of transportation.

I GREW UP in a small town in Northern California. My father was the world's most affable drunk, my mother the world's angriest enabler. He drank, she worked. He drank more, she worked more.

Which is to say, neither of them spared much thought for me. I ran around wild in the days before we worried about stranger danger and what kind of lone men lingered at playgrounds. Like most kids, I owned a secondhand bike with a rusty frame and a duct-taped banana seat. I rode it anywhere and everywhere. Though of course, there's only so far a girl on a bike can go. Which meant if I or the other kids wanted to make it to the five-and-dime to spend our spare change on two-cent Jolly Ranchers, we hitchhiked. Stood along the main thoroughfare and stuck out our thumbs.

Sometimes there might be six of us, piling on top of one another in the back of whichever vehicle took pity on us. Sometimes it might be me and my best friend, Sophie. Sometimes it was just me, because my dad was already passed out and my mom hours from getting home—and even back then, I had problems staying put.

I never worried about the safety of climbing into a random person's vehicle; it's just what we did.

These days, most parents would advise their kids differently, and yet, for many rural areas, hitchhiking remains a way of life. Mass transit only passes through major towns. Taxis, Uber, car rentals—those are amenities for city folks.

The town of Ramsey is thirteen miles from this final bus stop. A bit far to walk in the bright August sun, let alone the relentlessly dry heat. So copping a ride it is.

I approach the woman pumping gas. She glances up, nods once in greeting. She looks around my age, with sun-darkened skin and lean, muscled arms. Horsewoman for sure, I can tell by the way she's standing. I instantly like her, but this is one of my few superpowers. In my own loner-like way, I'm actually a people person.

Whether other people like me, however, is always an interesting question.

Now I keep it simple. "I'm Frankie Elkin. I'm looking to get to Ramsey. If you're headed in that direction, I'm hoping I might catch a ride."

The woman eyes me, my rolling suitcase, my battered brown leather satchel. I wonder what she sees, or maybe doesn't see. I'm not old. I'm not young. I'm not pretty. I'm not horrifying. I'm not from here, but then I'm not from anywhere.

Pump clicks off. She replaces the nozzle, goes to work on the gas cap.

"I have gas money," I offer, then try to remember how much cash I have jammed in my front pocket. I'm down to my last hundred and twelve bucks. It's okay, I've survived on less.

"Who are you?" the woman asks.

"Frankie—"

"No. *Who* are you?"

"Technically, I'm a professional bartender."

"Why Ramsey?"

"Because I also look for missing persons, and I'm interested in the Timothy O'Day case."

"You're a reporter?"

"Nope. Just a person who looks for other people." I shrug. "There's more demand for someone like me than you might suspect."

"That your gear?"

"Yes."

"Where's your pack? Hiking boots? Camping gear?"

I glance down at my roll-aboard suitcase, bruised from so many towns, miles, bus rides. The horsewoman raises a good point. No way I can take luggage on a hike into the mountains. So there might be a few flaws with my impulsive decision. That's never stopped me before.

"I'll figure it out."

The woman leans against her truck, folding her arms across her chest. She eyes me up and down. She hasn't said no, which in my world is as good as a yes, but requires more patience.

"How do I know you're not some crazy serial killer?" she asks at last.

"Because what are the odds of there being two crazy serial killers in the same vehicle?"

It's an old joke, but the punch line earns me a smile. Beneath the brim of the woman's Stetson, the corners of her blue eyes crinkle. She wears the dust, flecks of straw, and faint odor of horse manure well.

What if I got a job as a ranch hand? I'm tempted till I take a closer look at the rippling muscles on her arms, compared to my own scrawny sticks. I'm a very resourceful person. I've talked myself out of a fair amount of trouble. But no, I'm not winning any arm-wrestling contests anytime soon.

"All right," she says abruptly. "Name's Lisa Rowell. I'll take you to Ramsey. Climb on board."

I don't hesitate but scramble around the ancient truck and load up, luggage at my feet, leather satchel at my side.

"Nice to meet you, Lisa."

Just like that, I'm on the road again.

———

"DO YOU LIVE around here?" I ask her once we've headed out. The windows on both sides of the cab are rolled down, the wind streaming through my hair. I'm back to the happy side of my rash decision.

"Most of my life. Own a ranch near Ramsey."

"Horses?"

"Horses, cattle, a few other strays."

"Human or beast?"

I earn another flashing smile. "Bit of both, I suppose."

"Were you involved in the search for Tim O'Day?"

She nods shortly. "When he and his friend first went missing. Most of the locals helped out. I provided some of the horses for the search party."

"Do the locals have any theories?"

"Nature demands respect."

"Sounds like Timothy was respectful. Experienced. Well equipped."

She shrugs.

"Is it the booze?" I ask. "That he and his buddies hiked into a remote wilderness area, then pickled their brains with beer and whiskey?"

"What do you think the rest of us did during high school?"

Fair enough. "What do you think about wildlife? Grizzly bear? Mountain lion?"

"Possible."

"But not probable?"

"I don't head into the mountains without my rifle. There's a reason for that. But in all my years . . . I've never actually seen a grizzly. Black bears, yes, but they're not a problem. Besides, animals aren't the neatest eaters."

"In other words, if a grizzly or mountain lion had attacked Tim, there'd be more evidence. I thought the guys said they found blood, broken tree limbs, when they were looking for Scott."

"Search party found an area of disturbance, but no blood. Also, Tim was around for that part, not to mention Scott was found safe and sound afterwards."

"Maybe the disturbance was from an animal who'd wandered nearby, tempted by the scent of food. Maybe the fire kept it at bay, though." I'm thinking out loud. Bullshitting, really. Another one of my superpowers. "But then, when Tim hiked out, away from the safety of the fire . . ."

Rowell snorts. "You sound like the Bigfoot hunter."

"There's a Bigfoot hunter?"

"I thought you were part of the search party."

"I will be. Once I meet them and work my charm."

"Who are you again?"

"Trust me, the more I answer that question, the less anyone believes me. A Bigfoot hunter? Seriously?"

"From the North American Bigfoot Society."

This niggles at the back of my mind. I should know this. "Does Martin O'Day seriously believe Bigfoot took his son?"

"You'd have to ask him that question."

"And you?"

I'm expecting a sardonic retort, or even an eye roll. So Lisa's hesitation catches me off guard.

"What?" I finally prod.

"You say you find missing persons?"

"Yes."

"Then are you looking for all of them?"

"All of them . . . in the country?"

Lisa glances at me. "All of them who've gone missing in the

Popo Agie Wilderness. There's more than just some drunk groom. At least five people in the past twenty years."

I realize again how much I don't know. "Is that a lot for an area this size?"

"To never be seen again? It's not a little, that's for sure."

"Bigfoot?" I can't help myself.

Again the pause, followed by a shake of her head. "Or something. But take it from a local, you want to be damn careful headed into those woods."

CHAPTER 3

THE TOWN OF RAMSEY, WYOMING, looks like an Old West movie set transported to the dusty foothills of very real mountains. The picturesque Main Street is lined on both sides by wooden storefronts whose jutting rooflines appear like puzzle pieces against the deep-blue sky. I spot a yellow-painted general store nestled shoulder to shoulder with a deep-green five-and-dime and a faded red saloon. Coffee shop, feed store, touristy T-shirt depot, leather goods, and of course a storefront advertising all things cowboy.

On a bright, sunny August afternoon, the sidewalks are jammed with people. Some clearly tourists, families in shorts and flip-flops. Some probably locals, given their denim and cowboy boots. Mostly white, many strolling hand in hand, smiling and carefree.

In my line of work, it's been a long time since I've been surrounded by a sea of Caucasians. It's interesting to me, then, that I feel as self-conscious here as I do in a Haitian community in Boston or a predominantly Black housing project in Memphis. These people with their shiny lives and fashion-forward clothes and FOMO vacations . . . I don't know how to identify with them.

I wonder sometimes if there's anyplace that would feel like home to me. I started out playing the outsider. Now I simply am one.

I drum my empty water bottle against my leg restlessly.

"Make sure you drink plenty of fluids," Rowell comments. "Summers are arid, with afternoons prone to scattered thunderstorms. Don't know what you got in that bag, but you're gonna want layers. Temperatures can swing fifty degrees in a day, and nights are damn cold, even this time of year."

I nod. I travel light, meaning my roll-along suitcase contains just the basics: three pairs of pants and six shirts, all interchangeable. For shoes, I have a pair of sneaks and a pair of sturdy brown boots. I also have pj's—really men's boxers and Paul's old T-shirt—plus seven days' worth of socks and underwear.

My boots will work for hiking. The socks are definitely too thin. And I have only one coat, a medium-weight green army jacket. In the winter months, I add a hat, gloves, and scarf for warmth. I hadn't thought to make those purchases yet, given that it's August.

I should stay here, I think, to work and build up money if nothing else. But maybe, also, I'm tired. That kind of exhaustion that never really goes away. I think of Paul, as I often do when the weight of the years catches up with me.

But I also think of a Boston detective and former Marine, Dan Lotham, the whisper of his hands across my body. I think of a silent bar owner, as steady as his name, Stoney. And Piper, the homicidal cat, and an energetic fry cook and a sixteen-year-old Haitian girl, Angelique, the first and only person I've ever found alive.

My thoughts scatter and spin. I feel both keyed up and totally spent. And as is my nature, I think how much I'd like a drink right now. Maybe an ice-cold beer to quench my dry throat. Or a tangy margarita where the liquid warmth of tequila is followed by the refreshing bite of lime. A rum and Coke. A gin and tonic. I was never picky about my booze. I just wanted lots of it. Till my nerves dulled and my racing brain became pickled and I didn't have to think so hard because I no longer cared.

As fast as I feel the impulse, I push it away. My sobriety is one of my only accomplishments over the past ten years. I can't afford to give it up now.

Lisa slows the truck. We've reached the far edge of town, where the pretty buildings end and the more commercial structures begin. A squat budget motel. A huge outdoor gear and apparel shop. And across from the motel, a diner. *The* diner, I realize. Where Tim O'Day's groomsmen arrived that first morning five years ago, babbling about bears and mountain lions and things that go bump in the night.

"I'll get out here," I tell Lisa as she stops at the traffic light near the diner.

"You're sure?"

"Yes."

"Good luck," she tells me. Then, when I reach into my pocket for the promised gas money: "Don't worry about it. I was driving through town anyway."

I smile in gratitude. She pulls away, leaving me outside the corner diner with my rolling luggage in one hand, my leather satchel in the other.

No time for hesitating. I head through the doors.

THE DINER SMELLS of coffee, bacon grease, and grilled hamburgers. Immediately my stomach growls. I had a stale Danish for breakfast, a chocolate bar for lunch. I could use food. As well as hiking gear, a night's lodging, and a fountain of youth.

It's nearly three P.M. now. According to the sign, that's fifteen minutes before closing, which would explain the nearly empty interior and the lone white-aproned fry cook scraping at the griddle.

At the rear of the diner, however, I spy a group of eight people sprawled across two booths, deep in conversation over an open map, with a collection of dirty lunch plates pushed to the side. Martin O'Day and his assembled search party. Has to be. They're all outfitted in serious outdoor wear, scuffed hiking boots, cargo pants, and flannel. On first glance they look rugged, healthy, and ready to go.

I glance down at my decidedly non-mountaineering ensemble of tennis shoes, faded jeans, and a threadbare T-shirt. At least I'm covered in a film of travel dust and sweat. It gives me an air of authenticity as I roll my suitcase toward the group.

The man sitting in the middle is doing most of the talking. He looks to be mid-fifties, with the whip-lean build of a person always on the move. Across from him sits an older gentleman with steel-gray hair and equally weathered features. A bushy-bearded, red-headed male and a dark-haired female are to their left, four younger men to the right. Up close, I spy a ninth member of the party: a yellow Lab mix wearing a bright orange scarf, sprawled under the table, head on paws.

The dog looks up at my approach. Thumps its tail. The lone woman, a stunningly gorgeous Latina with almond skin and thickly lashed dark eyes, glances in my direction; I'm guessing the dog is hers.

I have a sense of déjà vu. Three years ago, different woods: a missing six-year-old boy who'd been playing tag with his eight-year-old brother around their campsite before he disappeared. Me, tramping through those woods with fellow volunteers day after day. Still searching, weeks later, long after all hope of recovering the child alive was gone. Because having started the hunt, we couldn't give it up. We had to seek. We had to find.

A family has to know.

I remember the mom's scream when news of the discovery reached her. I remember the father, a guy in his twenties, face ashen, voice thick as he shook the hands of all the volunteers and thanked us for bringing his little boy home. As if anyone could be grateful to have their child back for a proper burial. And yet, you can be. You absolutely can be.

I understand the woman's role now. I know what her Lab mix does. Cadaver dog. Because five years later, Timothy O'Day's bones are all that will be left.

Why do I do what I do? Searching for the missing long after hope is lost. Town to town. Heartbreak to heartbreak.

At any given time, hundreds of thousands of people have disappeared. Some left of their own volition. Some ran into trouble. And some, given the circumstances of their birth, never stood a chance.

For me, the question isn't why have I dedicated my life to this? The question is why hasn't everyone? So many of our children, who deserve to come home. Loved ones who need to know what happened to their family member. Communities forever haunted by what might have happened, paired with what could've been.

I know who I am. I know why I do what I do. It's the rest of the world that's confusing to me.

Now I approach. The man leading the discussion finally looks up. He has hazel eyes to go with his thinning dark hair.

"Martin O'Day?" I ask, plopping down on the closest counter stool. This is it. I am both excited and nervous. Determined and fearful. It's always like this.

I stick out my hand. "My name is Frankie Elkin," I state. "I specialize in working missing persons cold cases. And I'd like to help bring your son home."

AN OLDER WOMAN clad in a white apron comes bustling out, gray-shot hair pulled up in a pile of curls, wiry build speaking of a life-time on the move. I recognize her immediately from her photo in the paper: Marge Santi, owner of the diner and participant in the main event. She frowns at me, then looks askance to the table, as if I might be bothering them. Protective, then. Five years later, I wonder how many of the locals feel the same: This is their tragedy; outsiders need not apply.

No one in the group speaks right away. Martin O'Day, the clear leader, glances at my travel garb, rolly luggage. He scowls.

"I'm not taking questions at this time," he says.

"I'm not a reporter."

"I'm still not taking questions."

The older man with the cap of thick silver hair has twisted around to regard me. Gotta be Nemeth, the legendary local guide. He gives me an assessing glance, then glances up at Marge.

"We're good," he says, clearly speaking one local to another.

Marge gives me the side-eye, clearly less convinced. But when Nemeth continues to be unconcerned, she finally stacks up a pile of dirty dishes along one arm, then disappears.

I notice the four younger men remain disconnected from the entire exchange—present but distant. They must be the bachelor party buddies, given the palpable weight of their collective guilt. That left the gorgeous female dog handler and the massive, red-bearded male for me to sort out.

I peg Bushy Beard as the North American Sasquatch hunter,

though I'm cheating a little. Add body hair, and Bushy Beard could *be* the Sasquatch. An interesting example of owners matching their pets.

So this is the dream team. An experienced local, a grieving father, four guilt-stricken friends, a search-dog handler, and a Bigfoot hunter. Interesting combination.

"I have experience in woodland searches," I volunteer now.

"No, thank you." Martin O'Day returns his focus to the map, tapping the tabletop pointedly. Just like that, I've been dismissed. Not the first time. I'm an unknown variable. People don't care for unknown variables.

I start my case with the least judgmental member of the group. I slide off the stool, squat down, and stick out my hand toward the yellow Lab. The dog, not currently garbed in its working vest, gets up and crosses to me. The dog isn't leashed, but apparently no one—including diner owner Marge—cares.

"Name?" I ask, scratching the dog's ears.

I was right; the gorgeous Latina is the dog handler. She answers immediately: "Daisy."

"You named a cadaver dog Daisy?"

The fact that I recognize Daisy's role earns me a longer assessment from the exotic beauty, and a frown from Martin O'Day, who clearly wants to get back to the business at hand.

"Daisy is a rescue from the Philippines," the woman provides. "My partner and I started feeding her scraps while we were working a mudslide there with our professional canine crew. We ended up bringing her home to be a pet. But she gravitated toward training immediately. Next thing we knew, she'd outpaced our official roster of Belgian Malinois. Her problem-solving skills are second to none."

"Your name?"

"Luciana. Luciana Rojas."

I flash her a smile, then turn my attention to the enormous redheaded male. Want to know a trick for dealing with unfriendly alphas such as Martin O'Day? Don't deal with them. Ignore them completely. Ultimate power play.

"You're from the North American Bigfoot Society," I address Bushy Beard.

"Bob," he provides cheerfully, ignoring Martin O'Day's warning grumble.

It clicks then, what I'd been trying to remember earlier: "Your organization has the most complete picture of missing persons on national public lands," I burst out. "You guys know more about what's going on in the woods than even the authorities do."

I'm not making this up. If your loved one goes missing in the wilderness, the best data on potentially related cases comes from Bigfoot hunters, not the federal government. The world works in mysterious ways.

Then the second piece of the puzzle falls into place.

"Hang on. You're BFBob, aren't you? In the missing persons forums. Bigfoot Bob. You're working on the North American Project, mapping all the disappearances in this hemisphere. So nice to meet you!"

I rise to standing as Bigfoot Bob's eyes widen in recognition.

"Wait. Frankie Elkin? As in FElkinFinds?

I nod vigorously, pleased to meet a fellow amateur searcher in person. "You're conducting an operation in Wyoming? I thought the latest Sasquatch theories were focused on the Pacific Northwest. You'd been working the Olympic Peninsula."

"If you don't know where a creature is, then you don't know where it isn't. Plus, this search is"—Bob hesitates, glances at Martin—"in an area of particular interest."

I get it. The other missing hikers Lisa Rowell mentioned. Which would show up on the Bigfoot Society's national map as a cluster of red flags. A hot zone missed by the official government types, but credible fodder in the fringe community where Bob and I live.

"We need to get back to work," Martin interjects sharply.

"Just a sec, Marty." Bob turns to the team leader. "Frankie here is the real deal. We know each other from online. She doesn't just work cold cases; she solves them. Like dozens of them."

Closer to sixteen, but who am I to argue?

Martin doesn't seem to know what to make of that statement. He has his plan, probably months in the making. Viewing it as a series of steps and logistics, versus a mission to bring home his son's body, is how he's getting the job done. Now here I am, messing with his tenuous hold on sanity.

I understand. All of my missions start with this moment—coming out of nowhere, ripping the Band-Aid off a family's wound and hoping it doesn't lead to arterial spray.

At the other end of the table, Tim's college friends continue to ignore the interaction, which I find fascinating. They are a group within the group. A separate pod of agitation and grief. One of them, a pale blond, is downing copious amounts of coffee, his hand trembling so hard he can barely bring the mug to his mouth. The friend closest to him whispers something in the guy's ear. "Easy, now," would be my guess.

"You have search and rescue experience?" Nemeth speaks up for the first time. His tone is doubtful as he takes in my appearance. I don't blame him.

"I've assisted with line searches. And I've worked with dog teams." I nod toward Luciana. Daisy has returned to her place under the table, leaning her square head against Luciana's knees and sighing blissfully as her human scratches her neck.

"Got a pack? Camping gear?" Nemeth gestures to my luggage.

"This is a backcountry expedition. You need to be experienced, know what you're doing."

"I can rent equipment." Assuming it doesn't cost more than a hundred and twelve bucks.

"Why?" Martin this time. He sounds less belligerent, more tired. "We don't know you. You're clearly not prepared. We don't have time for this. We're headed out first thing tomorrow."

"I'm here to help. I read about your son. I read about your wife."

A spasm of grief across Martin's face.

"I'm here to help," I repeat. "I have experience. I'm good at what I do."

"She's good at what she does," Bob repeats.

"Sorry." Nemeth this time, clearly not convinced of my bona fides. "Gotta have permission for these kinds of expeditions, and our permit only covers eight."

"You'll still be a party of eight," I say.

Martin looks around. "There's eight here, which makes you number nine."

"He's not going to make it." I jerk my head toward the shaky blond.

"Josh," one of the bachelor buddies exclaims sharply as Josh's hand jerks violently and dumps coffee on the table.

"Shit. Josh."

Three men, leaping up as hot brew hits their laps.

"What's wrong? Man, you're burning up!"

Josh remains sitting, staring at the spilled coffee as if he can't get it to compute. His face is flushed, covered in sweat. His whole body is now trembling.

"He's sick," one of his friends says. "I think he has the flu."

"He doesn't have the flu." I don't have to be a recovering alcoholic to recognize the DTs.

Martin sighs heavily, exchanges a look with Nemeth. So they both knew about Josh's drinking. Which he must have recently sworn off in order to assist with the final attempt to bring his friend home.

Except Josh hadn't been drinking a little heavily before this. By the looks of things, he'd been a hard-core drunk, now entering the first stage of detox.

"I can help," I repeat to Marty. "I can use Josh's gear. I won't slow you down. I promise."

"Shit!" Fresh exclamation as Josh now slumps to the side, then slowly slides onto the floor.

Martin doesn't say a word. Just closes his eyes.

Nemeth does the honors. He turns toward me. "Guess you're in. Goddammit."

CHAPTER 4

"CAN YOU SHOOT A GUN?"

"God no. I rely on my charm."

"And when a bear charges?"

"Um, run faster than the next person?"

Nemeth glances at my scrawny form, as I observe his sinewy build. He looks like he's been hewn from the mountains themselves, a blend of rippling tree limbs and hard granite formations. He's average height, around five ten, but there's not an ounce of fat on him. I didn't look that good in my twenties and certainly can't imagine being that fit in my late sixties, early seventies. Nemeth may be my new hero. Though I kind of want to toss a brownie at him just to see what he'll do.

"Last time I had a conversation this stupid was with an arrogant ass by the name of Bobby Monfort. Moved here from back east, swearing he'd grown up in the mountains and there was nothing he couldn't handle. We tried to warn him these woods were different, but he set off on a seven-day hike anyway. Know what happened to Bobby Monfort?"

"Um, he lived a long and happy life?" I try.

"We removed him from the woods in pieces. Took weeks to find all of him. Looks like he was originally attacked by a grizzly. But then the racoons had a go at it, as well as the scavenger birds, et cetera. We're talking skull picked clean, bones cracked open for their marrow, fingers and toes chewed down to nubs."

I know he's being purposely graphic just to scare me. Doesn't mean it's not working. "I'll carry bear repellent," I amend.

Nemeth rolls his eyes. He and I are in the college friends' room at the motel across the street from the diner. The three still standing have left with Martin to take detoxing Josh to the closest hospital, which apparently is an hour away. In the meantime, Nemeth is bringing me up to speed, including helping me pillage Josh's supplies. I'm not sure what Bob the Bigfoot hunter and Luciana the dog handler are doing, but Bob didn't look too sad about having some time alone with a beautiful woman. Or he's really into yellow Labs.

"Stand up," Nemeth orders.

I stand up. He hooks Josh's metal-framed pack around my right shoulder, then my left. He lets go. I stagger slightly. Just manage not to tip over backward.

Nemeth regards me with his glacier-blue eyes. I haven't fooled him for a minute.

"Just needs some adjustment," I tell him.

Another long-suffering sigh. Seriously, the man could use some chocolate.

He takes the pack off, sits across from me on one of the two queen-sized beds.

"I'm guiding this team," he states. "Their safety, your safety, is my responsibility. So you might as well start confessing now, because

I'm not taking you into the woods like this. Woodland searches, my ass."

"I have done some! More than one."

"Two?"

"Possibly."

That look again. I have a feeling Nemeth has dealt with some stupid people in his time, and not just as a professional guide. Good news: My own idiocy is at no risk of breaking him.

"I walk," I offer up. "Everywhere. All the time. I don't own a car and have spent the past ten years in areas where mass transit only gets you so far."

"Sidewalks don't equal mountains."

"I'm fit. I won't slow you down. Better yet, I'm sober. Going on ten years. That puts me ahead of Josh, and you were willing to take *him*."

"*Marty* was willing to take him. I voiced my concerns. Show me your footwear. I can get a pack better fitted to your frame and lighten the load to accommodate the fact you're what—a hundred pounds soaking wet?"

"A hundred and five!" Maybe.

"Boots are everything on a seven-day trek. You need ankle support and decent tread for where we're headed."

His voice is so grim, I hastily unzip my bag and produce my lone pair of boots. They're battered on the outside, somewhere between fashion footwear and Nemeth's rugged pair. I find myself holding my breath. I've never had my shoes judged before. I feel nervous on their behalf.

Nemeth lifts the pair, turning them over to inspect the heavy soles, testing out the sides for durability, support, something. He frowns, hands them back to me. "You wear these for long periods of time?'

"I've spent days in them. They fit well, never blister."

Those seem to be the magic words. "Fine. They'll do."

We move on to the contents of Josh's enormous pack. Attached to the outside is a rolled foam pad secured with bungee cords, then a long nylon drawstring bag with the mouth pulled tight. I feel the contents with my fingers, identifying the shape of thin rods and squishy fabric.

"Tent," I declare triumphantly.

"Do you want a prize?"

"Maybe."

I check out the water bottles and a dangling red emergency whistle—something I carry in urban environments. Moving on to the front zippered pocket, I discover a first aid kit, plus a separate blister kit with sheets of moleskin. Snacks—protein bars, granola, mini peanut butter cups. At least Josh has taste. Then comes a whole host of miscellaneous supplies—waterproof matches, Bic lighter, utility knife, headlamp, flashlight, water filtration system. Finally, I pull out a sandwich bag with what appear to be greasy cotton balls.

"Cotton balls dipped in Vaseline," Nemeth says. "Preferred fire starter for most."

I nod as if I knew that. Now I am nervous. Have I bitten off more than I can chew? It's hard to know. I'm always out of my league. Always someplace new where I don't know where I'm going or what I'm doing. All these years later, I'm comfortable with being uncomfortable.

I don't want to interfere with Martin's final effort to bring home his son, however. Nemeth may be a hard-ass, but he's also correct. If I'm going to join this search, I need to pull my own weight.

I switch gears as I open up the hooded cover of the giant bright yellow pack to reveal a treasure trove of clothes.

"What do you think of Martin?" I ask Nemeth as I pull out pair after pair of heavy wool socks. These, combined with my own boots, will get the job done. Next, I pull out two jackets, one thin and windproof, one lined and waterproof. They'll be big on me, but beggars can't be choosers.

Watching me from his perch on the other bed, Nemeth shrugs. "What do you care?"

"Because I do. Because I head off into the woods with complete strangers to retrieve their loved ones."

"Obsessively butt into other people's business, you mean?"

"Exactly."

"What do you want?" Nemeth pushes, his tone skeptical. I'm used to it. I stop digging around in the bright yellow pack to look him in the eye.

"Same thing you and Martin want. To bring Tim home. To bring a family closure. To . . ." I hesitate slightly, then add with a small shrug, "To heal someone else's wounds because I don't know how to heal my own."

"How many times have you done this before?"

"Sixteen."

"But not search and rescue?"

"Cold cases. All over the country. Tribal lands, inner cities, small towns. You have no idea the number of people who've gone missing that no one is even looking for."

"How do you hear about them?"

"The news, which is what brought me here. Or online forums, such as the one where I met Bob. There are entire websites dedicated to bringing attention to such cases."

"You don't know any of these victims? Have any personal connection to the families?"

"You never met Timothy O'Day. You're volunteering your time."

Nemeth frowns, studies the brown carpet.

"I led that operation," he says at last. "I didn't bring Tim home. His fate is still my responsibility."

"What about the other missing people?"

He glances at me in surprise. "You already gossiping with the locals?"

"It's a gift."

"Do you know how big the Popo Agie Wilderness is?"

"I'm going with large."

"Try fucking huge."

"I like you more and more."

"We have woods, mountains, streams, lakes, gullies, cliff faces, wild animals, not to mention some man-eating carnivores—"

"Bigfoot?"

"This is nature," he says. "Raw. Powerful. Vast. Over a hundred thousand acres. Simple matter of statistics, not all will make it out alive."

"How very *Hunger Games* of you."

"Practical. Man can progress as much as we want. Mother Nature still owns our ass."

"What are your thoughts on chocolate? I feel like you could use more decadence in your life."

"You're not qualified for this search party. Do us all a favor and bow out now."

I take a moment. I can be too cavalier. I can be a total bitch. But I can also be honest, and I think Nemeth deserves that much.

"I'm not as experienced with camping as you would like. But I'm healthier than Josh and I have decent boots and great socks. If you can get me a pack that fits, I can do this. I won't complain, I won't slow you down, and I can help. I don't know why, but finding the missing? I'm good at it. I just am."

"You're damn stubborn."

I smile. "Thank heavens, right? Otherwise, how would those other sixteen people have ever made it home?" I return my attention to Josh's pack, pulling out more clothes, pants, long johns, items that definitely won't fit me.

"Martin O'Day." I return to our previous conversation. "Grieving father, experienced hiker. You like him? Trust him?"

"I do."

"Which brings us to the bachelor party buddies. What do you think of them?"

"Decent enough young men. Screwed up, paid the price. Are still paying the price."

"What exactly was their screwup? Drinking?"

That shrug again. "I've been a guide long enough to know most camping parties are carrying more booze than water. Drinking happens. Stupid but rarely deadly. Now, splitting up, on the other hand, losing track of each other—"

"Leaving a man behind?"

"Scott's disappearance was bad enough. After that they should've stayed put, regrouped at daylight, not sent another member of their party to stumble around dangerous terrain at night."

"Scott went missing first, right? They were all roused from their alcohol-induced comas by sudden noises. Looked around frantically with their flashlights, then realized belatedly that Scott was gone. So what happened to him that night? Has he said?"

"Scott claims he doesn't remember anything after retiring to his tent. My personal theory? Kid was drunk. Wandered out of his tent in the middle of the night and staggered about. Till he came to the river and passed out cold. Which was why he never heard his friends searching or other sounds of commotion. He didn't regain consciousness till morning, when he did his best to find his way back."

"Do you believe his story?"

Nemeth shrugs. "Don't have a reason not to."

Which is not the same as saying yes. "Okay, so bachelor buddy Scott got lost in earnest. A casualty of the night's drinking escapades. But what about the reports of animal screams and blood in the trees?"

"We found trampled brush, broken branches, areas of disturbance. Could be from a beast—"

"Bigfoot?"

Nemeth rolls his eyes. "In my *expert* opinion . . . we found damage consistent with four drunk dudes smashing through the woods in pursuit of their missing friend. Could it have been a grizzly bear or a mythical bipedal beast? Only if they're very tidy eaters. Same with a mountain lion, which we do spy from time to time. But they're shy creatures by nature. They don't bumble all over the damn place, smash up small trees, and drag off their prey without leaving a blood trail. And given Scott wasn't the target in the end—"

"Timothy O'Day is the one who vanished."

"Tim was six feet two, one hundred and eighty pounds. Fit, strong, well equipped, and, according to his buddies, packing a handgun."

"He was armed?" This wasn't in the paper.

"Glock nine. Carried it with him anytime he was in the woods. Now, most of us locals prefer rifles—you want distance and stopping power. Not to mention Tim carried the handgun in his pack, which is just plain stupid. Like a wild animal is gonna let you pause and retrieve your firearm before attacking. But by all accounts, Tim was experienced. He knew what he was doing." Nemeth hesitates. "Spend enough time in the wild . . . you know when you're not alone. You know when it's time to get the hell out. And you know when it's time to stop, assess the situation, and prepare to fight."

"Remove your pack, grab your handgun," I fill in quietly. I shiver slightly. I don't have Nemeth's wilderness savvy, yet I understand what he's saying. There are things you just know. Myself, walking a family farm, first day of arrival. Three generations prattling on how four-year-old Johnny just up and vanished one night. Kidnapped by strangers, abducted by aliens, who knew? Myself, striding from decrepit outbuilding to decrepit outbuilding, piles of rotten lumber, mountains of cattle refuse, knowing—just knowing—little Johnny never left these grounds. The key to what happened to him existed right here, and space invaders had nothing to do with it. Six months later, I was proved right.

"You never found any of Tim's gear," I say now. "Not his pack, headlamp, coat, nothing."

Nemeth nods. "Which is unusual. Forty years ago, when I first started guiding, search and rescue focused on bodies. Did you see the person or not see the person? Some real tragedies later, we revised tactics. SOP when we launch now, we're not just looking for the missing hiker; we're looking for signs of the hiker. PLS is place last seen—say, the campsite. Part of the search, however, is to refine that to LKP—last known position. Which could be miles from that campsite, given a broken branch here, discarded water bottle there."

"It's like losing an earring," I think out loud. "You start by retracing your steps from the entire day. Then you stop and think about it. Wait, I remember wearing it at this restaurant, or while watching TV. You narrow your search field, which allows you to focus more intently. Comb every square inch of the sofa, versus tossing the entire house. And voilà, you emerge with pretty bauble in hand."

"Assuming people are jewelry," Nemeth deadpans. "First step of any rescue operation is to deploy hasty teams. As their name implies, they start broad and move fast. Generally speaking, they have a fifty to sixty percent probability of detection rate—POD. Meaning we're sixty percent sure our missing hiker isn't here. Good enough in the beginning when you're racing from strategic area to strategic area."

"What's a strategic area?"

"That's one of my first jobs. Looking at a topographical map, I consider where the lost person was last seen, then identify places where he or she would've most likely gone off course. For example, trail intersections where Tim might've headed left instead of right. Or areas of low vegetation where, given nighttime conditions, he confused an opening between the trees for the continuation of the trail and headed deeper into the woods. There's not enough manpower in the world to comb through the entire Popo Agie. My job is to consider areas that are most likely and deploy my teams accordingly. With luck, that gets the job done."

"Except it didn't."

Nemeth nods. "At a certain point, it's time to slow down and switch gears. Think about dropping a quarter in a sandbox. First step is to quickly run your fingers through the sand—the hasty searches. Failing that, you break the sandbox into quadrants and go through each one grain by grain."

"Line searches," I speak up. "That's what I did. We were like the sweepers, scouring the area for every last crumb."

"Which hopefully results in locating the person. Or . . ." Nemeth eyes me expectantly.

"Or signs of the person." I get it now. "Which would refine their last known position. Allowing you to revisit the map, identify more high-probability areas, and adjust efforts accordingly." I bounce on the balls of my feet. I'm getting this. "Except"—my enthusiasm dims—"you didn't find Tim."

"Not even signs of Tim. Hundreds of volunteers, weeks of effort.

Dog teams, pilots, people on ATVs, locals on horseback, the National Guard. At a certain point, these woods were crawling with able-bodied volunteers. Myself and Sheriff Kelley, we pored over these maps. There's science to these kinds of operations, but there's also instinct." He eyes me. "Generally speaking, I have damn good instincts."

"Small children take shelter," I murmur. "The elderly head downhill. The inexperienced follow the path of least resistance."

"And the tech addicts head up. We have no cell coverage here. As in zero. But civilized folks can't fathom such a thing. They think if they just get up high enough—say, the peak of that chimney formation—they'll magically find reception and can call for help. Unfortunately, it can also result in them falling to their death. We considered all the factors and searched accordingly. Five years later, we haven't found so much as a boot print. A discarded carabiner. A strand of hair. It's as if Tim, a well-experienced, well-equipped young man, left that campsite and dropped off the face of the earth."

"Is that why we're now looking for Bigfoot?"

Nemeth gives me a look. "That's Marty's deal. I don't care. The Bob guy knows how to conduct a proper wildland search."

"In other words, is more qualified than me. So if you don't believe in Bigfoot, what do you believe happened?"

"I don't know." Nemeth's glacier-blue eyes are troubled. He shakes his head. "Go home."

"I don't have a home."

"Then take a vacation."

I have to smile. "This is my idea of vacation." I return my attention to Josh's pack, removing the last of his clothing, to reveal a final layer of dehydrated meals.

"When do we leave?"

"Six A.M. tomorrow."

"Given that you've already searched most everywhere, what's our target?"

"Devil's Canyon. Will take us a whole day of hard hiking just to reach it. Long shot, but it's one of the few places never thoroughly explored."

"And once we get there?"

"We let Daisy take the lead."

The cadaver dog, Martin O'Day's final hope of discovering his son's remains.

"Not too late to learn how to shoot a rifle," Nemeth tells me.

I reach the bottom of the pack, feeling beneath the piles of MREs to pull out a final item in a long black sheath. I yank on the handle to reveal a viciously serrated knife. Like something a Navy SEAL would carry. Or Rambo. It's both terrifying and awe-inspiring.

"I don't normally play with sharp objects," I inform Nemeth, my hand already shaking slightly. But I don't put it down. The double-edged blade, jagged on one side, razor-sharp on the other, gleams wickedly.

"Word to the wise." He nods at the blade. "Bottom of the pack is piss-poor planning. Gonna bring it along, at least strap that to your leg, where you can grab it instantly. I might not believe in Bigfoot, but where we're headed . . . Mother Nature is a fickle bitch and don't you ever forget it. Now, let me see what I can do about getting you a right-sized pack."

Nemeth stands up, heads for the door. I'm left alone in the guys' hotel room, holding a deadly tactical knife jammed into the bottom of the pack by a drunk.

I wonder what Josh was thinking when he threw this in. His idea of basic survival gear? Something more?

Or something worse?

CHAPTER 5

TWELVE HOURS BEFORE OUR EARLY morning departure, I'm starving, nervous, and clueless as to where I'm spending the night. The motel, I suppose, except I'd prefer not to spend that kind of money.

I wonder if Luciana, as the only other female, would let me crash on her floor for the evening. Nemeth had shown me the party's street-level row of hotel rooms, so I start knocking. The third time is the charm, as Luciana appears in the doorway. Behind her I spot Daisy, sitting before the shuttered closet, one paw raised in the air, body taut with expectation.

"You're just in time," Luciana informs me.

"I am?"

"Yes. Daisy is showing off her skills, and she always appreciates an audience."

Luciana gestures for me to enter. Daisy remains perfectly poised, staring so intently at her target it makes the fine hairs rise on the back of my neck.

"Is there a dead body in your closet?" I ask.

"Close." Luciana draws back the accordion-style door. In the next instant, Bob bursts from the tiny space in full bushy-bearded glory.

"Ta-da," he booms.

Luciana rolls her eyes, but she's grinning ear to ear. "Okay," she declares brightly, and Daisy leaps to her feet, tail wagging wildly. The Lab mix prances all around Bob, who fusses over her accordingly. Then Daisy races over to me for additional praise.

"Daisy is a fully trained SAR dog," Luciana informs me as she produces a long, brightly colored squeak toy for her ecstatic charge. "She's skilled in live, cadaver, and water searches. Our team specializes in disaster recovery, meaning we don't know what we'll discover on-site—could be living people, could be deceased, could be both. Our canines need to be able to identify all. Even dogs prefer happy endings, however—too many cadaver recoveries in a row make them depressed. Given Daisy's next week will be about human remains, we'll need to take turns letting Daisy 'find' us to keep her morale up. Bob was so taken with the idea he volunteered to be her first target."

"She's certainly very excited," I observe as Daisy tosses her squeak toy in the air and catches it again.

"She has a natural drive to find. You can't train a dog without it."

Bob goes down on his knees to scratch the yellow Lab's entire body. She huffs in pleasure. "Who is the best dog? *You* are the best dog. Yes, you are. Yes, yes, yes!"

I've never seen such a huge man reduced to baby talk, but I like it. After my very sobering conversation with Nemeth, this room is a happy place to be.

"I thought search dogs normally barked to signal they'd found something," I say to Luciana.

"Many do. It's a trainer's prerogative. I'm not a fan of the barking myself; I think that can be scary for the missing person. Can you imagine being a lost child in the woods or someone buried under rubble, and having a strange dog suddenly appear and bay at you? I teach my dogs to sit as an alert system. Daisy added the raised paw. She has a flair for the dramatic."

Daisy wags her tail again. She is clearly quite pleased with herself. Given my last animal roommate liked to rake her claws across my ankles and leave trails of disemboweled mice across the floor, Daisy seems particularly charming.

"I'm starving," I state now. "I was thinking of one last, ginormous hot meal before a week of freeze-dried rations. Any takers?"

"I can always eat!" Bob climbs to his feet.

"How much food do you have to carry with you to last seven days?" I ask him in wonder.

"Not as much as I'd like." He pats his rounded belly mournfully. At six foot seven, Bob more closely resembles Paul Bunyan than, say, wiry superhikers such as Nemeth and Martin, but he's clearly fit, not to mention that one of his legs is about as tall as my entire body. I have no problem envisioning him powering through the mountains. He probably clears small forests in a single bound.

"I wouldn't mind a hot meal," Luciana agrees. "Let me feed Daisy first."

"Um, one other question. Any chance I could crash on your floor tonight?" The room has two double beds, but I don't want to sound presumptuous. "Seems silly to shell out motel money for a matter of hours."

Luciana isn't fooled. "I take it going from town to town solving other people's problems doesn't pay so well?"

"Let's just say being rewarded with a squeak toy would be a step up."

"Maybe Daisy will share hers."

The dog trots back over to me. I obligingly scratch her ears as Luciana starts fiddling with travel bowls and pre-portioned bags of kibble.

"Keep doing that, and she'll sleep in your bed tonight," Luciana tells me.

"Does she prefer the right side or the left?"

"More like the middle. Welcome to the life of a spoiled work dog. But, sure, you can bunk here for the night."

"Daisy can sleep with me," Bob offers excitedly. "Just don't tell my husband."

Upon seeing my startled expression, Bob shrugs affably and explains: "His name is Rob. Rob and Bob. Seriously, could we be more confusing? But soul mates are soul mates."

"Is he a Bigfoot hunter, too?"

"Worse. A neurosurgeon. All science all the time. What was I thinking?"

"That Rob would let you one day get a yellow Lab like Daisy?" I venture.

"Yes! I'm going to tell him. When I get home, time for a new member of the family."

"Does Bigfoot like dogs?"

"I like to think Sasquatches are friendly toward everyone, being high on the evolutionary food chain."

"Herbivores or carnivores?"

"Omnivores."

"Hedging your bets."

"Can't know what we haven't met. But current cryptozoologists theorize Bigfoot shares many traits with the ape family, which would make them omnivores." Bob speaks matter-of-factly, no doubt accustomed to skepticism. We are kindred spirits in that regard.

Daisy finishes scarfing down her food. Luciana takes her out to water the bushes, then instructs the yellow Lab to go to bed. Daisy seems less of a fan of this order, but obligingly curls up on the carpet where she can monitor the motel room door for signs of her handler's return.

I finally get to set my rolly bag aside, then we're off to dinner. Three new friends, I like to think.

Enjoying the calm before the storm.

WE HAVE TO wait an hour to get a table at the steak house that is walking distance from the motel. We watch a steady stream of tourists flow into the western-themed establishment. Families, couples. Some glance up and smile; some never take their eyes off their cell phones. All sidestep noticeably upon nearing Bob. At one point I notice him noticing. He shrugs back at me as if to say, what can you do?

Once seated, Luciana and Bob order a beer each. I fixate on the food. I'm not picky. I eat anything and everything. I suppose my broad-mindedness will come in handy when subsisting on MREs for the next week. Just the idea of future deprivation, however, has me wanting everything on the menu. Nachos. Skirt steak. Fajitas. For that matter, I wouldn't mind a beer.

You'd think eventually the cravings would go away. They don't. I can be around others who drink. For that matter, my only employable skill is bartending, so I continue to spend my life surrounded by booze. Certain things, however, still whisper to me like words from a long-lost lover. The scent of hops. The clink of ice cubes hitting a glass. The creamy richness of perfectly poured foam.

I should go to a meeting after this. I should also sleep through the night, find joy in my heart, and relive a happy memory.

But I remain me. A woman capable of dining with two new acquaintances, and yet who still feels alone in a crowded room. I don't remember the exact age I had my first drink. I was young, very young, but then plenty of kids steal sips of their parents' drinks, trying to unravel the mysteries of adulthood.

Most recoil at the lighter-fluid punch. Whereas for myself . . .

I don't remember my first kiss. I don't remember my high school graduation. Even the phone call informing me of my parents' deaths is a hazy affair, like something that was happening to someone else.

But my first stolen sip of my father's drink . . . Liquid gold, burning down my throat. A seeping warmth that made my restless limbs and racing brain slow, steady, quiet.

Alcohol is my first love and most abusive relationship. All else has paled in comparison. Even my love for Paul.

The waitress arrives for our orders. The restaurant is so loud and crowded we have to semi-shout to be heard. I go with fajitas. Luciana orders grilled chicken. Bob requests nachos, rib eye, and a side of maple-fried Brussels sprouts. For the table, he says.

The waitress pauses mid scribble. She looks up for the first time. I recognize her harried attention span from my own lifetime in food service. Her gaze travels up Bob's enormous torso to his beaming face.

"I'll bring you extra bread," she says.

"Excellent!"

She walks away, still appearing a bit nonplussed. I smile, already imagining the stories she'll be telling in the kitchen.

———

THE BREAD ARRIVES. Bob dives in, butters up. None of us are talking, but it feels companionable. Luciana is texting someone on her phone. Bob is happy with his bread basket. I'm content to study my fellow diners and imagine how happy and perfect their lives must be, even if I, of all people, should know better.

Eventually the food arrives: a plate for myself, a plate for Luciana, half a table for Bob. Luciana puts away her phone and we all dive in.

Between bites of food, I learn that thirty-something Luciana is from Colombia, though her family moved to the States when she was eight and she doesn't remember much before that. She always loved animals and started out volunteering at the local animal shelter, where she met a woman who specialized in animal training. Eventually, Luciana started working with Belgian Malinois, which led to SAR dogs, which led her to Daisy.

Rescue work pays as well as my job does—or Bob's for that matter. Many people don't realize this, but even supplying world-class SAR dogs is a volunteer gig. Luciana doesn't frequent missing persons boards such as Bob and I do. Being part of a larger disaster response team, when her phone rings, she and Daisy are off. There is a network of volunteer pilots who ferry the teams for free. In international situations, the primary agency, say, the Red Cross, might pay for food and lodging—but that's about it.

Professional project manager for an online insurance company by day—she smirks—training in the Batcave at night.

Bob's turn. He grew up in Idaho, one of five kids, and swears he's the runt of the family. We don't believe him till he produces a family photo on his phone. Technically speaking, his mother and sister are slightly shorter, but they also appear significantly rounder.

His father and brothers are truly massive, looking like the defensive line of a professional football team. The entire family gravitates to horticulture and animal husbandry, which makes Bob's interest in cryptozoology understandable.

Bob lives in Washington now, where his daytime gig is teaching: biology at a local high school. Summers are reserved for Bigfoot hunting.

"Why Sasquatch?" I ask now, expecting some personal story of a close encounter of the ape-like kind.

"Why not Sasquatch?" Bob replies, scarfing down the last of the nachos. Then, when I'm still peering at him skeptically, "Why missing persons cold cases?" he challenges me.

"Because someone has to find them, and sadly, the authorities often aren't looking."

"Exactly." Bob beams at me. He has cheese in his copper-colored beard. If anyone can pull off the look, it's a Norse god.

I turn to Luciana. "How did you become a member of this party?"

"I've worked with Nemeth before, finding an elderly man who wandered off into the mountains. Nemeth called, I answered."

"And you?" I quiz Bob.

"Marty contacted me a few years ago, looking for information. We've been in touch ever since."

"And you know about the other missing hikers?"

"Yep. Six in total."

Lisa Rowell had said at least five. So six sounds right.

Luciana is nodding, so apparently she's familiar with the bigger picture as well.

"What do you put our odds of success at?" I ask no one in particular.

Luciana does the honors. "I think we'll find something—or

really, Daisy will find something. Want to know an interesting fact involving large-scale searches of wilderness areas?"

"Sure."

"Volunteers almost always discover a body. Just not the body they're looking for. There's that many human remains in the woods."

I don't know what to say to that.

Bob, on the other hand, has no such issues. He regards both of us hopefully. "So . . . dessert?"

IT'S NINE P.M. by the time we return to the motel. True to Rowell's prediction, the temperature has dropped sharply, and I have my arms tucked tight against my torso for warmth. The sun has set. Above us, the stars spread out against the dark blue sky like a scattering of diamonds. It is beautiful and mesmerizing and humbling.

And I have that fizzy, restless feeling I get right before a new case. Nerves. Anxiety. Basic personality. Even as a kid, I couldn't sit still. I was always seeking something more, looking for anything but what was in front of me. Which translated to twenty-plus years of hard-core drinking before I met Paul and he showed me the patience and acceptance I couldn't show myself.

Now I have this, a job few understand. Standing in the parking lot right now, however, Bob to one side and Luciana to the other, I think this might be the closest I'll ever come to discovering like-minded souls. The only difference being they pursue their efforts as side projects, whereas I've walked away from everything most hold dear just to be here, with people I've never met, looking for a person who'll never come home alive.

I'm tired. I'm hyper. I want to plunge into the woods and recover Timothy O'Day's body so his mother can die in peace. I want to run all the way back to Boston and place my head against Detective Dan Lotham's solid shoulder and . . . let go. Fall just so he can catch me. My body will melt into his. He will stroke my skin and it will feel better than anything I've ever found in a bottle.

Except then it will be morning.

There's always morning.

And he will want to keep holding me, because he's that kind of man. A solver of riddles, a fixer of broken things.

But I'm not really a riddle and I am definitely not broken.

I'm just . . . me.

Nemeth is waiting in the lit parking lot. He has two packs at his feet—the giant yellow one that belongs to Josh and a smaller, hopefully lighter-weight one that I'm guessing is now mine.

"How's Josh?" Luciana asks first.

"Detoxing. Others are back, prepping for tomorrow."

Nemeth picks up the two backpacks, hands them both over to me.

"Organize your supplies. Know how to find what you need. Vans will be here at six A.M. Don't be late."

Then that's it. He's gone. Bob retires to his room. I follow Luciana into hers, where Daisy greets us with body-wriggling delight.

And I have nine hours to learn everything I don't know about spending a week lost in the woods.

CHAPTER 6

LUCIANA CLAIMS THE BATHROOM FIRST.

"Last hot shower for a week," she announces, grabbing a small bag of toiletry supplies. "Don't wait up."

I hadn't even thought about that. Now I'm desperate for a hot shower, too. Instead, I take a seat on the floor with my personal bags to one side and the two hiking packs on the other. Daisy gazes at the closed bathroom door with longing, then sighs heavily and collapses next to me.

"Do you know anything about camping supplies?" I ask her.

She thumps her tail but offers no advice.

I start by emptying out Josh's pack, making a pile out of the food, usable clothes, and miscellaneous camping supplies. I add my own meager collection of belongings to the mix and optimistically stuff everything back into the bag. Except it rapidly becomes impossible to zip. Who knew that a woman who can fit her entire life into one suitcase would suddenly have too much stuff?

I make a second attempt at paring down to bare essentials. Trim my six shirts to four. Likewise with the rest of my clothing.

I'm still debating pants options when Luciana emerges from the bathroom. She runs a comb through her wet hair as she eyes my project.

"Those are your clothes? All of your clothes?"

"I travel light."

"No, I mean, no hiking pants, quick-dry shirts, wicking tank tops?"

"There are wicking tank tops?"

She sighs heavily, looks me up and down. "You're smaller than me, but not by much."

Height-wise, maybe. But build-wise, the Colombian beauty has curves I've spent my entire life pining for and haven't managed to grow yet.

Now she crosses to her own gear, piled near the closet. "First up, don't bother with the jeans," she informs me. "Denim gets too heavy, leads to chafing."

"Chafing?" I eye my jeans warily, having had no idea of their hidden dangers.

"Try these." She throws me a pair of olive-colored pants. They are incredibly lightweight, with a drawstring waist, a multitude of pockets, and zippers that encircle both pant legs. To turn the pants into shorts, I realize. I'm already impressed. Talk about a clothing item designed for the minimalist on the go.

Next, Luciana throws me two tank tops and one button-up baby blue shirt. The fabrics are lighter and silkier than anything I own, clearly some kind of quick-dry blend. I finger each piece in admiration as Luciana heads back to my hiking bag and yanks out everything I've managed to wedge in thus far.

"But," I protest, "Nemeth approved these items. I swear it. We already reviewed them!"

She ignores me completely, continuing with her inspection. "All right, Josh might be a drunk, but at least he knew what he was doing. Notice you have redundancy. Waterproof matches plus a butane lighter, first aid kit plus moleskin, headlamp plus a flashlight. Hope for the best but plan for the worst, as the saying goes."

"Sure."

"Now, you want to spread out what you're carrying. Say, stash the matches in your pack, put the butane lighter in your pocket. That way if you and your pack are ever separated, you still have the power to make fire."

"Nemeth told me to strap the knife to my person." I unsheathe the tactical blade, holding it up for her inspection.

"Holy shit. I carry a basic wilderness knife, but it's half this size and not nearly so serious." She takes Josh's knife, the overhead light of the motel room winking off the wicked-looking serrated edge. "I'd put this up there with an assault weapon. Something a special ops team might carry."

"Is that a good thing?"

"I don't know. Guess it means Josh has serious tastes in knives."

There's something in her voice, however, a slight hesitation, that leaves me unsettled. In my line of work, it's not what people tell you but what they don't that is often more important.

"Okay, back to Wilderness One-oh-one." Luciana returns her attention to my pile of gear. "When it comes to basic survival, you want to remember the rule of threes: You can go three minutes without air, three hours without shelter, three days without water, and three weeks without food. Prioritize accordingly."

I'm already skeptical. "I can last longer than three hours without shelter."

"Assumes adverse conditions—say, a blizzard or torrential downpour or absurdly hot temps. Hyperthermia is a bigger killer than you might think."

Now I get it. "The rule of threes is about prioritizing. My first job is to get air. Then shelter, then water. Don't worry so much about food."

"Exactly. This one-dollar lighter"—she holds up the Bic—"represents fire. Which will assist with shelter—keeping you warm at night—and boiling drinkable water. This magnificent if slightly terrifying survival knife can assist with building a shelter as well as creating kindling to start a fire. These two items alone can go a long way toward keeping you alive."

"Hence I should carry them on my person."

"See, you're a natural. Now, the emergency whistle."

"I have a whistle!" I'm genuinely excited. "I carry it around tough neighborhoods all the time."

"Your idea of self-defense in an urban environment is a whistle? Are you trying to die?"

I do not answer that question.

"Whistles are too bulky for pants pockets. I recommend this instead." Luciana throws a thickly corded bracelet in my direction. I catch it in midair, finger the camo-colored weave.

"I've seen these. Some kind of nylon rope, braided into fashion gear." I unclip the plastic buckle and discover a stainless steel tongue of surprising strength.

"Notice the slightly serrated edge?" Luciana points at the metal tongue. "That can serve as a small blade. Now blow in the other half of the buckle."

I give her a look but obediently purse my lips for a short puff. A faint whistle emerges from the hollow plastic. I try again, with more force, and am rewarded by a sharper sound. "It's a whistle!"

"A whistle you can wear on your wrist that also provides a small razor and utility ropes." Luciana beams proudly.

I don't blame her. I'm slightly in love with the bracelet. Reminds me of my five-dollar utility hair clips that include serrated edges on one side and tool options in the middle. I wouldn't go so far as to say they'll save me in the wild, but they have come in handy for some basic breaking and entering.

"So butane lighter in one pocket. Knife at your waist. Paracord bracelet on your wrist," Luciana summarizes. "Final item, that small pencil flashlight, which you can tuck into one of the pant-leg pockets. You don't want to be wandering around the woods in the dark, and not just because you'll most likely kill yourself, but because other creatures will regard you as food and do the honors for you."

"Do you really think a grizzly bear cares about a bobbing flashlight?"

"I'm hoping to never find out."

"Do you carry a gun?" I ask curiously.

"No. I don't like them and I'm not sure I could bring myself to shoot another life form, even a charging bear."

"What if the bear went after Daisy?"

"Then I'd kill the grizzly with my bare hands and the gun would be redundant."

I don't doubt her for a second.

"Nemeth has a rifle," she adds now. "It's part of his responsibility as the guide. I have bear repellent in my kit. The size of our party will be our most useful weapon, however. Wildlife is shy. They don't want to take on eight people and a dog. Just don't wander too far from the campfire at night. Pick the closest bush, squat, pee, and get back."

"There's no toilet paper in my pack."

Luciana rolls her eyes. "Seriously, woman, by the end of this week, you're not going to recognize yourself."

I pick up one of the few items scattered on the carpet that she hasn't mentioned yet. "Why does a guy have a maxi pad in his wilderness kit?"

"Field first aid. Perfect for stopping heavy bleeding. Press against the wound, secure in place with bandages. Tampons work, too."

I rub the relatively new scar on my shoulder absently, then start picking up each item and reloading them into my pack.

On the other side of the room, Luciana does the same. I notice she rolls each item of clothing, allowing her to cram more in. I follow her example and this time manage to zip the pack closed when I'm done.

I heft it up. The weight is real, but better than Josh's original load.

I can do this, I tell myself. Butane lighters, wicking fabrics, rule of threes. Nothing here I can't handle.

Then I bolt into the bathroom so Luciana can't see the panic on my face.

TEN THIRTY. LIGHTS out. Luciana and Daisy already sound asleep in one bed. Myself, totally awake in the other.

Daisy snores. A slight woofing exhale. It's rhythmic and soothing. I try to focus on that. Mostly, I wonder what would happen if I called Lotham right now. Two-hour time difference, making it after midnight in Boston.

He's probably asleep. Or working a major case. Either way, would he take my call? The number of times I've flipped open my cheap Tracfone, finger hovering over the buttons. Then closed the phone. Put it away.

The number of times I have thought of him, and forced myself to move on.

Now I order myself to let go. Be in this moment. Honor Timothy O'Day and the task I have undertaken. Sleep. Tomorrow will be hard enough.

But I don't drift off.

I remain wide-awake, staring up at the ceiling, wanting things I can't have. Missing a man I chose to leave behind.

Eventually I roll onto my side. I picture Patrice O'Day, waiting for her son to come home. I imagine the lines easing in her face when her husband finally returns with their son's body. I visualize the bachelor party friends sagging in collective relief and setting down the weight of their guilt.

A loved one recovered. A mission accomplished.

It will be good, I tell myself. It will be enough.

And that lie gets me through to morning.

CHAPTER 7

No one speaks when the alarm shrieks morning wake-up. Luciana rolls out of bed the second it sounds and is on her feet, pulling on clothes, tending to Daisy. I follow in a fog of sleep deprivation. In my world, five A.M. is for going to bed, not getting get out of it.

No small talk, no breakfast. Just get dressed, gather up personal possessions, and move. Then we are outside, where two white-paneled vans are idling and Nemeth is standing in the middle of the parking lot like an air traffic controller, motioning half of us here, half of us there. I end up in the same vehicle as Luciana, Daisy, Bob, and Nemeth. Martin and his son's friends ride in the other.

Separate, I think again, as the sun just starts to break over the horizon. Tim's college friends and his father equal one pod; we are another. I should follow that thought, but the hour is too early, my mind too fuzzy. I lean my head against the cold side window and close my eyes instead.

Then, just like that, the van stops and the door slides open. Nemeth steps out.

"Leave your extra luggage in the van. Marge will keep it safe for the rest of the week."

Which is when I realize our older female driver in full camo regalia is also the diner owner. Nemeth places a light hand on her shoulder, which would seem collegial for a normal person, but I'm guessing in Nemeth's understated world is a public declaration of intimacy. Marge doesn't even look at him but regards us with a cool, assessing stare.

I'm pretty sure they're soul mates. On the other hand, dear God, where is the coffee?

Bob is moving. Luciana and Daisy, too. They seem to know what they're doing, so I follow their lead, stepping out of the van, dumping my gear on the ground, then, belatedly, digging out the insect repellent. The others are spraying it on heavily. Even Daisy is subject to some minty-smelling, canine-friendly mosquito napalm. Once that's completed, everyone pulls on their packs. Again, Daisy fits right in, adorned in a red vest with bulging pouches and a single water bottle.

If a dog can do this, I tell myself, then I can, too.

Of course, the dog has had way more training.

Marge nods once at Nemeth. Some kind of all-set signal. I'm still trying to figure out how she got all of her bouffant curls tucked under her khaki-green hat, when he nods back, and that is apparently that. No lingering kiss as they part for the next week, not even a peck on the cheek. She heads back to the van; he turns toward us.

I'm thinking that this might be the most romantic thing I've ever witnessed, when Nemeth pauses before me, inspects my gear, then tightens straps here and there. With a final nod, he steps back.

"Today is about hiking into our target area," he announces.

"First eight miles aren't so bad, but don't let them fool you. The altitude we don't gain then we gotta make up the second half. I won't lie. Final mile is a bitch."

So much for a pep talk.

"Remember, slow is smooth, smooth is fast. We got a week of hard work ahead of us. No need to be stupid day one. Luciana, Daisy"—Nemeth nods in their direction—"you set the pace. Of all of us, Daisy has the hardest job. What she needs, we will accommodate."

I notice that Daisy's red hiking vest is not the official harness most SAR dogs wear when on task. Which makes sense if today is just about hiking into our search destination. Scenting is hard work. No point in exhausting the most valuable member of our party before we must.

"Here's the deal," Nemeth continues, his voice totally commanding. "When I say stop, you stop. When I say drink, you drink. When I say snack break, eat a snack. I don't give a rat's ass if you want to or not. We're a group. I'm the leader. What I say goes."

I wake up a little more, stand a little straighter. Damn, this guy is good—and not just because he has a rifle slung over his shoulder.

"Any foot discomfort"—he pauses, repeats—"*any* foot discomfort, you will speak up. We will stop, you will adjust your boot, change your socks, apply moleskin, do whatever it is you need to do. Number one cause of expedition failure isn't grizzly bears or falling off ledges or breaking a leg; it's blisters. There will be no blisters. Got it?"

We nod obediently. Martin and the young men appear less impressed, having no doubt sat through this lecture before. I'm mentally cataloguing every inch of my feet and informing them they will be healthy and happy because Nemeth says so. I want to believe my feet are impressed.

"Your back starts to ache, your shoulders get sore, you will speak up. We will stop, I will personally adjust your pack." Nemeth stares at me. "When everyone feels comfortable, we will resume our pace. But again, seven days. What bothers you now might kill you later. There will be no dying on this trek."

I'm totally and completely convinced. Whatever this man says, I'm on board. Maybe I should've tried boot camp when I was younger, because I'm actually a little turned on right now. Soon enough, I know, I will hate him, as I have a long and troubled history with authority figures. But at this precise moment, I'm drinking the Kool-Aid and hoping for another glass.

"You get tired, speak up. You get thirsty, speak up. You need to take a break for whatever reason: Speak. Up."

We nod as a single unit.

"Final rule: Pay attention to the body in front of you. We're starting off on an established trail, but soon enough we'll be in the backcountry, where markings are few and far between. By the end, we won't be following an official path at all, just trekking up through the magnificence that is the Popo Agie Wilderness. Unless you've been here before, or are really good at navigating your way through the middle of nowhere, don't get separated from our party. We got enough to do without having to waste time dealing with stupid."

He stares at me again. I'm tempted to stick out my tongue at him. But I'm also scared of what he might do to me next.

When no one else asks questions, talks backs, or engages in childish insults, Nemeth nods once, claps his hands.

"Gear up. Fall out." He gives us about sixty seconds to finish adjusting equipment, clothing, boots, then without another word, he turns and heads up the trail, Martin already at his heels.

I find myself glancing around. One last look at civilization? Bob nudges my shoulder, then smiles encouragingly, as if he can read my thoughts. He gestures for me to go first, the giant Bigfoot hunter clearly intending to bring up the rear. I don't have time to consider the matter, as the fellow members of my party are rapidly hiking away and Nemeth's words of warning are fresh in my mind. I don't know where I am or how to navigate forests. City streets, yes. Rows of trees, no.

I scamper to fall in line. And just like that we're off and running.

Ready or not, Timothy O'Day, here we come.

HOW DO YOU find a missing person?

I don't have any real training or even a codified approach. Not being a cop, I don't utilize forensics, though generally by the time I've gotten involved, anything significant in terms of physical evidence has been collected, analyzed, and crossed off as useless by local authorities. I'm not a computer hacker, so there's no diving into the dark ocean of the internet to discover the victim's sordid secrets, which led to their escape to a whole new life. To be honest, I've yet to encounter a situation where the missing person staged the whole thing or left of their own accord.

Sometimes the cases have garnered a certain level of police interest, meaning the obvious possibilities have already been pursued without yielding results. Other times—especially in underserved communities—the local authorities never bothered to open an active case file. Those situations make me the angriest: an entire life, written off without a single question asked. But even then, months or years later someone has done some basic digging. A loved one, a troubled friend, a concerned neighbor.

Generally, the first step of my involvement in any case is to review the work, whether it be rigorous or cursory, that happened before me. Sometimes, that results in a whole new line of questioning: Wait, no one ever asked about the new guy who moved in upstairs? Other times it leaves me scratching my head and knowing this case is going to be a doozy.

Which brings me to my highly unscientific second step: Show up. Walk around the community. Ask questions of anyone and everyone. No focus, no direction, just start picking up random stones and flipping them over. You never know.

Police will tell you they don't have the time for such a scatter-shot approach. Family members will tell you they're often too embarrassed.

This is where it's good to be me: I have neither concern. I work one case at a time to obsessive resolution, versus even the most dedicated detective, who has dozens at a time. I have no personal connection, meaning there's no question I won't ask, no boundary I won't cross.

How to translate all of this to a one-week expedition to recover skeletal remains? As I huff along the hiking trail, comfortable enough with the pace, delighted by the fresh mountain air, smiling at Daisy's sheer joy over . . . everything . . . I struggle with this answer. I'm here to help. I promised I would. But how?

I have no neighbors to question, no city streets to walk, no base motives to consider. Tim set out to get help for his friend in the middle of the night. Honorable. What happened after that. Terrible. And given the circumstances, too much area to search, zero witnesses to question, no thread to tease or bread crumbs to follow.

Nemeth is the expert on the topography—where Tim might have

veered off the trail. Martin is the expert on his son's problem-solving skills—once Tim went off course, what decisions he might have made next.

How the hell do I add to that? Another pair of eyes? Even I don't believe that; if we find anything, it will be thanks to Daisy's extraordinary nose, not our highly limited human vision.

Not that that makes me the only semi-useless member of this party. Tim's groomsmen, according to their witness statements, have no idea what happened after Tim left the campsite. Scott, who initiated this tragic chain of events by vanishing first, doesn't even remember how he disappeared. And none of them were known for being outdoor enthusiasts—camping was Tim's passion. They were merely humoring him.

Yet here we are, tramping through the woods, halting when Nemeth tells us to halt, force-feeding protein bars when he orders us to snack. I find it fascinating how the three guys keep to themselves: Scott, Neil, and Miggy.

They introduced themselves this morning, their manners perfunctory. I haven't heard them speak since, though our party of eight has quickly broken into a series of separate groupings. Nemeth and Martin are in the front, a twin pair of leaders, with Nemeth hiking ahead with the rifle, then passing it off to Martin to do the same.

The three buddies drift along behind them in a tidy row. They keep their heads down, their faces shuttered. They do what they're told, question nothing. Have all three of them returned every summer on this same hopeless mission? I wonder if it's the yearly searching that drove the fourth member of their group, Josh, to drink. Or the guilt over that one night.

Or something else entirely?

Luciana and Daisy follow the young men, a separate unit of two.

Luciana is letting Daisy relax off leash, though I notice she's quick to call the dog back anytime Daisy darts into the woods after squirrels. Luciana is the dog-manager version of Nemeth, forcing her charge to pace herself.

I follow shortly behind Luciana and Daisy. So far, so good. My calves ache slightly and I've been out of breath since we started, but not in an awful sort of way. Of course, it's still early in the day. I have no idea how many miles we've covered and I don't want to. Like any addict, I've spent the past ten years perfecting the one-step-at-a-time approach. I refuse to surrender my only competitive advantage now.

Bob brings up the rear. When we pause for snacks, he confers with Nemeth and Martin, which leads me to believe he's third man on the leadership totem pole. As a Bigfoot hunter, he should be nearly as wilderness savvy as the other two. Hence his strategic position as sweeper—ensuring no member of the team falls behind.

He doesn't speak much as he idles along behind me, but there's an energy about him that's reassuring. Of all of us, only he and Daisy appear to be enjoying themselves. Nemeth is an eagle-eyed scout, never resting for a moment. Martin appears to be strung tighter than a drum. The three college friends are shut down, and Luciana is in work mode even if she's given her dog the day off, while I'm in my own little world of What the Fuck, which, to be honest, is my norm.

Which makes us an interesting group as we trudge along. The trail winds through the woods, a ribbon of hard-packed earth lined with sagebrush and grasses, dusted here and there with pine needles. The air smells like sun-soaked sap and icy streams, with an undertone of bug spray, sunscreen, and human sweat. It feels green and blue and brown, a caress against my face.

The occasional whine of insects. The whisper of wind among

towering pines. The chatter of squirrels fussing over our intrusion. Timothy O'Day loved these woods. Tim chose here, these mountains, these trails, to celebrate his final days as a bachelor with his closest friends.

Which makes me aware of the deeper, darker shadows lurking around the edges. The relentless pounding of boots striking the ground, the sight of the rifle, slung over Nemeth's shoulder, the silence of friends who won't even speak as they set out once more to search for their buddy's remains.

What can I add to this somber funeral party and recovery mission rolled into one?

Maybe in this case it's not about asking the right questions or having an ear for the wrong answers. Maybe it's simply that I know and accept in ways most people never do that for everything going on in this nearly impenetrable wilderness, the biggest danger comes from the eight humans who just hiked into it.

CHAPTER 8

WE BREAK NEXT AT A small clearing at the top of a knoll. We are encircled by woods still thick enough to block any scenic views. Sadly, that means we're nowhere close to emerging into the so-called Devil's Canyon. Given we haven't passed the midday mark, we probably haven't even started the challenging second half Nemeth warned us about. Meaning that refreshing feeling of working leg muscles, which is quickly turning into a burning fire, is a pain I'd better get used to.

Nemeth has a point: Hiking is not the same as walking. But speaking as one of those people who would let hell freeze over before admitting the other guy is right, I remain confident in my ability to carry on. If only to piss off the boss.

In contrast to their behavior at our earlier stops, which involved short pauses for warm drinking water and gummy energy bars, Nemeth and Martin head over to a downed tree, remove their packs, and take a seat. Does this mean we're on lunch break? Do backcountry expeditions get a lunch break?

The others quickly follow suit, college buds collapsing to one side, Bob, Luciana, and Daisy decamping on the other. My first instinct is to head over to them. I like them, not to mention we're a logical grouping of our own. The odd men out.

But it's not my job to belong. Meaning I gird my loins and cross over to where Marty and Nemeth sit, their heads nearly touching as they regard Martin's ubiquitous map.

Nemeth glances up first, his narrow blue gaze performing an immediate scan of my figure, then the surrounding woods. It's possible the veteran guide is part cyborg. Wouldn't surprise me at all, given I'm currently drenched in sweat, while his weathered features are covered in a light sheen of moisture.

His attention returns to me.

"How's the pack?" he demands.

"Good." Feels like a ten-ton house strapped to my shoulders, but I figure that's as it should be. Now that it's off, I'm acutely aware that my borrowed high-performance shirt is plastered to my back. It's not a pleasant feeling.

"Boots?"

I glance down. "Great. My feet are very happy with the socks."

"Knees, lower back?"

I hadn't even thought about those body parts, but now that he's calling attention to them I realize my entire body aches. "I feel fantastic!" I bite off and dare him to argue as I hobble closer.

He continues to study me up and down as if in search of an obvious problem. Apparently, the children are allowed to approach the adults only if they need something.

Martin hasn't even bothered looking up from the map. In his

world, I might as well not exist. Is he that obsessed? Focused? Grief-stricken?

Or is it just me?

"I was wondering how *you* were doing," I say.

Nemeth blinks, clearly flummoxed by my question. Martin finally glances up, as if just now noticing my approach.

"What do you mean?" Nemeth asks warily.

"Are you pleased with our progress so far?"

"We're on pace."

"Trail conditions seem good," I comment, as if I know anything about such things. "Weather pleasant, skies clear, temperature not too hot, not too cold."

"Yes." He remains suspicious.

"No complaints or group arguments," I continue.

"No."

Martin cocks his head to the side and stares at me as if I'm some alien life form. Why is this underling still talking?

I don't actually have a point. I'm simply trying to engage the two men in conversation. I spend so much time operating outside of my comfort zone, I don't expect to know what I'm doing. But I've learned to listen to my instincts. Nemeth, who holds our survival in his hands. Marty, who organized this party but won't speak to any of us. I want to know these men. It matters, even if I don't know why yet.

I take a seat before them, as if they'd sent me a personal invitation. Then I say nothing at all. Have you ever attended an AA meeting? We are experts at silence. So much of our drinking is about filling those gaps, smoothing over awkward moments, trying to feel like we belong when most of us have gone through our entire lives feeling alone in a crowded room. Meaning, it's one of the first things we must overcome. It's not enough to stop drinking. We must change who we are, because who we are, are drunks.

Now I retrieve from my pant-leg pocket some coconut almond high-energy power bar I've been chewing on since this morning. Being an actual human being, I don't care for it; mostly, I crave Josh's stash of peanut butter cups. But given I'm only four hours into a seven-day death march, I figure I should have something to look forward to.

Chew. Swallow. Chew.

Chug water, because to be honest, no matter how much you grind away, the bar still goes down as a solid lump.

"How are the others?" Martin says abruptly. Now he's the one who has caught me off guard.

"The others? Luciana and Daisy seem fine and dandy. Bob is clearly enjoying the hike. As for the guys . . . Do they actually speak?"

Martin glances across the small clearing, his expression troubled.

"They blame themselves," he states abruptly. "For what happened."

"Do you?"

"My son was doing what he loved to do. He . . . disappeared . . . doing what he enjoyed most."

I notice he doesn't use the word *die*.

"Do you know how I ended up meeting Bob and the North American Bigfoot Society?" Martin asks me.

I shake my head.

"I read about another case they were working. A young man who went missing in the mountains of Washington. The Bigfoot hunters are particularly focused on that area. Knowing the trails well, they volunteered to assist. Years later, they're still combing the woods. One of the guys gave an interview saying they didn't know what had happened to the young man, but they could see him taken in by a family of Sasquatch and living happily ever after.

"I am a carpenter by trade. A man who works with his hands, believes in things that I can feel and touch. But that quote . . ."

Martin looks at me. "When you lose your child, and I mean *lose* your son, as in you have no idea where he is, no idea what happened to him, what his last moments might have been like, you need some kind of hope to get you through the day, before the terror finds you again at night. I never even thought about Bigfoot five years ago. Now, I want nothing more than to believe."

"What was Tim like as a child?"

Martin smiles reluctantly, as if even the happy memories are now forced out of him. "Tim was one of those kids—why walk when you can run, why sit on a sofa when you can jump on the cushions, why talk when you can roar? He drove his mother crazy. That amount of energy . . . he was a force to be reckoned with from the moment he opened his eyes.

"It's why I took him camping for the first time. Tim had started kindergarten and was already getting into trouble—sitting still just wasn't his thing. School wanted to hold him back. But Patrice and I could tell that he was plenty smart. He just needed to move."

Martin shrugs. "I did some asking around and several of my friends suggested camping. Get the boy out, away, into the wild. The activity alone would be good for him. Plus, for many of us . . ." Martin pauses, looks at the towering trees, the endless expanse of underlying green, green, green. "Here is where we belong."

I'm envious. Forty years later, I still haven't found that.

"We didn't have a lot of money. Patrice had just gone back to work as a receptionist in a beauty salon; I'm a self-employed contractor. But twenty-five years ago, there weren't microfibers this, crazy-expensive-tents that. You borrowed gear, you headed into the woods with a can of baked beans, a package of franks, and that was it. You had fun. You got out, you got away, and you laughed like hell with your kid.

"That's what we did, Tim and I. We hiked into one of the canyons not far from our home, wore ourselves out exploring during the day, practically froze to death at night—and *goddamn*, there isn't a second I would change about any of it. Timmy loved it. No one yelled at him to slow down or lectured him about being too loud or begged him to be anything less than who he was. He shone that weekend. That's what I remember. My boy, with his wild hair and crazy dark eyes, grinning. Ear to ear. The entire two days. I'd never seen him that happy. After that, we were hooked. We escaped as much as possible. Good for Patrice to have some time to herself. Good for her madmen, she'd say, to have time romping in the wild.

"Later, when she was diagnosed with cancer the first time . . . I took Tim camping to break the news. Meant his mother couldn't be there, but both she and I agreed it would be better that way. Tim could howl at the moon. And I could howl with him. Because it wasn't fair. Nothing about cancer is fair.

"We didn't know it then, of course. We didn't understand. Those were the good old days. When we had only one battle to fight. Soon enough . . ."

Martin stops speaking. He doesn't have to continue for me to understand. Soon enough, he'd go from a terminally ill wife to a missing son. And now, in a matter of months, he'll be the only member of his family left. My eyes are moist. I notice, even if Marty doesn't, that the rest of the group is listening intently.

A noise. Scott, the bachelor buddy who disappeared first that night, stands up abruptly. "Gotta piss," he mutters, then turns and stumbles into the woods.

The two others, Miggy and Neil, exchange looks. Both stand, head after their friend, because surely it takes three guys to pee in the woods.

Nemeth resumes glaring at me. How dare I disturb the fragile equilibrium of his hiking party. He is both right and wrong. Searches such as this one are about way more than finding tangible remains. They are about gaining closure.

Sometimes that comes from finally having a body. Sometimes that comes from the journey along the way.

I stand up, stepping close enough to touch the back of Martin's hand as he clutches his map. He flinches, clearly not expecting the contact.

I'm a mess in so many ways. Can't sleep through the night. Can barely make it a single hour without craving a drink. Don't know how to live the way other people seem to know how to live.

But grief. Bone-deep pain, soul-searing rage. This I understand.

"Thank you for telling me about Tim," I murmur. "I will do everything I can to bring him home this week. But I will carry the stories of him with me always."

Marty glances up sharply. Quick enough I can see the feral nature of his pain. Quick enough he can see the feral nature of my own.

I pull back my hand. Martin folds up his map.

And like survivors everywhere, we continue on with our day.

CHAPTER 9

Bite me, bite me, bite me," I repeat. Then, just to switch it up: "Good goddamn!"

Screw these woods. Screw my pack. Screw Nemeth, who's *definitely* a cyborg. The last half is gonna be more difficult? Seriously??

I'm panting. Staggering forward, one careening step at a time. Leg up, leg down. Pant pant pant. Leg up, leg down. Pant pant pant. Sweat pours down my face, stinging my eyes with a toxic mix of sunscreen, bug spray, and human salt.

No pretty trail winds like a ribbon through the verdant woods. No leveling off of the topography. No end in sight. Dirt, boulders, pine trees. Sometimes, we get a switchback, which is to say a slight turn to the right or to the left before a new route through hell. Then there are steep patches of ledge where there's no path at all. Instead, we clamber up like spider monkeys, clutching at spindly trees and praying not to slide back down.

I don't know much about flora and fauna, but so far the forest seems to consist entirely of evergreens. Pine, spruce, fir. I'm basically hiking my way through Christmas. I fucking hate Christmas.

Nemeth and Martin have vanished from sight, leaving Scott, Neil, and Miggy gasping painfully as they trudge along. Even Daisy is reduced to being on point. No more mad dashes into the woods. Just one paw at a time with Luciana following slow and steady behind.

"Stand up," Bob murmurs from behind me.

"I am standing up!"

"You're bending at the waist. It's squeezing your diaphragm, reducing your oxygen supply. I could take your pack—"

"Touch me and I will fucking kill you."

"Then I recommend placing your hands on your hips, which will expand your chest capacity. Or leave your arms loose and focus on swinging them forward. Where your arms go, your legs must follow."

I growl. Snarl. Whimper. Then grudgingly swing my arms.

It works. And enables me to focus on something other than my burning calves and exploding heart rate. I can do this.

I fall farther behind.

"You can go ahead," I mutter to Bob, completely humiliated.

"I'm good."

"I hate pity."

"Then stop being so pathetic."

"I hope Bigfoot kicks your sorry ass."

"Wouldn't that be something? Please take video."

I try to snarl again, but it comes out more as a moan. There's no fun in insulting someone who refuses to be insulted.

A disturbance up ahead. A figure has stepped to the side of the trail as Daisy and Luciana plod silently past.

Miguel from the college trio. He's broken from the group to stand off to one side, bent over at the waist as he struggles to catch his breath. His short dark hair is plastered against his skull, his khaki shirt totally soaked through. He looks as good as I feel, which, given his considerably younger age and compact, muscular build, makes me feel slightly better about myself.

He glances up as we near, his hands planted on his thighs.

"Go . . . ahead," he manages.

"Fuck . . . that," I gasp back and halt beside him. Bob stops as well. Compared to us, the bushy-bearded Bigfoot hunter appears perfectly refreshed. I have a fantasy of him tossing Miggy over one massive shoulder, me over the other, and carrying us the rest of the way. I really wish he would.

"Water," Bob suggests now. "Small steady sips till you get your heart rate under control. Otherwise, you'll further dehydrate yourself vomiting."

"You think?" I snarl.

Miggy nods wearily. He fumbles with his stainless steel water bottle. I reach over and do the honors. As a show of gratitude, he does the same for me.

Luciana and Daisy have now disappeared from view, leaving the three of us behind. The weak links. Well, two of us, anyway.

Miggy's ragged breathing is starting to slow. The young man looks terrible, his tan face flushed, his shirt drenched. I wonder if he drinks as much as his buddy Josh. Or if he's simply a mere mortal, not accustomed to hiking a gazillion miles straight up.

Inhale. Exhale. Drink. The thundering in my ears begins to subside. I remain too hot, physically spent, and incredibly shaky. My feet—I didn't know they could hurt this bad, and I don't even have blisters. I'm not sure where I'll find the resilience to begin again.

Miggy hands me his heavy water bottle. I return it to its side pouch. He does the same for me.

He peers at the steep ridge of dirt punching relentlessly up through the hot, dry woods. Where the rest of our party has gone before us. Where we must now follow.

"I wanted to golf," he murmurs. "That weekend. I voted for golfing. Why the hell didn't we just go golfing?" Then, almost savagely: "I hate these goddamn woods."

Which is when I finally understand the real reason Miggy broke from his friends—there is more than sweat beading down his cheeks.

"I hate these goddamn woods, too," I tell him after a moment.

He laughs brokenly.

We trudge on.

BY THE TIME we reach the top of the endless incline, we have all retreated someplace deep inside ourselves. My mind is a carousel of discordant memories.

Myself dancing under hot lights, whirling, whirling, whirling, till the crowded bar was nothing but a blur of neon and a cacophony of wild laughter but I didn't care because this wasn't my body and this wasn't my life and I'd never have to feel any pain as long as I kept spinning.

First time I woke up in a pool of vomit and didn't remember how I got there.

First time I woke up in someone else's bed and didn't know how I got there.

First time I woke up in county lockup and recalled exactly how I got there but still wanted nothing more than another drink.

My twelve-year-old friend's dog Shaggy, a big, lovable mutt who roamed the neighborhood with his wagging tail and goofy grin, until one day there was a squeal of tires followed by a terrible thump and my father told me not to look outside. I went to my room and tucked myself way back inside my closet because I didn't want to know. Later, Sophie came over and I snuck us a six-pack of beers from the fridge. We drank one after another, never talking, and my father had to know what we'd done—two semiconscious twelve-year-old girls staring at him blurrily from my bedroom floor—but he didn't say a word. And I loved him for that.

The first time I saw Paul.

The last, last time I took a drink.

The sound of Detective Lotham's heartbeat, solid and steady, then increasingly rapid as I pressed myself against him just last year, after my first successfully completed case in a place that came as close to any as feeling like home.

I'm not sure why I'm recalling these particular memories. The good, the sad, the reverent, the humbling. I just know I have to focus on anything other than the agony that is my body.

By the time we arrive, the others have taken up position before a wide, rushing stream, packs off, bodies sprawled. Nemeth and Martin look like their usual stern selves. Like the rest of us, their shirts are soaked with sweat, hair plastered to their scalps. But unlike, say, Scott and Neil, who have collapsed on the ground and obviously plan on never getting up again, Nemeth and Marty look ready for another eighteen miles. Luciana is somewhere in the middle, withdrawn, marshaling her resources. Daisy lounges in the dirt at her feet. The SAR dog looks up at our approach, thumps her tail in greeting, makes no attempt to rise. I understand completely.

The terrain has opened up dramatically. A huge expanse of wild grass, beaten golden brown by the sun this late in the summer, and dotted with white, yellow, and purple wildflowers. The air is crisper at this altitude, limned with the promise of glacier peaks and even the first hint of winter. All around us sweep the green, blue, and brown ridgelines of rolling mountains, some modestly short, some staggeringly tall.

It is all heart-stoppingly beautiful. The kind of views that drew pioneers far from the security of the known into the wild promise of the unknown. I would've made an excellent explorer, assuming I didn't drop dead of exhaustion first.

It takes me a few tries to unclip the buckles around my chest and waist. My fingers are clumsy and swollen. I try to shake off my pack and nearly hiss from the pain in my shoulders. I bite it back quickly, not wanting to give away just how much I hurt.

To judge by the look on Nemeth's face, he's not fooled for a second. Beside me, Miggy has finally wrestled his bag to the ground. Without another word, he crosses to the river's edge, drops to his knees, and plunges his head straight in.

It gives me the incentive to ditch my gear and follow suit as fast as I possibly can.

The water is a total shock. Not just cold, but *cold*. It's bracing and brain numbing, perfectly refreshing and excruciatingly painful. I want to jerk away and gulp down entire mouthfuls. I hold steady, letting the water flow over my face and neck till I feel on the verge of an ice cream headache.

When I sit up and toss back my head, my long wet ponytail slaps between my shoulder blades and sends a fresh torrent of icy chills shivering down my overheated torso. It's about as close to orgasm as I've ever come with an audience.

Beside me, Miggy removes the blue bandana from around his neck, dips it in the water, then uses it to scrub at his face, neck, bare arms. After a final dunking, he ties the dripping cloth around the bronze column of his throat.

Sheer longing must be stamped in my face, because next thing I know, Bob is kneeling beside me. "Want it?" Orange bandana still folded into a fresh, clean square.

"Last time I wanted something that bad, it was a bottle of rotgut vodka."

Bob grins. "Take it, it's yours."

I copy Miggy's technique down to the last detail. I might be stupid, but at least I'm a fast learner.

"Water?" Bob asks me.

"You want some?"

"No. How much do you have left? This is a good place to refill."

I feel like I should know what he's saying, but my physical exhaustion has impaired my ability to understand the English language.

Bob dangles two giant water jugs from their straps. Next, he produces what looks like an elongated plastic pop top, attached to an empty bladder. The water filtration system. I have a similar one in my pack.

As I watch, he fills the empty bladder with running water from the stream. Screws on the filtration top. Then, turning it upside down, he squeezes the water out of the bladder, through the charcoal filter pop top, into his drinking flask. Now I get it. And I should definitely refill both my bottles. Except that would involve standing up, and moving.

I promised I would not be deadweight. I promised I would not slow down the team. I still have to bite my lower lip as I rise painfully to my feet. Miggy is not moving much better. My impression is that Scott and Neil also wouldn't mind being buried where they lie. There is thinking you're active and fit, and then there is Nemeth fit.

When I turn, he's standing right there. I try not to startle or flush guiltily. He hands me my water bottles and the filtration system from my pack.

"Final mile to go," he says. "We'll be camping tonight not far from a stream-fed lake. You can soak your feet in the water there. It'll help."

I nod.

"Today's the hardest. Once we reach the target area and start our search, we'll have to slow down and pay attention, not to mention respect Daisy's need for breaks."

I've never loved a dog more.

Nemeth steps back to take in the rest of the group. He might be a hard-ass, but clearly he's also an experienced guide who knows how to size up his audience. Marty would walk to the ends of the earth without ever stopping, to bring his son home. Bob would follow because his heart is as big as the rest of him.

But for the bachelor party buddies, myself, even Luciana, this level of exertion is pushing our limits. Day one, Nemeth can't afford for any of us to break.

"Ten more minutes," he announces now. "Then we'll gear up. Good news, we got plenty of daylight left, so you can take your time on the home stretch. Upon arrival, we'll make camp, have a hot meal, then Marty and Luciana will walk us through the game plan for tomorrow."

We nod as a unit. Nobody talking but everyone paying attention.

Then, in the distance: a strange, shrill scream that prickles the hair on the back of my neck. I drop my hand to the Rambo knife, feeling a jolt of fight or flight as the cry builds in intensity.

"Any questions?" Nemeth asks.

Scott, eyes wild: "What the hell is that?"

"Just an animal."

The second shriek echoes disturbingly. Daisy's ears prick forward, her body taut. I grip the handle of the tactical blade.

Nemeth remains unconcerned. "All right, break's over. Gear up."

That was not the ten-minute break he promised us. It makes me pay attention, catching the look Nemeth and Martin exchange while I note Bob's posture has taken on a tension I haven't seen before.

A third cry. Shrill. Building, higher, higher, higher. Then, a sudden sharp cutoff. Like a blade severed the sound. Or the creature making it.

Daisy whines, presses closer to her handler.

Another exchanged look between our two leaders, but no words spoken.

Nemeth shoulders the rifle, takes point. Bob prepares to bring up the rear.

They're lying to us. Wild animals, my ass. But why? What don't they want us to know?

Nemeth hops boulder to boulder over the broad stream before disappearing into the thick copse of trees beyond. Martin follows, then the others, one by one vanishing into the woods.

I grip my tactical blade. Very reluctantly, I follow suit.

CHAPTER 10

WHEN I WAS TEN, I became obsessed with camping. I don't re-member why. Probably the other kids in my class were talking about fun-filled family adventures and I grew jealous.

I pestered my parents relentlessly. My mom was firm on the subject: "You know I don't have time off, and if I did, I'm certainly not spending it sleeping on the ground."

My father, the appeaser, never said no, but also didn't say yes. So around and around we went, me convinced that I couldn't live another day without sleeping in a tent, my parents convinced that eventually I'd grow out of it.

My father had recently lost his job. Downsizing, he said as he popped open another beer. His unemployed days turned into weeks, his body slowly merging with the sofa into one hops-scented blob, while my mom, currently working two positions, returned late each evening in a state of tight-lipped rage. Furiously cleaning the kitchen, throwing in loads of laundry, collecting all the empties. She never said a word, but my father, watching her through his drunken haze, would do the talking for both of them.

"You're right. Absolutely right. I should find work. Get off this damn sofa. Tomorrow, honey. I promise. Tomorrow." Then he'd crack open another beer and return to his Naugahyde bliss.

One afternoon, I took it upon myself to tend the house. I scrubbed the counters, scoured the bathroom, vacuumed the floor. Was I protecting my father? Saving my mother? Can any child answer that question?

My mother arrived home late, her shoulders slumped with exhaustion. She peered tiredly at the spotless kitchen, then at me, sitting patiently at the table, even though it was nearly midnight. I thought she might smile in gratitude. Give me a huge hug. Burst into song?

She said, "For God's sakes, Frankie, at least learn from my mistakes."

Then she headed for her bedroom.

Later, I listened to them fight: "I mean it, Ron. Seven days from now if you're still like this, I'm out. And I'm taking Frankie with me. You'll never see either one of us again."

Then I listened to my father cry.

The next afternoon after school, I returned home to my father sitting upright, his back ramrod straight on the edge of the sofa. He had his hands clasped tightly before him, clearly waging some kind of internal war with himself. A tremor snaked through his frame. He screwed up his face in fierce concentration till the shaking stopped. Though his hands still gave him away.

Finally, he noticed me standing in the doorway. "You're home. Thank God, you're home!"

He exploded into a whirlwind of nervous energy, fixing me a snack, unloading my backpack, fussing over my schoolbooks.

I must have homework. Didn't I have homework? Let's do homework!

I didn't have homework. But I found some math worksheets and spread them out on the table. We did the problems together, first giggling lightly, then laughing hysterically because we were both so terrible at it. For weeks afterward, the phrase *carry the one* had us rolling on the floor all over again.

My mom came home to dinner. Frozen pizza, but still, my father took it out of the wrapper and baked it himself.

That night there was no fighting. That night, the house was so quiet, I couldn't sleep from the sheer agony of the unknown.

The following afternoon, my father had collapsed back into the sofa, covered in sweat and shivering uncontrollably. I bathed his forehead with a wet washcloth, fetching him blanket after blanket.

Eventually, my mother arrived. I waited for the yelling, the blame, the torrent of rage. But to my surprise—my father's surprise?—she took a seat next to him. She rubbed his back.

She said, "I'm so proud of you." She murmured, "I've missed you, Ronnie."

She whispered . . .

That I couldn't hear.

Couple of days later, my father's sweating and vomiting stopped. His color returned. He once more achieved the vertical position. I came home to more snacks. My mother gained a clean house and evening meal. And the house existed in a perpetual state of peace and quiet. So much peace and quiet. I couldn't figure out how people did it, living day after day with this amount of peace and quiet.

One day my father greeted me with a huge grin on his face. Surprise! He and I were going camping. Well, actually, we were going to spend the night in a borrowed tent in our backyard, but close enough, right? I bounced all over the house in excitement. Yes, yes, yes!

My mom actually smiled, caught up in our enthusiasm.

Saturday morning was all about prep. We were going to need all the makings for s'mores, plus hot dogs and baked beans. I thought we should definitely have a fire. My father thought we should definitely not. He spun some yarn about mythical forest sprites who would carry away our food and return it magically cooked. I was offended. What? Did he think I was still five?

Just yesterday, he assured me wryly. And the day before that, I was a newborn. Then he cleared his throat and ruffled my hair.

Late afternoon, we carried our gear outside.

My father attempted to assemble the borrowed tent. Much cursing and swearing ensued. I ran piles of blankets and pillows from the house to the yard because we didn't have sleeping bags, something my father hadn't realized till just now.

Everything took way longer than expected, my father's expression becoming less excited, more frazzled. But eventually, the sun just starting to descend, he had produced a tent-like shelter, while I had procured every piece of bedding we owned. I would organize our sleeping quarters. My father would inform the forest sprites of our dinner reservation.

He was gone a very long time. But then, I had a lot of blankets to arrange.

When my father finally reappeared, bearing a tray of cooked franks and baked beans, he was beaming from ear to ear. So pleased with himself. So happy. So very, *very* happy.

Just like that, I knew why he'd been in the kitchen for so long. His smile faltered. He opened his mouth as if to say . . . No! . . . You're wrong! . . . I'd never do such a thing!

But the words didn't come. He closed his mouth, held out the tray. We sat on the ground and ate our meal with our hands, dipping the franks into the baked beans and making a huge mess. I wanted to giggle at the baked beans dripped across my father's lap, the smear of ketchup on his cheek. I wanted to scream, "Carry the one!" just so he'd laugh uproariously and I could collapse beside him and we'd *both* be so very, very happy.

I wanted this moment to be real.

But my father was gone. In his place was a drunk who talked too fast. About childhood memories and random facts and oh, wait, look at the color of the sky. He always loved the smell of grass, there was nothing like sleeping under the open sky and we should do this again, wait, we should do this now, and hey, why had we never gone camping before this? Next week, Yosemite!

My father disappeared into the house with our dishes, eventually weaving and stumbling his way back out. He grabbed for the tent to balance himself. Both it and he collapsed to the ground. Never mind. Ghost stories!

By the time my mom appeared, I was carting the blankets from the tent back to the house, so I could drape them over my father's passed-out form. He and the sofa were one again. Which left my mother and me on our own. She stared at his prone form, still in her coat, clutching her purse. I couldn't read the expression on her face. Rage? Resignation? Relief that our household was finally back to normal?

I told my mother I was tired and going to bed. Then, clutching a pillow to my chest, I turned sideways as she walked by. I didn't want her to see the half-filled bottle of bourbon I had stashed behind my back.

Later, in the privacy of my room, I sat on the floor behind my bed and studied my father's precious bottle of booze. I twisted off the black cap. I inspected the amber liquid, sniffing the slightly sweet brew, dripping it across my palm, licking it off my fingers. I wanted to taste what my father tasted. I wanted to feel what my father felt. I wanted to understand this powerful liquid he loved more than anything in the world.

Even me.

I rubbed some of the bourbon at the top of my lip. I licked more and more off my hands, took tiny sips from the cap. I felt, bit by bit, the warmth spread through my veins. Then I inhaled until the boozy scent formed into the shape of my father, grinning beside me.

We are camping in the backyard. The night is cold but our tent is cozy thanks to my stockpile of blankets. My father tells me this is the best adventure he's ever had and look at that shooting star and oh, he has one more ghost story to share. And we talk and laugh and stuff ourselves with marshmallows straight out of the bag because he never let me build that fire. Then we chase down the marshmallows with chunks of dark chocolate and broken pieces of graham crackers and it tastes so good we declare we will never eat s'mores any other way. We fall asleep still laughing.

My father and me.

On the camping adventure that never happened. And the relationship that never was.

I never camped again. My father had more moments of sobriety. Followed by more moments of failure. Such is the ride.

My mother . . . she worked, she endured, she nursed her rage. First at him. Later at me.

Till the day I graduated. I don't remember it, being so well and truly wasted that even my father regarded me with pity as I stumbled home at four in the morning. Then soon enough, I was gone, off to bright lights and hard partying in LA.

Till one day, hundreds of miles away, a driver swerved across the center line. He hit a vehicle head-on, and just like that, my parents were dead.

I took the call standing outside a bar, one finger stuck in my ear to drown out the background noise as I listened to my aunt's words. I think I nodded. Then I went back inside, to the business at hand.

I never met my parents as a sober adult. I never got to show my father this disease could be beat. I never got to prove to my mother that I took after her more than she thought; I'm a good worker, I know how to get the job done, I can make a difference in this world.

She knew I loved my father. She died before I could tell her that I loved her, too. That I did admire her. That my father might have been my favorite playmate, but she was my hero, and I never would've gotten my act together if I hadn't had the example of her strength to guide me.

Unfinished business. An addict's life is filled with such instances. The coulda, woulda, shouldas that will never happen again.

It helps me relate to the families I assist. Enables me to understand why Martin is driving us now, step after brutal step, deeper into the mountains.

Until we finally arrive at this place, Devil's Canyon, where we stagger to a halt, half of our group still vertical, the other half of us dropping like rocks.

"This is it," Nemeth declares, gesturing to a flat clearing next to a vast blue lake. "Home sweet home for the next six days. Everyone, welcome to our campsite."

I think of my father and the backyard and the camping that never was, and I do my best to hide the exhausted tears running down my cheeks as I finally wrest the pack off my shoulders. I'm not the only one struggling; Neil, Scott, and Miggy appear equally wrung out.

"You are a goddamn asshole," Miggy bursts out suddenly. He points a finger straight at Martin. "Haven't you ruined our lives enough by now? We loved Tim, too, you know. Trying to kill us year after year doesn't change a goddamn thing."

He throws his pack on the ground and stomps off into a patch of trees.

Which is how I officially know this isn't the end of our ordeal, but just the beginning.

CHAPTER 11

DEVIL'S CANYON APPEARS TO BE a broad, flat expanse that spreads out . . . forever. The lake before us is framed by a staggering gray-brown cliff face and more red-and-green-streaked mountains in the distance. Up close are patches of dark woods interspersed with meadows of sun-dried grass and plains of dusty earth.

I understand at least part of Miguel's temper tantrum. An entire day of grueling hiking later, my feet roar, my shoulders have knotted into a solid bar, and I'm not sure where the pain ends and I begin. Hard dirt and an ice-cold lake? I want a soft bed and bubble bath. Even Daisy has plopped down with an exhausted sigh. I wonder how much Tim's former college friends still hike in their real lives, or if this is the yearly torture test, as Miggy claims.

I study Martin's face for his reaction to the outburst, but his expression remains inscrutable as he begins unloading his pack.

Nemeth starts pointing and commanding. Fire here, latrine there. First clump of tents here, second there, third over here. As the two females, Luciana and I are assigned our own little corner of dirt. The bachelor buddies form the next grouping of three, leaving our fearless leaders as the final trio.

I don't know what to do next. I have no idea how to set up a tent, establish a campsite. I never managed to spend a single night in my own backyard, so how the hell am I supposed to fake my way through this? Everyone seems to be unloading gear, so I follow their lead. Luciana already has her shelter spread out on the ground. Watching her, I'm filled with the age-old terror of making a mistake, looking foolish. How is it we all leave high school, but high school never leaves us?

Bob appears by my side. For a big guy, he moves with surprising stealth. He glances from my tent, still in its drawstring bag, to me.

"If you could start gathering wood for the fire, I can set up your tent," he says.

I've never been so grateful.

I walk circles around the emerging campsite, picking up kindling, then bigger sticks, then just random dried twigs, because at this stage of the game, to stop moving is to collapse, and I can't afford to drop dead. I spiral out farther, weaving through the closest screen of pines before eventually stumbling across Miggy. He's sitting at the edge of the massive lake, tucked behind wavy grasses and looking at nothing in particular.

I glance back at the campsite, a distant whir of activity I can barely make out through the trees. Then I set down my armful of dry twigs and take a seat next to Miguel.

I don't speak. In this day and age, we all talk too much and hear too little. Listening has become a forgotten art that the world is sorely missing.

"I'm sorry," Miggy says shortly. He picks up a rock. Throws it at the lake. It lands with a small plop.

"How are you feeling?" I ask him.

"Terrible. Like a guy who works a real job day after day, because that's the responsible thing to do, then once a year gets thrown back into the mountains because my best friend who disappeared five years ago happened to love camping, and his father has hated us ever since."

"You don't hike on your own?"

"What's your name again? Frankie?"

"Frankie."

"Take it from me, Frankie, I would never step foot on a trail again if I had my choice. And Josh, Neil, Scotty—they agree with me. We lost enough that night. Martin's yearly death marches don't make anything better. They just torture us all over again."

"Is that why Josh drinks so much?"

"Maybe. You'd have to ask him."

"Are you four still in touch?"

Miggy picks up another pebble. He slices it through the air, watches it skip three times across the water. "They were my brothers," he states quietly. "I thought nothing would break us."

I understand what he's saying. Or rather, not saying. That shared trauma can bond, but more often than not, it severs. The guilt. The pain. The need to move forward, the agony of letting go. Five guys went into the woods. One has never been seen again. And the other four . . . they are not who they used to be either. Life is like that.

"Do you still live relatively close?"

He nods. "Beaverton has quite a few major tech firms. Scotty, Neil, and I all work in that area. Josh went the manufacturing route, but his firm is just around the corner. Getting to be you can't throw a rock without hitting an enginerd in that town."

"But no catching up at bars after work, weekly game of hoops, periodic college reunions?"

"We tried, after we came back. But . . . it didn't feel the same anymore. No one knew what to say. How to act. Do we sit around and talk about Tim? Do we pretend it never happened? We couldn't figure it out. Josh broke first. Stopped coming around, returning calls. When Marty contacted us about a renewed search effort one year later, I was surprised Josh showed up. It was the first time any of us had seen him in months. He seemed distant, but who were we to tell him how to cope? He continued to withdraw after that, though. I heard rumors of a DUI. That he was having difficulty at work. I thought of picking up the phone, but I just couldn't do it. Two days ago was the first time I'd seen him since last year. Just looking at him . . . Goddammit. We fucking failed him. Again."

He throws another rock into the water, then a second, third, fourth, in rapid succession. No fancy skipping, just unfocused rage.

"We're all here because Marty owns our asses and he knows it," Miguel says at last. "But even assuming we stumble upon Tim's body tomorrow . . . will that actually change anything? Will Josh stop drinking? Will Martin finally hate us less than we hate ourselves?"

He glances at me but I don't answer because I already know it's not my words he needs. This kind of search is distinctly personal. For some, finding answers does bring closure. For others, finally knowing what happened to their loved one only makes their nightmares that much more specific.

Miggy returns to staring at the rippling lake. "I was scared that night," he states abruptly.

"Because Scott had already disappeared?"

"Because . . . because of the screams and that noise and . . ." He shakes his head.

I wait.

He picks up three more stones and fires them off.

"We were so damn drunk. Sometimes, I'm not sure what even happened. Was it a bad memory or a fragment of a nightmare or an alcohol-induced hallucination? We hiked in. We set up. Campfire, dinner, beer. Then . . . everything went to shit. Yelling and screaming, sounds from the woods. Scott's gone and Josh . . . Josh is so upset. And I know why except I don't know why. It's like a blurry movie reel, and the more I try to see, the more out of focus it gets."

"When you first think about that night, what immediately pops into your head? How do you feel?"

"Terrified."

"What do you want to do?"

"Get away. Get the hell out of the woods. Never look back."

"And the others? Josh, Neil, and Scott?"

"Josh doesn't speak of it. Neil and Scott are of the nothing-you-can-do-to-change-the-past school of thought. They've moved on the most." Miggy pauses, smiles at something I don't get. "Kind of."

I switch gears. "How'd you meet Tim?"

"Freshman year at OSU. We were waiting outside a TA's office, got to talking, learned we were both engineering students. Josh was my roommate. Tim was with Neil and Scott. We all started hanging out, given we had plenty of classes together. Junior year we rented an apartment together. Then, upon graduation, we all got a house in Beaverton. Dudeville, Tim called it. Home of Friday night beers, Saturday mayhem, Sunday recovery. God, those were good times."

"What happened?"

"Life." Miguel shrugs. "Promotions to more demanding jobs, casual dates turning into serious relationships. You can only be young and stupid for so long, though we certainly gave it our all."

"One of you introduced Tim to his fiancée, right?"

"Neil. He worked with Latisha. She was in marketing."

"Do you still see her?"

"The first year, sure. But it's difficult, when the only thing you have in common is what you lost. She didn't blame us. Not like Martin. She'll tell you, if Tim had to . . . meet his end . . . out in the mountains doing what he loved best was the right way for him to go."

"Why isn't she here? I read she was a big hiker as well."

"She's pregnant."

"She met someone? Good for her."

"You mean good for her and Scott."

I blink my eyes several times. "You mean . . ."

"Yep. They wed in March. Small ceremony. Tim's parents didn't attend. Neither did the rest of us."

"How do you feel about—"

"I don't."

"What about Josh and Neil? Surely they have opinions about one of Tim's friends marrying his former fiancée."

"You should ask them."

I can already read the answer on Miggy's face, however. The union between Scott and Latisha isn't a happy development for the rest of the crew. Which means: yet more tension in our group that isn't really a group.

"What is your goal for this week?" I ask Miggy now.

"You mean, other than to find Tim's remains and bring him home?"

"Do you want that?"

Miggy appears genuinely startled. "Aren't I supposed to want that?"

"That's not the question. You can want whatever you want. Just you and me here, and I won't tell anyone."

He pauses, remaining silent for so long I'm not sure he's going to answer me. Then: "I want to never walk these mountains again.

I want to no longer wake up screaming in the middle of the night. I want to stop thinking of my best friend and breaking down from the guilt. I want . . . to feel human again."

He looks at me. "Is that even possible? If we succeed this week, is any of that finally going to happen?"

"For some people it does."

"In other words, I'm shit out of luck."

I smile, then state as gently as I can: "In my experience, you won't ever feel the same. But eventually, you may find some things about the new normal that aren't so bad. One day, you might even like what your life has become. Then you'll know you have moved on, even if you didn't realize it at the time."

He tosses another frustrated pebble. "If only it was that simple."

"It's not really that complicated."

"Don't make me fucking hate you, too."

I grin at him, understanding completely. We sit in silence a moment longer, then Miguel rises to his feet, dusts off his butt. "We should head back. Before Nemeth comes to find us."

"Do you like him?"

"No. I don't like any of them. But then, I think we just established I don't like myself very much either. The search dog, Daisy? I can root for her. Otherwise, I'm just counting down the days till we head back to civilization."

"I like Bob," I offer, standing up as well. "He seems genuinely cheerful."

"Then you're an idiot."

This catches me off guard. "Sorry?"

"Isn't it your job to ask questions? Because why Bob? Why a Bigfoot hunter?"

"Because the Bigfoot Society has some of the best data on missing persons in America's wildlands?"

"And they get paid how much for that interest?"

"Paid? It's a hobby, an after-hours-enthusiast kind of thing—"

"Try five thousand dollars."

I'm totally baffled now. "Bob was paid five thousand dollars?"

"From Martin. I saw the check myself."

"But . . . why?"

"Based on what I overheard, to bring us out alive. Or really, to bring Marty out alive."

"But . . . I don't . . ." I frown, not quite able to make sense of this revelation. Bob was paid to ensure Martin's safety? From what?

Miggy follows my line of thinking perfectly. "Exactly," he says. "Still happy you joined our merry band?"

Then he picks up an armful of dried kindling and heads back to camp. I follow a moment later and quite a bit slower.

Martin's obsession, Miggy's guilt, and Bigfoot Bob's payday? My squirrel brain races and spins with all this new information. But try as I might, I can't make any sense of it.

Day one down. I'm already nervous for what happens next.

CHAPTER 12

THE CAMPSITE TAKES SHAPE QUICKER than I can imagine. By the time Miggy and I return, the tents are up in three clusters around a larger clearing with a ring of stones in the middle for the campfire. I drop my load of wood beside it as Miguel does the same. He takes the liberty of setting up the kindling, clearly knowing what he's doing.

I notice Neil and Scott staggering out of the woods with a massive section of tree trunk between them. They position it in front of the fire the way one might arrange a sofa, then disappear without a word to fetch more seating.

I walk over to my tent, which Bob has erected next to Luciana's. Daisy is sprawled on the ground before Luciana's small blue-domed shelter. She thumps her tail in greeting as I approach.

"Tired, girl?" I ask her, pausing long enough to scratch behind her ears. She yawns contentedly. The dog is clearly tuckered out by the long day but seems in good spirits. Puts her ahead of most of us.

Luciana pokes her head out of her tent. "Just in time."

"For what?"

"Water duty." She holds up several portable buckets. "I volunteered us." She gives me a conspiratorial look. "Grab fresh clothes, then follow me."

Who am I to argue? I sort through my pack till I find a long-sleeve T-shirt and my black yoga pants. The air is already starting to cool, dusk coming quickly now. I remember what Lisa Rowell said about nights being chilly this time of year. After the hot, sweaty day, I'm looking forward to it.

Luciana has her own bundle tucked under her arm as she leads me away from the camp. I'm really sorry to be moving. The ache in my feet has reduced each step to a painful hobble, let alone the sore muscles defining the rest of me. I don't have to be an experienced hiker to know that tomorrow will feel worse, especially after a night of sleeping on the ground. So I grit my teeth and remain quiet as Luciana threads her way through a bank of trees to the lake's edge, out of sight of everyone else.

She sets down her clothes, shakes out the collapsible canvas buckets. She hands me two, and I'm immediately impressed by the design. Hard metal rings give structure to the top and bottom, as well as pail handles. But the waterproof material folds down to almost nothing in the middle. Pretty ingenious.

We fill all of them. Several gallons' worth of water for the campsite—to boil for drinking water and dinner prep, I assume. Given my level of thirst and hunger, it all seems like a good idea.

Once finished, Luciana triumphantly holds up a small object I can barely make out in the shadows.

"Soap," she announces, then in the next instant starts stripping.

I don't have to be asked twice. Given I spent decades of my life waking up naked in strangers' beds, I'm not one to worry about modesty now.

The water is freezing cold. Stream fed, Nemeth said. Then I'm guessing that stream came straight down from a glacier as I recoil sharply and bite back a scream. But the pain is worth it to scrub the layers of encrusted sweat and grime from my skin. I've never felt so itchy or, for that matter, smelled so bad.

Luciana goes all the way under, emerging with the grace of a dark otter and flipping back her long black hair. Obviously a pro, she works the tiny bar of soap through her hair, across her face, down her body. It's a natural soap, she informs me, safe for lake water, but not so great at sudsing, so don't be put off by the lack of bubbles.

We both quickly rinse, then return to the lake's edge and drag our fresh outfits over our still-wet forms. Luciana attempts a brief wash of her dirty clothes, so I do the same. I'm starting to understand for the first time how thin my hiking wardrobe is, if we're going to sweat through an outfit a day.

"We can hang our clothes near the fire to dry," Luciana informs me. "Won't be perfect, but a couple of days from now, they'll smell better than anything else we own."

"Thank you," I tell her honestly. I don't really have friends, which makes me even more appreciative of people who are kind.

We return to the camp, where Miguel has the fire going. He's set up a cooking stand with a stainless steel pot dangling over the flames. Luciana dumps in the first bucket, and in no time at all, we have boiling water. My stomach rumbles expectantly.

"Exactly," Luciana says. "Did you notice the calorie count on your MRE options? Most contain several thousand per serving. Ridiculous in normal life. Totally awesome after a full day of hiking.

I'm telling you now, freeze-dried stroganoff is about to be the best thing you've ever tasted."

More noise announces that Scott and Neil are back again. This log is smaller but works equally well. Bob appears with another slung over a single shoulder, whistling cheerfully as he plunks it down next to Scott and Neil's labored delivery. They shake their heads at being so clearly outmuscled. But just like that, we have an outdoor living room, complete with fireside seating.

Nemeth and Martin emerge with their meal kits. The rest of us quickly follow suit. More water is boiled, instant food prepared, and by the time the daylight starts to fade, it's a regular dinner party. We sit on the logs, waving tiny sporks and extolling the sheer perfection of rehydrated lasagna. Luciana didn't lie: My pouch of macaroni and cheese is the finest meal I've ever eaten. I contemplate a second but figure I should pace myself.

Daisy scarfs down her own dinner, then hangs out in front of the fire, tongue lolling.

Conversation is light, with occasional bursts of banter. In this moment, we feel like a unified group. Eight people relaxing after a long day of physical exertion. The sky yawns above us, streaked with pink, then red as the sun works its way down the horizon.

I wonder if this is how the kids in my class felt when they went camping. This sense of awe and wonder, fear and excitement.

I think of my father, the intent look on his face as he struggled to assemble the borrowed tent. What do you remember most—the moments your parents genuinely tried, or all the times they definitely failed? I've never figured out that answer.

Sitting here now, I focus on the good. That this moment is beautiful and perfect, and I'm wise enough now to appreciate all the moments that came before it, even the less beautiful and less perfect ones, as they led me here.

The gift of gratitude, we say in AA. It took me a long time to find it, and I'm still not the best at remembering it, but every now and then, I almost understand. The grandeur of these mountains. The contented silence of my friend Stoney, wiping down the counter of his bar. The taste of the perfect hot dog, eaten street side.

I may not own much, but I'm a collector in my own way.

I finish up my rehydrated cheese and pasta, scraping morosely at the inside of the foil pouch. Nemeth has produced a heavy-duty, scentproof trash bag for our garbage. It and uneaten rations—similarly bagged—will be removed from the campsite and tied up high. Bear management, he explains. He looks relaxed for the first time all day. I was right before: He could've been carved from these mountains, appearing as natural in this habitat as the distant cliff face, the ramrod-straight pine trees, the towering peaks. He belongs to this world, I think, whereas the rest of us are merely visiting.

I expect Nemeth to be the one to break the mood first. Instead, it's Martin.

In the rapidly falling light, he brings out his ubiquitous map, snaps it open. "All right. Gather round. Over the next five days, this is the game plan."

MARTIN HAS DIVIDED Devil's Canyon into a series of quadrants. I'm no expert, but even I realize we can never cover all this ground in a matter of days. Hence each quadrant has been given a weighted value. What did Nemeth explain earlier? Probability of detection, something like that.

"We need to preserve Daisy for the heavy lifting," Martin explains now. "She can only search for forty-five minutes at a stretch, then she requires a fifteen-minute break before continuing. Given that, the humans need to target her efforts as efficiently as possible, working as the forward crew."

In the past ten years, I've found more bodies than I would've liked, but I've still never set out explicitly to recover bones. Given the dry climate and passing years, Timothy O'Day's remains have most likely skeletonized into a collection of dried bones, scattered by scavengers. In all honesty, they wouldn't appear much different from the kindling I gathered for tonight's fire. A sad testimony to what we all become in the end.

"We know when Tim headed out, he left behind his tent, sleeping bag, and food but had most of his other gear with him," Martin continues. "In the past few years, we've retraced several logical areas where Tim may have veered off trail, forking left instead of right, that sort of thing. Our assumption has been that someone as experienced as my son would quickly fall back to basic survival skills upon realizing he was lost. First and foremost is the need for shelter."

I had always thought water would be top priority, but according to Luciana's overview of the rule of threes, shelter came first.

"Therefore, we're going to start with these four quadrants, which include a series of caves on the far side of the canyon. Any one of them would be a viable option for taking cover. It's a solid two-hour hike to reach that destination. Along the way, I want everyone to pay attention. Remember, we're not just looking for Tim, but signs of Tim.

"His backpack was navy blue. He wore a dark green windbreaker. He carried with him a variety of khaki pants and predominantly long-sleeve white knit tops, which he layered with red, green, or gray flannel. Be on the lookout for fragments of color, scraps of fabric, anything out of the ordinary. This area is not heavily trafficked. Spot any boot prints, signs of human passage, speak up."

Martin pauses. We nod obediently.

"Tim also knew the importance of leaving a trail behind. Look for lengths of rope tied to branches. Maybe torn strips of cloth, or pieces of duct tape. He'd want to mark where he came from to manage his own orientation, as well as aid search efforts. Be aware.

"Also, while we're headed to the caves as a source of natural cover, Tim was well-versed in making shelters. He had a tarp in his pack as well as plenty of cord, so he could've erected something as official as a makeshift tent to something as temporary as a twig lean-to. Best way to spot something like that, look for hard lines or straight objects. Nature is rarely perfect. If something catches your attention, stop and take a second look. Often our eyes pick up on things before our brains can fully process the image."

I raise my hand.

Martin glances up, already appearing vaguely annoyed. "What?"

"How does that work for Daisy? If we get too far ahead, will that contaminate the scent field for her?"

Luciana answers the question. "If we were looking for a live recovery, then yes, I'd need Daisy to be in the lead and the rest of you to remain downwind. But cadaver recovery is very specific. Daisy isn't trying to catch the scent of human, but the odor of decomp. Trust me, she won't confuse us with that."

"Even if its bones? I mean . . ." Scott falters, looking self-conscious, if not a bit stricken, to have stated the obvious out loud. "Five years later, how much decomp is left?"

Luciana again: "The age of the remains is not a factor. There have been cases of canines hitting on hundred-year-old bones. Nor do they confuse animal bones with human."

This catches my attention. "Hundred-year-old bones must be nearly fossilized. What organic matter is even left for a dog to scent?"

"We don't know." Luciana shrugs. "A dog's sense of smell is ten thousand to a hundred thousand times better than our own. It's one of the reasons my team doesn't utilize synthetic cadaver scents for training. Trust me, you can buy entire kits—Pseudo-Corpse Scent, Drowned Victim Scent. They come with chemical ratings, mass spec profiles, and all sorts of scientific mumbo jumbo. At the end of the day, however, no one is really sure what it is that triggers the dog's response. Is there a corpse scent that still lingers on hundred-year-old bones? Certainly not that we can detect. For that matter, our training material of choice is human teeth. They're easy enough to obtain, legal to own, and much less disturbing than, say, severed body parts. Old teeth don't seem particularly decompy to me, especially after we've buried them a million times. But our dogs always know.

"When we get to our defined search area," Luciana continues, "then I'll need you all to stay put while I determine wind direction and pick a starting point for Daisy's efforts. She's an air-scenting dog, so whatever she detects will be brought to her on air currents. She'll work side to side till hopefully she detects the desired odor. Then she'll follow that smell backward to the source. The complicating factor, of course, is that she'll want to follow a direct line, regardless of topography. Our job will be to problem solve the best work-around for her. For example, if she comes to a steep gully or a heavily wooded thicket that's impassable, we need to figure out how to navigate that obstacle, then help her get back on scent on the other side. That can take some time. But she's good. If we can get her within the vicinity, she won't let us down."

I'm studying Martin's map upside down. Devil's Canyon is very long and wide. This won't be a simple search at all, especially with only five days to cover as much ground as possible. I imagine the limited timeframe is in deference to Daisy's stamina. Even working canines need a day off. But all in all, looking at this map, consider-ing the size of our group, this feels more and more like a fool's er-rand to me.

I wonder if Miggy might be onto something: Is Martin really convinced he can find his son's body, or does he just want an excuse to torture his son's wayward friends year after year?

"Why Devil's Canyon?" I ask Martin. "Seems far away from Tim's last known location."

"This is a long shot," Martin admits. I wait, because that doesn't answer my question. Marty finally taps at the map, his finger following a line from the campsite five years ago to where we are now. "Our working assumption is that Tim got lost, became disoriented."

I nod, understanding the theory—if Tim had met his end closer to the guys' campsite, someone would've found his body by now.

"The first few years, we focused on the most logical 'wrong' trails. If Tim headed west instead of turning east at this juncture, then he would've ended up on this trail, which could've led to that trail, et cetera, et cetera. Or having forked north, he would've come to this river, which he could've followed to that crossing, leading to this meadow."

I nod again.

"All of these options assume Tim stayed on the known byways. Safest course of action for a guy lost in the woods. Except . . ." Martin drags out the word.

"You never found him."

"Which got me thinking. What if he made a judgment call? What if something tempted him to abandon an easier-looking route and strike out on his own? Look at this section here." Martin moves his finger on the map. "If Tim missed the first turn as he hustled through the night, then he would've continued trekking north instead of south. Eventually, he'd find himself hiking along the bottom of this heavily wooded ravine. Nemeth and I did it last year. Tough trail. Narrow, densely wooded, real bitch. Tim would've found himself exhausted, disoriented, and desperate to get his bearings. Which brings us to right here. Where there's a break in the trees. Where a fit, enterprising young man might be tempted to turn off the trail and take a direct route up the side of the ravine in order to reach higher ground. Maybe he thought he could get cell reception or a better vantage point once on top. Of course, that didn't happen."

"Nemeth says cell phones are useless in these woods."

"Not even sat phones work worth a damn. But can't blame a guy for trying. Now"—Martin returns to the map—"Tim is off trail, traversing the top of a ravine. If he continued his northern route, that path would bring him to this canyon. It'd take him most of the day, but upon arrival he'd see flat land, a large body of water, and opportunities for natural shelter. Shelter, water, and food." Martin ticks the items off on his fingers. "Tim was smart. He'd recognize immediately this canyon presented his best shot at survival."

"You're hoping he took refuge here." I hesitate, suddenly unsure. Did Martin think his son might actually still be alive? Surviving on his own for five years?

"He wouldn't have made it through the winter," Martin says quietly, as if reading my mind. "He didn't have that kind of gear. Not for mountains this high, terrain this rugged."

I nod, feeling guilty for bringing it up. Martin straightens, folding up his map.

"We've been searching a long time," he murmurs. "Whether this next week can magically make a difference . . . For Patrice's sake, I hope so."

Marty heads back to his tent, while the rest of us remain huddled around the campfire for warmth.

No one talks. Bodies worn-out, bellies full, we succumb to individual comatose states. I move off the log to the ground, where I can stretch out my tired legs while leaning back and peering up at the night sky. The moon, probably three-quarters full, glows like a fat squash. And the stars. So many of them, stretching out forever. I'd nearly forgotten what they looked like, after my last year and a half in major cities.

These same stars spread across the tribal lands where I found Lani Whitehorse's body at the bottom of a lake. Over the farm where I discovered little Johnny in the trunk of a rusted-out junk car. Over the crack house where I located my very first missing person, a sad young woman whose boyfriend blew off her head rather than let her go.

I wonder if Timothy O'Day did make it this far, five years ago. Was he grateful to stumble into this slice of paradise, thinking he'd finally gotten lucky? Did he look up at this sky every night and think of his soon-to-be bride waiting for him back home, his parents, who had to be going crazy? Did he whisper his secret hopes and hidden fears to these distant pinpricks of light, trusting them to remember him, a lone human in search of comfort?

Eventually, one by one, everyone makes discreet trips into the woods, then disappears into their tents.

I get up when Luciana does, Daisy lumbering slowly to her feet. I follow them to our corner of the campsite. My long-sleeve shirt is comfortable enough so I don't bother to change. I climb into my borrowed one-person tent, the size of a cozy den. Then I zip myself inside my sleeping bag, the silvery lining reflecting my body's heat back on me till I'm my own little convection oven.

I hear the low murmur of voices from the college friends, still sitting around the fire. Distant noises echo in the trees while frogs sing closer to the lake, a woodland lullaby . . .

I BOLT AWAKE, panicked and disoriented, my heart already thundering in my chest.

Then I hear it for the second time.

Somewhere outside, a person is screaming.

CHAPTER 13

FUMBLE WITH THE ZIPPER of my tent, then finally tumble out, registering several things at once. The fire has burned down to glowing red embers and the camp is in a state of chaos. People are pouring from their shelters, twisting around wildly, trying to identify the threat we can all hear but not see.

Then, that scream again. Definitely human, definitely male.

Beside me, Luciana has emerged, holding a straining Daisy by the collar. The woman's face is pale, Daisy clearly distressed.

Nemeth strides forward, rifle in hand. "Everyone, stay here."

But our group that isn't really a group has already fractured. Bob disappears into one bank of trees; the college buddies grab flashlights and take off into the second. I jam on my boots with one hand, while digging around for a light source with my other. I come up with the headlamp. Good enough.

"Be careful," Luciana says in warning. She's already wrestling Daisy back into her tent, preparing to zip them both back in. I can understand her not wanting her dog racing through the trees after dark. I shouldn't be doing this either. It's not like I have a gun, or expertise, or any kind of training to offer.

But I've never been one to sit idly by. Even if it's crazy, foolish, and impulsive—*especially* if it's crazy, foolish, and impulsive—chances are I'm going to do it. No point in wasting time fighting the impulse.

Sound is disorienting in a canyon. I thought the last scream came from the direction of the pine trees, which is where most of our party headed. But then I hear something else from behind me. Not a scream. A distinct popping crack. Like a tree limb breaking. Or a human bone.

I correct course to the vast unknown on the other side of camp, the light from my headlamp swinging wildly as I glance frantically from side to side. Almost immediately, I wish I'd brought a flashlight instead. The beam from my headlamp slices the landscape into a disorienting mix of top of meadow grasses here, piece of tree trunk there, single curve of boulder over there. Meanwhile, I trip over every unseen object at my feet.

I power forward, ears straining.

Breathing. Heavy, deep. I turn toward it. Coming from my right side, near the lake. I stumble in that direction, barking my shin and nearly face planting as I catch the edge of a tree stump with my left leg.

Is that a darker shadow between the golden shimmer of dried meadow grasses? I slow, moving less certainly now. Man or beast? And in either case, what am I supposed to do?

I should've grabbed the emergency whistle or bear spray. Nemeth is right: My biting wit isn't going to do me much good in the wild.

I try my best to advance silently. Perhaps a stupid precaution given that my glaring headlamp advertises my every move.

The shape remains hunkered down. A crouched human? A bear on all fours? A baby Sasquatch? Now I hear a low groan. Followed by more rapid, panicked breathing. Sounds of a creature in distress.

I close the remaining distance, my light finally catching the shape dead on, illuminating a blue flannel shirt and a mane of shaggy brown hair.

"Scott?" I call out.

He turns. Throws out a hand to block my light. That's when I see all the blood.

I guide him back to the campsite by the arm. He can walk but is babbling incoherently. I let him be, needing to focus on our footing. His arm feels solid and warm. I use that to anchor myself in the moment as, bit by bit, I drag us through the dark.

Upon arrival, I seat him on one of the logs next to the fire. The woods around us are filled with noise, crashing, calling, cursing. My companions, still on the search.

I hand Scott a tin of boiled drinking water, then grab the whistle from Josh's pack and blow three times fast.

Luciana appears immediately.

"It was Scott," I inform her. "I got him back to the campfire, but he's hurt."

She ducks back into her tent, then returns with a first aid kit in hand, Daisy at her heels. Around us, the night grows louder as everyone answers the emergency signal by stampeding back to camp.

Nemeth arrives first. His headlamp is clicked on, making it hard to look directly at him, but I can just make out the rifle held in both hands, the battle stance of his feet.

"Scott," I yell. "Next to the campfire. Luciana is tending. For the love of God, turn that thing off!"

Belatedly, Nemeth snaps off his headlamp, twisting toward the glowing red embers. The others come streaming out of the trees.

Miggy, Neil, followed shortly by Martin. Still no sign of Bob, though given his size and speed, he probably journeyed the farthest away.

Everyone is breathing hard and in various stages of disarray. Once again, Nemeth takes charge.

"Fire," he orders.

Miggy is on it, building up the flames.

"Water."

I jump into action, refilling the cooking pot.

"Light."

Neil obediently holds up a flashlight, then points it down Scott's form, illuminating the other man's bloody face, torn shirt.

"I saw him," Scott babbles immediately. "I saw him."

"Who?" Martin, striding forward.

"Tim. I swear it! At the edge of the woods. He was right there, wearing his green jacket. I could see him, clear as day."

By the glow of the firelight, I watch Martin's face shutter.

"You were mistaken," he states curtly. "Tim's dead."

I haven't heard him say the words before. I'm not completely sure what they cost him now. Martin's not one to share his emotions. And yet, there's something about the set of his jaw, the rigid line of his shoulders. In his world, I sense, that single statement is a horrific mark of delineation. Whatever good happened in his life came before. Now, there is only after.

None of us move.

"I saw him!" Scott insists.

"How?" Nemeth asks.

"Had to take a piss. Minute I crawled out from my tent, I spotted him, straight ahead. Watching us."

"How did you see him?"

"What do you mean? He was standing there. Clear as day. I'm telling you."

"In the beam of your flashlight?" Nemeth prods.

"I didn't have . . . I don't have . . ." Scott looks down, seems to realize for the first time he's not holding any flashlight nor wearing a headlamp. In fact, he has no light source whatsoever.

Luciana dabs at his face with a wet bandana. His cheeks and forehead are a collection of scrapes and tears. About what you'd expect if someone went racing blind into night-blackened woods, careening off every tree branch along the way.

"Your shirt," she murmurs.

Scott pulls it over his head, hissing sharply. Across his chest are two long, deep gouges. Luciana fingers the first one, feeling out the edges, and he winces

Miggy glances away sharply. Feeling that horrified, I wonder, or that guilty?

"You were dreaming, buddy," Neil murmurs softly. "You got up to take a leak and saw what you wanted to see. What we all want to see."

Scott glances at his friend, losing some of his bluster. "But I swear . . ."

"You didn't have a light. How could you have seen him standing all the way over there?" Neil points to the edges of camp, where night has turned the surrounding landscape into a wall of ink.

"It felt so real," Scott says at last.

The water has started boiling in the cooking pot. Luciana gives it a second to cool, then dips in the bandana and resumes dabbing at his wounds. To give Scott credit, he doesn't flinch as she starts flicking pieces of dirt and debris from the gouges on his chest.

I speak up. "Do you have a history of sleepwalking?"

He glances at me. "Sometimes."

"Is it worse under stress? In unfamiliar places?"

"Yes."

"Is that what happened five years ago?"

"Maybe. I've had episodes off and on since childhood. I wondered if that night . . . Was I really that drunk, or was I sleepwalking? Maybe that's why I didn't hear anyone call. But, lately . . . it's gotten worse."

"Post–Tim's disappearance?"

Scott doesn't look at me. "Post-marriage."

"Guilt walking," Neil coughs, an edge in voice.

Scott doesn't answer. There is plenty of collective blame from that single camping trip, but looking at the friends now, it's clear Scott carries an extra load. If he hadn't disappeared, if Tim hadn't gone for help . . .

If Scott hadn't married his best friend's former fiancée? His actions, then and now, have further isolated him. Miggy was right. They are not a band of brothers anymore. They are the walking wounded, inflicting further damage as they thrash around in their pain.

"Why were you screaming?" I ask.

"Screaming? I wasn't screaming."

"Maybe when you ripped open your chest," Luciana comments soothingly. "That looks worthy of a yelp or two."

"I don't remember screaming," Scott says uncertainly.

I have another question: "If you started out chasing . . . your vision . . . into the woods, how did you end up behind us on the other side of camp?"

"I have no idea. I saw Tim. I remember *seeing* Tim. Then . . . I'm not sure what happened next. Maybe it was just a nightmare."

A fresh noise. We all spook, our nerves on edge. Nemeth immediately shoulders the rifle.

Bob lumbers into camp. He has boots on but unlaced and an open shirt revealing a torso covered with as much furry red hair as is on his face. There's a streak of blood on his forehead, but it doesn't seem to bother him as he snaps off his flashlight and asks, "What happened to our food?"

LUCIANA, MIGGY, AND Neil stay with Scott to finish tending his wounds. No need for stitches, Luciana offers up. But definitely the gashes need a thorough disinfecting before being glued shut.

I've stayed in communities where superglue is all anyone can afford for healthcare. I'm still not sure I want to watch someone have their chest closed up with a tube of adhesive.

So I follow Nemeth, Martin, and Bob away from the camp, to where Nemeth hung up our food and trash in scentproof garbage bags. Two of the three black bags are now nothing more than gutted piñatas, their contents strewn all over the forest floor.

Nemeth keeps the rifle at the ready as he squats down, inspects the ground, then the scattered trail of MREs. I click on my head-lamp and do my best to illuminate the surrounding area.

The bags were suspended by ropes to about eight feet off the ground. The rope is still intact and tied to its anchor point. Just the food sacks seem to have been destroyed, the plastic sliced into ribbons.

"I thought they were bearproof," I say.

Nemeth glances at me but doesn't answer. He duckwalks closer to the epicenter of the damage.

"Nothing is a hundred percent bearproof," Bob answers at last.

"Why hang everything up? Don't bears climb?"

"Bears aren't the only wildlife we're trying to dissuade."

I peer up eight feet again. "That's one big bear."

Bob shrugs, as if not particularly impressed. Maybe compared to Bigfoot, eight feet doesn't seem so big. Or compared to his own massive self. Personally, I'm rethinking my policy of relying on a plastic whistle.

Bob unties the rope now, lowering the surviving sack to peer inside. "Dog food," he declares. "At least Daisy still has her dinner."

"We'll need to gather what we can," Martin announces, indicating the tossed rations. "Take inventory."

"There are extra bags in my tent." Nemeth looks at Bob. "Grab a couple."

Bob heads off. I remain, bobbing my headlamp over all available surfaces. I do three or four passes before it finally comes to me. What I'm not seeing. What Nemeth has most likely already noticed.

"There are no paw prints." To be sure, I bang the toe of my boot against the dirt. The ground is hard and dry, but my efforts still yield results. One earthen dent, no problem.

Which is terribly confusing. Whatever beast did this had to leave evidence behind. Except I'm not seeing any prints on the ground, nor any fresh scratches on the pine tree.

Nemeth and Martin exchange one of their looks.

Bob returns, fresh bags in hand. Bit by bit, we collect the remaining meal kits. I don't need an exact count to know this is much less than what we started with. Eight people, two MREs a day . . . This is not a week's worth of food. At best, we now have enough for a couple of days.

"There are no paw prints," I whisper to Bob as we crawl on the ground side by side. "What doesn't leave a print?"

"Something light. Or"—he glances up at the canopy of trees—"something that flies."

"And brought its own grocery bag to cart off dozens of meal kits?"

He doesn't have an answer, but whereas I'm anxious on the subject, his expression is much more . . . considering.

We grab the final few MREs, climb to our feet. Martin and Nemeth have been huddled together in low conversation. Now they break apart, fall silent at our approach.

"We'd appreciate it if you didn't say anything to the others," Martin states.

"As in, we're now missing half our food and need to abort our mission?" I retort.

"It's been a long night. No need for alarm."

"Further alarm." I've never liked being told to stay silent. "First Scott, now this. Which would be cause for *further* alarm."

"We can take stock in the morning." Martin's tone remains placating, though I notice Nemeth appears less convinced. "Everything looks better in the morning."

"What is this, the bumper sticker guide to emergency management?" I'm revving up just as Bob lays a hand on my shoulder.

"There's no course of action that can be taken right now," he states calmly. "Safest option is to remain at the campsite. Regroup in the morning."

I scowl. He's basically agreeing with Martin, meaning I want to object on principle. Except the way he puts it, the decision makes more sense. As Scott and our flayed food bags prove, the mountains are no place to be wandering about after dark.

"Fine," I bite off. "But we need a team meeting."

"First thing in the morning," Martin agrees.

Then he, Nemeth, and Bob all share a look. Good job calming the hysterical female?

I don't like it. As we return to the beckoning glow of the campfire, I wonder more and more about what I've gotten myself into.

CHAPTER 14

MORNING ARRIVES TOO BRIGHT AND too early. Noises drag me forcefully to consciousness. I fight the pull, a lifetime of staying up half the night and sleeping through half the morning making the early bird hour especially egregious.

A bark, followed by two or three more. I rouse to sitting, raking a hand through my tangled hair, then rub my forehead. My head pounds; my mouth tastes like ashes. I haven't felt this bad since my heavy-drinking days and find myself reaching automatically for a bottle of vodka to ease my pain. Muscle memory is a bitch.

I crawl to the front of my tent, manage the zipper, and stare bleary-eyed at the outside world. Sun is up, sky is blue, birds are chirping.

Fuck it. I want to go back to sleep for about another six days. And Advil. I'd sell my soul for a couple of tablets of over-the-counter painkiller. I knew my body would be sore this morning, but this . . .

Daisy appears, wagging her tail and barking again.

"Figures you're a morning person," I grumble at her.

She wags her tail again, then licks my cheek, as we are at face level. I think her breath might actually smell better than mine.

Then another fragrance hits me, rich and beguiling. It pulls me from my tent to standing position. Coffee. Thank God, hot java. I might make it after all.

I appear to be the last one awake, but not the only person to be suffering. Scott, Neil, and Miggy have taken up positions on the longest log, clutching stainless steel thermoses filled with steaming brew and staring sightlessly at the dancing fire. Their hair is un-kempt, their clothes rumpled, their shoulders slumped. Scott has replaced his torn shirt from last night but still has bloodstains on his sweatpants. No one seems to notice.

Nemeth is working the fire. At my approach, he offers up a tin of instant coffee, followed by a box of instant oatmeal. I start with the coffee, spooning it into my stainless steel water bottle, then adding boiling water. I think I'm getting used to the cooking aspect of camping, as well as the one cup, one spork approach to fine dining.

Martin is puttering in front of his tent. He appears to be tidying up, though what exactly there is to be set to rights remains a mys-tery to me. I suspect he's mostly keeping himself distracted, funnel-ing his emotions into busywork. I recognize the technique.

I take a seat next to Luciana, who is appallingly gorgeous even at this hideous hour. Glowing brown skin, glossy black hair, thickly lashed eyes.

As if reading my mind: "Don't hate me because I'm beautiful," she intones perfectly and shoots me a wicked smile. I have to laugh, which quickly devolves into a wince.

Bob sits across from us on the ground. He lifts his cup as a morning greeting. I return the gesture, then take the first bitter swig of boiling-hot java and scorch my tongue. It burns, but I savor the pain.

Luciana holds out her hand to me. It takes me a moment to spot the two white tablets in her hand. "Ibuprofen?"

"Do you want a hundred for both, or a hundred per tablet?"

"I'll take your firstborn child."

"Deal."

I toss back the pills with more hot coffee, searing off some of the lining in my throat. Still don't care.

"How do you feel?" she asks.

"Best not to think about it."

"Agree. Daisy and I get out and about, but an entire day of hard hiking is still an entire day of hard hiking. Definitely a different experience from disaster recovery."

Daisy has left us for Bob, sniffing around the redheaded giant, before sitting and staring at him with clear expectation.

"Dogs don't like oatmeal," he informs her, clutching his cup of breakfast more tightly to his chest.

Daisy's expression disagrees.

"She's recovered nicely," I comment, gesturing to the yellow Lab mix.

"Daisy always bounces back. Hence her name. I've never seen anything that could keep that dog down."

Daisy wags her tail at Bob again. He stubbornly shovels several sporkfuls of oatmeal into his mouth.

I wonder if he or Martin and Nemeth have broken the news to the group yet about our missing food. Judging by everyone's sleepy looks, I doubt it. The mood is much too mellow for people who have woken up to impending doom.

Scott is rubbing absently at his chest.

"How are you?" I call over to him.

"I'll live." His tone is subdued. He doesn't look happy this morning, but neither do Miggy and Neil. I wonder if the three of them were able to go back to sleep last night. Or if they lay awake, thinking of that other night, five years ago. When Scott also went missing. And nothing was ever the same again.

Will they be relieved to learn their mission just got cut short? Or at this stage, do they just want to keep on trucking till they finally locate Tim's body and can then get on with their lives? I know which way Miggy would vote. Neil, I have no idea. And Scott . . . Assuming we stumble upon Tim's remains and Scott gets to gaze at last upon his best friend's sun-bleached bones . . .

How in the world was he going to go from that to his new life with Tim's former bride-to-be?

Scott rubs his chest again, stares at the glowing fire.

I finish my coffee, then hobble over to the breakfast pickings. Instant oatmeal it is, topped with almonds and brown sugar for extra energy. One thing I will say for this level of physical exertion, it makes all food taste amazing. I already want seconds and thirds—which isn't going to happen given last night's events.

I flicker a gaze at Martin, who is still avoiding us, then stare hard at Nemeth. He seems to take the hint, clearing his throat, rising to standing.

"We've had a development," he states. One by one, the guys look up at him. Across the way, Martin finally ceases his puttering. "Last night, an animal got into our food supplies, shredding two of the bags. Daisy's stash is fine. The rest of us are down several dozen meal kits."

"What?" Neil stands up. "Some beast got into our food? I thought those were animal-safe bags."

"What matters is that the same animal didn't enter our camp—"

"You mean like a bear?" Miggy, also rising to standing.

Nemeth's jaw tightens. "We're safe. We were also able to recover most of the MREs—"

"How much is most?" Neil again.

I have to admit, I'm enjoying the show.

"Several dozen—"

"We're a party of eight." Miggy, doing the same math I performed last night. "We're going to need at least sixteen a day. So basically you're saying we have, what, a two-day supply?"

"Three. Four if we're careful."

"Careful? What the fuck is careful? Last night, we supposedly did everything *careful* and Scott here is missing half of his chest, while you lost half our food."

Nemeth clearly doesn't appreciate that comment. He's just opened his mouth to argue, when Martin steps forward.

"Stop it." There's a tone to his voice. Nemeth, Neil, and Miggy shut up, and Scott finally looks up from the fire.

"I've counted the meal kits. We're good for four days. This might shorten our trip, but it doesn't change our immediate plans." Martin turns to Scott. "Can you still hike?"

"Yes, sir."

"Then there's nothing else to discuss. Finish up, get dressed. We head out in thirty."

With that, Martin is done. He turns back to his tent. After another tense moment, Nemeth follows.

"Well, that was interesting," Luciana murmurs beside me.

"You have no idea," I tell her.

The college buddies are already on the move. They may resent Martin, maybe even hate him, but they clearly feel obligated to obey him.

I finish up my oatmeal, down the last of my coffee. My entire body hurts. The idea of slipping my feet back into my boots almost has me undone. It's a two-hour walk to the caves, Martin said last night. I have no idea how I'm going to do that, given I can barely make it to my tent.

"Today, I'm grateful for this beautiful morning," I murmur, drawing upon my AA training. "Today, I'm grateful for the sun, and my new dog friend, Daisy, and the opportunity to be out in the great outdoors. Today, I'm grateful I haven't had a drink."

I give it a moment. For my shoulders to come down. For my buzzing brain to center.

Then I pull on my still-damp clothes from yesterday, strap my badass blade to my belt, and prepare for another long trek through the woods.

LUCIANA HELPS ME reorganize my pack with enough supplies for a day-trip versus a weeklong expedition. I refill my water bottles, reload snacks. Belatedly, I discover I never handed over Josh's secret stash of chocolate or dozen protein bars. Given the food bags' fate, I'm grateful I kept the snacks to myself. Though I may have to change my mind if I wake up to a grizzly in my tent.

Nemeth and Martin finish up the camp chores. Food secured, fire banked, tents zipped shut. Then we're off.

We start out much as we did yesterday morning, which was only twenty-four hours ago and already feels like another lifetime. Nemeth, slinging the rifle over his shoulder, takes point. Martin follows close behind. Then the guys, all of them wincing with each step. Next come Luciana and Daisy, with Daisy now clad in a black duty vest and trotting happily. The dog clearly knows she's off to work and is excited about it.

I trudge after them, grateful for my significantly lighter pack and telling myself my stiff, sore muscles will loosen up anytime now. Just one more step. And another. And another.

Bob plays sweeper, his long legs effortlessly gobbling up the trail. I slow to put a little distance between us and Luciana.

"You okay?" he asks as we start to lag.

"How long have you been a member with the North American Bigfoot Society?" I ask him.

"Ten years. Wait, maybe twelve. Awhile now."

"Isn't it a volunteer organization?"

"We have an elected board, that sort of thing. Given our size, most meetings are online. But local members often come together for group hikes, organized searches of a target area, that sort of thing."

"Help with lost hikers?"

"Sure. Most of us spend lots of time in the woods. If there's anything we can do to help . . ."

"Are there paid positions?"

He laughs. "Don't I wish. I'm currently the secretary. Trust me, it's all for love, not money."

"Then why did Martin write you a check for five thousand dollars?" I twist enough so I can catch the expression on Bob's face as he walks behind me. His red-gold beard is either that thick, or he's that cool under pressure, because he gives nothing away.

"Marty didn't pay me any money. Marty *did*"—Bob pauses to emphasize the next phrase—"write a check to the North American Bigfoot Society. A thank-you, for all the help we've offered over the past few years with his search."

"Five thousand dollars is one helluva thank-you."

"That would be a question for Marty, not me."

There's a note of tension in Bob's voice now. A curtness at odds with his normal easygoing manner. The Bigfoot hunter's sensitive on this subject. Why, if the check was nothing but an appreciative gift to his group?

I don't know Bob well. We are online acquaintances, virtual comrades in arms when it comes to seeking what others haven't found. But I know a liar when I hear one, and Bob is lying to me.

"Do you really believe there's a Sasquatch in these woods?" I ask after a second, as we pass the tip of the lake, start to loop around to the other side, en route to the caves.

"It would be a happy surprise, but I'm partial to the Pacific Northwest as natural Bigfoot habitat."

"But you're here, and not just because of Martin and his son. The other missing people?" I ponder. "The additional data points on your map that make these mountains an area of interest?"

"Searching for a mythical beast is like hunting for a lost hiker— you don't just look for the person; you look for signs of the person. Clusters of unusual activity in remote wilderness areas are as good a hint as any that something more may be living in those woods."

"Do you think Sasquatches are a threat to humans? That that's what happened to the six other missing hikers?"

"I think if Sasquatches were nothing more than giant bipedal apes, then they would've been spotted by now, snacking on local populations. They haven't. Meaning we're talking about a creature who's not just smart, but sophisticated enough to avoid discovery." Bob shrugs. "Call me romantic, but if they've gone this long without hurting us, then I'd like to believe they'd have an instinct to help us."

"Then why track lost hikers?"

"If you saw an enormous hairy beast rise up out of the woods ahead of you, what would you do?"

"Pee my pants. Wish I had eaten that last piece of chocolate cake." I concede his point. "Run for my life."

"Leading to possibly plunging over a cliff, or careening face-first into a boulder, or getting well and truly lost in the woods."

"So hikers end up dead, but not because of any evil intent on Bigfoot's part?" I arch a brow dubiously.

"You never know."

I've had enough. I stop suddenly, bringing us both up short. "I don't know about Bigfoot, but you're lying to me, Bob. Why are you lying to me?"

"I am here to help Marty."

"For five thousand dollars?"

"I didn't—"

"Yes, you did. Someone saw. The check was in your name. Admit it."

"Who?"

I smile. He just proved my point.

"What happened last night?" I ask him, point blank. "The food bags. They appeared to be shredded by claws, but what kind of animal leaves no prints? I know of only one creature clever enough to cover its tracks, and it's of the *Homo sapiens* variety."

"You think someone in our party did it. Sabotaged our supplies. Why?"

"I don't know. That's why I'm grilling you."

"I didn't touch the food bags. I wouldn't do such a thing." For a moment, he sounds so earnest, I want to believe him. He sounds like the Bob I thought him to be, which is a joke, because I only just met him in person forty-eight hours ago. Maybe Miggy's suspicions are correct, and Bob's lovable-giant routine is a ruse designed to put the rest of us at ease till he reveals his true diabolical intentions. Except what would those be?

"I wasn't the only one who took off last night," Bob continues now. "Last I saw, everyone was headed into the woods, trying to figure out what was going on. Meaning the food was left unattended for a good twenty, thirty minutes. Would've been easy enough for any one of us to cycle back, tamper with the bags."

"Luciana stayed behind. Last I saw, she and Daisy were zipped up tight in her tent. She didn't want Daisy getting out and getting hurt."

Bob says what I'm already thinking. "None of the dog food was touched."

"What would Luciana have to gain from destroying our food stash? She needs to eat as well."

"What do I have to gain? And I need to eat, too. Even more than the rest of you." Bob pats his large frame self-consciously. He has that overgrown-puppy-dog vibe working again. The sweet blue eyes, the faintly pleading expression.

I can't buy it; I can't reject it. Did I hike too much yesterday or not sleep enough last night? Because my instincts are failing me. My ability to quickly size up people is one of my few life skills. But now my thoughts are clouded, my brain spinning.

I scrub at my temples, willing some semblance of plausible narrative to gel in my head. I got nothing. I'm heading deeper and deeper into the wilderness, beyond all contact with the outside world, and I have no idea who these people truly are, and what their real intentions might be.

I feel vulnerable in a way I haven't felt in a very long time.

"Do you know what it takes to spend your life looking for Bigfoot?" Bob speaks up abruptly.

I look at him.

"Faith. It takes huge bucketloads of faith. I have no idea what happened last night, how Scott got injured or our food stash destroyed. But I'm not the problem here."

I smile. I want to believe him, if only so I can sleep better at night. But what I notice most in his little speech is that he doesn't mention the check Marty wrote to him. Yet more proof that payment did happen and Bob is hiding it.

Why?

Eight people head into the woods. A grieving father, a hiking guide, three college friends, and three semiprofessional searchers. On the surface, it makes sense. So why do I have a feeling eight of us won't be coming back out?

A disturbance up ahead. Neil appears, the person I'm hoping to speak with next.

"Are you two okay?" he calls out.

"Just adjusting our packs," Bob answers. Covering for us and our conversation. He doesn't look at me; I don't look at him.

"Then hurry up. We've found something. Straight ahead."

CHAPTER 15

THE GROUP HAS DISCOVERED A makeshift campsite about twenty feet off the main trail. Martin spotted it first—though, *how*, I have no idea. It's a crude setup: a barely body-sized lean-to fashioned from hand-cut pine branches. A few feet from its narrow opening are the charred remains of an old campfire.

"Placing the fire at the opening captures the heat," Martin murmurs to no one in particular. "It may not look like much, but a shelter like this can maintain a temperature above fifty degrees, regardless of conditions. I taught him this. For a while, he'd practice them in the backyard, teach his friends on the school grounds. Kids love building forts."

There's a tone to his voice. A man who is seeing both the present and the past. A father who is feeling both proud and gutted.

The site is too small for eight people, so the rest of us stand back, letting Martin walk the area.

"You think Tim made this?" I ask Nemeth in a low voice.

He doesn't answer right away, his gaze scouring the surrounding area. "It's possible," he allows at last. "Could be five years old, could be from earlier this summer, though." He frowns, stares at the shelter, frowns again. "I doubt that. I'm thinking it's at least a year old. How much beyond that, I can't tell."

"Why at least a year old?"

Martin is now walking around the lean-to. He pauses occasionally, touching the dense covering of pine needles, the sliced ends of the gathered tree limbs. Nemeth is looking at the scene, but Martin is *feeling* it.

"The ground, for one thing. Notice the light covering of detritus. Whoever built this would've disturbed the entire area. We'd see churned-up earth, impressions from a person sitting before the fire. We don't. It looks . . ."

"Ghost towny?" I fill in. "Not just abandoned, but in a long-gone sort of way?"

"Exactly." Nemeth squats down, regards our surroundings from this new vantage point. "Then again, five years later, I'd expect more of the shelter to have collapsed, branches to be knocked down. This is in pretty good shape for a ramshackle construction."

"I thought you mountain-guru types were supposed to be able to sniff the dirt, lick a pine cone, then state unequivocally who came here at what date and time, not to mention their favorite food and astrological sign."

Nemeth stares at me. "I know you're a Virgo; does that help?"

"How do you know that?"

"Cuz you're a pain in my ass. Stubborn, critical, overthinking—"

"Okay, okay, okay, let's call it a draw."

Martin has moved from the lean-to to the fire. He picks up a piece of charred wood, turns it over in his hand.

Luciana and Daisy, I notice, are now walking a larger circle around the campsite—as best they can, given that we're in the middle of a clump of straggly, half-dead pines. Bob trails behind them. Neil, Scott, and Miguel are standing to the side, doing what they do best, which is nothing at all.

"Why build it so far off the trail?" I ask.

"Generally, you look for some kind of natural starting point. Say, a few collapsed trees that already form a frame for the structure, that kind of thing. But to leave the trail and walk this far in . . ." Nemeth glances behind us, where the hiking path is barely visible through the fence of matchstick tree trunks. His expression is troubled. "I don't know," he says at last.

I think of the screams we heard yesterday when hiking up. The cries Nemeth said came from an animal but didn't sound like any kind of cute, four-legged creature that I know. I wonder if the person who sheltered here heard those shrieks as well and felt a need for a less conspicuous shelter.

Nemeth rises to standing, dusting off his pants. He directs his next comment to the group: "While Devil's Canyon is hard to access for your average hiker, a fair number of people still pass through here during any given season. Best bet is to see if we can find some trace of Tim's gear or remnant of the person who stayed here. Otherwise, all we got is evidence of a single person who camped here at some point at least a year ago."

Martin speaks up. "It's his."

We all look at him.

"The tree branches forming the lean-to. They haven't been just hacked down. Their tips are cut at a precise forty-five-degree angle, as one might expect from an engineer. Then there's the way the stones are arranged around the fire pit. They're all similar in size and shape. No need for that. Requires extra effort. But Tim liked things uniform, balanced to the eye. Son of a carpenter, you know."

I don't know, but the more I learn of Tim, the more I wish that I'd had a chance to meet him. My life is filled with ghosts. Images and stories of people I never knew and, in most cases, never will. They haunt me. And yet I keep coming back for more, collecting memories that aren't even my memories and clutching them tight to my chest. If you hoard other people's tragedies, does that make your own easier to bear?

I'm still waiting to find out.

"We could search from here." Luciana speaks up softly. She and Daisy are standing at attention twenty feet away, Luciana holding a small bladder in her hand. I've seen it used by trackers before, puffing the orange powder in the air and watching how it drifts to determine the direction of the wind.

Martin stares at her a long, long time. Once again, his face is shuttered. Once again, he's seeing things only he can see.

The three amigos shift restlessly. Bob adjusts his pack. We wait.

Still, Martin doesn't answer.

Now that we're here and the moment is at hand, does he really want to proceed? To stumble upon his child's bones? To learn once and for all what happened to his son, realizing he can never un-know it?

Closure is such a tricky, tricky thing.

A single snaking tremor, rippling through his entire body. Martin turns to Luciana.

He says, "Yes."

"SEARCHES WORK BEST as a team of three: canine, handler, and support person." Luciana eyes our group expectantly.

Martin immediately raises his hand. "Support person."

Luciana regards him for a moment, clearly considering. Then abruptly: "No."

Martin blinks. This is the first time I've heard someone tell him no. It's clearly not his thing.

"Wait just a damn moment—"

"Do you even know what a support person does?"

Martin scowls. "No."

"You plot progress using compass points and are in charge of communicating with the rest of the group to ensure we don't intersect one another or duplicate efforts. Do you feel like staring at a map and compass, or do you want to keep your eye out for signs of Tim?"

That scowl again. Martin doesn't have to speak for us to know his answer. Luciana waits for it anyway. This is her area of expertise and she's establishing her dominance right out of the gate. I want to applaud but I worry it might be in poor taste.

"Fine," Martin bites out, graceful to the bitter end.

Bob speaks up. "I'm good with a compass."

Luciana nods at him. "Perfect. You're support. So this is how it'll work." At the word *work*, Daisy perks up. Luciana acknowledges her canine companion with a pat on the head. "Yes, work, work, work," she coos. "We're getting ready to work." Now Daisy positively vibrates with excitement.

"It's important to get her revved up. The more engaged she is, the better she'll do," Luciana informs the rest of us. "Not that Daisy ever needs much. She genuinely loves the hunt.

"Now, Daisy is our tracker. Bob is our recorder. That makes me the navigator. Most of you probably have real hobbies. I do things like watch how mist rises off the water, the movement of fog as it eddies through a canyon, the waft of smoke from a backyard grill. Scent behaves exactly the same way, as it is captured by the same air currents. It rises up with temperature and open expanses. It pools at barriers, such as fence lines, mountain ridges, thick outcroppings. Cooler mornings you want to start downwind in a gully. Hot afternoons you want to be at the top of the same gully." She pauses. "I put our current conditions at base neutral, not too hot, not too cold. Meaning I'll start Daisy downwind"—she holds up the puffer—"then keep an eye on topography. The rest of you can assist with that as well. A downed tree, a steep rise in elevation. Look for anyplace you can picture fog collecting. Those are great targets for Daisy, increasing her probability of picking up the trail.

"Your next job: Stay out of Daisy's way. You should spread out behind us, like sweepers on a soccer field, where you'll serve as extra sets of eyes. Daisy will be tracking for human remains, meaning she'll go straight past everything else—a discarded backpack, a scrap of cloth, a bit of cord, et cetera. For that matter, she could be standing three feet from the body, and if it's even slightly downwind, she'll walk right past it. Her focus will be on what she can smell. Our focus needs to be on what we can see."

We nod obediently.

"I recommend arranging yourselves in three teams of two. Partly for safety's sake. We don't need anyone staring at the ground so hard he or she loses their way and steps off a cliff. You might think I'm being silly, but trust me, it happens."

"It happens," Nemeth agrees.

"Daisy, are you ready to work?"

Daisy prances again. She is so ready to work. Her entire being screams, *Work, work, work.*

"So, in a moment, I'm going to give Daisy her search command. You're going to think I'm crazy, but it's an inside joke. Immediately afterwards, Daisy's going to race around, desperate to discover the scent trail. So be prepared, and stay out of her way. Then you'll see her settle, grow more methodical in her approach. We'll give her two hours, standard protocol. If she hasn't discovered anything by then, we should probably move on." Luciana glances at Martin. "This particular site does seem temporary in nature, versus the caves you've identified as possible long-term shelters."

Martin nods. He appears mollified to have his master plan acknowledged.

"Any questions?" Luciana asks us.

We shake our heads.

"Pair up."

I already figure Martin and Nemeth will partner, being superior beings and all. That leaves the four members of the B team—myself, Neil, Scott, and Miguel—to sort out. I've been looking for a chance to talk to Neil, so I turn to him automatically. But he and Miggy have already closed ranks. And not subtly at all. They take a definitive step away from Scott, leaving him standing alone. I watch the sting of rejection play across his face. Then the squaring of his shoulders as he accepts his fate.

He gained a wife from the events of the past five years, but it clearly cost him dearly. I wonder if he ever thinks the price was too high.

I cross to him, stick out my hand in formal recognition of our partnership, and say, "You chose wisely, my friend. I have Josh's secret candy stash."

He flashes me a grateful smile, while Miggy blusters, "Candy stash?"

"First one to help Daisy pick up the trail gets a peanut butter cup."

Nemeth and Martin roll their eyes—kids! But Luciana and Bob are definitely in. I'm sure Daisy will earn mucho rewards from Luciana, so it seems fitting the humans have something to look forward to.

Luciana pulls out a map, reviews it shortly, then hands it to Bob, who already has a compass in hand and a pencil tucked behind his ear. She holds out the puffer. Releases a plume of orange powder. We all watch it float through the air, curling sinuously, and I realize the dog handler is right: There is something incredibly mesmerizing about wind flow.

Luciana heads closer to the original hiking path. Releases a second puff. Corrects her position slightly, till the orange powder is drifting directly toward her.

"Direction?" she asks Bob.

"Wind is coming from the northwest."

"Have our start point on the map?"

"X marks the spot."

"All right. Behind me. Spread out. Make sure you're tracking your own positions. Are we ready?"

Martin's face shutters, while beside me Scott trembles so hard, I grab his hand. The only one of us who appears happy is Daisy, who is one hundred percent fixated on her handler's face, body tense, ears forward.

"Time to work," Luciana announces to her eager mutt. Then to the rest of us: "The command word for cadaver searches can be tricky. *Search, seek, find it,* are too general. Adding *corpse* or *dead person* too gruesome. So one of my teammates came up with something a little different, based on a code word her daughter used for her menstrual cycle—another training tool is used tampons. Now that the rest of you are good and freaked out, ready, Daisy? Time to work. Find *Fredericka.*"

We are totally surprised.

Daisy bolts forward, and just like that, we're on the hunt for human remains.

CHAPTER 16

TRUE TO LUCIANA'S PREDICTION, DAISY is anywhere and everywhere. Sniffing, running, sniffing some more. Scott and I both have to leap back as she comes barreling at us. Then it's Neil and Miggy's turn to scramble out of the way. We're all so fixated on the dog's explosion of energy and effort, we quickly forget our own tasks.

"Eyes," Luciana snaps, and we belatedly jump to it. Luciana hasn't moved yet, just tracks her dog with her gaze. Bob has his map and his compass and looks as eager as the dog to find the trail.

Scott and I retreat, trying to put more space between us and the crazy canine. "Natural barriers," I mutter. "Places that would pool scent."

This seems to galvanize Scott, and we start moving in unison. Neil and Miggy have headed back toward the main path, so we track in the other direction, eyes on the terrain. I try to think like a wafting fragrance. Where would I go? Where would I linger? But in this flat terrain, with its collection of skinny, half-dead pine trees,

I'm having a tough time identifying any kind of collection point. I move on to searching for random spots of color—say, a scrap of fabric, as Luciana mentioned. Mostly I see muted neutrals. Reddish brown dirt. Silvery gray tree trunks. Small patches of green growth. The woods here have a rich, loamy smell. Not the glacier crispness of our campsite, but something earthier. I wonder how it must register for Daisy, and her exquisite nose that is at least ten thousand times better than ours.

Scott has drifted farther away from me. He is looking down so hard, he snags a strap of his backpack on a broken branch and is momentarily caught. I cross over to help.

"Doing okay?" I ask him.

"Sure," he says in a tone that indicates he's not okay at all.

The others have become distant figures, people we can hear more than see. I loosen the strap, then wordlessly remove his water bottle from its side pocket and hand it to him. Whether he knows it or not, he's sweating profusely.

"How's the chest?"

"I'll live." He rubs it self-consciously.

"Your face is flushed. Sure you're feeling all right?"

He unscrews the cap of his flask. Drinks deeply. Replaces it. "No."

"Present injury or past regrets?"

He flashes a smile. "Wouldn't I like to know."

"If you need to go back to camp, I'll go with you. I don't mind."

He shakes his head. "I can't," he says quietly, and I think I understand.

"So how shall we approach this? You want to monitor our location, or be on the lookout for signs of human passage?"

"You mean stare at the map versus look for my friend's body?"

"This can't be easy."

"No." Scott turns away from me, peers into the desolate woods.

"Marty wants nothing more than to retrieve Tim's remains," Scott murmurs. "I've tried to picture it in my head a hundred times. What that might look like. A mummified corpse still clad in Tim's clothes? A pile of bones topped by a skull? A single clump of dark hair? I just can't imagine. Do you mind me asking—how many dead people have you found?"

"Too many."

"Is it awful?"

"Yes. But not so awful that I don't go looking again."

"But you don't know them; it's nothing personal. Whereas for the people who loved them . . ."

"And yet you keep showing up year after year."

Bitter laugh. "Have you met Marty?"

"Miggy said the same."

Scott pauses. A fresh spasm rocks his features. We haven't resumed our search. We should, but I don't push. He wants to talk. He *needs* to talk. And I want to listen.

"They blame me," he whispers.

"Do you blame you?"

"Yes."

"Why? Sleepwalking is sleepwalking. It's not like you wanted to get lost in the woods in the middle of the night. Or meant for Tim to head off in search of help and never be seen again."

Scott doesn't answer for so long, it is its own kind of answer. Guilt trumps logic. Always has.

I give him another moment, then I start walking again.

"Tell me about Tim," I say, peering along a fallen log, studying a low clump of vegetation. This particular area has an almost ghostly feel with its sickly trees and barren ground. It keeps me on edge as I try to sharpen my gaze, pick apart the colors and shapes around us.

"Tim's that guy," Scott says at last.

His voice is rough. Clearly, while I've been looking, he's been thinking.

"Smiling, happy, life of the party," he continues. "People noticed him, that whole girls-want-to-sleep-with-him, guys-want-to-be-him thing. Saint Timothy, we called him. Because the heavens opened and choirs sang every time he walked into a room. Nickname pissed him off, but he couldn't deny it. He had presence. Knew where he was and where he wanted to go. And man, his thirst for living. A guy with his looks and smarts could've been a complete arrogant asshole. But he didn't want to own the world; he wanted to experience it. All of it. Let's kill this exam. Let's crash this kegger. Let's take off into the woods for a weekend. He led, we followed. We were just so excited to be along for the ride."

"Dudeville," I comment.

Scott laughs. "Miggy tell you that? Those were the days." But then his laughter fades, and a different, more painful emotion flickers across his face. Because those days didn't last and would never be again.

"My family lives in Connecticut," he says now. "Didn't make sense for me to travel all the way back east for the shorter holidays, so I'd go home with Tim. Thanksgiving with his folks, three-day weekends at his house. Patrice and Martin always made me feel welcome, any-friend-of-Tim's sort of thing. Tim and his dad were clearly close, but Patrice, she was the center of their shared universe. The two of them doted on her. Tim brought her flowers, would pull out her chair when she sat at the table. Martin was always fussing, offering up extra food, grabbing her favorite sweater. They were the first family I ever met who seemed to actually like one another. It blew my mind, while adding to Tim's luster. He was the perfect guy; of course he had the perfect family."

"I take it your home crew in Connecticut are different?"

"My parents divorced when I was five. I have one full sister, two half sisters, and one half brother. Households are many and varied. Holidays numerous and scattered. I gave up tracking it all years ago."

I think I spy something near the trunk of a tree. I head closer, tossing over my shoulder, "I hear congratulations are in order."

"You mean on my wedding? Or that Latisha and I are expecting?" A pause, then: "Who told you?"

"Does it matter?" Upon closer inspection, my visual target is nothing more than a clump of fallen moss. I straighten, look around, and realize we're truly alone now. Like isolated and possibly lost in the middle of a forest, straight out of a scary movie. Nope. Don't like it. I head to our right, hoping that'll bring us back to the others.

"Miggy and Neil are just jealous." Scott falls in step behind me.

"Of you and Latisha?" This is interesting.

"If you ever met her, you'd understand. Latisha has this smile . . . One look and all you want is to make her smile again, just so you can feel the glow. She used to volunteer in the children's cancer ward. Needless to say, she was the kids' favorite. She's generous like that. Warm, genuine. Not to mention successful, smart, and gorgeous."

"How long have you been in love with her?"

"From the first moment Neil brought her home."

"But she took to Tim?"

"Everyone takes to Tim."

"And you were okay with that?"

"I accepted that. I was happy for them. Truly."

"And the others?"

Scott doesn't answer right away, which, of course, makes me wonder. "Tim had this thing," he says at last. "He was a good guy, a great guy. But he could also be a total jerk."

"Thank God. The Saint Timothy thing kinda freaked me out."

"That's one way to look at it. Tim always got what he wanted. But he had a tendency to want the things other people had."

"Such as Latisha?" I peer at Scott's face. "Who did she belong to first?"

But he won't take the bait. "This is a different story. End of senior year, we're all desperate to land jobs. OSU has this co-op program where you get to spend time working for other companies. Often, if all goes well, this leads to an official job offer. For Josh and me, this is looking good. But Tim didn't love the places he worked, while Miggy is being his usual indecisive self. He liked his final co-op experience, could see himself working there. But then he's reading about an engineering position at this other new and exciting start-up and maybe that's what he should pursue? On and on. Clock is winding down. He still hasn't heard from the start-up. He finally makes his choice, going with the co-op company.

"A week later, he learns from a friend he did get contacted about an interview at the start-up. Call came the day after he accepted the co-op position. He never got the message. Tim did. And Tim went to the interview instead."

"Wait, Tim took Miggy's place in a job interview? At Miguel's dream company?"

"Tim didn't get it, thank heavens, but it was not a good time to be sharing an apartment with the two of them. But Tim, he also had this way about him. Sure, he didn't tell Miggy about the interview. But Miguel had already accepted another job. So no harm, no foul, right?"

"What did Miggy think?"

"Same as the rest of us. Asshole move. But . . . but Tim is Tim, and Miguel *had* already made his decision. Maybe Miggy is being too harsh. Maybe he should just let it go, accept the case of beer, and hit the basketball court with Tim. We all got it, had been there ourselves. You try to stay mad. Tim was the one who screwed up, of course you have the right to be pissed off. But somehow . . ." Scott shrugs. "Even when we hated him, we still forgave him. He was a jackass on occasion, but he was also the guy who'd bring you home each and every holiday and never once make you feel like an outsider. How do you stay angry with that?"

Voices. Finally. I exhale a sigh of relief. We've done a terrible job searching. Have nothing useful to report. And yet, I've found this conversation enlightening, making our jaunt productive in its own way.

I make one more push for the answer Scott has so far refused me: "Tim loved Latisha. He ended up dating her and getting engaged to her. But he wasn't the one who saw her first. So who did he steal her from? You? Josh? Neil?"

"I had a major crush on Latisha," Scott replies carefully. "I tried not to, but I couldn't help it. And as you can tell, I'm not exactly a subtle sort of guy. Tim could've backed off, acknowledged my interest, given me a chance. But that wasn't his style. Once he decided he wanted her . . .

"Well, you know how that went. I wanted to blame him for my broken heart. But at a certain point . . . I think Latisha is the most extraordinary person I've ever met. And back in those days, I could tell that's what she thought every time she looked at Tim."

"You came to terms. Were even willing to stand beside Tim as he married her."

"I never tried to sabotage their relationship. And I didn't set out to marry her after Tim was gone. But this is what Josh, Neil, and Miggy don't want to talk about. After Tim disappeared . . . we weren't the people we were before. None of us. And the people we became, the people Latisha and I became . . . We clicked. First, over our mutual grief and, yeah, shared memories of Tim. Then as friends helping each other get through. And then . . . We love each other. We're good together. Now we're starting a family. I wish the guys could accept that, but if not, fuck them."

"Ironically enough, they would've come to terms if it'd been Tim marrying your ex-fiancée."

Scott laughs harshly. "There is that. At least Patrice understands."

"Tim's mom?" This catches me off guard.

"Patrice has been battling cancer for over fifteen years. That's a long time to contemplate dying. It's made her much more practical about these things. Death happens; life goes on. She sent us a card for our wedding, giving us her blessing. She wrote that she'd long considered me a second son, and that she loved us both, and it made her heart happy to know something good had come out of something so awful. She looked forward to one day meeting our children. Though realistically speaking, I'm not sure that will happen. Last time Latisha and I visited, Patrice looked like a walking skeleton. First Tim, now her. Goddammit. They were my family, too, you know. Hell, I like them better than my own relatives."

Scott can't speak anymore. He pinches the bridge of his nose, then wipes at his eyes. We're almost back to the others now. I pause, giving him a moment to recover.

"This is all so shitty," he whispers. "The way Josh and Neil and Miggy look at me. Martin's total hatred. I know finding Tim won't magically change any of that, but at least it'll finally be over. We can lay his bones to rest. And someday, Latisha and I will take our kids to visit his grave and tell them about this really great guy we both loved. We'll share stories. We'll keep his memory alive.

"That's what Patrice wants. She knows Martin is too pissed off to remember. So we're the keepers of Tim's flame. And maybe it's twisted that Tim's former fiancée now married to his friend are the ones carrying it, but I don't see the others stepping up."

"Then my best wishes to the two of you," I tell him honestly. Because I also know what it's like to love someone so much that, years later, the loss still feels like a razor's edge. And the only person I can share my sadness with is his widow. The woman Paul loved, calling the woman who loved him. Scott's right: Grief makes for strange bedfellows.

"I need this to end," Scott declares with a final rub of his tear-stained face. "I need Daisy the SAR dog to be brilliant. I need all of us to get this done. Then I need to go home to my wife and baby and never think of these damn mountains again."

"Sounds good."

A sniff and a nod. "All right, let's do this."

We can hear talking. The rest of our party is just beyond this wall of trees. Scott points himself toward them.

At the last second, I grab his arm. "Quick question. Do you know anything about Bob the Bigfoot hunter?"

"Never met him till two days ago. Why?"

"Luciana and Daisy?"

"Also just met. More acquaintances of Martin, I guess. He never quits this. Never."

I let his arm drop, just in time for him to now stop me.

"Wait, does this have something to do with our diminished food supplies?" he asks.

"That's what I'm trying to figure out."

"I thought an animal did that."

"That's what I'm trying to figure out."

Scott studies me. "What aren't you telling me?"

"No idea. But if I ever solve the puzzle, you'll be the first to know."

He blinks at me, but I really don't have answers. I shrug. He stares at me and I shrug again. Then, finally, we thread our way through the line of ghost trees and join the others.

CHAPTER 17

IN THE END, OUR IMPROMPTU search is a bust. Daisy doesn't pick up any scent trail. The humans don't stumble upon any visual evidence. We have the makeshift campsite, that's it. Daisy is clearly forlorn and requires much patting, as well as a twenty-minute break. Martin is equally frustrated, but nobody pats him. I eye the chocolate in my pack with longing but, figuring the day will only grow more torturous, settle for another protein bar instead.

Day two in the wilderness and I'm already making deals with myself: If I just survive this trek, I will never eat protein bars ever again. It's the little things that get you through.

Nemeth must be timing us, because I no sooner crumple up my wrapper than he's standing expectantly. There's a collection of low groans, then one by one we rise to our feet, adjust our gear, and stagger forth.

We are a wordless procession, snaking through the woods, then crossing a broad stream into a vast meadow. The sun has climbed higher, warming our faces and glittering off distant snowy peaks. In this moment, it's easy to believe we are enjoying a gorgeous day hike, complete with dancing wildflowers and gentle flowing streams. After the desolation of our last search area, I want to appreciate this beauty. Bask in the scent of meadow grasses, the singing of birds, the feel of the wind on my cheeks. The sky so impossibly blue and stretching out . . . forever. So very different from the last few places I've stayed. It beckons and I can feel our answering call in the fresh bounce of our steps. Even Daisy has recovered and is prancing along, snapping at blowing grasses and pouncing on random insects.

Walking through this section of the canyon, I can understand the mountains' appeal. What would draw someone like Tim—restless, adventuresome, confident—to test himself against the great outdoors. I am starting to build a picture of him in my mind. I can imagine him striding along, knowing he was lost, but still taking a moment to admire the scenery, still upbeat enough to think he was one footstep away from solving this latest problem. From saving himself.

I can see him thinking if he could just make it to those cliffs . . .

Did he amuse himself by thinking of the stories they'd soon be telling of this camping weekend gone awry? Or was he still panicked and worried about his missing buddy, Scott? At what point did he realize—or did he ever realize—that it was his survival that was now at stake?

We can walk his last steps. We can retrieve his bones to be laid to rest next to his mother's. But we'll still never know everything that happened to Tim. Sooner or later, his father and his friends will have to come to terms with that. That the quality of their future sleep won't be determined by a visit to his grave, but by their ability to let go.

I'm panting by the time we complete our meadow crossing, traverse more patches of evergreens, then start winding our way back up. I don't know why we're going up. I'm very sorry to be hiking up.

Once again, Miggy, Neil, Scott, and I fall back, Bob slowing to maintain his position as rear guard. No one talks. We're all swiping tiredly at our sweaty, dripping faces when we finally clear the rise and discover ourselves in the middle of a dusty boulder field, face-to-face with a solid wall of jutting rock.

The cliff. Taller and broader than I ever imagined from the other side of the canyon. Like trying to take in the entire length of a football stadium in a single glance from five feet away. Can't be done.

"Holy shit," Miggy breathes as we stagger to a halt beside the forward members of our party.

Already I can see the dark opening of a cave here, then another there, peppering the base. Some appearing to bore into the cliff face itself, others formed from collapsing piles of rock. Easily a dozen if not several dozen possible shelter sites.

"Fuck me," Scott groans.

For once, his friends don't argue.

LUNCH BREAK. MARTIN doesn't want to; Nemeth doesn't give him a choice. Clearly, we have our work cut out for us. Now is the time to drink, eat, prepare for the coming battle. While we get situated, Luciana and Daisy take off for a quick recon. The dog picks her way easily among the sea of smaller stones and larger boulders. It looks to me like year after year, pieces of the reddish brown cliff have broken off and rained down below, until we're surrounded by hot, dusty rocks, some the size of footballs, others Volvos, with lots of grit and sandy particles in between.

The sun that felt so lovely just an hour ago now feels like a broiler, radiating off the stones around us. I wish I had a brimmed cap to shield my face. I notice Bob dampening the bandana around his neck, then tying it around the lower half of his face. I follow his example, giving him a thumbs-up when he nods in my direction.

Everyone is dousing themselves in more bug spray, adding a chemical tang to our exciting lunch of nuts, granola, and dried fruit. I make a new deal with myself. Survive this mission, never eat granola again. At least the limited food choices keep us from lingering.

Luciana and Daisy return with an update. "I lost count at eighteen openings, and that's just what I can see from standing in one place. Some are probably too small, some may be quite deep. Impossible to tell without checking each one. Daisy is a skilled rock climber from working rubble piles, but the sheer size of this wall . . . We could use a team of search dogs, not just a lone canine."

Martin nods, takes out his map, and snaps it open on the rock before him. "Our original plan broke this area into four quadrants. Now that we're here looking at it . . . I say we ditch that and go with a standard hasty search strategy—two of us will start at either end of the cliff face and work from the outside in, while the remaining members of our party start at the midpoint and work from the inside out. We'll do a quick study of all the possible cave openings, mark ones that have signs of habitation as worthy of further exploration by Daisy."

He pauses, we nod.

"Now, according to the map, midpoint looks about a hundred yards that away." He points to my right. "We'll set up there. Two of us will hoof it in opposite directions to the far ends. Two more can head out for halfway down. Leaving the final two hikers to start at the middle, working toward the ends. Make sense?"

I get what he's doing, trying to cover as much of the massive protrusion as quickly as possible. We arrived later than planned, given our impromptu search of the lean-to area. All of us, including Daisy, will tire soon enough. Not to mention in these hot, dry conditions, water will be an issue. No pretty lakes and meandering streams for refills in the immediate vicinity. I've already chugged my first bottle, while Daisy looks like she could go for another bowl or two.

Martin looks at Nemeth. "You and I will take the endpoints." They're the fastest hikers, so that makes sense. He glances at Bob next. "You get one of the halfway downs, head northwest or southeast, I don't care."

Bob nods. Martin's gaze goes to Luciana and Daisy, the next most qualified hikers.

Luciana's already shaking her head. "No. Daisy needs to rest so she can be ready for the main event. We'll hold down the fort. That's it."

Martin doesn't love the news but surrenders to the realities of the cadaver dog's limitations. That leaves him with myself and the three bachelor buddies. If we didn't realize we were the B team before, we certainly know it now. If Nemeth and Martin were picking hiking teams on a mountain playground, we'd definitely be the last kids they tapped.

"Someone needs to hike to the opposite halfway-down point from Bob."

Scott raises his hand. "I'll do it."

"No. You're injured. Someone else."

Neil speaks up. "I got it."

Miggy grumbles briefly, but not too seriously. He and I suffered the most on yesterday's hike in. We're the logical fits to start searching from the middle. Which leaves Scott as the odd man out once again.

Marty doesn't pretend to care. He waves a hand in Scott's direction. "You can either assist one of them"—a vague gesture at Miguel and myself—"or remain with Luciana."

"I can help search," Scott states stubbornly. He eyes me, then moves closer to Miguel. I nod in understanding. At this stage, I might be the more comfortable pairing option, but best friends are best friends, and Scott is trying hard to rebuild a relationship with his.

We all rise to standing. My sore muscles, having stiffened up, scream in protest. Miggy, Neil, and Scott don't look like they're doing much better. But no one protests, even as Martin greets our muffled moans with a look of contempt.

"We only have a matter of days. You can do this."

It's delivered less as a reassurance, more as a command. It might just be me, but Martin seems to be turning into a bigger asshole by the minute. I can't decide whether it's the anxiety of being this close to discovering his only child's remains, or if he just hates his son's former groomsmen that much.

"If anyone spots anything of note, or gets into trouble, use your whistles," Nemeth instructs. "Stay close to the cliff face and you can't get lost. Also, pay attention to your footing. Easy enough to twist an ankle on these rocks. Oh, and don't step on any snakes."

"Snakes?" I freeze, mid backpack shrug.

"Don't worry, they're more scared of you than you are of them."

"I sincerely doubt that."

"Then you'll be happy to know we don't have much in the way of venomous snakes around here. Prairie rattlers don't care for this elevation and most of the midget faded rattlesnakes live to the south."

"Most?"

"Pay attention to your footing," Nemeth repeats crisply. "You'll be fine."

I don't feel fine. Rats and cockroaches I've learned to live with, given some of my housing options. Even tarantulas on occasion. But snakes. I've never been a fan of snakes.

I finish shouldering my pack, then we all follow Martin to our new base of operations.

Luciana and Daisy settle in near a circle of particularly large, flat boulders. Daisy is eyeing Luciana with clear expectation of something. Probably more treats.

Nemeth glances at his watch. "I want everyone back here in two hours. Got it? If you haven't met up with a fellow searcher by then, mark where you are along the wall, then return. And no going too deep in any of the caves. You never know what kind of creature considers it home."

Great, now I'm navigating boulders while keeping an eye out for snakes and creatures.

Apparently, that was Nemeth's version of a pep talk, because without another word he turns and strides away. Martin immediately heads out in the opposite direction, his steps equally rapid. Watching the two men power effortlessly around and over the mounds of sand and rock, I realize for the first time how much they've adjusted their pace over the past two days to accommodate the rest of us. Which confirms that they are indeed superhuman.

Bob nods once at Neil, then takes off after Nemeth. Neil in turn heads out in Martin's direction. Leaving me, Miggy, and Scott to work from the inside out.

"I'll go left, you go right," I offer, putting the two friends on the path that doesn't intersect with Martin. They nod gratefully.

Then we all get to work.

IN THIS CONTEXT, I'm not a great searcher. Ironic, given my job. But working cold cases generally comes down to people skills. Knowing who to ask what, how to spot a lie. Why someone might do what they did. This kind of discipline—peer underneath a rocky outcropping here, stick my head in this opening there . . . Let's just say I wasn't the kid who excelled at Easter egg hunts.

I'm feeling extra squeamish now that Nemeth has planted the image of snakes in my head. I also have a difficult time maintaining focus. The more I plod along the brown, gritty rocks, the more my mind wanders. I pay less attention to particulars, while contemplating larger issues.

Would Tim really hunker down here? Sure, the collection of caves makes for natural shelter, but it's so dry and desolate. Where's the water supply? Possibilities for food?

Knowing the importance of finding shelter in a survival situation doesn't mean Tim acted accordingly. According to Nemeth, leaving his companions and taking off in the middle of the night was already a break from the safest course of action. Meaning that when push came to shove, Tim's first instinct wasn't to wait and see but to go and do.

Assuming he made it all the way to Devil's Canyon, I can definitely see Tim continuing on to the cliff face, as it dominates the landscape. Upon discovering the network of caves, maybe he chose one to hunker down in. The nights were cold when he vanished, winter already nipping at fall's heels. From that point of a view, a nice sun-warmed cave made sense.

It's the hunkering-down part I'm having trouble picturing. By all accounts, Tim was the kid who could never sit still and who grew into a man of action. A guy like that, staring at this massive rock wall . . .

I remember Nemeth's comment on how people often assume they can get cell phone reception if they just get up high enough.

The more I think about it, the more I'm convinced Tim wouldn't be looking to shelter in this rock wall. He'd be looking to climb it.

Watching my footing—snakes, snakes, snakes, please God no snakes—I strike a path perpendicular to the cliff face, trying to get far enough back to view it more as a whole. Then I drift over to where our trail first opened up into the rocky terrain.

Tim O'Day would've been hiking for miles by the time he hit Devil's Canyon. An entire day spent traversing a ridge while knowing he was lost and that Scott needed help. Night would have been falling by the time he made it this far. So maybe he did build that lean-to once it grew too dark to keep moving. Marty certainly seemed convinced it was his son's handiwork.

Which meant if Tim set out the next morning, he would've hiked a mere mile before arriving here. Day was young. Tim was fit.

I stare at the wall. Shift left, stare some more. Then head even farther right, study that portion. The cliff face isn't sheer, but layers upon layers of rocky protrusions. I can spot a wide outcropping here, decent enough ledge there. Bit by bit, I can piece together some semblance of a workable path, rising to the top. Skinny, to be sure. And too scary for me. But Tim? Worried about his friend? Knowing he was lost with limited supplies?

He would've tried that path. I just know it.

I walk closer to the wall, where the first logical upward path protrudes. I follow the line of rocks to the next outcropping. From there it would be tricky, but if Tim trusted himself enough to jump, he'd land on a narrow ledge that ran a solid thirty feet northwest. More protrusions, another rocky outcropping. Tim's a third of the way up the wall now, going strong. He's gonna make it. Climb to the top, phone for help, rescue himself and his friend . . .

Oh, the stories they'd tell after this. A bachelor party that would forever live in infamy.

There, a glimpse of green on that top ledge, where no green should be.

I get out my whistle, preparing to blow in triumph, when:

A different whistle sounds. Shrill. Three times in rapid succession. The universal signal for help. The sound bounces off the canyon wall, echoing all around me. But by the third shriek, I'm pretty sure it's coming from the northwest, where Martin and Neil had set out.

I grab some of the smaller rocks at my feet and quickly build a cairn on a larger boulder to mark this location.

The whistle again. One. Two. Three.

Followed by the sound of a male voice, booming down the canyon.

"Help, help, help. Someone, we need help."

I forget about snakes and race toward them.

CHAPTER 18

I AM GASPING FOR BREATH by the time I find them. I spot Scott first, standing up on a huge boulder, waving his arms frantically with a bright orange whistle pursed between his lips. I have a moment of confusion—Scott was supposed to be headed in the opposite direction with Miggy. How the hell did he end up here? And how did he cross from south to north without me seeing him?

Then I spot the blood. So much blood, splattered across the rocks.

For a split second, my restless mind hopscotches across too many memories at once. Paul, on the ground, staring up at me with an apologetic smile as he bleeds out. A shot-up gangster I barely know, resting his head on my lap while gasping out his last words. A young boy, a teenage girl, a new mom. The progression of their images from official missing photos to unofficial death masks dances across my vision.

I am more than a finder of lost people. I am a repository of final moments, with too many of them having been seared into me.

"Water," Scott's babbling. "Do you have water? He needs water."

I blink my eyes, focus on the matter at hand.

Scott is standing over Neil's body. The young man's face is covered in blood, his spiky brown hair matted at one side, his eyes closed. He moans. First sign that he's still alive.

I scamper onto the rock beside Scott, dropping my pack and grabbing my thermos. "What happened?"

"I don't know. I found him like this. I'd been with Miggy, but he, um, he suggested I might want to talk to Neil."

I yank my bandana off my face, soaking it with water. My hands are shaking so badly I splash it all over the boulder. I start dabbing at Neil's face, looking for signs of the core wound.

"Keep blowing the whistle," I instruct Scott. "We need more help."

Just then, Neil's eyes fly open. He stares right at me as I recoil sharply.

"Shhh," I murmur. "You're okay now."

He's lying at an awkward angle, having fallen with his pack still on. Maybe he stumbled and whacked his head. I want the explanation to be that innocent, even as I already doubt it. I already noticed smears of red on the stones around us. As if Neil staggered around, shaking his bleeding head—fighting off an attacker—before collapsing.

Neil blinks at me several times, clearly trying to get his bearings.

"What . . . what happened?" he asks. He licks at his chapped lips. I grab my water bottle and pour some liquid straight into his mouth. He swallows gratefully.

"We were going to ask you that."

"'We'?" For the first time, he notices Scott. Something tightens in Neil's face, then disappears before I have a chance to grasp it.

"Scott found you. He called for help."

On cue, Scott sounds the whistle again. I can hear more sounds bouncing around the canyon. Rocks sliding, footsteps pounding. The cavalry arriving. I hope.

Neil winces at the sharp noise, raising a hand to his head. I grab it before he can touch the sticky mess.

"Not yet. I'm still trying to inventory the damage. What hurts worse?"

"My head. The . . . back of my skull." Neil shudders slightly. "Jesus."

"Can you move your limbs?"

He lifts his arms and legs. Then, before I can warn him not to, he twists his neck from side to side.

I can see the back of his cranium now. Definitely the source of the carnage. I give up on the bandana and pour the last of my water straight onto his hair. As a bloody river flows away, I can make out an ugly gash up high. Probably a couple of inches long. Probably in need of stitches, or at least superglue. Though how you crazy-glue someone's head, I have no idea.

A rush of heat and gasping breath, then Martin bursts upon us. I don't look up, intent on delicately probing the wound. Neil grimaces but holds steady as I examine the damage.

"What the hell . . ." Martin draws up short as he spies Neil, blood and more blood.

"Head versus rock," I announce. "The rock won."

Beneath my fingers, Neil laughs faintly. Or maybe hysterically?

"What happened, son? You trip and fall?" Martin squats down in front of Neil, peering at the young man's face.

"I don't think so."

"You don't think so?"

"I was staring at an opening. Trying to decide if I should

investigate. Then I heard something. A noise. I turned . . . I don't know. Here I am."

Martin thins his lips, frowning. "Rocks rain down from these cliffs all the time. How do you think we got so many at our feet? You shouldn't have been standing so close. It's dangerous."

I stop examining Neil's wound long enough give Martin a pointed stare. "Now is not the time."

"Asshole," Scott mutters, much less diplomatically

"I wasn't standing that close to the cliff," Neil bites off, batting at my hands and struggling to sit up. "I know what I'm doing. Five years of chasing you through these goddamn mountains, you think I don't know what I'm doing?"

"Shhh," I try to steady him, but he's too pissed off. Ready or not, Neil sits up. More blood immediately wells at the back of his head. I thin my lips at my disobedient charge, then glare at Martin again.

At least Martin has the decency to appear contrite. For now.

"Careful," I murmur to Neil as he shifts to a more upright seated position. "Head wounds bleed a lot."

"I know. I played soccer. Not my first split skull." He stares at me. "What happened? Who are you?" Then, as my eyes widen in alarm: "Just kidding. It takes more to scramble my brains than you think."

Noise from behind. Luciana and Daisy are weaving their way rapidly toward us. Not far beyond them come Miggy and Bob, leaping frantically from rock to rock. Well, Miggy is leaping. Bob is just stepping. But they're both hustling as fast as they can. Maybe our group that's not a group is stronger than I thought.

Still no sign of Nemeth, but he'd probably made it to the far end of the cliff wall by the time Scott blew the whistle. Without any means of contact, there's nothing we can do but wait for his return.

The remoteness of our location. The lack of access to out-side help.

Kneeling before a wounded man, I refuse to think about it.

Daisy and Luciana arrive first, followed shortly by Bob and Miggy. Miguel takes one look at his injured friend and immediately looks like he's going to be ill. He turns away sharply. Daisy, on the other hand, scrabbles onto the rock and heads straight to Neil. She stops mere inches from him, whining intently, as Luciana arrives thirty seconds later, panting heavily.

Neil gives Daisy a reassuring pat. "I'm okay. I promise."

Daisy licks his cheek.

Abruptly, Neil draws the dog toward him and buries his bloody face in the ruff of her neck. After another second, his shoulders start to shake.

He's crying. Because of his injury? The intensity of the moment? Grief over what last happened in these mountains so many years ago?

It feels wrong and intrusive to watch. We stare at anything but the sobbing man and consoling dog until finally Neil pulls away, swiping at his eyes with his dirty hand. Daisy licks his face again. He laughs roughly.

"Honestly, best kiss I've had in years." He laughs again, hugs her close, laughs even harder.

Forget his physical recovery; I'm no longer certain he's mentally with us. But he lets the dog go, then stares straight at Martin and declares in a defiant tone, "All right. We only have a few days, right? Let's do this."

WE DO NOT do this. Neil may think he's all well and good, but the second he stands up, gravity proves problematic. Bob has to grab him, while Scott scurries forward to prop him up from the other side. It takes both of them to get Neil slowly back to our temporary base camp at the midpoint of the wall.

Miguel trails far behind, looking at anything but his injured friend. Neil doesn't seem to notice, but I do.

We arrive just as Nemeth does.

"I thought I heard a whistle. What happened?" Then, gazing upon Neil's bloody face: "Crap."

Neil's laugh again. "Yes, sir. That's me. Mr. Fuck-Up. Pity when you could've had Saint Timothy instead."

Scott and Miggy exchange startled glances.

"Let's get him back down to sitting," I instruct. "And water. He needs more water."

My supply is out, but between the others, fluids are rapidly produced. As the resident first aid experts, Luciana and Nemeth take turns inspecting Neil's bashed skull.

"Nauseous?" Luciana asks. "Headache? Tunnel vision?"

"I've had concussions before," Neil mutters, raising a hand to block the sun. "Scale of one to ten, give this a four. Rest. Just need to rest."

Daisy takes up position next to him, while Luciana sits on Neil's other side. Martin and Nemeth walk a short distance away from the rest of us. As if that will keep us from hearing what they're saying in the middle of an echo chamber.

"We need to abort and get this kid down the mountain immediately," says Nemeth, hands planted on his hips.

"Get him down the mountain? How? He can barely walk. You know we don't have enough daylight left."

"Then we head back to camp. Right now. Make him comfortable, trek out at sunrise."

"I found the remains of a campfire." Martin, voice tense. "Right before the whistle blew. Near the opening of a large cave."

"Old campfires are a dime a dozen in these parts. Plenty of people enjoy building a fire and hanging out after a long day's hike. Doesn't mean a thing."

"But the one I found was encircled by perfectly matched stones. Like the one at the lean-to. I'm telling you, Tim had a thing for balance and symmetry. It's his. I know it."

Nemeth, staring hard at Martin: "First hazard of any search and rescue—seeing what you want to see versus what's really there."

Heaven help me, I raise my hand. "I found something, too."

Both men stop arguing, turn to stare at me. Nemeth is scowling while Martin regards me with the kind of feverish intensity only a grieving parent can know. I'm now the center of everyone's attention.

Deep breath: "I'm not convinced Tim would take shelter. I thought he might try to climb the cliff face instead."

"You didn't even know him." Miggy speaks up, tone hostile.

"I didn't. But I've been learning about Tim through all of you. And all of you loved him very much."

Neil chitters, "Saint Timothy!" Scott glares at him.

"Tim didn't have any rock-climbing gear," Nemeth states at last.

"Maybe he didn't need it. Pulling back, I was able to identify a path of sorts. Tricky, and probably terrifying. But the cliff wall is riddled with protrusions and ledges. If someone was desperate enough, he could think it worth trying."

"No way," Nemeth says, just as Martin speaks up. "What did you find?"

"Something dark green. Maybe an article of clothing? It's about a third of the way up. Too high for me to see clearly. But there's definitely something there. I marked the spot with a cairn. You can take a pair of binoculars and check it out for yourself."

Martin reaches immediately for his pack, as if to retrieve said binoculars. Nemeth grabs his arm.

"For God's sake, man, the living matter more than the dead."

"Take him back to camp." Martin jerks his chin at Neil. "Do what you gotta do. But I'm not walking away. Not with this much daylight left."

"So you can get your head bashed by the next falling rock?"

"She said dark green. Tim was wearing a green windbreaker. You know that. This is what we came here for. Now, let go of my arm, if you plan on keeping yours."

My eyes widen at that, while the group swallows a collective gasp. Nemeth remains exactly as is, face set, hand wrapped tight around Martin's wrist.

Then—

"Uh, guys." Neil with his little laugh, sloppy, concussed grin. "Before you kill each other, might wanna consult with the rest of us."

Nemeth and Martin remain fixed on each other, not inspired by the suggestion.

"I'm not going back to camp," Neil continues breezily. "Not cuz I don't want to. Sleeping bag? God, that sounds good. But, no way I can walk. The rocks are moving. Racing like a current. Do stones eat brains? I've never thought about it, but I think they enjoyed mine."

Martin is startled enough by this new level of insanity to stop growling at Nemeth and regard his son's injured friend. In response, Nemeth releases Martin's arm, also considering.

"I'm gonna sit here," Neil continues. "No. I'm gonna sit over there. Nice, shady spot where the sun can't stab me in the eye. More water. More rest. Then maybe the rocks will hold still. And eventually I can make it back to camp. But right now? Not gonna happen."

Neil pauses. "Whoa. Why is my head bloody? Who are all of you? What the fuck?" Longer pause. "Never mind. Psych!"

We are all alarmed now, but Neil has a point. He's in no shape to move, and given the rough footing here . . . I'm not sure we can even carry him out.

Bob tentatively raises his hand. "I don't mind checking out the green fabric Frankie spotted. I mean, as long as Neil needs to rest . . ."

"You can't make it up that path," I inform him. "It's meant for modestly sized humans, not aspiring Bigfoots."

Bob bursts into a smile, clearly delighted by the comparison. Some of the mood lightens.

"We can go." Miggy and Scott, united again.

We all take another breath, glance at Nemeth.

Martin speaks first: "I'll go with Miguel and Scott to check out Frankie's discovery." He hesitates, then looks at Nemeth. "Maybe you, Luciana, and Daisy would like to explore the area around the cave I discovered. Given how the campfire's been constructed in a certain individual style."

"Someone should stay with Neil," Luciana points out.

I raise my hand. "I can do that."

Another moment. Then, short nod from Martin, short nod from Nemeth. We all exhale.

Miguel, Scott, and Bob move toward Martin. Nemeth, Luciana, and Daisy become a team of three. And Neil and I are now bosom buddies.

Neil starts laughing softly again.

"Saint Timothy," he murmurs. "Oh, Saint Timothy, Saint Timothy. Everyone loves Saint Timothy."

"Shhh," I try to tell him.

But he only laughs harder as the others walk away.

CHAPTER 19

ENJOY . . . THE SHOW?" NEIL ASKS me, as the others depart, leaving him and me tucked in a domed shelter created by a pile of collapsed boulders. Luciana produced an instant cold pack, which I wedged between the back of Neil's skull and the rock he's leaning against. His hair and neck are too bloody for me to tell if the laceration is still weeping or not, but at least he's conscious.

"I put my money on Martin," I say as I take a seat on the ground beside him. Smaller, scrabbly stones dig into my butt, and I shift around to get comfortable. "Nemeth is tough, but Martin is just short of crazy, and I never bet against crazy."

"Nemeth is unbeatable."

"You know this how?"

"Local gossip. Hiking group got lost twenty-something years ago, end of October. Volunteers were activated, Nemeth leading the charge. An unexpected blizzard hit above nine thousand feet, caught Nemeth and his team. They were a party of eight. Four days later, only Nemeth was recovered alive. Pretty much a human Popsicle, but he recovered fully in the end. He isn't from the wilderness, the locals like to say. He's of the wilderness. And mountains never die."

I'm impressed, then notice my charge's drooping eyelids. "Uh-uh-uh. Eyes open. Sorry, but that's the way it's gotta be. More water?"

Neil's eyes open. He sighs harder. "Fine."

"Have Nemeth and Martin gone at it before?" I ask him as I remove the cap from the thermos. He drinks long and hard. His color appears normal, but I'm worried he's running on the adrenaline rush following his initial injury. Once that fades . . .

"Directly? Not that I know of. But both are stubborn old farts. Tim used to say . . . his mother survived cancer first time cuz Martin willed it."

"I don't think his will is working out so well these days," I say quietly.

"Guess not. Or maybe he's stopped telling his wife what to do. Poor Patrice."

Neil shifts restlessly, then promptly winces from the pain.

I give him more water. Nemeth left us with one of the largest bottles. Now is not the time to be stingy.

"Nauseous?" I ask my charge. "Headache? Bellyache? What's your name?"

"Fuck you," he mutters without any heat.

"That would be my name. I asked for yours."

A reluctant smile. He blinks his eyes several times, seems to be forcing himself to rouse. "Last time I split open my scalp"—he fingers the top of his caked hair—"they used staples to close it up. I still have the dents. Six of them. Duh, duh, duh. That hurt. This . . . I'll live."

"You've broken your skull that much?"

"Let's just say . . . I was a clumsy kid." He emphasizes the word *clumsy* enough for me to understand.

"I'm sorry."

"Not your fault. My old man was a drinker. The stronger the booze, the quicker his fists. At least he finally drank himself to death. Couple of decades later than my sister and I would've liked, but done is done."

"Younger or older sister?"

"Younger. Four years. Baby of the family."

"I take it you were especially clumsy when she was around?"

"Ding, ding, ding, give the woman a prize."

"My father loved his beer," I volunteer. "And Jack Daniel's and anything else he could get his hands on. He wasn't a violent drunk, though. Just an unemployed one."

"Your mom?"

"Worked two jobs. Hated him, loved him, resented him. But didn't kick his sorry ass out the door. I've never known why. First, I was too young to ask the question. Then I was too drunk to care. And then . . ." I shrug. "They were too dead for me to ask."

Neil twists his head to study me, moving slowly to keep the ice pack in place. "You got the drinking gene?"

"Started early and went at it hard," I assure him. "I don't remember most of my twenties. Given I spent them in LA encouraging strange men to pay my bar tabs, it's probably better that way."

"Drugs?"

"In my drinking days, I'd take whatever you were offering. But liquor remains my first love. The rest, I can walk away from. I'm lucky that way."

"My sister, Becca, loved it all. Drink it, snort it, smoke it, inject it. Nothing she didn't try. I blamed my father. If you can't beat 'em, join 'em. But then he died, and she was still a train wreck. Lost her license. Lost her job. Picked up a new loser boyfriend. The two of them . . . like the meth-head version of Bonnie and Clyde, racing their way to the bottom. My mom and I tried. Interventions, rehab, AA, substance abuse counselors. For a while, every penny I earned went to my sister's latest treatment. But Derek the Douche always reappeared. And she always went away with him."

"You can't help someone who doesn't want to be helped."

"You?"

"Sober ten years, five months, and"—I've lost track of dates—"eighteen days. Took me a couple of tries, though. And I did have help, someone who believed in me until I was strong enough to believe in myself. I take it your sister . . . ?"

"Drank herself to death?" Neil smiles thinly. Despite my best efforts, his eyes are at half-mast. I snap my fingers, forcing him to focus.

"Remember. No sleeping."

"No dying," he finishes.

"That's the spirit."

"She OD'd. My sister. Two years after I graduated from college. Police found her body in some abandoned warehouse. Derek the Douche was long gone. Probably grabbed the rest of their drugs and booked it while her body was still warm. I always thought the call would come in the middle of the night, but no. Eleven A.M. on a Tuesday. I was sitting at my desk at work. Saw my mother's number and picked up without suspecting a thing."

I squeeze his hand.

"Called Tim next. I didn't know what to do. My mom was sobbing hysterically. And I was just . . . numb. After everything we'd done. It's like half of me knew this was always going to happen. But the other half . . . She was my baby sister, the one who'd sneak me Popsicles after my father passed out. The girl who saved her Jell-O from school lunch because she knew how much I liked it. She used to swing so high, my mother would scream at her to get down. I loved her. Even when she was at her worst."

Wordlessly, I wipe the first tear, followed by the second, third, and fourth, from his cheeks.

"Thank you," he whispers.

"Did Tim help you? When you called him?"

"Tim took care of everything. Called the other guys, spoke to his parents, organized the funeral. My mom was useless. I knew I should be helping, but I just . . . couldn't."

"Sounds like Tim was a great friend," I say at last.

"Saint Timothy."

"'Because the heavens opened up and choirs started to sing every time he walked into a room,'" I quote. "At least, that's what Scott told me."

"Scott's an asshole." But Neil's smiling faintly.

He sighs, eyelids drooping again. I shake his shoulder till he peers at me groggily.

"Your head hurt?"

"Like a son of a bitch."

Adrenaline's worn off. Here we go. "Nauseous? If you're going to vomit, please do it in the other direction."

"Don't suppose you have a stapler?"

"Sorry, this is a superglue-only ER. Come on. I know it's hard, but you gotta keep talking. Tell me about Tim."

"Can't."

"He was your best friend. First one you called when you got terrible news. Guy you introduced to his future bride. I wanna hear all the details."

"Latisha was my date. He was supposed to entertain her friend."

I pause, remember Scott's earlier coyness, and feel like an idiot for not connecting the dots sooner. "You're the one who dated Latisha first."

"Only a couple of times. Took me forever to work up the courage to ask her out. Then I was so damn nervous, couldn't get out of my own way. Spent the first date tongue-tied. The second sweating like a freak show. She was so nice about it, too.

"I was desperate to succeed. So I consulted Tim. His idea, turn the next outing into a double date. Less pressure. I'd relax, make a better impression. So I did. And it was way less pressure. Especially once Latisha stopped paying any attention to me. One look, and just like everyone else, she was all about Saint Tim."

"Awkward."

"Yep." Heavy sigh.

"You must've been very angry with him."

"Yes. No. I don't know. He knew how much I liked her. But then, not really his fault if she didn't feel the same about me. That's what I told myself. Once I stopped crying into my pillow." A feeble smile.

"He could've backed off," I say quietly.

"Not his style."

"He could've excused himself from the date, given you more time to work your magic."

"Not his style."

"He wanted what other people had. Even what his best friends had."

"Tim was one of those guys . . . you could love him even when you hated him. Which we all did, sooner or later."

"Love him or hate him?"

"I'm tired. Can't I just take a nap?"

"No sleeping. Come on, Neil. Keep talking. Saint Timothy who stole your date. What about Scott? Clearly, he wanted Latisha, too."

"Scott was a putz, pining for something he was never gonna have."

"But he did end up with her. Once Tim was out of the picture."

"I don't think a rock fell on my head," Neil says abruptly. He rubs his temple, winces, squeezes his eyes shut against the pain. "I wasn't that close to the cliff."

"What do you think happened?"

"I heard a noise. I turned. And then . . ." Neil shudders, shifts uncomfortably. "Water, please."

I give him the bottle, watching as he drinks deeply. He's definitely paler now, with a sheen of moisture across his face. My concern ticks up several notches.

"This is it," Neil mutters. "The four of us, we agreed. After this trip, we're done. No more looking for skeletons. Once we walk out of these mountains, we're never coming back. It's what motivated Josh to crawl out of the bottle. Make one last push. Except then he got out of the trip. Lucky bastard."

"Why is this the last time?"

"Because we can't take it anymore. None of us. Josh is the most obvious, but all of us . . . He knows. I don't know how he knows, but he knows. And now . . . This isn't a recovery mission anymore. This . . ." He stares at me blearily. "This is a reckoning."

I have a sinking feeling. Followed by a chill. I have to ask the next question, even though I'm not sure I want the answer.

"What did you guys do, Neil? What really happened five years ago?"

Then, just as I feared:

"We lied. We lied about everything." Heavy, heavy sigh. "And our lies killed Tim."

CHAPTER 20

N EIL'S EYES SHUT. HE SLIDES sideways. I grab his shoulder before he can hit the ground and jerk him back to sitting.

"Wake up, wake up, wake up." I'm still in the process of chanting when Nemeth suddenly appears out of nowhere, looking tense.

"We gotta go. Thunderstorm rolling in. We need to take shelter at the tree line."

"I don't think he can walk."

"Not an option. Slap him if you have to, but he needs to move." Nemeth peers over his shoulder, as if the storm is right behind him. Now I'm spooked. If Nemeth is worried about something, then the rest of us should be terrified.

"Neil!" I shout. His eyelids flutter. I tap at his face, then give up and throw water on him.

"Wh-what?"

"Come on. Time to stand. We're going for a little walk."

Nemeth gets on the other side of Neil and helps me heft him to standing. It's awkward, especially given I'm half their size. But Nemeth is already dragging Neil forward, forcing both Neil and me into motion. Is the torrential downpour about to pour through the boulder field? I don't want to find out.

Together, we manage to get Neil out of the den. Luciana and Daisy are already waiting. Luciana appears as agitated as Nemeth, while Daisy prances nervously beside her.

I feel a gust of cooler wind. Peering into the horizon, I can see the dark clouds. A line of them headed straight toward us, a black wall devouring the blue sky. It is both beautiful and horrifying. I can't help but stare, even as my skin prickles with the promise of impending lightning.

"Luciana," Nemeth barks. "Take Frankie's place. Frankie, grab the gear."

Luciana and I quickly switch places. Daisy whines again.

"What about the others?" I ask.

"Marty's in charge. Hopefully he's paying attention."

Nemeth grits out the last sentence. Because Martin's focus has been one-dimensional all day. Hell, maybe for the past five years.

Neil is trying to lift his feet. The cool wind has pulled him back to consciousness, helping him muster his reserves. With Nemeth and Luciana serving as walking sticks, he starts hobbling forward. Daisy remains glued to Luciana's side, head down, tail tucked between her legs. I wouldn't think a SAR dog would be put off by weather. Or is it something else? Because Luciana's expression remains shuttered, which isn't like her at all.

I'm still trying to sort through what Neil told me. Or sort of told me. Lies. Which means secrets. One of which most likely stole our food and bashed Neil over the head.

Scott had been missing when the food bags were sabotaged, and present when Neil was struck. Meaning I'll be starting my next round of questions with him. In front of others. Whatever happens next, I want witnesses.

A fat raindrop lands.

Then a crack of lightning forks across the bruised sky, followed almost immediately by a concussive boom of thunder, so close it causes me to jump. Dark roiling clouds sweep over us, casting the entire canyon into immediate shadow. No more time for admiring the wild beauty. We gotta hustle.

"Just need to get to the trailhead," Nemeth says, encouraging. "We can hunker down in the trees, let the storm pass. Few more feet. You got this."

He's totally lying. The trailhead is at least thirty yards, if not more. But Neil picks up his feet again.

People, straight ahead. I make out Martin and the others. They're shouting and waving their arms to get our attention. They've already made it to the woods. Bob, however, clearly recognizes our predicament and immediately bolts from cover to help. Within minutes, he's taken over for Luciana, and together he and Nemeth half carry Neil the rest of the distance.

We make it to the woods just as a fresh bolt of lightning electrifies the sky. Then, with a second massive boom, the thunderstorm explodes into the canyon. Rain falls in sheets, soaking our hair, sluicing the dust from our skin.

Nemeth and Bob get Neil situated under a small cluster of pines. The spindly branches aren't thick enough to block out the downpour, but Neil doesn't seem to mind. He lifts his face to the sky, the dried blood on his head turning fresh crimson, then running off him in gory rivulets.

Washing away his injury. Cleansing him of sin. If only.

He looks at me then, with the bone-deep exhaustion of a person who's been carrying a heavy load for far too long. I want to tell him

I understand. I want to promise him it'll be all right. But I don't want to add to the lies.

He smiles wanly, as if he can read my mind. Then he closes his eyes and surrenders to the rain.

THE STORM DISAPPEARS as quickly as it struck. The clouds roll past us, taking their light show with them. Soon the thunder is a distant boom and the air no longer tingles with electricity.

Bob shakes out his hair and beard, then brushes the beaded raindrops from his pack. Just like that, the Bigfoot hunter is ready to go. The rest of us follow suit much more slowly. No one is talking. I go from face to face, searching for any hint of what's going on. I stare the longest at Scott. His face flushes. With guilt? Remorse?

I turn my attention to Miggy next, who quickly becomes equally flustered.

When we get to base camp, there's going to be one helluva discussion.

"We need to fashion a travois to get Neil back to camp." Nemeth steps into the middle of the trail, already pulling a blue emergency blanket from his pack. "You two," he snaps at Miggy and Scott. They jump to attention. "I need two sturdy branches of roughly the same diameter and approximately three feet longer than your friend here. Move it."

They hustle away, clearly motivated by Nemeth's urgency.

"You." He pins me with his gaze. I'm tempted to twist around to see if there's anyone standing behind me, but I already know better.

"Time to learn how to use that knife."

Dear God.

He tosses me a coil of thin nylon rope. "Cut this into segments eight feet long. Next, I need you to make holes along the edge of the tarp Martin's going to hand you. A simple X will suffice, big enough for the rope to pass through."

Nemeth turns to Luciana, delivering additional orders. Martin throws me a folded-up tarp, and I have no choice but to unclip the monster blade from my waist and eye it warily. The textured handle feels comfortable enough. And I appreciate the broad guard protecting my hand from slipping down the blade. But the thing is still a beast, razor-sharp on one side, wickedly serrated on the other.

My hands are shaking. I have to take several deep breaths. Then I head out of the tree line, back to the now glistening gray rocks. I unfold the tarp on a large boulder, uncoil the rope, and get to work. It takes me a few moments of trial and error to find my courage and put some muscle behind the blade. In the end, the serrated edge seems to work best for slicing through the nylon. Just to be fair, I use the straight edge on the tarp.

I like the knife more and more. Cuts easily, feels solid and reassuring in my hand. I heft it a few more times just because. Then I have to wonder once more: Did Josh pack such a hard-core tactical knife because he was worried about self-defense? Or because he had his own score to settle in these mountains?

Miggy lost a potential job because of Tim. Scott and Neil lost their chance at the woman they liked. And Josh? What did he lose? And how bad was it, given it sounds like he's been drowning in a bottle ever since?

I carefully resheathe the double-edged blade, then return to Nemeth with my homework.

Martin grabs the tarp. Nemeth takes the rope. In a matter of seconds, they've fashioned a sling of sorts between the two branches Miggy and Scott have fetched. While they fine-tune their invention, I wander over to Luciana, doing my best to appear casual.

"What happened at Martin's cave? You guys find something?"

I keep my voice low because I already sense she's not eager to share with the group.

"Maybe." Her voice is terse and equally quiet.

"Daisy pick up scent?"

"Yes. We started to follow, but it didn't make any sense. We kept running into dead ends, a giant rock here, a boulder there. Natural barriers should pool the scent. Instead, Daisy kept losing the trail." Luciana shakes her head. "I don't know. She started spooking. Then I started to get twitchy, too."

"How so?"

Luciana glances around to ensure no one's close enough to hear. "I felt like I was being watched. Like someone was studying us."

"What about Nemeth?"

"You know how he is—never said a word. But he seemed unusually jumpy, kept looking behind us. By the time he spotted the storm rolling in, we were grateful for the excuse to bug out. I don't like this place. I don't like these woods. I just . . . don't."

Beside her, Daisy whines her agreement. Luciana places a soothing hand on her head. "When we get back to camp, I need to tend to her. And I don't mean food and foot care. I mean she's rattled by the conditions and dejected she never found her target. She needs to end on a good note. Morale matters." Lucy looks around at our group. "For all of us."

I nod in understanding. This has been a long, strange day. Unfortunately, I have a feeling it's about to get worse.

Nemeth rises to standing. "All right," he states. "Time to head out."

NEMETH SPREADS THE blue emergency blanket in a diagonal pattern across the makeshift litter. Miggy and Scott help Neil lie down on top, then Nemeth uses the edges of the blanket to wrap up the injured man like a human burrito. Pretty slick, I think. Neil's conscious again, but clearly in pain. Luciana activates a second instant cold compress and tucks it behind his head. Neil smiles gratefully. Final step, using sections of the rope to secure Neil's form in the carrier.

Now Bob positions himself at the front right pole, while Miggy grabs the left. On the count of three, they lift as one, raising the front of the litter off the ground. The back ends of the two poles are left to drag, which is when I finally get it—travois versus litter. Because Neil doesn't need to be fully immobilized, such as someone with a bad break or spinal injury. He just needs transportation assistance. Not to mention, given we are now a party of seven mobile persons, we can rotate out two carriers much more easily than four.

With everyone in position, Nemeth starts walking, Daisy and Luciana following on his heels. Next comes the travois, with Scott trailing behind it. Martin glances at me impatiently; he's clearly waiting to bring up the rear now that Bob has medic duties.

I take the opportunity to fall in step beside Scott. He's immediately skittish, looking at anything but me.

"How was the cliff climb? Did you see the green thingy, up high?"

"Yes." His voice is as terse as Luciana's. Apparently, everyone had a fun-filled afternoon.

"Who did the climbing?"

"I did. You were right. Too narrow for Bob, and Miggy's afraid of heights."

"What about Marty?" Because I could see the man scaling the Empire State Building if he thought it would help him find his son.

"Bob ruled him out. Told him he needed to stay below and help direct my path."

"And Martin accepted this?"

"A chance to watch me suffer more? You bet."

"You seem to have a complex on this subject."

"What did Neil tell you?"

"What do you think?"

Scott doesn't take the bait. He falls silent, then, abruptly: "I couldn't do it. Follow the cliff trail? There's this section, only way to continue is to jump."

I nod, having seen it myself.

"I wanted to. I tried to. But every time I went to launch . . . I kept seeing Latisha, and all I could think was, what if I slipped and fell? What if she had to receive that phone call a second time? I couldn't do that to her. I couldn't . . . I couldn't do that to me."

I don't say anything, letting the silence drag out. Soon enough:

"I want to do better," he whispers. "I want to *be* better. You have no idea. Ever since that night . . ." A deep, shuddering sigh. "Goddammit."

Again, I wait.

"I didn't make it all the way up the path. I couldn't retrieve whatever's there. Marty screamed at me. Bob physically restrained him from attacking me. Then we felt the wind change, glanced to the south, and bolted out of there. Thank God."

"Martin will want to go back."

"Yep."

"You?"

"I want to do better. I want to be better," he repeats with a sad grimace. "Goddammit."

"Did you brain Neil with a rock?"

"No! Why would I do that?"

"You tell me, because clearly you and your friends have been holding back."

Scott shakes his head. "I didn't attack Neil. I have no reason to hurt him. I found him already bleeding on the ground. Swear on my unborn child."

"And the food bags?"

"No idea. Last night happened just as I said. I left my tent, thought I saw Tim, and took off into the woods, and then . . . you found me. And Luciana superglued my chest. You don't think . . ." Scott pauses, finally turns toward me with wide eyes. "You don't think it could've actually been Tim? That somehow, after all these years, he's still alive?"

"Is that possible?"

"I don't know. Maybe. Oh Jesus." Scott sounds more terrified now than ever before.

"What did Josh lose?"

"What?"

"Tim was generally a good guy and a great friend. But he had a habit of wanting what others had. And you guys had a habit of forgiving him. Until you didn't. Was it Josh? Was that the breaking point? What did Josh lose?"

I don't think he's going to answer me, but then, suddenly, bitterly:

"His faith in his friends. His trust in humanity. His self-respect. After that, what's left?"

I don't have an answer, which is just as well, because Scott refuses to speak again.

We trudge back through the woods to base camp. One man down. Seven people lost deep in their own thoughts.

And one terrible suspicion growing in my head.

CHAPTER 21

I'VE NEVER BEEN SO GRATEFUL to arrive anywhere as our damp collection of tents. The sun is starting to set as we enter the campsite, light falling, temperatures cooling. My rain-soaked clothes that felt refreshing two hours ago are now cold and clammy against my skin.

After the physical and emotional exertion of the day, I want nothing more than to crawl into my sleeping bag and collapse. Camping, however, doesn't work like that. Neil needs tending; the fire demands building; water requires fetching.

No one speaks as we fall into our roles. Nemeth and Scott unbundle Neil from the travois. Miggy hits the fire, working some kind of magic that gets wet wood burning. I fetch pails of water, while Luciana tends to Daisy. Martin retrieves our food. We're like a dysfunctional family, ignoring the nearly palpable tension till chores are finished and food is on the table.

When I return with the final two buckets, Neil is situated in front of the now roaring fire, blanket wrapped around his shoulders like a blue shawl while Luciana carefully rinses the back of his head. She touches. He flinches. She touches again. He flinches again. Still, no one says a word.

Martin appears with the scentproof bag of remaining meals. He sets it down, opens it up, and just like that, dinner is served. We take turns choosing main courses and adding boiling water. I am both hungry and not hungry. I have a squirrel brain under the best of circumstances. After today's events, I can't concentrate. My mind hums, my skin feels too tight, and my nerves thrum wildly. These are the moments I most crave a drink. To save me from myself. Or at least escape for a little while.

Fortunately, there are no bars in the middle of nowhere. Unfortunately, there's no cell phone reception, sat phones, or radios either.

I have spent most of the past ten years on my own, but I've never felt so vulnerable and alone as I do now.

Miggy and Scott sit on the ground on either side of Neil. He sips water; they chew on rehydrated pasta. Luciana has crossed to the other side of the fire, closer to me. Daisy lies at her feet, but the dog's deep brown eyes are open, watching.

"Does she still need to play hide-and-seek?" I ask softly.

"Not now. Too dark." Luciana sounds distant. She's made a decision. I already know what it is and don't blame her.

"When will you and Daisy leave?"

"At first light." She glances at me. "You're welcome to join."

"Not sure yet." But like her, I've reached a decision as well. Mine just makes less sense. A dry drunk. That's what Paul accused me of being when I first started doing this work. Substituting one dangerous addiction for another. I want to think there's more to it than that. More to *me* than that. But times like these, even I'm not sure.

Martin steps closer to the fire, clears his throat, opens his mouth. I don't wait.

"Did you attack Neil with a rock?" I ask in a loud, clear voice. It's enough to stop him and startle the others.

"What?"

"Did you try to kill Neil out there in the boulder field?"

"No." Martin sounds genuinely bewildered, if not a trace indignant. "I was conducting my own search."

"And the food? Did you rip open the bags?"

"Why would I rip open the bags? You were with me when I discovered them—"

I'm already moving on to Nemeth. "And you, where were you this afternoon?"

"At the other end of the cliff face." He speaks up, equally defensive.

"And you, Bob?"

"Chasing after Nemeth."

"Miguel?"

"Headed in the other direction; you saw me."

My attention homes in on Scott. "That leaves you, buddy."

"I already said—"

"He didn't do it," Neil interrupts tiredly. "He wouldn't do it. Not him or Miggy. For God's sake, it's time. It's five years past time. Tell them. Just tell them everything. While we still can."

I KEEP MY attention on Martin while Scott, Miguel, and Neil whisper among themselves. I spare a glance for Nemeth and Bob to be sure, but Martin is the one I'm most interested in. He knows, Neil said. I assumed he meant Martin. Martin figured out the secret the guys were hiding. But so far, Martin looks confused and angry. That good an actor?

Nemeth is wearing a reserved, wary expression, as if he knows something bad is headed his way and is trying to predict the blow.

Bob's expression is the most thoughtful, the least surprised. He seems to have expected some sort of grand revelation. In theory, he's the person I should know the most about, given our past acquaintance through virtual forums. But as I'm sure the three college friends are about to reveal, there's a big difference between thinking you know someone and actually knowing them.

The boys stop their whispered huddle, sit back, peer at the rest of us.

Miguel seems to have been appointed primary speaker. Deep breath, then: "We lied. About that night. Not about everything, but about enough."

I appreciate the strategy. Once you've been found out, stop with the petty denials and cut to the chase.

Across from me, Martin's eyes widen in apparent surprise. But for once, the man shuts up and listens. Nemeth and Bob are already on that page.

"We were drinking. All of us."

"Even Tim." Neil speaks up. "A lot. More than we should've. More than anyone should."

"We were off-our-asses drunk," Miguel clarifies, in case we weren't getting the picture.

Martin nods slowly, the fact that his son was drunker than originally reported not being of the greatest relevance.

"Josh especially," Neil murmurs.

"We should've stopped him," Scott sighs.

"What happened?" I push, trying to move them along.

"Tim got to talking—"

"Making a speech," Miguel corrects Scott.

"Whatever. He was pontificating—"

Neil laughs hoarsely.

Good God, I want to kill all of them. I study Martin again. He still looks like he has no idea where this story is headed. Nemeth is blank-faced, while Bob nods along encouragingly.

"He wanted to thank us for being his closest buds. You know, now, on the eve of his marriage." Miguel, still sounding bitter after all these years. "He told us he knew he wasn't perfect, hadn't always been the best friend. He started with me first, apologizing for stealing my job interview."

Martin's mouth gapes open. He shuts it again.

"He told me he was sorry for stealing Latisha." Neil's turn. "He'd gone on the double date with every intention of being a good wingman. But then he saw her. And he knew he was being an asshole, but he couldn't have behaved any other way. He knew in the first instant, she was the woman he'd spent his life waiting to find."

"Wait a minute." Bob raises a hand. He looks at Neil. "You dated Latisha first?"

"Briefly."

"But you're married to her now." He points to Scott, who nods shortly. Next Bob turns to Miguel. "What about you?"

"Three out of five of us is enough!"

Bob nods. "And your other friend, Josh?"

"Josh doesn't date much. Or at least, he's not one to talk about his love life."

"He's not one to talk," Neil mutters. The three friends exchange glances again.

Miguel closes his eyes, takes another deep breath. "Speaking of which, Tim's apology to Josh."

Now I'm interested.

"Tim's best man," Bob clarifies, which also grabs my attention. I'd never thought to ask that question. They were all Tim's grooms-men, but of course, one of them had to be the best man. Presumably, the one Tim felt closest to. The man now detoxing in a Wyoming hospital.

"Josh has a sister two years younger," Miguel is explaining. "She started at OSU our junior year. She's pretty."

"How Josh ever ended up with a sister who looked like that . . ." Neil shakes his head.

I can't even remember what Josh looked like before his collapse. Dirty-blond hair, sweat-covered face. I noted his symptoms, not the man, which leads me to believe he wasn't that striking. Another backdrop piece to Tim's larger-than-life personality.

"We helped Julianna move in," Scott picks up the story. "She immediately starts making googly eyes at Tim while he's doing his whole big-man-on-campus routine. Second Tim ducks out of the room, Josh exits right behind him. I walk out into the corridor in time to find Tim shoved up against the wall. Josh, who, for the record, is four inches and thirty pounds smaller, has Tim pinned in place, staring him right in the eye. 'No,' he says. 'Touch my sister and I will kick your ass.'

"Tim laughs it off. 'Of course. No problem, bro. Never mess with family. Got it.'" Scott mimics college Tim's placating tone. "Tim untangles himself, walks away. But I can tell Josh is still worried. Before Latisha, Tim was a player. Never knew which gorgeous girl was going to walk out of his bedroom Saturday morning, never to return again."

Neil and Miguel both nod.

"Classes got going and that was that. Sometimes Julianna would come over to our place to hang out, but not often. She had her own friends, social circle. I never even saw Tim and her interact much." Scott looks at Neil and Miguel.

"I never noticed anything," Miguel agrees.

"I certainly never put two and two together." Neil shrugs.

"Tim hooked up with Josh's sister," I fill in, trying to skip to the punch line. "But Josh never knew about it."

Scott stares at me from across the fire. "Julianna dropped out for a semester her sophomore year," he says quietly. "She was pregnant. Ended up getting an abortion. She never told anyone, including Josh, who the father was."

My eyes grow wide. I glance at Martin, who appears equally stunned.

"Are you saying"—Martin speaks up slowly—"that Tim got Josh's sister pregnant?"

"Tim never said anything at the time," Miguel says, "not even when Josh was going out of his mind over what had happened. His parents took the news hard. They didn't approve of abortion, but they also didn't want their daughter dropping out of college. It was a big mess. Josh spent the first half of senior year trying to console his parents one moment, then support his sister the next. He personally drove his sister to the clinic, held her hand while what was done was done. Afterwards, he shut himself up inside his room, didn't emerge for a week. We were all wondering if we should start sliding food under the door when he finally stepped out. Looked like hell. He never brought up the subject again, so neither did we, but then, that was Josh for you. Still waters run deep."

"Tim never came clean?" I push.

"Never." Scott this time. "He was all 'Let me help you with this,

Josh; hey, I can take care of that, Josh. Here are my notes for the exam. Don't worry about the latest homework.' Maybe he was too nice? But then, Tim was the guy who stepped up when you needed him most. Gave you a home away from home for the holidays—"

"Planned your sister's funeral," Neil murmurs.

"Loaned me a thousand bucks to fix my car." Miggy's turn.

"None of us suspected a thing."

"I don't understand," Martin says, but I can tell by the bleakness in his tone that he does.

"We never should've opened the Maker's Mark," Scott mutters thickly.

"Tim never should've opened his damn mouth!" Miguel states more angrily. "Seriously. Ten years later, he magically wants to come clean? Repent his youthful indiscretions? Walk down the aisle with a clear conscience? Did he think about Josh for one second? How Josh would react to learning his best friend had not only gone behind his back and screwed his sister, but had also gotten her pregnant, and *never said a word*? Of course Josh lost his shit."

"Tim apologized for his past wrongs against each of you," I say slowly. "Most of which you already knew, so whatever. Until he got to Josh. Who had no idea about Tim and his sister. What did Josh do?"

"What did Josh do?" Miguel asks incredulously. "What do you think he did? He tried to kill Tim with his bare hands."

CHAPTER 22

J OSH LAUNCHED HIMSELF AT TIM," Miggy continues. "Knocked him to the ground and beat the living shit out of him. Took the three of us to drag him off, though we weren't exactly moving that quickly on our feet."

"So damn drunk," Neil whimpers.

"Tim was taken aback," Scott provides tightly. "He thought Josh would be mad, but not like that. Water under the bridge, he'd figured."

"Josh slugged him again," says Miguel.

"And then it got ugly," Neil murmurs.

"*Then* it got ugly?" I'm officially flabbergasted. Martin moans in distress.

"It all came pouring out," Scott says. "Saint Timothy. The way he'd take and we'd forgive. He could steal jobs and girlfriends and, hell, date the one person his best friend asked him not to. Then smile, shrug, and move on."

"We ended up screaming and yelling. I don't even remember . . ." Miguel, holding his head as if still pained by the memory. "Josh said he was done. His and Tim's friendship was over."

"I might've said something similar." Scott, looking at the ground.

"Basically," Miguel says, "we quit."

"You brawled with my son?" Martin, still sounding completely stunned. "You all . . . quit as groomsmen?"

"Drunk. So damn drunk." Neil again.

"What *happened*?" Nemeth speaking up for the first time.

"Tim grabbed his pack. Stormed off into the woods."

"Which direction?" Nemeth stares at Scott.

"Back the way we came. We didn't think about it. We just . . . weren't thinking."

"We went to bed," Miguel says. "We knew we were drunk and stupid. So we crawled into our tents."

"Except for Josh," Scott interrupts. "He was still sitting by the fire."

"That's right." Neil nods. "The rest . . . it wasn't so far off from what we later said. There was a terrible noise."

"Some kind of animal," Miguel chimes in, shivering.

"And Scott had disappeared."

"I still don't know why," Scott offers. "Sleepwalking, I guess."

Miggy picks up the story. "By the time it was morning, Scott was still missing and Tim hadn't returned. We didn't know what to do. So Neil, Josh, and I grabbed our packs and hightailed it for civilization. We fully expected we'd either pass Tim sleeping somewhere along the trail or meet up in town. But then we got to the ATVs and realized his was still parked there . . . We started to freak out. This was bad, really bad."

"Who came up with the idea of saying Tim had set out to get help for Scott?" I ask.

Neil, Miguel, and Scott exchange glances. "The story just kind of evolved," Miguel says vaguely.

I roll my eyes at them, protecting one another to the bitter end. "It was Josh, right? He didn't want others to know he'd punched out his now missing friend. You were all more worried about Tim than Scott. Why, because you guys had beat up Tim?"

"Josh didn't hit him that hard," Miguel grumbled. "But . . . we were just plain scared. Tim had taken off and was now God knows where. Scott had disappeared around the same time as those terrible animal sounds. We needed help. And we thought . . . we thought if we admitted what we'd done, people would be less likely to want to search."

"We always step up." Nemeth frowns at them. "Even when the lost are idiots, we still commit to finding them."

Martin steps closer to the fire, peering hard at the three men. "You lied about the happy evening."

As a unit, they nod.

"You lied about why Tim left."

More nods.

"But he headed back toward the main trail. You're sure of it?"

A slight hesitation. Miguel nods.

"Did he have his headlamp on? Windbreaker, pack full of gear?"

"Yes, sir."

Martin swings his gaze to Scott. "You really wandered off in your sleep? You honestly don't remember anything after that?"

"I truly don't. I wish I did. You have no idea—"

"Shut up." Martin raises a hand. "You understand what your lies cost the original search efforts? We thought we were looking for an experienced hiker in a sound frame of mind. Not a half-drunk and injured young man stumbling around in the dark. Every minute matters in a rescue operation and you cost us *years*."

Neil, Scott, and Miguel don't say a word.

"Did you know?" I ask Martin.

"About what?"

"About what really transpired that night?"

"Hell no. If I did, I would've taken that into account when planning my own search efforts. And maybe have had success." He glowers at the former groomsmen again.

Good point. I can't see Martin sabotaging his own expeditions just to cover up his knowledge of their lie.

"Who have you told?" I address the trio in general. Because someone must know. Hence the food tampering, Neil's bashed skull. Not to mention the sense of being watched. That we're here, but we are not alone.

Scott finally raises a hand. "I told Latisha. Everything. Before we got married. I felt I had to."

"So you're a better husband than friend," Martin comments bitterly.

Scott returns the man's stare. "I wasn't that bad a friend. I'd never blamed Tim for Latisha. And once we all sobered up, I'm sure we would've sorted this out, too. Maybe not Josh and him, but . . ." Scott shakes his head. "But the rest of us . . . Tim wasn't the only one who could be an asshole, not to mention, most of his 'sins' happened when we were young and stupid. He'd grown up since then. I liked to think we all had."

Except Tim hadn't made it out of the woods and they hadn't told the truth and now, five years later, they were still living with the guilt.

"How did Latisha take the news?" I ask Scott, very curious about this woman who'd captivated three different friends.

"She understood. She forgave. Some people know how to do that." Scott's turn to glare at Martin.

"You two tell anyone?" I look at Miggy and Neil. Both shake their heads. Which leaves us with: "What about Josh?"

"Don't know," Miggy provides. "He's pretty much gone his own way since."

Clearly, Josh's path involved a lot of drinking. Which is worth considering. Drunks talk.

"This changes nothing," Martin states finally. "Either way, Tim vanished in these mountains. And now, for the first time, we've discovered signs of his passage. Nemeth says your dog picked up scent near the cave." Martin regards Luciana.

"Daisy picked up a trail, but I can't say of what, given we weren't able to trace it back."

"Tomorrow, then." Martin's tone is firm. "We'll head back to the cliff. Give ourselves plenty of time to search."

"Daisy are I are leaving in the morning." Luciana's voice is equally resolute. "This isn't what I signed up for. I need to put myself and my dog's safety first."

"Now, wait a second—"

Luciana doesn't let Martin finish. "He needs real medical assistance." She points at Neil, then changes her focus to Nemeth. "When I get down, I'll notify the sheriff. There's plenty of places to land a chopper in this canyon. They can medevac him out."

Nemeth nods.

Martin gets flustered. "Just wait. No need to make any decisions right now. It's been a long day; we could all use some rest."

Nemeth is looking at me. "Are you going with her?"

"No."

"No one should be hiking alone, especially on backcountry trails." He turns to Bob. "You?"

"I'll stay." His gaze slides to Martin as if for confirmation. What is the deal with them? Five-thousand-dollar donation to the Bigfoot Society, my ass.

"We'll stay with Neil." Miggy and Scott speak up without being asked. "We learned our lesson about leaving a man behind. We're not making that mistake again."

Nemeth nods, purses his lips, clearly still moving the players around in his head. I understand him wanting someone to go with Luciana. I even have an idea on the subject. But I'm already guessing Nemeth is the kind of guy who likes to arrive at solutions on his own.

"Let's sleep on it," Nemeth says at last. He stands, stretches out. "You two, take turns monitoring him. Wake him up every hour." Miggy and Scott nod.

"Keep your eyes out," I add. "For anything moving in these woods, sounds that don't belong. Something else is going on here."

Everyone glances at Nemeth, who slowly but surely nods. "These aren't the woods I know," he says.

Luciana climbs to her feet, Daisy appearing happy to be moving. I follow them to our tents.

"I'll touch base with you in the morning," Luciana says, "in case you change your mind."

"How long before this chopper arrives?"

"It's a solid eight-hour hike out, given the terrain. Then Daisy and I will need to hitch a ride to town, contact the sheriff. Depending on chopper availability . . ." She wags her head, considering. "My guess, as early as tomorrow evening or as late as the following morning."

"Roughly twenty-four hours," I murmur. I'd like to think I can survive anything for twenty-four hours. "Sleep tight," I tell her.

"You, too."

But we both know that's not going to happen.

WHEN I FINALLY tumble into sleep, it is a train wreck of old fears and new anxieties. I'm stumbling through a pile of bones, struggling to climb out while skeletal hand after skeletal hand latches onto my ankles.

I can hear the bones whispering in glee. I belong to them. This is my home. Then I'm staring at a grinning new skull as Timothy O'Day pulls me into his bony embrace.

I JERK AWAKE, breathing hard. First I check that my knife is still tucked under my pillow. Then I take a long sip of water. Finally, I realize the walls of my tent have brightened with daylight. I've never been so grateful to get up.

I unzip my tent and climb out to discover three things at once:

Neil is still alive.

Luciana is packing up her tent.

And our remaining food is gone.

CHAPTER 23

You didn't hear anything? You didn't see anything? Are you sure one of you stayed awake all night long? You didn't doze off, abandon your duties?" Martin is practically foaming at the mouth as he drills Scott and Miggy.

Both men shrink back. It's already clear that whatever they say, Martin won't believe them. Martin swings away, pacing furiously in front of the fire.

"Goddammit!" he explodes at last.

"We need to leave." Nemeth, the voice of reason. "Remember, most injuries occur on the way down. We can't afford to be too weak or hungry given the hike out of here."

Scott and Miggy exchange glances. Miggy must lose the bet, because he grimaces, then raises a tentative hand. "I don't think Neil can do it. Look at him."

We all turn our attention to Neil. He's awake, kind of. His face is drawn and pale, his eyes squinted tight against the onslaught of sunlight. If I had to guess, on a scale of one to ten his headache currently scores an eleven. Miggy's right. No way Neil's going to manage a grueling all-day hike over rough terrain and down treacherous descents.

"We'll wait with him." Scott this time, still desperate to make up for past mistakes. "You guys can go. I still have some PowerBars and granola in my pack. It's enough to make do if there's just three of us."

Miguel speaks up. "I've got some snacks as well."

Which makes Nemeth grimace: So much for his speech on basic bear safety. But thank God we're all poor listeners or we'd be completely screwed.

"We can manage till you guys reach town and arrange for a chopper," Scott continues.

Martin's already shaking his head. "I'm not going anywhere."

"You're going to stay with Neil—" Nemeth starts.

"I'm not babysitting. I don't care what the rest of you do. But I'm going back to the cliff face. Tim was there, I know it. Like hell I'm giving up now."

"You're willing to risk your life and the lives of others for the sake of someone who is already dead?" Nemeth growls.

"He's my son!"

"What about your wife? She needs you, too."

Martin thins his lips. For the first time, his anger breaks. Beneath it is something far more awful to see. "I can't help her anymore," he whispers.

Nemeth frowns.

"She's reaching the end. She and I both know it. It's just a matter of time now."

None of us know what to say. Even Nemeth is clearly shocked. He recovers first. "Patrice is *dying*, and you're a thousand miles away in the woods?"

"Yes! And this is exactly where she wants me to be, fulfilling her dying wish! You think I don't want it to be otherwise? That I haven't begged God to take me instead? But in case you haven't been paying attention, God isn't listening to me these days. Or maybe he listened too well the first time around, when I promised him anything if he'd just let my wife live. But I didn't mean my son. I never meant *our* son." Martin's voice breaks. He whirls away from us angrily, stalking back several steps.

It all makes more sense to me now, Martin's relentless drive over these past few days. All obsession comes from pain, but Martin's anguish isn't just the five-year-old grief over losing his son, it's his current agony over losing his wife. Where there was once a family of three, soon there will be only one.

"I'm staying," Martin repeats, his back still to us.

"If he's continuing his search, then we still need to take care of Neil," says Scott.

Nemeth turns to Bob. "Then you go with Luciana and Frankie. Get back to town, contact Sheriff Jim Kelley. He'll know what to do."

Bob sighs, a massive rumble in his chest. "I can't."

"What the hell—"

"I only take orders from my boss. And that's him." Bob points to Martin. And finally I get it. What I'd been missing all along.

"You're no biology teacher in real life!" I sputter. "You're a private investigator, aren't you? Wait, who brings his own PI on a wilderness hike? Unless . . . Oh shit! You two, start talking. Now!"

MARTIN'S STILL NOT in a speaking mood, but he nods at Bob to do the honors. He reveals that Martin hired him a few months ago, after a string of disturbing incidents.

"First, his house was broken into. These things happen." Bob shrugs. "But it's not so common for the thieves to take mostly sporting goods equipment, including camping gear."

Martin's pack is in excellent shape. I'd figured he owned top-of-the-line products, given his passion. I didn't realize the piece is also brand-new.

"Then he got a series of anonymous e-mails, telling him to stay away from Ramsey. The locals didn't want him there anymore—he was bad for business. Martin first hired me to trace the e-mails. I couldn't, as they'd been bounced all over global servers. I've seen Russian hacking jobs that were less sophisticated. Which seems out of character for a bunch of small-town shop owners."

Nemeth nods his agreement.

"Then Martin's car died a few weeks ago. Turned out someone had poured bleach into the gas tank, destroying his engine with corrosive rust. Cars can be repaired, but it takes time and money. And when you're a guy whose wife is dying and you're trying to organize a final search party to find your son's remains . . ."

"Someone wanted to make it too difficult for Martin to come," I fill in. "Make him abort the trip."

Bob nods. "We think so. I am BFBob from the online forums," he tells me apologetically. "And I do have a fascination with Bigfoot and a passion for working cold cases. I don't want you to think it's all been a lie."

I give him a look. Too little too late.

Bob concedes with a shrug. "Either way," he continues, "it's been clear for a matter of months that someone hasn't wanted this expedition to happen. Who, however, I haven't been able to determine. To be honest, I was wondering about Josh, given he's always been the most reluctant participant. Now, after that story the three of you gave last night . . ."

"How sick was he?" I ask abruptly, glancing from Martin's back to the college buddies. "When you took him the hospital, he appeared to have the DTs. But could he have been faking it?"

No one seems to know what to say to that. "Was he shaking and sweating and trembling?" Miguel speaks up at last. "Sure. You all saw that. But could he have been faking it, or maybe have taken something . . . ?" He looks at Scott and Neil for confirmation. "Honestly, I have no idea." Scott shakes his head, clearly taken aback. "But even if it was Josh, are you thinking he followed us up here? How? You were there for the hike up. Not exactly a hop, skip, and jump. Let alone . . . why would he be attacking us? We already know what happened that night, and we've never told anyone."

"Good point."

Miggy is also frowning. "Besides, it's not like slugging your friend for getting your sister pregnant and leading her to have an abortion is a criminal offense. Tim still took off on his own. What happened after that remains an accident."

Martin snorts derisively.

I ignore him. "Another good point. Except . . ." I study the three friends. "Didn't you all say you went to bed first, after Tim left? But not Josh. Last you saw Josh, he was sitting in front of the campfire."

One by one, they nod.

"Meaning you don't actually know if that was the end of the story. Maybe Tim did return. Or Josh went after him."

They clearly don't like this thought.

Miguel speaks up. "And did what? Chased Tim down, killed him with his bare hands, then returned to camp and went to bed? Wouldn't we have found the body by now? I mean, that particular area." Miggy looks at Nemeth for confirmation. "Those woods have been gone over dozens of times."

Nemeth nods. "Course, we were looking for a missing hiker. Not something like, say, a shallow grave."

"The dogs would've found it," Luciana provides. "Any SAR dog, even one not specifically trained for cadaver recovery, will react to a dead body. You had to have been using dog teams."

"We used half a dozen different dog teams."

"Then whatever happened, it wasn't in that area, or . . . I don't know. This Josh kid knew some particularly ingenious method of body disposal we'd better hope no one else ever figures out."

"Josh is smart. The smartest of all of us," Miggy comments.

"Josh is clever," Neil agrees tiredly. "But he's not vicious. Never."

No one has an answer for that.

"I'm leaving," Luciana states levelly. "I am taking Daisy, and whomever else, with me. Once I get to town, I'll notify the sheriff of the situation. In addition to organizing a rescue chopper, I'm sure he can check into Josh's status."

Nemeth nods, returns his gaze to me. "That leaves you," he says. "You go with her."

"There's another solution."

"To you staying here with no food or survival experience?"

"I have peanut butter cups."

Nemeth gives me a pointed look, as if that says enough about my survival skills.

"You should go with her," I tell him.

"I'm the leader—"

"Yes, meaning you're the one responsible for getting us help. Neil can't make it down on his own. Given that, it makes sense to have Miggy and Scott stay with him, as they aren't the strongest hikers anyway. That leaves Martin, who's clearly gone rogue. No way you should be putting his safety ahead of the rest of the party. Bob would be a good choice to accompany Luciana, but turns out he's working for Martin. So why not let him earn his keep? He can starve up here with the rest of us while you and Luciana hightail it down. You two should be able to reach civilization and summon the cavalry in record time." I shrug, concluding bluntly, "Face it, at this stage, we need a medevac chopper more than we need you."

Nemeth doesn't flinch. I respect that about him. I deal with so many people who lie, it's always nice to meet someone who can handle the truth.

"Why are you doing this?" he asks me quietly.

I reward his honesty with my own. "Because I don't know how to live any other way."

He nods thoughtfully. He sees me. I see him. But mostly, I long for a detective in Boston.

Nemeth never says yes. He simply turns and hands the rifle to Bob. Then he takes in Luciana and quivering Daisy.

"How long till you're ready?"

"Twenty minutes."

He regards the rest of us. "Hope for the best, plan for the worst. That means start rationing your remaining snacks right now. Then look for the chopper come nightfall."

We nod. I'm feeling shaky and queasy and far less brave than I want to be. Secrets and lies I understand. But this, alone in the wilderness. Off the grid. Out of touch. Food gone, companion injured, whole party under attack by person or persons unknown.

I'm used to being the hunter.

Never before have I been the prey.

CHAPTER 24

THE CAMP FEELS DIFFERENT THE moment Nemeth, Luciana, and Daisy depart. With their tents whisked away, the leadership grouping has been reduced to two, while my shelter now sits alone, a sad little blue dome. I think I should move it closer to the others, except I have no idea how to do such a thing. And I'm still not sure that's a good idea. So far, I've caught all five of my remaining companions in at least one lie. That doesn't exactly inspire confidence.

I head back to the low-burning fire as the sun rises and warms the air around us. Neil looks exhausted and gray. Miggy wrung out. Scott depressed. He keeps rubbing at his chest and wincing each time he does so.

Bob and Martin are in front of their tents, talking in low voices. No doubt planning their new search strategy for the day. Or really, Martin is dictating next steps, and Bob, his paid employee, is nodding along.

The question is, what will I do? Remain at the campsite with the boys, or head back to the cliff face with Marty and Bob?

I take the collapsible buckets and refill them at the lake while I war with my inner demons. When I return, Bob and Martin are zipping up their packs.

They look at me in wordless inquiry. I sigh heavily. Luciana has left a small pile of chemical cold packs, which she pillaged from our collective gear. Now I pick up the top one, crunch it into activation, then offer it to Neil for his head. Next I turn to Scott.

"Remove your shirt, please."

This earns me a round of a stares. Scott hesitates, then gingerly raises his arms and pulls off his faded cotton top. As I suspected, the glued edges of his chest wounds have turned an angry red.

"Shit," Miggy mutters.

Scott touches the swollen flesh, grimaces. "Kinda figured. Still doing better than the other guy." He gestures to Neil, who smiles at the comparison.

"Cold compresses for him." I point at Neil. "Ibuprofen for you." I point at Scott. "Which makes you head medic." I point at Miggy.

"You're going to go with them?" Miggy asks me.

"Sadly, yes. Anything else you three need?"

They glance at one another, then shake their heads. "I have granola bars. We'll be okay for a bit," Scott says.

Given the hiking distance to the canyon wall, Martin, Bob, and I will be gone for ten to twelve hours. More than a bit, but no one corrects him. We'll also be splitting up our party, without any means of communication. Another not-so-smart move that no one is acknowledging.

Bob steps forward, holds out a red canister to Miggy. Bear counterassault spray.

"Just in case," he says, and we all know he isn't referring to bears.

A final strained moment. We who are about to die salute you.

I have too many memories in my mind. As always, Paul leads the pack. The man who ten years ago lifted me out of the gutter and tried to give me the world. The man I had to leave because even love feels like prison to me.

Except I couldn't quite let go. Until one phone call later, he's in the liquor store, trying to talk me out of my latest mistake as a kid walks in, pulls out a gun, and everything goes wrong at once.

Paul, who tried to save me.

Paul, who clutched at his bloody stomach and whispered his wife's name with his dying breath.

I know too much of ghosts. Of past mistakes and better intentions. The drive to get things right the second time around, regardless of the cost. And the way such obsession can make each and every subsequent decision that much worse.

We are all haunted here. Heaven help us.

Martin shoulders his pack, stares at Bob and me pointedly. I give the three friends one last bolstering smile.

We who are about to die, we who are about to die, we who are about to die . . .

Miggy gives me a thumbs-up. Something about the gesture makes me shiver.

Then I turn and follow Marty and Bob out of the campsite.

TWO DAYS OF strenuous hiking hasn't made me magically faster or stronger. Adrenaline, on the other hand, coursing through me in alternating waves of terror and anxiety, has my legs pumping and my muscles firing. Everything still hurts, but I'm too wired to care.

My mind is blasting ahead to the canyon wall. Attempt the climb up to retrieve the green fabric? Head to the mysterious cave where Daisy picked up a scent trail? So little time left; how to make the most of it?

Marty isn't talking, but I don't care about him anymore. This whole thing has become something bigger than discovering Tim's body. Something more sinister.

An act of reckoning, Neil had said. By whom? For what? And how? The groomsmen's big confession was interesting, but to Martin's point, not necessarily dramatically different. The end of the story remained the same—Tim grabbing his pack and heading back to the trail in the middle of the night. Drunk, not sober, which probably explained why he got lost, but lost is lost. Same end, just a better explanation as to why.

Unless Josh really did do something after the others returned to their tents. Except how far into the woods could he have gotten in the small window of time before the crazy noises roused the entire camp? And if he'd somehow harmed Tim, why wasn't Tim's body discovered immediately?

Spinning. The wheels of my mind racing around and around while my legs pump, up-down, up-down, up-down.

Next thing I know, we burst free of the scraggly pines, and there it is. The sprawling gray-brown cliff face. The infamous piles of rocks. And, maybe, the answer to all our questions.

"WE'RE HEADED TO the cave I discovered yesterday," Marty informs me as he changes course toward the northern end of the wall.

"No more attempts to climb up?"

"Too much risk for too little reward. Daisy picked up scent near the cave, making it a more definitive target."

I nod, trucking along behind him. Entering the rock field, I have to pay attention to my footing, alternating from stepping on boulders to skirting around the larger piles.

"Why did you stay?" Martin asks me abruptly.

"Why did *you* stay?"

Marty frowns at me. "Tim's my son."

I shrug. "Plenty of parents lose children. They don't all spend five years combing the woods regardless of the danger to themselves and others. Not to mention—"

"They don't abandon their dying wives?" he bites out.

"You said it, not me."

Martin doesn't answer right away. His stride has grown faster with his agitation. I can't keep up and don't even try. I figure he'll pull away, storm off to his target, while Bob struggles to decide if he should power ahead with his boss or stay behind with me. I'm surprised, then, when Marty suddenly stops and whirls around, his weathered face glowering.

"Are you scared?" he demands to know.

"Terrified."

"Accidents happen in the wild. Could be that simple."

"And the person who broke into your house, sabotaged your car?" I push back.

"Childish pranks."

"Then sent you threatening e-mails routed around the globe? I prefer my reality served straight up, thank you."

"You can be a real bitch," he clips out.

"And you're a real asshole."

"*Goddammit!*"

Martin's curse explodes across the space, echoing off the towering cliff face. Both Bob and I draw up short, Bob taking up position behind my left shoulder. I want to believe it's a show of solidarity, but it could just as easily be to block my retreat.

Martin's breathing hard, his hands clenched into fists at his sides. His expression has finally cracked, and beneath the surface I don't see molten rage, but something worse. The pain of a man who knows he is wrong, and has done wrong. The agony of a man who still can't do things any differently.

I recognize that anguish. It robs me of my own breath. Failure, in its harsh, cruel entirety. I know it intimately. And just like Martin, I still can't stop myself from making the same mistakes.

"I know," Martin shudders out roughly, "that I'm obsessive and arrogant and controlling. I speak when I should listen. I act when I should let go. I'm hard on those I love. Hell, I'm a hard man to love. I *know* I am these things. I also know I was all of those things before my son disappeared."

I nod slowly. Bob places a steadying hand on my shoulder.

"I don't know how to watch my wife die. I don't. I tried. I failed. I can't spend one more second at her bedside, holding a hand that no longer feels like her hand. Listening to her struggle to talk in a voice that isn't her voice. Looking at a body that is supposed to be my Patrice but . . . isn't. I have loved her since I was eighteen years old. I don't know how to just sit there now and let her go."

Bob and I say nothing.

"So I left. I told her I'd bring her our boy. I promised her we'd be together again. Our family. You don't understand . . . We were so good once. We loved each other so much." His voice breaks; he can't continue. Tears streak down his heavily lined face. He makes no move to wipe them away. "Patrice . . . She is the love of my life," he whispers. "She is the best part of me, the decision I got right, the person who gives meaning to my days. And Tim . . . Maybe he wasn't perfect. Maybe he screwed up and hurt his friends, Josh's sister. But he loved us and he cared about his friends very much. Once he met Latisha, settled down, got engaged, I could see the husband and father he was going to be . . . I wanted so badly to meet that man. I couldn't wait to share him with the world."

Martin releases another shuddery breath. He wipes at his face, swallowing hard to get his composure back.

"So, yes. I'm an asshole. I should've done what Patrice told me to do—let Tim's friends move on with their lives. Blessed Scott and Latisha's marriage. But I didn't. I dragged everyone here instead. Despite their hatred. Despite threatening e-mails and stolen camping equipment. This is where I need to be. This is what I gotta do. This is who I am."

"And if we don't find Tim's remains this afternoon?" I ask quietly.

"We're close. I can feel it."

"So close someone else feels compelled to stop us?" I push.

Martin shrugs. He doesn't seem put off by the idea. If anything, he leans into it. "You two take care of yourselves. If something happens to me, so be it. I've made my peace. No need to worry about hauling down my body. This canyon's as beautiful a place as any to rest in peace. Hell, maybe Patrice's parents would give permission to bring some of her ashes up here. Then the three of us would be together, just as she wanted. Tim would like that, I think. Forever under the wide-open sky. There are worse places, worse ways, to die. Just ask Patrice."

I dart a nervous glance over my shoulder at Bob. He's looking nonplussed at the morbid turn to the conversation.

"Let's just focus on reaching that cave," Bob says now.

Martin gestures toward the rifle slung over Bob's shoulder. "Keep that close."

Bob nods soberly.

"Can you feel it?"

I don't understand what Martin's talking about, and then in the next moment . . . I do feel it. Like an itch between my shoulder blades. The sense of being watched. Of no longer being alone.

I glance around wildly. Bob does too. The towering cliff face, the exposed boulder field, a distant bluff. I can't make out a single sign of life, not even a bird soaring overhead, though now that I'm aware of the sensation, I can't let it go. I want to whirl in circles. I want to scream at the top of my lungs, "Show yourself."

But nothing moves. No one appears.

"Let's get to the cave," Bob suggests quietly, the urgency in his voice unmistakable.

Martin is already walking north. But then I spy what I've been looking for. The bloodstained rocks from yesterday afternoon.

As much as it pains me, I turn in that direction. Because I understand Martin way better than he realizes. I also have to do what I have to do, even when I know it'll lead to nothing but heartache.

"I'll meet you there," I tell them, gesturing toward my new destination. I hold up my red emergency whistle. "I'll stay in contact. One is good. Three is bad."

"Separating is already bad," Bob states.

"And yet here we are. You heard the signal yesterday, right?" I glance at Marty, who nods. "Then you'll be able to hear me now."

"Frankie, no—" Bob grabs at my arm. I pull away.

"You have your job, I have mine."

"You don't have a job!"

"Yes I do. I work for the dead. And my path takes me over there."

I don't wait. Though my hands are shaking and I have a queasy feeling in my stomach, I head for the bloodstained boulder where we discovered Neil's collapsed form yesterday afternoon. I hope Bob doesn't follow. I wish desperately that he will.

But Martin has already resumed his beeline for the mysterious cave. After another moment of unhappiness, Bob succumbs to his employment agreement and follows.

In a matter of minutes, they are nothing but a cloud of dusty footsteps drifting farther and farther away.

I wait to see if our invisible watcher will go with them. But I'm not that lucky. Martin and Bob disappear. The itching between my shoulder blades remains.

I take a deep breath, then I get to it. My personal quest for the day.

I don't like feeling like prey. Which, after much consideration, leaves me with only one option. To hunt the hunter. And hope I find him first.

CHAPTER 25

TWO THINGS HAVE BOTHERED ME since Neil was attacked. Who and how? Then it occurred to me that maybe those questions go together. Neil's attacker had to have materialized right here, on this bloody boulder, inches behind his target. Meaning it had to be the only other person in the immediate area—college buddy Scott. Or there's something else we're missing.

The sun is already high in the sky, heating up the canyon. The air is so dry and dusty, I feel each breath like a coating of grit in the back of my throat. I don't drink any water just yet, however.

I need to marshal my resources. For all my best guessing, there are too many things I don't understand and too many bad things that can still happen between now and our nighttime chopper rescue.

The top of the bloody boulder is completely exposed. No trees for a stalker to hide behind, no nearby clumps of grass for shelter. I jump down, landing not so gracefully on a strip of sandy pebbles below, then take a fresh look at my surroundings. The rocks around here are completely helter-skelter. Some have collapsed together close enough that it's easier to stay on top, leaping from one to another. But other boulders are so massive, or rest so askew, there's no choice but to work around them. The area I've landed in is nothing more than a narrow ribbon winding here and there. Wide enough for two people across, or one Bob. It doesn't allow me to see much ahead, which only heightens my nervousness.

I walk around the base of the boulder Neil had been traversing. If someone had been down here in this corridor while Neil stood up top, would he have noticed? I would think movement would attract his attention. But on the other hand, standing where I am now, I'd be invisible to anyone watching from the other side—say, the direction I'd come from.

I can't circle the entire boulder, as it abuts a curved rock of equal size. I try exploring the pebbled path instead, realizing belatedly I should have first checked for signs of boot prints. Then again, I'm not sure this kind of surface would retain any. The loose stones shift so much beneath my feet, I feel like I'm swimming as much as I'm walking.

I make it fifty feet along the path before hitting a pile of rocks that require me to clamber up again. I try another direction but meet the same fate.

Fifteen more minutes of aimless wandering and that's that. Sure, there are these makeshift corridors that would allow someone to traverse between the boulders and be less visible. But none of the paths get very far before forcing the person to return topside.

Scott or I should have been able to spot a stranger appearing or disappearing among the rock piles like some dusty gopher. Not to mention Martin racing in from the north, or Miggy and Bob closing ranks from the south.

Meaning Scott was lying? Meaning he had to be our perpetrator after all?

I don't like it. What does he have to gain? He already won the girl. Even if his buddies feel put out by the new happy couple, I can't see their disapproval being something worth killing over.

I wind my way back to the original boulder, very thirsty now. And hot. My lips are cracked, my fancy wicking shirt glued to my back. I don't want to be a hiker anymore. I want a hotel room and a hot bath and pitchers of water and a greasy cheeseburger topped with crisp dill pickles. And not necessarily in that order.

I look up, squinting against the sun. I can just make out my hand, coated in fine particles of dust. Feel the grime down my arms, streaking my legs, powdering my hair.

Just like that, it comes to me. I've been looking up and to the side. What about down? Where already, I'm a near-perfect match for the sand beneath my feet?

I heft off my pack. Then, crouching low, I start an awkward duck walk, peering along the bases of the rocks around me. My knees have just started screaming when I see it. Where Neil's crime scene meets the other, more massive boulders. A black opening, not quite two feet tall. Like the narrow mouth of a subterranean cave.

I stick my arm forward. Then I remember snakes and snatch my hand back. I dig around in my pant-leg pocket for the pencil flash-light instead. I aim the thin beam into the dark space. The light illuminates an endless well of space.

Deep breath in. Anything coiled and forked-tongued comes popping out of that opening, I'm going to personally hunt Nemeth down and kill him. Assuming I don't die of fright first.

I scoot forward on my hands and knees, wincing against the rock shards digging painfully into my flesh. I'm close enough now that I can feel a waft of cool air from the opening. That seems encouraging. I sniff experimentally. Smells like dirt, which is better than other options. Where's Daisy when I need her?

Another deep breath. I have no choice now but to flatten out and stick my head and shoulders in. I squeeze my eyes shut. Count to three. Thrust forward.

Forcing my eyes open, I see it's an underground cavern of sorts. Or maybe *cavern* is the wrong word. More like a cave-sized air pocket formed eons ago as these boulders collapsed. It's deeper than I expected, maybe five to six feet tall, and surprisingly wide.

I hesitate. This space is plenty big enough to house a person. A perfect underground hunting den, where an opportunistic predator could lie in wait, then scramble up to attack before dropping back down to obscurity.

Scott could've been telling the truth after all.

I should enter and explore. Check for signs of human passage.

I don't want to go in there. And not just because of snakes. But because nothing good comes from exploring underground tombs. Everyone knows that.

My only other option is to fetch Bob and Martin. I already know Marty won't come, and Bob . . . Well, the space isn't that small, but neither is it that big.

No guts, no glory, I tell myself.

I turn around and scoot backward, feetfirst into the opening. Then I allow myself to fall into the abyss.

I HIT THE ground with a puff of dirt that promptly makes me cough. I wield my flashlight like a weapon, stabbing first that dark corner, then that one, that one, that one. A spinning circle of lighted jabs.

When nothing leaps, bites, or rattles, I finally release a shaky breath. I'm here. I'm alive. Fuck, how am I getting back up?

I stare at the opening overhead. Not five or six feet up; more like eight.

Another shaky breath. I'm here now. Might as well tend to the matters at hand.

Using my flashlight, I turn my attention to the space around me. The floor isn't really flat, but a sandy mound of dirt and pebbles that have collected in the crevices between the jumbled rocks. It shifts beneath my feet, which makes it a challenge to walk.

This time, I check for boot impressions before taking a step. There's a depression very close to me, then another and another. The soil is too loose to hold something as distinct as tread patterns, but from a layperson's perspective, it certainly looks like someone has been moving around in here.

I take a first tentative step, sliding to one side, before I find a more solid base, probably a larger rock beneath the shifting sand. I make it to the wall, where I feel the craggy edge of a bus-sized boulder. Did it break free from the cliff face a millennium ago? Was it delivered here by glaciers? Tossed by a giant?

Bit by bit, I pick my way around the uneven perimeter. I'm not sure what I'm looking for, just evidence of human occupation.

Nothing immediately jumps out. And yet the space doesn't feel abandoned to me.

Then I come across the first gap in the wall.

Two huge boulders toppled against each other, leaving a V of empty space between them. It's tall enough for me to wedge myself through.

To where? Another void? Or a tighter and tighter space till my chest compresses and my lungs seize up, and I . . .

I can't go there. At the thought alone, my hands are shaking so hard I've turned my flashlight into a disco ball. I'm breathing too shallowly, my heart starting to race. All at once, this space is too dark, too scary, too empty for me.

Forget snakes. I am already in a grave. If I can't reach the opening above, claw my way out, Bob and Marty will never know. They'll walk right over the top of me. Then they'll be gone and it's not Marty who will be joining his son forever in Devil's Canyon.

Why did I come to Wyoming? Why do I keep doing this to myself? Paul is dead but I'm still chasing the bullet, waiting for it to finally punch into my gut, spill my own blood. All these searches, these strangers I help find and bury. It never changes anything.

Other people find closure, other people move on. Not me. Every place I arrive, I already see myself leave. Every door that opens, I already know will close.

I don't want to be me anymore. I want to be the kind of person who falls in love and stays. Who has a job other people actually understand. Who returns night after night to a place I call home.

I want to build a time machine and go back to the night my father and I went camping. Except this time, I won't be hungry. My father won't have to head to the kitchen and pretend magic wood sprites are fixing us dinner. Instead, he and I will stay next to our adorably unstable tent. We'll gaze up at the sky and watch the stars appear. We'll share stories and he'll know what he's saying and who he's saying it to.

He'll remain himself with me.

Maybe I'll lean my head against his shoulder. He'll pat me on the top of my head. And then we'll fall silent. We'll just be.

My entire life, I have always wanted to just be.

I'm crying. I can feel the moisture on my cheeks. More salt tracks through the endless layers of grime. I don't know why. There's no point to my tears, no use in wishing for the lessons I never learned.

I'm a drunk who followed in her father's footsteps.

Until one day he was dead. And I became sober.

Now I live every day, spinning and wanting and wishing. But sober. Each and every day.

Even when it hurts.

I look up at the opening above. It appears too high, too hard. But my panic is receding, my resolve returning. If I can go each and every minute without taking another drink, then I sure as hell can do this.

I've seen what I needed to see. Someone could've very well been hiding here, waiting for Neil. Furthermore, there are more than just the caves in the cliff wall for taking cover; there appears to be at least some kind of warren of subterranean hideouts.

Most likely, Scott was telling the truth and someone else attacked Neil, then disappeared into this hidey-hole without any of us being the wiser.

Someone who wasn't just watching us, but knows this area intimately. An enraged local? Ghost of a past hiker?

Or Timothy O'Day himself? Having made it this far, maybe he did survive. And all these years, he's waited for his revenge?

That doesn't make sense to me either. But one thing's for certain. I'm climbing my scrawny ass out of this damn tomb. Then I'm racing like hell toward Marty and Bob. Not just to tell them what I've learned, but to warn them as well.

Danger is everywhere.

And we're much more vulnerable than we knew.

CHAPTER 26

'M A PANTING, HEAVING, SWEATY mess by the time I careen into Bob. He's standing outside the opening of a large cave when I crash into him. He grabs my shoulders reflexively, then widens his eyes at my disheveled appearance.

"Rocks. Air pockets. Den below. Caves above. Hideouts. Everywhere," I manage to gasp out. I can't breathe. I've been running ever since I crawled my way out of the underground chamber. The climb up to the opening hadn't been so bad, with the craggy rocks providing plenty of handholds. Having to wriggle back into the exposed sun, however, wondering if our watcher was standing there, waiting for me. With a gun. Or a knife. Or a venomous snake.

It had taken me nearly as much mental fortitude to force myself out of the subterranean cavern as it had taken me to blindly plummet into it. Then, standing up, my shoulder blades starting to itch, the fine hairs standing up on my arms . . . I'd grabbed my pack and bolted north. Veering around boulders, stumbling up rock piles, just running, running, running. The hunted hare desperate to reach safety.

"You're okay," Bob says. "I got you. Here." He reaches around me to remove my water bottle from the side pocket of my pack and hand it to me. I unscrew the top and drink desperately, water spilling down my chin in filthy rivulets.

"Stop." Bob pries the metal bottle from my hand. When my breathing has calmed another notch, he gives it back. "Now, come inside where it's cooler. You can talk to Marty and me at the same time. Something about air pockets?"

I manage to nod. My heart is slowing, my adrenaline fading. I feel faintly foolish, but still shaky. I pick my way slowly into the impressively large cave, Martin's great discovery from yesterday.

The space is so tall not even Bob has to worry about head space. It's wide, too. Like, gather-twelve-of-your-closest-friends-and-enjoy-the-bonfire kind of wide. Which is where Marty is now, sitting on the rocky ground, staring at the charred remains of wood and ash, encircled by two dozen perfectly symmetrical, golf-ball-sized rocks.

Marty's right: The stone fire ring is a work of beauty, showing an aesthetic touch when none was required. Is this Tim's signature? Particularly pretty campfires? Or is this how a lost, lonely hiker distracted himself? By searching through the endless supply of rubble to find the pebbles that were just right.

Marty looks up as we approach. He isn't just studying the rocks, but once again touching them. As if he can still feel his son's fingers upon them. Now he takes in my grimy appearance and frowns.

"What the hell happened to you?"

I do my best to explain. About subterranean pockets beneath some of the boulder piles. The potential for our watcher to be anywhere, everywhere. Above us on the cliff face. Beside us in one of the caves. Below us in a hidey-hole.

My voice grows agitated as I speak. But Marty shows little expression. His attention appears miles away. I'm not sure he's even listening, then I wonder if it matters.

I don't think Martin's searching for his missing son anymore. He's holding vigil for his lost family.

"How big was the opening again?" Bob asks me when I'm done.

"Maybe two feet high?"

"So big enough for a male or a female."

"Yes. Though, couldn't be a huge guy." I glance at him pointedly. "But Martin- or Nemeth-sized would definitely fit."

"It would have to be someone who knows this area well. Even Nemeth never mentioned anything like an underground den."

"Gotta be a local," I agree.

"But why would one of the townspeople attack Neil?" Bob asks.

"Why would anyone send threatening e-mails to warn Martin not to return? Then go through additional steps to sabotage this search before it ever began?"

Martin finally manages a shrug in answer to all these questions. Then he returns his undivided attention to the circle of stones. I focus on Bob, who seems to be the only other functional adult.

"Was Devil's Canyon always the target of this year's expedition?" I ask him.

He nods.

"And how many people know that?"

"It's public knowledge. Nemeth filed the paperwork requesting permission months ago. It's a matter of protocol when leading an expedition into a wilderness area. Lets district rangers know what's going on. Also, the permit can be used to launch rescue efforts if your party doesn't return after the listed timeframe."

"In other words, plenty of people would know." I pause. "Five years later, Martin's efforts aren't a new variable, right? And he's never gotten threatening messages before."

"No."

"Then it's gotta be this area. That's what's new. Devil's Canyon itself. Someone doesn't want outsiders here."

Bob remains thoughtful. "Nemeth said this area wasn't well trafficked but that other hikers do pass through. What would make our presence so special?"

"We're not passing through," I guess. "We're staying and searching. And we brought a cadaver dog."

"But attacking us would only bring more attention and people into this canyon."

"Unless Neil wasn't supposed to end up incapacitated. More like wounded enough we'd have to abort our efforts and return to civilization. Same with stealing our food. Further motivation for us to depart."

"Except Neil can't hike out. Most of us stayed, and the two other members of our party are now summoning the cavalry. That doesn't bode well for our attacker's mission."

I gaze at him with troubled eyes. "Or it doesn't bode well for us."

"What do you mean—" Bob stops himself, arriving at the answer before he finishes asking the question. "You're worried now the person will have to grow more serious, get rid of us once and for all."

"I wish this canyon could talk," I say quietly.

"Me, too." Bob nods slowly. Then: "I think we should get back to the others now."

"Agreed."

We both turn toward Martin. Then our real work begins.

———

MARTIN DOESN'T ARGUE, but neither does he agree. He pretends to listen but doesn't appear to register any of our words.

I understand grief. I've witnessed its ravages before, felt its sharp teeth myself. I still don't know what to do with Martin's silent surrender. He's gone from totally obsessed to completely shut down. I'm not sure which is worse.

In the end, Bob gives up on discussion, goes with a command. "You have twenty minutes," he informs the man. "Then we're leaving. All of us. Even you."

Bob walks off, heading deeper into the cave to give Martin some space. I follow after him. The ceiling slopes down the farther away from the opening we get. There's still plenty of distance before Bob has to duck.

We curve around slightly, then approach what appears to be the end, where the cave narrows down into a den-like space not so different from my domed tent. There's another, smaller campfire that's been built here. I peer behind us, just making out a piece of the vast opening where Martin still sits. Living room, I think. Making this the bedroom.

With two sources of heat, this place would feel cozy even as the temperatures plummeted. Had that given comfort to its inhabitant—say, Timothy O'Day—before the first winter storm arrived and buried all his available firewood in feet of snow?

"What have you found?" I ask Bob quietly.

"Just this. Someone's clearly camped out here. But who? When?" Bob shrugs. "Marty has his symmetrical-stone theory. Believes it's proof it was Tim. But I've been all through the cave, as well as the area outside of it. I can't find any traces of Tim's pack, gear, clothing. There's also no sign of bedding."

"I thought Tim didn't have his sleeping bag or tent."

"No, bush-craft bedding. A layer of harvested moss, or a mat of thin pine boughs. If Tim stayed here for the long run, he'd want something other than stone to sleep on, and not just for comfort, but for insulation as well."

I nod. "Having a second fire back here implies this was a resting area. But you're saying not for the long haul."

"That would be my guess. There's no food refuse either. Say, bones from small animals or discarded roots, dried mushrooms."

"Do you really know how to live off the land?"

"I know enough." Bob shrugs. "Like I said, I didn't lie about everything."

I still don't feel like letting him off the hook just yet, but nod in acknowledgment. "Nemeth said plenty of hikers liked to take shelter in these caves, enjoy a campfire."

"I found several more used caves," Bob confirms. "Though to be fair, this is the only one with such a distinctly aesthetic approach to the stones ringing the campfires."

"Maybe we're all right. Tim did make it this far. Took shelter long enough to catch his breath, recoup his strength. Then he headed back out. Attempted to climb the cliff face, knowing he'd never survive through the winter."

"If his journey ended here," Bob says carefully, "we should've found his pack. That implies he moved on, if he was ever here at all."

"Daisy caught a scent," I murmur.

"We walked through that area; it's right after this cave. I didn't see anything."

I sigh unhappily. "Did you happen to look down low? You know, for any underground openings?"

"I don't do down low very well."

Now we sigh together, knowing what we have to do next.

———

WE LEAVE MARTIN to play with pebbles as we exit the cave. I hesitate for a moment, not just because of the heat awaiting us, but because I can't stand the thought of once more being so exposed.

Bob seems to share my concern, both of us drawing to a halt right before the cavern opening. Here, we have a thin cover of shadow before bursting into full sun. The view is gorgeous from this vantage point, the gray-brown expanse of the boulder field rippling like a dry riverbed right before the green explosion of the abutting woods. A blue-tinged bluff rises to the right, not nearly as impressive as the cliff face, but offering up its own patchwork of forest shadings. If I squint hard enough, I think I can almost make out water in the distance. One of the streams we crossed or maybe even the lake near our campsite.

Or it's all just wishful thinking.

I return my gaze to the piles of rocks strewn before us. Midafternoon now. Do this, return to base camp, welcome the rescue choppers.

Only a handful of hours left.

WE JUMP DOWN from the cave entrance without speaking. Bob heads straight for the cover of the largest boulder and I follow. We don't put our mutual fear into words, just watch each other's back as we thread our way to the place where Daisy detected the odor of decomp.

According to Luciana, the dog kept losing the scent trail. Now that I'm walking the terrain, I get Luciana's point. It feels to me like the rocks themselves would trap the scent in places such as this corridor, making for an easier time, not more difficult.

We hit a dead end at a particularly large boulder. After a moment's hesitation, we both scramble up to the top of it, leapfrog our way quickly another ten to fifteen feet, then drop down again. I feel a patch of coolness against my ankle.

Sure enough, there's a thin black void beneath one of the rocks. Too small for a human to wiggle through, but further evidence of air pockets. We continue on more slowly.

Back and forth. I start sweating heavily again, using my bandana to blot at my forehead. It's about as dirt-stained as I am. I long for civilization, running water, hot showers. I wonder how Luciana, Daisy, and Nemeth are doing.

Moving fast, I'm sure. As cavalries go, we couldn't have chosen better.

"It's been more than twenty minutes," Bob says behind me.

I nod. I'm hot, tired, and defeated. And I have that twitch back. Bob is looking hinky as well. There's something about standing in the middle of a barren rock field that feels so vulnerable. I have images of a wild-eyed human popping up to surprise us. Maybe even now the predator is hunkered down low, watching our progression, waiting to attack.

I was never one for haunted houses, and this is starting to feel an awful lot like that.

I lead the way back up to a section of massive boulders, staying low as I scurry my way across. I don't have to look at Bob to know he's doing the same. Of course, a guy of his size still remains a considerable target. We reach the end, jump down into one of the dusty corridors. The rocks here aren't tall enough to shield us completely, but it still feels better than being topside.

This section is wide enough that we could easily walk side by side, but Bob remains behind me. Covering my back? If I'm being honest, I understand Bob fibbing about his true profession. As lies go, it's not the biggest I've ever heard. At heart, he seems to be a good guy with a natural protective instinct. Which explains his actions now, as he stalks behind me like my own personal guardian Sasquatch.

We're approaching the base of the cliff, where we'll have to scamper up a steep rock pile to make the final, open-air traverse to Martin's cave. I come to a halt, preparing to climb, then I feel it. A kiss of cold wind against the back of my neck, causing me to shiver.

I turn around, frowning. Bob draws up short as well. There are four or five particularly large boulders that form a jumbled pile behind us. Like the rest of their craggy brethren, they're tilted this way and that, a compact grouping at first glance, but the more I look, the more gaps appear between the stones. I pause before a particularly tall, narrow crack. Cool air wafts out.

Definitely there's a void inside this rock pile. But this opening is far too skinny for human access, and I say that being a particularly skinny human.

"What?" Bob asks.

"Hold up your hand."

He does as I instruct, nodding as he registers the breeze. I continue to study the opening. What is it that's bothering me? What am I not seeing?

Then I do. It's not the opening. It's the enormous boulder itself. What appears to be a giant slab protrusion along the side of the rock . . . isn't. I can just make out a fine line of cracks all around it. This piece isn't connected to anything. It's a free-standing, five-foot-high, four-foot-wide section. In shape and dimensions, it's a door. A stone door.

I gaze up at Bob, then gesture to what I've found, tracing the edges of the slab with my fingertips. I don't speak a word and neither does he. Because, having found the door, we now have to worry about what's behind it.

Bob thins his lips. To open or not to open, that is the question. Except it's not really much of a debate. Both of us are seekers. Of course we have to know what's on the other side.

He shrugs out of his pack. I follow suit. He digs around in his gear until he emerges with fresh can of bear repellent, holding it up for my attention. It's as good a weapon for self-defense as any. I have my knife attached to my belt, but I'm not that confident or blood-thirsty, so I retrieve my own canister of high-octane pepper spray.

We nod at each other. Then, as if we've been partners forever, I take up position to the right of the opening, where I can pepper spray first, question later, while Bob takes on the door, clutching the edge with both hands and preparing to slide it left.

The slab should be incredibly heavy, nearly impossible to move. Instead, it pops to the side so quickly, Bob nearly tumbles to the ground.

Which is when we make our second discovery. The gateway isn't chiseled stone after all, but some Styrofoam-like substance, painted and covered with a thin layer of pebbles and sand to make it both look and feel genuine.

Man-made. Placed here with purpose. Hiding this chamber.

We stare at a jagged gap that's now appeared between the rocks. More cool air wafts out, and with it, a faint odor. Musty. Earthy. Fetid.

The bear spray rattles in my hand.

"I'll go," Bob says.

A guy with a good heart, but there's no way he's fitting into an opening that at four-feet high, is even tinier than the dimensions of the fake door.

I smile. I once more take out my pen flashlight.

"Tell me there are no snakes."

"There are no snakes."

"All right. I can do this."

I don't give myself another moment to think about it. I duck my head and go.

CHAPTER 27

LATER, THIS IS HOW I will tell the story: Once, while searching fearlessly for a missing young man, I entered a crawl space underneath a jumble of boulders. It was tough going. No smoothly carved tunnel, but a series of opportunistic gaps that enabled me to work my way forward piece by piece. I forged bravely on for what felt like forever but was probably more like ten minutes.

Until suddenly the space opened up. Enough that I could straighten to my full height with plenty of clearance, and wave my flashlight over the entire room. Which I did, bit by bit, until finally . . .

Later, this is how I will tell the story. Assuming I survive long enough to speak of it again.

BY THE TIME I stumble back out into the light of day, I'm no longer shaking. There are no tears on my cheeks, or bile in my throat.

Inside me, there's a scream building but it can't come out. To make a sound would be to jar myself back to consciousness. To speak words would be to give voice to something I can't bear to be real.

Instead, I stare at Bob. I stare and stare and stare. I think of Marty and his silent surrender. I wish it for myself.

"Frankie?" Bob prods with concern.

But I can only shake my head.

"Did . . . did you find him? Was Tim's body in there?"

I shrug, because I honestly have no idea.

Bob hands me my water bottle. He forces me to take a drink. Then, when I remain a silent statue, he wraps his huge arms around me. He pulls me into his massive sweaty form and I don't mind. I focus on the feel of him, solid and warm.

I start to shake then. And once I do, I can't stop. Then I'm crying. And once I do, I can't stop.

Bob whispers words of soothing. He strokes my hair. He cradles me against him as if I'm a child.

I cling to him. In the way I was never allowed to cling to my parents. Harder than I even clung to Paul, because I knew from the very beginning his love would be too much.

But now, I don't let go. I absorb every last ounce of Bob's comfort. I soak it in and reach for more, leaching from him wave after wave of compassion, demanding it. Till he's shaking, too, though he doesn't know why. Maybe he's also crying, because tears can be contagious. We shudder together like shipwreck survivors, desperate to feel saved.

I don't want to pull away. I want to stay here, plastered against my own personal Bigfoot.

But there's no security here. We need to retrieve Marty, then hightail it back to camp and hurl ourselves into the first chopper that appears. We need to get the hell out of this valley and never come back.

Slowly, I pull away. Till only Bob's hands remain on my shoulders, lending me strength.

He peers at me with solemn blue eyes. "Frankie? Did you find Tim? Is that what this is?"

I lick my lips. Take a deep breath and let the words come. "I don't know. I didn't find one body. I found eight."

WE MAKE A break for it. Both of us moving fast and low as we scramble up the steep rock pile. Eyes everywhere. That's all I can think. If we're being watched, then our hunter knows we've discovered his lair. Eight bodies later, what's a few more?

We burst topside, and I feel an immediate gust of cold wind, while in the next instant, the daylight dims dramatically. Another thunderstorm rolling in. Meaning we really have to hustle. Grab Martin. Race for camp. Go, go, go.

Bob is still behind me, trying to make himself as small a target as a bear-sized human can be. I run flat out, leaping across the gaps between these larger stones, stumbling over smaller stones. I can see the cave entrance just up ahead.

Martin appears, frowning at us. We've been gone far longer than twenty minutes, and no doubt he's also noticed the incoming storm. He seems more alert, which makes me feel guilty for the news I'm about to deliver. But there's no time for niceties anymore.

I burst into the cave, careening past Martin, Bob hot on my heels. Marty falls back with us, clearly perturbed. Then in the next instant, as if some internal radar has pinged to life:

"Did you find it? Was it Tim? Take me to him. Now!"

He's already whirling for the cave entrance when Bob grabs his arm. "Stop. Listen. Frankie, tell him."

"We discovered another boulder chamber," I babble. "I crawled inside. There were bodies. Eight bodies. I saw them. I have no idea if one of them is Tim. I'm so sorry."

Martin doesn't move. He peers at me as if I might've spoken English, but it came out as gibberish. "Eight bodies?"

"Yes."

"You mean like an ancient burial chamber for Indigenous people?"

"I don't think there's anything ancient about this."

"But if it's recent . . . how can there be eight?"

I hesitate, glancing at Bob. "We've heard of other missing hikers. I don't know. But there were eight."

Martin cocks his head at me, clearly trying to process what I've said, but coming up short. I take another deep breath, then do my best to describe something I never want to see again.

"The remains appear mummified. No clothing, no gear. Some probably male, some female, though I'm judging by hair length." Bile rises in my throat. I force it back down.

"Um, I'd guess some of the remains have been there for a while. They were . . . further along. Others appeared more recent, but not . . . fresh." I don't know how to explain it exactly, and I don't want to try.

Bob and Martin remain silent.

"The bodies were laid out next to each other. A progression of sorts, oldest to newest. I could see damage to either their skulls or their chests, sometimes both." I blink rapidly. "Maybe gunshot wounds. Also, some kind of mark on their necks . . . I think . . . I think maybe their throats had been slit."

Bob murmurs, "Bled out?"

Martin is staring at both of us. "You're saying these people were murdered?"

"I think there's a reason someone tried to warn you away from coming here. Then did their best to get us to leave again."

"But that person wouldn't want to have called too much attention," Bob follows my line of thinking. "Hence starting out with threats, sabotage. He wants to keep people away, his secret safe. Except now that we know . . ."

The wind has picked up outside, the sky falling darker.

"We need to go," I plead urgently. "Get back to base camp. We don't want to be trapped here." And by *here*, I don't just mean the cliff face and surrounding boulder field. I mean in this cave, where if someone appeared right now with a rifle, there'd be no place for us to go, nowhere for us to run.

But Marty isn't reaching for his pack. "Do you think one of the bodies belongs to Tim? My son was shot and killed?"

"I don't know. Without any clothing or gear to go by . . ." I shrug helplessly. "Look, the rescue chopper will arrive in a matter of hours. Once back in town, we can summon experts. A good forensic anthropologist and DNA test later, you'll have all the information you need."

"I'd know," Martin states. "Take me to see them. Right now. I'll know if one of the bodies belongs to my son. A parent always knows his child."

The look on his face would've broken my heart if I didn't want so badly to slap him.

"Martin, we've stumbled upon a killer's hunting grounds. For now, forget identifying your son. We need to save our own skin. Let alone Miggy, Scott, and Neil. They're sitting all alone back at camp, two of them partially incapacitated and none of them with a clue about the real danger. We need to *move*."

The first crack of lightning flashes across the canyon, making me jump, followed immediately by a boom of thunder and sheets of rain.

"Fuck!" I have an explosion of my own, turning wildly to Bob for support. "Let's leave anyway. We can use the storm to cover our retreat."

"That's not a bad idea."

"I want to see the bodies—"

"I'm not taking you and you'll never find them without me. So shut up and let's go!"

I head for the cave entrance. I'm shaking again. From nerves, horror, the building electricity of the storm. From an overwhelming sense of panic and doom. I just know we have to get out of here, and we have to do it *right now.*

I'm almost to the opening when Martin grabs my arm. His eyes are too bright. I recognize the look from his previous altercation with Nemeth. He's beyond the reach of reason, a man who's lost so much, the only dream he has left involves a pile of bones.

"I'll pay you."

"I'm leaving."

"Anything you want. My house, my car. You said you don't have a home. Take mine. Take all of it. I'll give you everything. Just show me . . . You have to show me . . ."

"Tomorrow," I attempt to placate him, as arguing isn't working. "We'll return tomorrow. With more help."

"Now, I need to go now."

"It's raining and I'm clumsy enough on dry rocks. You've seen me hike, Martin. You know I'm a disaster."

Behind Martin, Bob is slowly advancing, an intent look on his face. He's clearly planning something. I have no idea what, but I hope it involves knocking Martin over the head, then dragging his unconscious body out of here.

Martin clutches both my shoulders, his hazel eyes fixated on me. Grief. It's etched deep into his features. He is drowning in it, drunk upon it, crazed with it. I understand, but we don't have time.

I try to twist away, shrug out of his grip. While lightning cracks and more thunder booms.

Except Martin is suddenly staggering back, and rain splatters across my cheek within the shelter of the cave. Then the thunder roars again and rock shards explode from the rock wall beside me, driving into my skin. Bob screams at me to get down. Martin clutches at his chest where a red stain is now blooming across his shoulder.

Blood. Gunfire. Bullets.

The facts finally penetrate my shocked brain.

We didn't get out in time. And now the hunter is here.

CHAPTER 28

S HIT, SHIT, SHIT." BOB IS dragging Martin away from the opening. Belatedly I scramble after them. More thunder, so loud and close the entire cave seems to shake with the concussive boom. This storm is definitely bigger than yesterday's. I don't know whether to be terrified at its wild power or grateful for its protective cover. For now, I crawl over to where Bob has Martin on the ground, ripping away the man's shirt.

I swipe at the moisture on my face. My fingers come back stained with blood. Martin's. All over me.

I gag, then recover. I will not think of liquor stores or dark alleys. One horror at a time, and this one is hard enough.

"First aid kit," Bob snaps at me.

I dig frantically through my pack, producing the small mesh bag packed by Josh.

"Not good enough. My pack. White box. Grab it."

I go plowing through Bob's belongings. Sure enough, front

pouch, a hard rectangular kit, much more robust than what I have. I hand that over, then remember Luciana's explanation on the first aid uses for feminine hygiene products. I return to my pack, never so happy to whip out a tampon and a maxi pad.

Bob is already nodding at me. "Good idea. But first I need you to open up the medical box and remove the antiseptic wipes and plastic gloves. I'm too filthy to be handling an open wound."

My attention bounces to Bob's massive hands, which are coated with a mix of red gore and black dirt. He's right: First things first.

Martin isn't screaming or moaning. His breathing is ragged, shock kicking in. But his face . . . He doesn't look scared or anguished. He looks furious; his gaze is fixed on the cave entrance. As if he can see the sniper across the way. As if he's already planning on killing the hunter with his bare hands, for daring to come between him and his son.

I fumble with the plastic first aid kit. There are some kind of fancy red tabs I can't make sense of in my frazzled state. The more I tell myself to hurry up, the less coordinated I become.

"Frankie, slide them back!"

I manage that, but the clear lid remains glued to the blue base. I feel like I'm wrestling with the Tupperware container from hell.

"Tape. On the sides. It's brand-new."

Sure enough, the kit is still taped shut. Martin is going to die because I'm an idiot.

While I fight with inanimate objects, Bob dumps water across Martin's shoulder. The blood bubbles out of a wound higher up than I originally thought. More muscle and sinew, less heart. But it's still bleeding profusely.

I finally have the kit open, pawing through with my shaking hands. Antiseptic wipes, blue surgical gloves, got them.

Bob eases Martin back down, the man's shirt balled under his shoulder to keep it out of the dust. I don't detect a single tremor in Bob's fingers as he rips open the wipes, quickly scrubs both hands, then pulls on the surgical gloves.

"All right, this is going to hurt." He's speaking to Martin, not me, but I still take the words to heart. "Frankie, the alcohol prep pads."

Oh shit, this is going to hurt.

"Count of three. One, two—" Bob forgoes three and slaps the saturated isopropyl alcohol pads simultaneously to the front and back of the bubbling wound, gripping tight with both hands. Martin screams, back arching, toes curling, as outside, more thunder booms.

"Pad," Bob barks at me. I belatedly free the maxi pad, being careful not to touch the surface with my own filthy hands. Bob rolls Martin roughly to the side. "Good news, man. It's a through and through. You're lucky."

I'm pretty sure that's an ironic statement, but I don't argue.

With Marty half folded to the side, Bob lets the alcohol pad on the back of the man's shoulder fall to the dirt, replacing it with the maxi pad. Once more, he eases Marty onto the folded ball of his shirt, holding the absorbent pad in place.

"Tampon," Bob clips out.

I don't want to watch what's going to happen next but can't seem to look away as I hand over the product and watch Bob drive the tight cotton roll straight into the bullet hole. Marty howls again while the sky roars its answer.

I lean over and gag.

"Do not vomit here," Bob states so coldly and commandingly it slices through my light-headedness. Gone is the amiable, puppy-eyed Bigfoot enthusiast. This is a man who can leap mountains in a single bound and thank God, because I need one of us to know what the hell he's doing.

I force down the rest of my bile, wiping my mouth with the back of my forearm.

"I'm okay," I manage.

"Yes, you are. Now, scrub in."

"What?"

"Antiseptic wipes. Hands. Start cleaning."

I do as instructed, but with a growing sense of trepidation. I'm a naturally squeamish person. It's not like working missing persons cold cases is a front-line sort of gig. There's a big difference between interviewing people and . . . this.

But Bob is waiting, and Martin, his jaw clenched in pain, his eyes narrow slits of watchfulness. I scrub the dirt and blood from my hands as best I can, then look at Bob for my next orders."

"Grab the compression wrap and unwind the first quarter of the roll."

"Okay."

"Now set it all down in the lid of the kit and come here. I need both your hands."

I'm still not sure I want to know, but I scoot closer. Bob once again twists Martin's torso to the side, the man gasping out a string of curses, but complying.

I understand the issue almost at once, grabbing at the absorbent pad at the back of Martin's shoulder to hold it in place while simultaneously slapping at the tampon plugging the front of the bullet wound as Bob untangles his own fingers. With my hands now pinning the bandages in place, Bob grabs the wrap.

"Hold the pads steady while I secure them in place."

I will not be sick, I will not be sick, I will not be sick.

More forked lightning. More rolling thunder. I can hear the rain, sounding hard and smelling fresh just outside the cave opening. While inside, my senses are coated with the sticky feel and rusty odor of blood.

Martin's lips are moving, but I can't make out his words. A final prayer? A call to his wife, a promise to his son?

Bob is both beside me and over me. He moves fast and efficiently, not speaking as he weaves the first aid wrap over, under, and around Martin's shoulder. I keep my fingertips in place till the final second, then release my grip on the rear pad, then the front tampon as Bob snugs them into place. Within a matter of seconds, Martin's shoulder is bandaged and we are all sitting back, breathing heavily.

I feel covered in blood, but then so is Bob, with streaks across the backs of his arms, down the front of shirt, even dripped into his beard. Ironically enough, Martin is the cleanest of the three of us, his wound now contained in a sea of tape.

Bob pours water onto his hands, scrubs them clean as best he can. Then he's back to the first aid kit, digging around for a foil packet of painkillers. He rips it open and dumps two into Martin's hand. The man takes them without protest.

"Drink more," Bob orders, after Martin's first swig. "Nope, more than that. Okay, to quote Frankie, we need to get the fuck out of here. Because the moment that storm passes, we're sitting ducks."

I nod rapidly.

Martin smiles. Actually smiles. His breath is ragged, his skin nearly gray with pain. And yet there's a certain glow about him. His fanaticism lives on. "I got a clean shirt in my pack. Get it out."

Bob retrieves a simple blue microfiber top and helps Martin wrestle it on. I can't even imagine the pain as Bob forces the man's injured left shoulder to move, sliding his left arm into place. But Martin merely grits his teeth in determination.

"Rain coat," he requests next.

It takes both Bob and me to tuck him into the jacket. No draping it over his bandaged side. Coat must be all the way on, both arms in the sleeves. "Gotta . . . be able . . . to get on my pack," he states.

"I'll carry it for you."

"My pack. My back." At least it's something new for us to fight about.

The thunder booms again, but no longer so loud. The epicenter has already passed over us, the storm fading away. I glance nervously at the cave opening, where I can still see the rain coming down, but lighter. It's only a matter of time now. The afternoon thunderstorms are a short-lived affair. Hit hard, move fast.

Which is what we need to do next.

Martin makes it to his feet. Bob wrestles the pack onto his hissing form. Then we're ready to go.

My body is shaking. I'm a mess of adrenaline and terror. But I also feel focused and razor-sharp. Survival has a way of doing that to a person.

There are no good options left. We are the rabbits, about to bolt into the open and race across the predator's field of view. I am the slowest and clumsiest. Then again, there's already-injured Martin and big-as-a-barn Bob.

I think our hunter is about to have the time of his life.

Martin is staring at us intently. Whether he knows it or not, he's swaying slightly on his feet. "You see where the initial shots came from?" he asks us.

I'm still shaking my head when Bob answers. "Across the way, forty feet to the north, is a bluff. Halfway up, I saw a gleam, like from a rifle scope."

"Good shot at that distance," Martin says, gesturing to his shoulder.

Bob nods.

"But it's always more difficult to hit a moving target."

Bob nods again.

"I go first," Martin instructs. "Give me a minute or two, then follow." He reaches up to his neck, roughly tugs off his orange bandana with his free hand. He appears one hundred percent focused and intent. But also . . .

He gives us one final look. "Get to base camp. Summon help. Get justice for my son."

Just like that, he turns and bolts for the opening, orange bandana waving like a flag.

"Hey, asshole. See if you can hit this!" Then he's bounding forward, but not toward the safety of the tree line. Instead, he cuts due north, bolting in the direction of eight dead bodies. Forcing the hunter to track away from the cave in order to keep him in sight.

The storm's weakening rumble is now trailed by Martin's own battle cry. "You kill my son, you bastard? Face me, goddammit, face—"

The first rifle crack. Pebbles explode near Martin's feet. But he zigzags, running and weaving, bandana high in the air, taunting at the top of his lungs. "Missed me!"

Another shot, two, three, four.

Bob has my arm, pulling me forcefully out of the cave and into the lightening rain. But I keep looking at Martin. A fresh spray of blood, his body spinning. Another primal scream.

"You asshole! I'm coming for you! For my son. I'm coming, *Timmy!*"

Then the rifle booms again and Bob is shoving me across the rocks, off the edge, down into the first corridor, where we race forward before clambering up, bolting across. Up, down, across. Up, down, across.

Rain slashing at my cheeks. The sounds of Martin's enraged yells. More cracks of the rifle. Followed by a fresh scream, sharper, higher. Another direct hit. The hunter taking Martin apart in pieces.

"Timmy!" Martin shouts in a garbled tone.

I don't turn around anymore. I keep my head down and shoulders hunched, my hair plastered with rain, my cheeks coated in tears. I do as Martin hoped we would do.

I race for safety. I bolt desperately, breathlessly, for the tree line and the trail back to base camp. Where the choppers will arrive. Where help will finally come.

Where other people, heavily armed and much better trained than us, can return to these rocks and do what must be done.

Recover the missing.

Carry out the dead.

I run for a very long time, Bob right behind me, till the trees have swallowed us and the storm clouds have cleared and the sun steams the wet from our clothes. Finally I hit a stream, where I slip on the first stone and fall into the ice-cold water. And Bob, far from fishing me out, collapses into the water beside me, his chest heaving as hard as mine.

We still don't speak. There are no words to say. We let the freezing water wash over our bloody clothes and sweat-stained faces. We let it sluice across our eyes hoping that will carry the images away.

When it doesn't, we rise, and much more slowly, aware of our surroundings at all times, we work our way back to the three men we left behind.

Praying they're still alive.

CHAPTER 29

WE FOLLOW THE TRAIL AROUND the vast lake, homing in on base camp. At the last moment, I find myself drawing up short, straining my ears. From this position, crouched down behind a green veil of lake grass, I can make out the colorful domed tents of our camp, but not the people. A thin line of smoke indicates the campfire still burns. Meaning Scott, Miggy, and Neil are still huddled around it?

Bob doesn't question my decision to halt, but squats beside me. Our impromptu dip in the stream had felt both visceral and spiritual. But once on the other side, Bob had paused long enough to grab huge handfuls of squelching mud and smear it across his glow-in-the-dark fair skin, then rub it into his golden-red hair. I'd followed suit; my coloring might be darker than his, but not by much.

Now I picture us as a pair of badass commandos in some cool action movie, but maybe that's the hysteria talking.

We wait. I see tents. I smell smoke. I still don't hear people.

We exchange nervous glances.

Bob points to the right, veering us off trail toward a dark copse of skinny pines. More cover. I nod my understanding, and we creep through the waves of grass to our next destination.

I don't have a watch, but my internal clock pegs the hour somewhere around late afternoon, early evening. Sun no longer straight up, but several hours till its full descent.

And our impending rescue?

Three hours is still three hours. Especially if we're being stalked by someone with a high-powered rifle.

Martin . . .

I refuse to think of his last moments. I choose to picture him, Tim, and Patrice, all together again. They are somewhere where the sun is always shining and the grass is green and the breeze is perpetually pleasant. But mostly, they are a family again.

We hit the strip of woods, weave our way through the skinny trees and the low-growing bushes. I'm still listening for voices.

Then, all of sudden: "Who goes there? I have a gun and I'm not afraid to use it."

Miggy, thank God! I step forward, hands already in the air. "It's us. Bob and me. Are you guys all right?"

Miggy appears from behind a moss-covered boulder, holding not a gun, but the red can of bear spray.

"Where is Martin?" he asks.

"Where are Scott and Neil?"

Which leads to our next discussion.

"AFTER YOU GUYS left, we tended to Scott's wound. Coated it in a triple antibiotic ointment, replaced the bandage. But within an hour or two, I could tell he was spiking a fever, while Neil started vomiting."

Bob and I blink our eyes at Miggy. We're tucked at the edge of the woods, close enough to the camp where Miggy can survey his kingdom, while also keeping watch on the perimeter. I notice he never loses his grip on the pepper spray and his gaze has taken on the intent alertness I once associated with Nemeth.

"Worse," Miggy said, "I kept hearing noises in the woods. Something moving. A big something. I ventured away from camp a few times to investigate, but never saw signs of anyone. I did, however, find some recently disturbed bushes, that kind of thing. Then, when I returned to the fire, I noticed the flap to Martin's tent was open. I knew it hadn't been open before, so I made my way over."

Miggy's voice isn't so steady. I can't imagine how that must have felt to him. Approaching the tent, knowing he must peer inside and check for monsters. That his two best friends were depending on him. And he'd already lost another in these woods.

"There wasn't anything inside," Miggy says. "I mean, there wasn't *someone* inside. But I saw a pile of ripped-open foil pouches, like the kind our dinners come in. Sure enough, in the middle of the tent, a bunch of our missing meals had been returned, the contents shaken out onto the floor. A pile of wasted food." Miggy grimaces.

I'm still confused, but Bob does the honors.

"Bear bait," he states.

"Yeah. Which got me tossing the other tents, then tearing around the perimeter. Sure enough, piles of exposed food everywhere."

My eyes widen. I'm getting it now. The perpetrator who'd originally stolen our food then turned around and used it to sabotage the entire camp. Attract the attention of a grizzly, which, stumbling upon three fire-warmed humans, would've considered it quite the buffet.

And the kind of thing that, when discovered by our too-late rescuers, could be chalked up as an unfortunate accident. The type of tragic mistake made by inexperienced hikers left on their own once their guide went for help.

"What time was this?" I ask Miggy.

"I'm not sure. Noon, maybe? I was starting to picture all my favorite lunches. A nice roast beef sandwich, heavy on the horseradish. My mom's shrimp tacos with sliced avocado and fresh cilantro . . ." Miggy shrugs, his remembered cravings making all of our stomachs growl. "Scott was still feverish, Neil nauseous and incoherent. In the end, I dragged them into our tent, zipped it up tight, and then used a shovel to scoop up as much of the food as possible. I didn't know what to do with it, so I dug hole at the other end of the lake and dumped it in. I'm thinking bears have a good sense of smell? And if so, I want the beast dining on his unexpected buffet as far away as possible. Though, of course, I couldn't go too far away, because what if Scott got worse, or Neil vomited again? Or the crazy person returned and hurt them while I was gone?"

Miggy's voice starts to wind up with a new bout of anxiety and stress. This is not a day any of us would choose to repeat.

"They're still in there," he says now. "But I've been keeping watch from out here, in case that person returns. Or, you know, a grizzly. I check on them every thirty minutes or so, bringing them water. I'm down to the last instant cold compress for Neil and a handful of ibuprofens for Scott. Help is coming, right? Nemeth and Luciana should be talking to the sheriff right about now and he'll call search and rescue and the chopper will launch and we'll be saved. Any moment now. Any moment."

Miggy stands, paces back and forth in sheer agitation, then plants himself on the tree stump again, staring at the trembling can of bear spray. He's breaking. Given his afternoon, I can't blame him.

He takes a deep breath, exhales slowly. Then, glancing up: "So, where's Martin?"

I LET BOB do the talking. I'm not sure I can handle revisiting the details just yet. Bob keeps it simple, though that doesn't make it any less horrible.

"What do you mean there's eight bodies in this canyon? Murder victims? Hunted? Are you fucking kidding me?"

Bob raises a calming hand. He gets to the sniper, Martin's initial wound, then the man's choice to bound off into the boulder field, leading the hunter's attention away from the two of us.

"There's some freak show with a high-powered rifle waiting to kill us? Jesus Christ. He could be here right now, any moment. *Fuck!*"

Miggy is back on his feet. Forget pacing. He's bent over, head at his knees as if to keep himself from passing out. Bob doesn't say anything. I find, hearing the story of our day out loud, I'm starting to hyperventilate myself. Returning to Martin, then trying to save him, then finally fleeing in the opposite direction from him.

Those hadn't been moments for thinking. Those had been moments for doing. And doing is a cushion of sorts. Now, all action stripped away, I am forced to confront what happened, what I'd seen, what we'd lost.

I pace a small circle and will myself to hold it together. Miggy is losing it enough for all of us. Not to mention it sounds like Neil and Scott are in even worse shape, and we're still hours from sunset and, oh yes, our hunter friend should be arriving at any time, is maybe even stalking us as we speak, creeping his way from tree to tree, rifle butt pressed tight against his shoulder.

I pace six more loops before I hear a very real sound from behind me and whirl in fresh alarm.

It's Scott, standing at the edge of the camp, his pale face covered in sweat. "Neil's vomiting again," he says. "We gotta get him out of here."

BOB GOES TO check on Neil. I remain with Miggy, who's staring at the ground. Scott has taken a seat on a dead tree. He doesn't look good at all, but he's clearly trying to pull it together for his friend.

"I heard you," he says now. "I heard you guys talking. Some guy has been killing people up here, and we . . . found it?"

"I think Daisy did yesterday. But having the remains so deep beneath the rock pile confused her." Though I'm not sure why that would be an issue, given all her experience working mounds of rubble.

"I don't think we can stay here," Scott murmurs.

I nod, worrying about the same thing. "Do you think Neil can travel?"

"If we load him back into the travois," Scott says, "and all take turns carrying."

I give Scott a look. Like he's capable of carrying anything right now. But he raises a good point. We have the travois, and it's better than nothing.

"We leave the gear," Miggy fills in now. "The tents, even a low-burning campfire with the cooking pot on top."

"A false target." I nod slowly. "Trying to keep his focus here, while we sneak away."

"We could even fill the sleeping bags. You know, pretend we're kids again, leaving behind clothing dummies for our parents to find while we sneak out of the house." Scott smiles wryly.

"Where do we go?" I ask. "We can't get Neil, or you"—I gesture toward Scott—"all the way down the mountain. Especially not before nightfall."

"What if we made it just one mile?" Miggy speaks up thoughtfully. "Back to the river at the base of the last, hard climb that brought us into this canyon? That area's not as exposed as this, making it more defensible. It has a readily available source of water, while being close enough we'd see the choppers when they arrived. We could signal them with our flashlights."

"I don't think that ravine's wide enough for a chopper to land," I counter.

Scott uses the hem of his shirt to blot the moisture from his face. "Doesn't have to," he provides. "They can lower down a stretcher, not to mention rescuers. Harder, but doable. And yeah, the smaller area . . . Position ourselves with a dirt embankment or a grove of trees at our backs and we could at least see the threat coming."

"We have a rifle," Miggy adds. "Not to mention half a dozen cans of bear-grade pepper spray. Hit someone in the eyes with that shit and they're not peering down the barrel of anything."

I nod. I'm not sure how feasible any of this really is, but it's a plan, and we need a plan. Plans give you a list of tasks to keep you from drowning in your own fear. Plans give you a feeling of control, even if it's just an illusion at the time.

Miggy picks up a stick, starts sketching out defensive options in the dirt. Scott ticks off things to do. By the time Bob returns to tell us what we'd already guessed about Neil's condition, we're ready for him.

Miggy does the honors, tapping the ground in front of him. "Okay, this is how we're going to survive till the choppers get us out of here."

CHAPTER 30

WE MOVE FAST. BOB AND Miggy need to make adjustments to the travois to prepare it for a steep descent. Notching poles, adding a crossbar, creating a rope system to help lower it down from above, as it will be too much weight for two people to try to control from the bottom.

I start out as errand girl, riffling through Martin's tent for any and all available rope. I grab a roll of duct tape, then any empty water containers. Once Bob and Miggy have what they need for their engineering project, I join Scott in disguising our camp. We roll up dirty clothes and stuff them into the sleeping bags in some close approximation of human forms.

I feel my fake campers are superior to Scott's in every way, but then I logged a lot of hours perfecting such skills during my misspent youth.

Next up, Neil. The tent reeks of vomit. He really doesn't look good, his skin color somewhere between ashen and pallid. He's only semiconscious, enough to regard us through heavy-lidded eyes as we lift the edges of his sleeping bag and wiggle him out of the tent as carefully as possible.

I inspect the back of his head. The wound is no longer weeping, but there is one hell of a lump. I worry about swelling inside his skull but don't magically have any more medical knowledge than I did a minute ago. Water for the patient, ice for the head injury. No ibuprofen, as it's also a blood thinner and could increase bleeding. That's it, all I know, and I'm not even sure how I know that much.

Scott and I exchange nervous glances. He's also pale and sweaty, but he's clearly resolved not to repeat the mistakes of five years ago by leaving a buddy behind. And maybe equally determined to get himself to his new wife and soon-to-be baby. Love and regret. Can't get much more powerful motivation than that.

Bob lifts Neil into the new and improved travois, lashing the man to the carrier, sleeping bag and all. Final look around, conscious that our hunter could appear anytime, that maybe we are already standing in the crosshairs of a rifle scope . . .

Miggy tends the fire, trying to bank it just enough to still look good, while reducing the risk of it flaring up and out of control. It's a huge violation of sound woodland practices to leave a fire burning unattended. But given the imminent danger to our own lives, it's a risk we gotta take.

We load the last of the boiled water into our thermoses. I dump the final bit of lake water into the cooking pot, which Miggy leaves strung across the low flames. Look at this active campsite, where dinner prep is already underway!

Then the hard part. Miggy and Bob assume the position, one at each of the forward poles of the travois. Count of three, they lift the front, Neil's head coming up, his feet remaining down low, to reduce the pressure on his skull.

Scott takes point, mostly because we need to keep his feverish form in sight. Which puts me, the weakest hiker, as sweeper. I would laugh if I wasn't so terrified.

Our humble party of five. One injured but at least vertical. One completely incapacitated. Two who must now shoulder the load of carting that one around. And me.

Miggy had thought we could make it one mile. I hope he's right.

So many things I didn't know about true wilderness hiking that I now wish I still didn't know. For all the muscle-burning, heart-racing, chest-heaving pain ascending this impossibly steep section caused me, going down is worse.

Footing is lousy. Little pebbles and loose dirt breaking free beneath our feet, till we slide more than we step. Awkward for me and Scott, dangerous as hell for Bob and Miggy trying to manage the travois.

Short, sharp declines turn out to be the easiest. Bob jumps down first. Then, given his superior height, he can pull the front of the travois nearly onto his shoulders, while Scott, Miggy, and I scramble to assist with the back end. It's excruciating given our fatigued muscles, but at least it's a quick burst of pain.

Whereas the incredibly long steep sections, where we once had to scramble up hand over foot . . . Now I understand the logic behind the modifications. Bob has a rope system forming a triangle at the top of the travois. The rope extends from the tip of the triangle back to Bob, where he gets to form a human anchor point, slowly unspooling the rope through gloved hands. For the truly extended segments, he recruits a nearby tree to help him bear the weight. But either way, it is painfully slow, muscle-straining, teeth-clenching work as Neil is lowered on the travois feetfirst. Miggy and I are in charge of catching the end poles, one of us on each side trying frantically to buffer the descent. It's made even worse by my significantly smaller height, which tilts the travois dangerously to one side. After the first section, Scott takes my place. But the first real impact of the carrier's descending weight sends him to his knees.

By the time we hit the third sharply plummeting stretch of trail, I'm ready to cry from exhaustion, while Neil is moaning softly from all the bumping and banging. I doubt we've made it even a quarter of a mile. No way we can keep this up much longer.

Scott is on his knees, head hanging down, either trying to regain his breath or trying not to vomit, or both.

Miggy is standing, but clearly strained. Even Bob looks haggard, having borne the brunt of our exertions this entire way.

"Leave . . . me," Neil gasps out. "Just, stick me . . . aside."

"No," Miggy states sharply.

"When help . . . comes. They can . . . retrieve me."

"No," Scott groans.

"Need . . . more people . . . to carry. Not enough . . . people."

Now I almost do cry. Because we're not enough people. I am not enough people. I have never been enough people.

Bob speaks up. "We can do this. Just . . . need a moment."

"Fuck that." Miggy turns to Scott. "We don't need more bodies. We need better physics."

Scott straightens up, his gaze sharpening. "Rope and pulley? But we don't have pulleys."

"We do have rope." Miggy turns to Bob. "Don't suppose you have any anchor plates, D rings, or mechanical grab devices in your pack?"

"Um, I have a few D-shaped carabiners?"

Miggy contemplates. "Rope, carabiners"—he glances around—"and all the trees and boulders a person could desire. What do you say, Scott?"

Tired, strangled moan. "Nerd powers activate."

"That's the spirit. All right. New plan."

WE ALL COMB through our packs, producing every carabiner we can find. I had no idea carabiners came in so many shapes and sizes, not to mention pretty metallic colors, but no one except me seems impressed by that detail. Miggy and I take up position with the piles of gear beside Neil's semiconscious form while Scott and Bob stumble off to recon available woodland features. I unsheathe my evil blade, ready to attack rope, though my fingers are so thick and swollen it might result in the loss of a digit. Miggy doesn't want shorter segments, however, but longer.

In the end, I play go fish with nylon cords, matching them by approximate width and flex as Miggy starts tying together the similar pieces in a series of lightning-fast knots.

"Fire and knots," I mutter. "Former Boy Scout?"

"Yep."

"But you don't love camping?"

"Hey, I was there for the soapbox derby cars. Even from a young age, I had a need for speed."

I don't know car design, and I've never been good at physics. But as Miggy explains it, the intent of this particular rope-and-pulley system is to use the pulleys to create enough friction to lighten the load of the descending weight. Given we don't have actual mechanical pulleys, Miggy plans on using two to three natural formations handpicked by Scott to wind the rope through and around in a fancy figure-eight.

Rope will be forced to twist left around this tree, then right around that tree, creating the friction necessary to naturally slow the descent of the travois while easing the burden on the two bottom hikers trying to catch it.

Sounds good to me, though given all of Miggy's muttered cursing, I gather it's not quite that simple. Or maybe even possible.

Scott and Bob return with their tree choices, and after one final sigh, prayer, and expletive, Miggy declares we're ready.

Miggy and I glove up. Miggy will be the primary for slowly feeding the rope into the elaborate tree-trunk system. I get to serve as backup, in case the friction isn't enough and the rope starts uncoiling too fast. Which leaves Bob and Scott to serve as the descending hikers. If Miggy and I do our job right, Miggy explains, the weight should be low enough for Scott to handle.

Miggy threads the rope through the system, using a few carabiners to guide it around select trees, then connects the rope to the head of the travois. Then Bob and Scott each take a pole at Neil's feet and start their initial descent. Within seconds, the travois is tilted sharply upright, with Bob and Scott having to fight to keep it from plummeting down. Miggy yanks the rope hard to the left as it wraps around the tree closest to him, creating a temporary brake. Then the adventure begins.

In the beginning, I'm a big fan of the system. For one thing, I get to stand around and do nothing, which is about all I feel capable of. For another, even Miggy seems at ease as he unwinds the rope bit by bit through the first carabiner, around the first giant tree trunk.

I can hear the rope as a thin whisper against textured tree bark. Then the sound becomes a little louder. Miggy grimaces, the rope definitely unspooling faster now. He leans back, putting more weight into his makeshift braking system.

"How . . . much . . . further . . . ?" he shouts out. But there's no answer.

He gives me a single look and I spring into action. But my weight barely makes a difference.

"More . . . friction."

Standing behind Miggy, I spy a skinny fir near me and run around to the other side, adding a small cog to Miggy's tree-based pulley system. The rope slows slightly before once more starting to accelerate as the racing cord shreds the bark from the anchor trees, reducing the friction and increasing the weight of the load. Miggy grits his teeth. We both throw our weight against the pull, Miggy's muscled arms bulging, my scrawny sticks screaming. Then . . .

The rope goes slack. So much so that Miggy and I both almost topple over. We don't hear yelling or cursing. Quickly we scramble forward and peer down.

Bob and Scott are standing way beneath us. Bob is wearing a huge grin, while Scott is partially keeled over, laughing hysterically.

"That was fantastic!" Bob booms up at us. "Again!"

Miggy sways. Before I can catch him, he falls to his knees. I stumble down in alarm. But he's not collapsing, he's not crying. He's just shaking his head.

"I can't believe that actually worked," he mutters. Then his eyes rise to meet mine: "I'll be damned if Tim wouldn't be proud of us right now. Son of a bitch, he would've loved this."

CHAPTER 31

THE SKY IS DARKENING BY the time we finish our strenuous descent. We're an exhausted, messy group of misfits as we splash our way across the stream at the bottom of the hill and stumble our way into the clearing. Bundled in the travois, Neil opens glazed eyes.

"Please tell me . . . done."

"Almost," Scott soothes his friend. Scott's feverish coloring has now faded to ash white, and he's spent the past twenty minutes shivering uncontrollably. The temperature has plummeted with the sun, but Scott's shaking clearly has more to do with his internal thermostat than the outside.

"I need *out*," Neil moans.

I can't blame him. We've been banging him about like a human doll for hours. If he wasn't in pain before, he certainly should be by now. I'm not sure I've ever felt so wrung out, but then, I've been saying that for days. Apparently, physical exertion is a never-ending scale, and as fast as you think you've reached your limit, there's still more to go.

Now we all stare at the growing shadows self-consciously. Bob has the rifle slung over his shoulder, trigger at the ready. I tell myself nightfall is good. The dark offers cover. The late hour meaning we're that much closer to imminent rescue. Surely Nemeth, Luciana, and Daisy have hit the town by now. I picture them on the phone with this highly respected Sheriff Kelley. Then some cool, movie-set airfield where a chopper is even now revving to life, filled with eagle-eyed search experts who are heavily armed and bearing platters of hot food. While I'm at it, I add a steaming bubble bath to the rear cargo section, even if it does strain credibility.

In real life, we make our way to a line of pine trees, then stare at one another uncertainly.

This is the same area where we broke for snacks just two days ago. When we were younger and fresher. When Martin was still alive, and the college buddies had only their grudges to nurse and I thought my impulsive decision to join a wildland search was an adventurous lark. Now we look like earthquake survivors, and not all of us made it out of the rubble.

Bob peers up in the direction from which we came. He holds up a hand for silence, and we do our best to quiet our labored breathing. We listen for sounds of crashing tree limbs, advancing footsteps, sliding rocks. Mostly, I can hear my thundering heart. Then, as my pulse slowly calms, the sounds of night emerge around me. The whine of insects, a growing chorus of frogs, a lone owl's inquiring call.

My pulse slows more. Such a busy place, the grand outdoors. We are the interlopers with our enormous appetites and booming guns. I wish we could truly settle, spend a single evening savoring the cacophony of life all around us.

But while we don't hear any sign of our pursuer just yet, it's only a matter of time. Once he investigates the camp closer and realizes we've abandoned our post, his next logical step is to pursue us down the lone trail leading out of the canyon.

Maybe our hunter will decide he has all the time in the world to catch such wounded prey, and not rush on our account. Stop and have a hot meal first. Take a nap. Wash up in the lake. Make himself look his very best before tracking down and shooting five innocent people. More wishful thinking on my part, but it's all I've got.

Scott is shivering so hard his teeth are clacking. Miggy digs through his own pack, then produces a thin, lined jacket. Scott accepts it gratefully.

"What now?" Miggy asks Bob.

The Bigfoot hunter hesitates. "We should get out of immediate sight. Find shelter somewhere deeper in the trees."

"Where we're not sitting ducks?" Scott speaks up wryly.

"Help will come. We just need to hold on a bit longer."

Miggy nods. He has a small flashlight in his hand. "My memory is the meadow is that way. Not much cover in a meadow, so I'll head this way first, do some recon. Be back in a jiff."

He heads into the pines, turning himself sideways to slide between the trees. I hate that we're once again separating, but don't see a way around it. To keep myself occupied, I retrieve my water filtration system and use it to refill everyone's bottles from the stream. We are going through massive quantities, given our brutal exertions and parched conditions.

A few days ago, I'd never heard of the rule of threes. Now, I'm living by them. Find shelter—Miggy's task. Procure water—my job. Produce food—Josh already did that with his stash of peanut butter cups. I've never looked forward so much to candy for dinner, even if it's only a few pieces.

I return with the filled bottles just as Miggy reappears from the woods.

"Not far," he says, which is probably all we can manage with the travois.

Bob grabs one corner, Miggy the other, and we're off again.

The woods are dark. Deep dark. Like take-a-left-at-the-witch's-hut dark. The sounds captured within these thickly branched evergreens already feel more ominous. Less chirping, more slithering. Fewer hoo-hoos, more shrieking.

Poor Bob is nearly folded in half as he struggles to pull the travois through the dense forest. I grab the end of the litter, lifting it awkwardly to help get it over one rock, then a large bush, then a particularly steep rise. After a few more feet, Scott does his best to assist from the other side as we heave and curse our way forward, slipping and sliding on all the pine cones underfoot. I hope our tracker is miles away, because we must sound like a herd of elephants, trampling our way through the forest.

Miggy draws up short. We come to a crashing halt beside a slight bend in the stream. In the falling light, I can just make out a pile of moss-covered rocks, then a giant hollow formed by a toppled pine tree. Half its roots are now ripped out of the ground, standing at attention like a massive, fan-shaped wall. Between the gentle cradle in the ground and the thick backdrop for defense, it is the perfect resting spot for a group of humans looking to disappear.

Miggy has done good.

We start setting up camp in the dip of cool earth. We left our sleeping bags and tents behind, but I'd grabbed all the emergency blankets I could find, given the nighttime temps. Now I pull them all from my pack and start doling them out. The blankets are thin and crinkly, but with a silvery lining designed to reflect body heat; they're warmer than they look. Bob removes a heavy-duty black

garbage bag and spreads it on the ground to create a barrier between the damp earth and his body. We all quickly follow suit.

"Out," Neil moans from the travois. "Please!"

Miggy and Scott work on untying Neil from the travois and help
him sit up. He winces, holding his head.

"Fuck me," he states. He tries to stand. Miggy catches him just
before he falls. This time, Neil stays seated next to the travois. "Not
getting back into that . . . ever again."

None of us argue.

"We don't have any of the instant cold packs left," I offer up
finally, "but I could ice down a bandana in the stream."

"We're near a river? Freezing-cold water?"

"Pretty cold."

"Take me . . . to it."

He holds up his arms. Miggy grabs him from one side. Scott attempts the other, then gasps as it pulls at the infected wound in his
chest.

I nudge him aside and take over. One invalid at a time.

It's only ten feet to the stream, which is good, because I don't
think Neil could've made it an inch farther. Now unwrapped from
his cocoon, he's shivering hard. When we get the water's edge, he
collapses onto all fours.

"How deep?"

Miggy shines his flashlight on the water. I stick my hand in and
move it around. "Shallow," we declare at the same time.

"Awesome. I'm gonna . . . on my back. Can you . . . put head.
Just let water . . . flow over. Need cold. Very cold. Please . . . be
fucking freezing."

I get what he's doing. Using the stream itself as an ice pack to
both clean his wound and help reduce the swelling. Not a bad idea,
especially given the day's abuse of his already-concussed brain.

It takes both Miggy and me to get him in position. We all end up wet. And yet, the second the back of Neil's head makes contact with the cool stream, his sigh of relief is palpable.

Miggy and I stay on either side of him, squatting in the rocky streambed to help cradle his neck. We'll need to get out of these wet clothes the second we return to the tree hollow. Bundle up for the impending chill. But for now, witnessing Neil's badly needed respite, it's worth it.

"If the chopper doesn't make it tonight . . . tomorrow I walk. No travois . . . litter . . . death trap. Done."

Miggy and I both nod, then exchange glances above Neil's head. Rescue chopper had better make it tonight.

Finally, Neil's had enough. We help him sit up, then give him a moment to get his bearings. Miggy examines the head wound by the beam of his flashlight. I think it looks slightly better, but that could be more fanciful thinking on my part.

Neil holds out his arms; we help him to standing. At least his steps back to our little encampment are stronger than the ones he took away from it.

We lower him onto a trash bag. Miggy peels off Neil's soaking-wet T-shirt. I dig out a long-sleeve top from his pack, then add a flannel shirt and jacket over that. Miggy handles the redressing, then tends to his own clothes.

I turn my back to the men to strip off my top layers. Then realizing how much I soaked my pants in the stream, I change out of them as well. We're all much too exhausted to worry about things like modesty.

I pull on all the layers I have left in my pack, then grab one of the crinkly blankets and wrap it around my shoulders. I'm still cold. We all are.

"Fire?" Miggy asks Bob softly.

"The smell of the smoke . . ." Bob shrugs. In other words, no.

We all nod morosely, no one surprised. We're a pathetic little crew. Terrified and wrung out, but hanging in there. One by one, we peer up at the sky. Looking, listening, for a sign of our imminent rescue.

Not yet.

I recover Josh's stash of chocolate candies and start doling them out. We each get three mini peanut butter cups, though Bob tries to wave his off.

"I'm not that into chocolate."

"Everyone's into chocolate. Come on, we all need each other to remain as strong as possible. Take them."

Bob eyes the gold foil with longing, then caves with a sigh, snatching up the candies and cradling them like precious gems. I understand. I can't decide whether to eat mine or simply inhale the intoxicating scent over and over.

Just yesterday, I promised myself that if I survived this expedition, I'd never eat granola again. Now, I think if I just survive this trip, I'll never complain about granola again.

One by one, we polish off our treats. Scott produces two Power-Bars. We break them into thirds, creating six shares for five people. Scott hands the extra share to Bob. "Because you're, like, twice our size."

Bob looks tempted to argue again, but Scott's voice is firm, his logic sound.

We finish dinner, such as it is, and return to staring at the sky.

"Time?" Neil asks quietly. So far, he's managed not to vomit up dinner. More signs of progress.

"Nine thirty," Miggy supplies.

"How long, do you think . . ." Scott, glancing at Bob.

"Not sure. I've never been medevaced before. They gotta locate an available chopper, summon the volunteers, arrange some supplies. Might be closer to midnight. Or"—he hesitates—"they'll launch first thing in the morning."

"Nemeth will push them to come sooner versus later," Miggy murmurs.

We all nod. What Nemeth wants, Nemeth gets. Finally, we're grateful he's such a stubborn ass.

"Either way, we have a few more hours to kill." Bob pauses, clearly regretting his word choice. Then Neil starts chuckling and Scott starts laughing and next thing, we're all rolling on the ground like punch-drunk hyenas because he said *kill* and that's probably exactly what's going to happen next.

Bob manages to pull it together first. "Sorry."

I giggle again, slap a hand over my mouth. Hiccup.

"Guard shifts," Bob manages this time. "Watch duties."

Miggy glances around our encampment, then back at Bob. "We could set up an overwatch position. One of us in a tree, with the rifle. Better line of sight, not to mention better angle for shooting."

Bob looks around. "Um, yeah. Is now the time to say I don't do trees? Or trees don't tolerate me? Something like that."

I raise a hand. "I can climb." More advantages of a youth spent running wild.

"Can you shoot?" Miggy asks.

"No. Can you?"

"I know how to load a gun and pull the trigger."

"In other words, you can't hit bupkes."

"Is bupkes a big-ass target? Because if so, you're right."

I'm feeling stronger now. I prefer doing to waiting, participating to watching. This is something I can offer.

"You're in luck," I volunteer. "Monkeying up trees and staying awake all night happen to be two of my core strengths. I'll take overwatch, but I don't want the gun. I have my whistle. First sign of approach, I'll signal. Those of you who can handle a rifle, have at it."

"I have a handgun in my pack," Miggy says, opening it up. Well, well, the man is full of surprises. "Not so great for stopping grizzly bears, but . . . other kinds of predators."

He gives us all a look.

"Still, your gun, I'm tree duty." At the last moment I turn toward Bob. "And if I hear the chopper?"

"*When* you hear the chopper"—he corrects—"blow the whistle. I have a flare in my pack. I'll activate it to reveal our new position."

Or attract our happy hunter, I might say. But I don't want to ruin Bob's optimism.

I tuck my whistle into my jacket pocket, grab my blanket and water bottle, and head out. I still have my knife at my waist. Not sure if that's a good thing or bad, but more and more I've come to appreciate the feel of it against my hip.

I'm already vulnerable. I don't want to be completely defenseless.

Conifers don't make for great climbing. Too many thin, prickly branches, not to mention sticky pitch. In the dark, it's hard to tell my options, but I can't seem to find anything close to a sturdy oak or statuesque maple. In the end, I settle for a particularly large pine tree. I have to scramble up a rock to reach the lowest branch, but once I swing up and get going . . .

Just like riding a bike. In my mind, it's me and Sophie again, on a sunny California afternoon. I'm escaping from a father already passed out on the couch. She's escaping from an empty home where her parents arrive late and leave early for reasons neither of us know. But none of that matters as we climb until the thinned-out limbs groan ominously and yet we continue on because we're young and immortal and the sun is high and summer is good.

Up up up. Top of the world. Shrieking with laughter.

Nothing can catch us up here. Nothing can hurt us. Nothing can go wrong.

It was only on the ground that the world failed us.

I'm not sure what happened to Sophie after I headed to LA. Is she alive? Happy? Does she still remember those sunny afternoons? Miss her dog? Think of me as a childhood friend?

One of these days I should look her up. Except, of course, a woman who never stays is hardly likely to become a woman who finally returns.

Now I find a perch nestled against the sticky trunk, high enough that the skinny branches can still bear my weight, low enough that I can just make out shifting shapes in the darkness below. I'm physically tired, but mentally ramped up. Exactly perfect for night watch.

Bit by bit, my companions wrap up in their blankets, lie down like a row of little cocoons. The creatures in the woods resume their nocturnal song. A breeze wafts through the trees. The stream gurgles beneath me.

I hold my whistle. I look down and study. I glance up and wait.

As hour turns into hours.

But the chopper never arrives.

ONLY WHEN THE sun rises do I carefully clamber down, my limbs heavy, my mind overfull. Was the rescue effort delayed? Is the chopper just now taking off? Do we stay camped here, do we try to continue on? What to do what to do what to do?

My attention is so distracted I almost don't see it at first. Then, just out of the corner of my eye, a spot of red. Bright red.

Carefully I creep my way through the trees, till I have a better view of the object. I cross over, pick it up, cradle it in my hands.

My stomach plummets. My blood runs cold. I don't want it to be. It can't be. It shouldn't be.

And yet it is.

Much more slowly, I return to the others, my sad discovery clutched tight against my chest.

CHAPTER 32

EVERYONE IS SITTING AROUND THE hollow when I first approach. Miggy glances up sharply as a twig snaps beneath my foot. I wave my hand frantically before he starts pointing his firearm. It would figure that I survived all of yesterday's trials just to be shot by a paranoid companion now.

"I'm sure the SAR team will be here anytime," Bob is saying as I join the group. My water bottle is nearly empty. At least I had a moment to pee behind a bush before reappearing. Luciana was right—outdoor life is changing me.

I don't really know how to announce what I've discovered, so I simply hold out the torn red fabric.

Bob's voice fades. He blinks his eyes several times.

Scott beats him to the punch: "That's Daisy's vest."

I nod.

"The one she wears when not working. She had it on yesterday morning."

I nod again.

Scott takes it from me, fingers the fabric. "It's been ripped. Several places. Like . . ." He pauses, looks up at me. "There's some blood."

I will not cry I will not cry I will not cry. I nod again.

Now Bob takes the vest, then Neil and Miggy after him. All of us must see it for ourselves, feel it for ourselves. Process the significance, all by ourselves.

"Where did you find this?" Bob asks finally.

"Near a pine I'd climbed up, opposite side of the stream. It looks like it got snagged on a downed log."

Neil takes a deep breath, then states what the rest of us have realized but don't want to know. "They went off trail. Like us. Meaning . . . they were most likely being pursued. Like us."

Reasonable assumptions.

"When did you first start hearing activity at the camp yesterday?" Bob asks Miggy, Scott, and Neil. "When did the stolen meals start reappearing?"

Miggy shrugs. "Late morning, maybe? Elevenish?"

"This is only a mile from the campsite. Nemeth, Luciana, and Daisy took off shortly after seven. If someone was following them . . . They could've been attacked here. Killer would still have plenty of time to hike back to the canyon."

"We have Nemeth's rifle," Neil murmurs quietly.

Meaning the guide would've been unarmed. "Luciana told me she didn't do guns," I speak up now. "Still, I wouldn't want to take on the three of them. You know they'd put up a helluva fight."

"Unless he ambushed them like he did Martin," Bob says slowly. "Had already taken up position with his rifle. Shot Nemeth first, eliminating the biggest threat, then hit Luciana. After which Daisy would've taken off into the woods. Maybe she snagged the vest herself, ripped it pulling herself free."

I feel both nauseous and hopeful considering Bob's words. Ill because of what it meant for Nemeth and Luciana. Optimistic for Daisy, who might still be out there, racing through the forest.

"We should go back to the main trail," Scott says. "Look for signs of violence. We could've missed them last night in the dark."

"And walk straight into the killer's sights?" Miggy counters. "No way. Whatever happened, happened. Real question is what do we do now?"

"Hope for the best, plan for the worst," I murmur. "Meaning . . . if we assume Nemeth and Luciana didn't make it, then we also have to assume no chopper is about to magically arrive. We're on our own."

"I want to go," Bob states suddenly. "I need to see for myself what happened. I need to know."

We all stare at him, uncertain how to argue with a crazy man, let alone a crazy man twice our size.

"I'll go on my own," he continues. "Sneak back to the clearing, do some investigating, then return."

"And if you get shot?" Scott asks.

"Then you'll have your answer. Hunter is here and ready to rumble."

"Don't get shot," I inform Bob, rubbing my shoulder self-consciously. "I can, um . . . I can return to where I found Daisy's vest, see if there's anything more to discover."

"To what end?" Neil asks tiredly. "Either way . . . on our own."

Scott raises a hand. "I, uh, I need some help."

We watch wide-eyed as he slowly unpeels his top layers, then pulls off his T-shirt. I might've gasped first, but the others weren't far behind.

The wounds on his chest, the two jagged gashes superglued by Luciana two nights ago . . . They aren't just red and inflamed. I can see yellow pus now weeping out the edges, let alone more pockets of infection sitting there, right under his skin.

"Dude, how are you even sitting up?" Miggy asks him.

"Are there supposed to be two of you?"

Neil pats Scott's knee. "Course not, buddy. There's three of him."

Miggy shakes his head at his wounded friends. So we're on our own with . . . this.

"Do we still have first aid kits?" Scott asks.

Bob nods.

"Then I just need someone to disinfect a knife and play surgeon. Figure a little slicing, draining, fresh cleaning, I'll be good as new."

Now we're all horrified. But Scott is dead serious. And maybe not so irrational after all.

I slowly reach down to my waist. "I have a knife."

"Perfect, you're hired. Both of you."

"All three of her!" Neil chortles.

And I'm terribly envious that Bob's the one walking away, even if it's into a possible death trap.

"I DON'T KNOW what I'm doing." I want this clearly established up front.

"Ever have an ingrown toenail?" Scott replies. "Then you know what you're doing."

We've all moved closer to the stream, including Neil. I'm not sure I'd call his lurching gait from prickly tree to prickly tree exactly a workable stride, but he's better than yesterday. Speaking on behalf of the group, we'll take all the breaks we can get.

Miggy is carrying the larger first aid box from Bob's pack. Initially, he was taken aback by the trashed contents.

"When Martin first got shot," I murmured, and he immediately tucked the kit away from Scott's and Neil's gazes. Hearing about something terrible still isn't the same as seeing direct evidence of the tragedy. Bloody fingerprints on plastic. Packets of alcohol wipes and antibiotics ripped open and emptied out.

Fortunately, Bob's fair-sized kit still contains adequate supplies. Miggy found fresh surgical gloves in his own modest medical bag, while I have my knife and a butane lighter. I don't want to consider either item. I order myself to keep moving. Rational thought is overrated anyway.

Neil collapses at the side of the stream—intentionally, this time around. He manages to lie down on his back and slide the top of his torso into the icy-cold water. He sighs happily. The chilly bath is clearly working for his head wound. I hope it can work similar wonders for Scott.

"Okay." Miggy has appointed himself boss. His brains, my brawn. "Scott, shed the clothes. Frankie, cauterize the blade."

I obediently flick open the butane lighter and start waving the tiny flame over the straight edge of my double-sided tactical blade. The guys all had smaller, less dangerous-looking options, but even Scott agreed my knife was the one, as its slicing edge is incredibly thin, wickedly sharp.

"Has Josh brought this each year?" I ask them as Miggy starts tearing open the alcohol wipes and antibiotic ointment in preparation.

"Never seen that before," Scott answers, carefully pulling off his shirt. "But he might've had it in his pack the whole time."

"Was he an experienced hiker?"

"Kind of. He and his father went elk hunting once a year. And for a while, he got into bow hunting. Felt it was more sporting than a rifle."

"He brought down an elk with an arrow?"

"No. But he did an excellent job trekking through the woods while holding a bow and wasting lots of arrows. Does that count?"

I slowly release the lighter flame. The edge of the blade has taken on a dull patina from the smoke. Now Miggy hands me the first alcohol swab, which I use to wipe the knife. I swap him the used wipe for the blue surgical gloves.

"Why can't it be Miguel?" I whine even as I glove up.

"Miguel once passed out witnessing another guy's nose bleed on the basketball court. No way I'm trusting him with a knife."

"Miggy's going to faint?"

"Notice he's prepared everything in advance."

Miggy nods. "Normally, we'd make Josh do this. Tim would assist. I'd already be hiding behind a bush while Neil supplied the wiseass comments."

"Working on it," Neil calls out from the stream.

"That's why you turned away when you first saw Neil's head wound," I fill in the blanks.

"Note I was the first to grab one of the front poles of the travois. All the better to ignore the gore."

"Remember the swimming hole?" Scott comments now. "We'd heard about it from others. Hot summer night after Ultimate Frisbee, we decided to check it out. Tim jumped in first, and the rest of us followed."

"I'm already going to vomit," Miggy moans.

"An old rusty pipe was sticking straight out near one of the rocks. Tim smacked it with his arm swimming to the surface. Tore open this nice long gash all the way down his right triceps."

"Stop," Miggy warns.

Scott's grinning now. The good old days. A perfect distraction from the not-so-great here and now. "We drove like bats out of hell to the ER, Josh and me sitting in the back, holding a wrapped T-shirt around the wound to staunch the bleeding. Except every time we hit a bump, Tim would shout obscenities and more blood would spray out. Within minutes, Miggy is vomiting out the passenger's window and Neil, poor Neil . . ."

"'Not my car!'" Neil intones readily from the stream. "Why did I have to be the one to drive? I threatened to burn it afterwards. My first brand-new car, too. A BMW X3, black on black. Drove that off the lot feeling like The Man. Then, months later with these goons . . . Probably should've torched it."

"Josh went in with Tim while he got stitched up," Scott relates. "I called Tim's parents. And two weeks later, we hit the swimming hole again. This time with much less bodily harm."

"How old were you guys?"

"Twenty-six, twenty-seven. Old enough to know better, young enough not to care."

Scott smiles and I catch it now, the bittersweet edge on even his carefree memories. For the longest time, I couldn't think of Paul at all. I couldn't say his name or I was back there, on the sticky floor of the liquor store, and he was smiling apologetically as the blood poured from his stomach and I screamed and screamed.

In the beginning the awful memories block out everything, a total eclipse of happiness. But, bit by bit, the good times sneak through again, and the pain becomes less a feral beast and more a wise companion. I don't know if that's peace, but it is progress.

"We would've worked it out," Scott murmurs now, as if reading my mind. "We were all assholes. We'd all done stupid things. We would've fought a bit more, forgiven a lot more, then got on with it. Twelve years of friendship . . . You don't just give up on that."

"He would've married the woman who's now your wife."

"Yeah. And I would've lived with it. I was infatuated back then, captivated by the idea of Latisha. I didn't truly know her, so I couldn't really love her, not the way I do now. We became real to each other only in the past few years. We fell in love only in the past few years. I understand the difference." He's speaking more to Miggy and Neil now than to me. I let him have his speech. I let the three of them feel this joint memory, probably one of their first moments of solidarity since Tim's disappearance.

Why do I do what I do? Because at the end of the day, the people left behind matter as much as the ones who are missing. We mourn the ones we've lost, but we agonize over the pieces of ourselves they took with them. The identities we'll never have again. The emotions we're certain we'll never feel again. The sense of our own selves, becoming undone and disappearing just as completely and suddenly as those who vanished.

Now I present Scott with a bolstering smile.

"You're a very considerate man," I assure him.

"I like to think—"

I stab him in the chest.

And Miggy drops like a rock. While from the stream, Neil starts laughing.

CHAPTER 33

WE'VE LAUGHED, CRIED, AND DONE everything short of weaving friendship bracelets by the time we hear approaching footsteps. We immediately hunker down behind the enormous felled pine. Miggy has his gun out, pointing straight up. The Charlie's Angels pose strikes me as hysterically funny, and I have to duck even lower, my shoulders shaking with suppressed laughter.

Maybe it's low blood sugar or sleep deprivation or sheer terror, but we've all gone a little batty.

Bob appears in the middle of the encampment, holding a pack. One by one, we pop up like a row of prairie dogs. He looks at us, blue eyes widening.

"What happened to you?" he asks Miggy.

"Rock."

"He fell," I provide.

"He passed out cold," Neil clarifies.

Scott giggles slightly.

Bob's eyes widen further. He holds up the pack. I recognize it immediately. "That's Luciana's!"

Bob nods, taking a seat as we all scramble forward. "I didn't find any bodies," he states bluntly. "Or blood. But I found an area of disturbance and this."

He digs around in his pocket, emerging with a thin piece of looped cord.

"A snare," Miggy provides.

I've heard of them for hunting rabbits. While I don't like to think about it, I imagine the same principles apply for targeting human prey. "You think they were ambushed?" I ask.

"Luciana made it one mile from camp, then set down her pack and simply walked away?" Bob shrugs.

I want to say that's absolutely plausible, but of course I can't. The truth is just so hard to take.

"Do you think . . . they're still alive?" Neil asks.

"I didn't find bodies," Bob repeats. "Then again, given the chamber we stumbled upon yesterday . . . I'm not sure this person likes to leave his kills behind."

I shiver now, rubbing my bare arms. Kills. Is that all we will be in the end? We enter life with such grand illusions, then exit as notches in some serial killer's hunting belt?

"No blood?" I quiz.

"No. But if he used some kind of trap, such as a snare . . . maybe he didn't have to shoot first."

"Maybe he tied them up and left them tucked away someplace," Neil brings up hopefully. "While Daisy ran off."

Bob doesn't say anything. Neil pretty much abandons his theory the moment it's spoken out loud. The odds of a man who'd already killed eight people and laid out their bodies in an underground chamber simply tying up two more victims and walking away . . .

"How are you?" Bob asks Scott.

In reply, Scott raises the edge of his T-shirt to reveal a fresh white bandage. "Don't let her fool you"—he points at me—"the lady loves her knife."

"He made me do it."

"She sliced open my chest," Scott provides. "Didn't warn, didn't count down, just did it."

"Is there a good way to slash someone across the chest?" I pose.

"Pus." Miggy is already making a face. "I don't want to remember, you don't want to know. Lots of pus."

"Very cool," Neil chimes in. "Afterwards, Scott joined me in the stream. Dropped chest first. Let the icy water work its magic." Neil sighs happily, a clear testament to the power of glacier runoff.

"I had no idea what I was doing," I admit with a shrug. "Sliced him open, let the water rinse him out. Then wiped him down with the alcohol—"

"There was some screaming," Miggy interjects.

"I did not—"

"Total screaming, like a little kid who lost his ice cream cone," Neil and I back up Miggy's assessment.

Scott glowers at all of us.

"Then we gooed him up with the ointment, slapped on a bandage, and hey, he almost looks like a real person," I finish up.

"Lucky me," Scott grumbles.

Bob reaches out and lays the back of his hand against Scott's forehead, then his cheeks. "You feel better."

"Power of ibuprofen."

"And you?" Bob turns to Neil.

"Down with the death sled! The two-legged walk again."

Bob leans back slightly.

"Yeah," I agree. "We've been like this all morning. It's possible we're officially cracked."

"Can you walk?" Bob asks Neil quietly.

"Ab-so-lute-ly!" Neil stands boldly. Promptly sways and grabs at the top edge of the root ball, then sits down hard. "I got this."

Bob doesn't laugh or speak or sigh heavily. Which finally cuts through my illogical giddiness and brings me crashing back down to earth.

"No travois!" Neil blurts out. "Fuck the travois! I'll stay here. Hold the line, make my own fucking snare. But no travois! Can't make me."

Now Bob regards me seriously. I get it. I just don't want to understand.

"We're not safe," I state quietly.

"We watched Martin get shot to death. Nemeth and Luciana have clearly been ambushed on their way to get help. The chances of them still being alive . . . We stumbled upon something horrible. But also, something that's been going on a very long time if your assessment of the bodies is correct."

I nod quietly.

"Whoever's been doing this, he has to know using this canyon as his hunting grounds is over. Chasing us away with a series of accidents might've protected him and his lair. But the moment he fired that first shot at Martin . . . A party of eight disappearing in these woods? Sooner versus later, this area will be swarming with SAR volunteers, forest rangers, county deputies. Even if our hunter isn't caught, he won't be able to resume his game anytime soon."

"Making this his last hurrah," I murmur.

"Then why hasn't he attacked yet?" Miggy brings up, his own voice somber.

Bob shrugs. "He's had a busy twenty-four hours. Maybe he

decided to take a short rest before the final blitz. He knows we have an injured party in a litter and are moving slowly. Though by now . . ."

Bob glances at his watch. It's probably already ten in the morning. Once, I'd barely considered that hour worthy of rise and shine. But in the world of outdoor living, half the morning has already passed. If our hunter has been recuperating, he should be good and ready to strike.

"How far are we from bottom?" I murmur.

"Too far." Bob glances at Neil, who's now studying the damp earth.

Miggy speaks up. "We could abandon the trail. Pick a less obvious path."

"Any hunter knows how to track. Do we look like five people who can cover signs of our passage?"

We get his point.

"Then we hit the main trail," Scott proposes. "Make a run for it. There are five of us. He can't take us all."

"I can bring up the rear," Neil says, and the fact that he offers it without hesitation, even knowing the likely outcome, makes me blink hard.

"No," Miggy snaps impatiently. "I'm not doing this again. Fuck these woods! I've lost enough. No way, no how, am I going to turn this into some kind of horror movie where if we're really lucky, one of us plucky souls finally staggers into town to tell the story of the others' demise. No. No, no, no. No."

Scott waits a beat. "I believe Miggy is saying no."

Miggy throws a clump of moss at him. "Fuck no," he amends.

Neil smiles. "That's the Miguel we all know and love."

"If we choose not to make a run for it," Bob ponders much more sensibly, "then what?"

"We have a rifle," Miggy says. "And a handgun."

"Bear spray," Scott adds.

"Scary dual-edged blade," I offer.

"Five of us, one of him," Neil concludes. "Or in my world, fifteen of us, three of him. Either way . . ."

Bob regards us solemnly. "You're voting to take a stand."

"Do you seriously think we could run for it?" Miggy counters. "Martin, Nemeth, Luciana, and Daisy—face it, they were the professionals. If they couldn't make it . . ."

Bob nods slowly. "Just for consideration . . . we're down to our last few snack bars. Our gear is limited. Our shelter, if we're ambushed in the middle of the night . . ."

I look behind us at the giant wall of earth, which in a matter of minutes could turn into the backdrop of the St. Valentine's Day Massacre.

"Maybe we can't hold out forever." Miggy shrugs. "But maybe one of us gets lucky and takes him out first."

An experienced hunter on his home turf. Bob doesn't have to express his doubt for us to know it.

Slowly, I raise my hand. "If we don't have the strength to outrun or the supplies to outlast . . . what about the brain power to outsmart?"

"How?" Bob asks.

I shrug. Eye the three engineers. "We build a trap."

CHAPTER 34

I HAVE FIFTEEN MINUTES TO feel good about my grand idea, before our scheming devolves into bad *Scooby-Doo* story lines. We'll bury a giant net that will scoop up the evildoer when he goes racing by. Except we don't have a net, let alone Shaggy and Scooby to lead a trained outdoorsman racing over a trip line.

We'll dig a pit, cover it with leaves. With what shovels? Let alone the half a day it would take to dig anything sizeable enough. Guy might as well pick us off one by one while we labor. We'd be grateful to be put out of our misery.

Fine, our own snare to grab him by the ankle. Possible, Miggy allows, assuming we get him to step exactly where we want when we want. The main trail was perfect for ambushing Nemeth and Luciana as it limited them to a specific path. We're now in the middle of the woods, exposed on all sides, with a guy who's probably going to put some thought into his approach.

"One of us can sit before the campfire to lure him in that direction," I attempt.

"Great, till he stops a hundred feet away and takes aim with his rifle," Scott counters.

"Then I'll shoot him with my gun," Miggy finishes.

"Except one of us is dead, and, oh yes, you can't shoot," I retort.

"I'll play the bait," Neil volunteers.

"Shut up," we inform him crossly, moving on.

"We need eyes." Bob brings us back to practical matters. "A sniper's perch of our own. Some hope of seeing him before he sees us."

"I can climb," I offer. "But visibility is limited. This whole area is too thick with pine, spruce, and other prickly trees. None of them make for great scaling, and higher elevation just gives you a view of more needles."

"If I were him," Miggy murmurs, "I'd have a ghillie suit. Experienced hunter? Probably made his own, covered in local brush and leaves. Something like that, he could belly crawl right into our encampment, pick us off one by one."

"This isn't helping," Scott says.

"Unless we make our own." Miggy purses his lips, clearly thinking. "Forget a pit. Too much time and labor. But a series of shallow depressions, say, in a starfish pattern around this area." He gestures to the tree hollow. "We each hunker down individually, covered in debris." He looks up at us. "When he appears, we spring. Each of us armed. Attack as one."

"We're the teeth of the trap," Bob states.

"What if he waits all day?" Scott argues. "Makes his move at night?"

"He could have night goggles." Neil speaks up. "Everyone likes a pair of kickass night goggles."

"Yes," Miggy exclaims in exasperation. "He probably has night goggles. And for that matter, hydration built into his suit, space diapers to absorb urine output, and high-protein gel pouches to keep him fueled and awake. He *is* fucking better prepared. Now, enough about him. What are we going to do?"

"Daisy's red vest." I hold it up. "He doesn't know about it yet. He wouldn't have left it there."

Everyone stares at me.

"We take Miggy's idea, but move it. This campsite as ground zero is too passive—you're right, he could hunker down and watch for hours, content we'll eventually return. We need something that draws him out, forces him to move where we want him to move. Something unexpected." I glance at Bob. "Even if he got Nemeth and Luciana, there's a chance Daisy got away. Meaning, she's a loose end for him. Spotting this remnant . . ."

"He'll want to go check it out," Bob fills in.

"He won't be expecting five bodies scattered around its location. He won't even be looking for us. A scrap of red in the woods. No reason for him not to walk forward and grab it. I did."

Miggy starts to nod slowly, then Scott. Finally, Neil and Bob.

"As plans go, it's riddled with holes, uncontrollable variables, and way too many assumptions." Miggy looks around. "On the other hand, anyone got a better idea?"

We all remain silent.

"All right. Clock's ticking. Let's make this happen."

MY HEART IS pounding by the time I lead them to where I first found Daisy's vest. With each step, I wonder if the air behind me will crack with rifle fire and the ground explode at my feet. We've already wasted most of the morning between intelligence gathering, first aid, and strategic planning.

Our tracker is way ahead of us. He knows roughly where we are, how many we are, and how completely unprepared we are. At any moment . . .

Once again, Bob brings up the rear, this time to try to cover our tracks. Not his best skill, he confessed, but he's still the most qualified.

We left some gear loaded into the travois, as if we were planning to return to the tree hollow. We wanted our hunter to feel calm, like he had plenty of time to catch his inexperienced prey. Play to his ego.

Psychological warfare is as important a strategy as any.

When we arrive at the fallen log where I first spotted the red vest, I gingerly return it to its snagged position on a broken branch. The log is half rotten, pieces of bark having fallen away to reveal the smooth, ivory-colored flesh beneath. I trace the exposed wood with my fingers. It feels like bare bones. What we all become in the end.

Miggy walks a circle around the area. There's only a small patch of open ground before we encounter more trees, a clump of bushes, et cetera. It takes me only a second to realize we're not digging five depressions in this ground anytime soon. There's no way we'd be able to hack our way through all the tree roots, let alone the level of disturbance that would make.

"Plan B," Miggy states, looking at Scott. "We use the terrain."

Scott points up, wincing only slightly, as he gestures at a V formed by two branches at the trunk of a rough-looking fir. "One perch."

"The bushes," Neil offers. He's leaning against the fallen log, clearly having to recover from the walk over. He's still doing better than yesterday. "Dig out a little beneath them, that'll be perfect."

"Not for a person my size," Bob warns.

Which brings up a good point. How do you hide a glow-in-the-dark Paul Bunyan? These trees aren't particularly large or old.

Growing this densely, they are a collection of thin to medium-sized trunks. Nothing suitable for Bob.

"I'll find a place between here and the camp," Bob says at last. "Closer to the stream, I saw some more open spots. I can signal when he's coming. Close in from behind."

"How are you going to signal?" I ask. "We don't have walkie-talkies and the emergency whistle will give you away."

In response, Bob trills. Then makes four or five other birdcalls that have us all rocking back on our heels.

"My husband says it's what made him first fall in love with me," he says sheepishly. "I also play a mean ukulele."

"Um, okay," Neil offers. "So which of those would sound most natural in these woods?"

Bob repeats an option that sounds pretty close to the birds I've been hearing in the morning. Not knowing my species, I've been referring to them mentally as the happy birds. Versus crows and ravens, which are never happy. And seagulls and pigeons, which are just plain annoying.

Happy birds it is.

"We need more cover," Miggy says, still looking around. "Tree branches, boughs of needles we can use to further obscure our hide-outs. We'll need to keep it loose and natural-looking—no neat rows of twigs, maybe living branches, downed logs."

I unsheathe my knife. "I can hack off some lower pine boughs."

"Perfect, but not around here. The fresh cut marks will be a dead giveaway."

I didn't even think of that.

Scott sets down his pack. "I can go to work on these bushes, dig out beneath them."

"I'll help Frankie with the branches." Neil stands, bobbling slightly. "You cut, I gather."

I think that's a mighty generous offer, given he appears ready to fall over.

"I'll backtrack," Bob announces. "Select a size-appropriate lookout option for me."

That lightens the mood, makes us all smile. Just in time for Neil's stomach to grumble. Then Scott's, as if in sympathy.

We all hesitate, gaze longingly at our packs. We're down to nearly crumbs. Going through Luciana's bag produced two more protein bars, which felt ghoulish, but she would have been the first to hand them over.

"No," Bob states firmly. "We don't know how long this will take. Assuming we win this fight, we still have to get down this mountain."

I really wish he hadn't said that. Such a demoralizing thought.

"Let's get through this. When we know we're making the final trek home, then we'll snack. Celebratory protein bars for all."

That sounds more promising.

We nod in agreement, then get to our tasks.

NEIL AND I need to hack down tree limbs away from the initial area. But which way? Strike out to the left? The right? What if our guy is already in either of those places and we walk straight into him?

We suffer a solid minute of analysis paralysis, then Neil simply takes a step forward and I follow him. What can possibly go wrong by putting the guy with a concussion in charge?

We come to a thick clump of spruce, their prickly limbs all snarled together. I curl my nose.

"Ouch. My kingdom for a nice, sturdy oak."

"I see a bunch of lodgepole pines over there. Softer needles, stickier sap. But in this area, hardwood trees are few and far between."

Evergreens it is. I decide to start with the spruce, crawling beneath the ring of low-hanging branches on my hands and knees. I unsheathe my blade, give it a hard stare.

"You be good to me, I'll be good to you." I think it gets the message.

The first branch snaps off easily, turning out to be half dead. But that also means the moment Neil tugs it out, half the needles shed onto the forest floor. I pay more attention after that, trying to stick to branches around an inch in diameter, and moving around so there aren't a bunch of fresh nicks all in one place.

I saw, heave, saw some more. Neil tugs, sits down to rest, tugs some more.

We're both a sweaty mess in a matter of minutes, my arms stinging from a thousand needle jabs. I think wrestling a porcupine might be easier. I have to take a break to put on my gloves, wishing I'd done so sooner, as my palms are already red with fresh-forming blisters, while my fingers have become sticky with sap.

I give up on the spruce sooner versus later. Just too difficult. We cross to a more open area where there is a spread of picturesque soft-needled pine trees adorned with pine cones.

I hope they are friendlier than the spruce as I hunker down and crawl forward. My hands hurt, my arms are tired. The knife and I are no longer such great friends as I resume sawing through a sticky mess of branches. I learn the hard way that placing a knee on a fallen pine cone really smarts.

I finally sit back on my haunches, breathing heavily.

I find myself gazing fretfully all around us. Is the hunter close? Watching, laughing? Or preparing his ambush of someone else? Maybe stalking Daisy herself?

I can't have that thought; I start feeling ill.

"Tell me about yourself," I say abruptly, returning to a particularly stubborn limb lined with forked tongues of green needles.

"Me? Like what?"

"Do you miss Latisha? And how exactly does one woman en-snare an entire group of guys, anyway? Is she like some millennial version of Helen of Troy?"

"Was Helen of Troy a six-foot-tall Black goddess with an intoxi-cating laugh, a great sense of adventure, and a wiseass wit?"

"I never read the book."

"I have a girlfriend," Neil says abruptly.

This is more interesting. None of the guys have talked about other girlfriends or wives.

"Her name is Anna Hajlasz. I'd just started dating her before . . . I was going to bring her to the wedding as my plus one."

"You haven't brought her up before."

"I, um, I haven't told the others about her."

I stop sawing long enough to glance at Neil. "Hang on a sec. You've been dating this Anna for over five years, and you haven't even *mentioned* her to your friends?"

"It's a sore subject between her and me," Neil admits.

"You think?"

"My family has all met her. And my other friends, coworkers. It's not that I keep her hidden away. I just . . . I don't talk about her with Scott, Miguel, and Josh."

"Because of Latisha?" I'm honestly confused.

"No. I don't even think of Latisha anymore. Yeah, I had a crush on her. But seriously, three dates? I understood what Scott was say-ing. There's a difference between infatuation and love. Once, I was infatuated with Latisha. Five years later, I'm in love with Anna."

"So why don't you tell them?"

"I don't know."

"Sure you do."

Neil is quiet. I return to sawing, calling over my shoulder. "You know, we're probably gonna die soon. Might as well get it off your chest."

"I don't want to share her," he blurts out.

"You're afraid one of them might steal her? Like Tim did with Latisha and then Scott did with Latisha?"

"Not that. I don't want to *share*. I want her to be just mine, to belong to only me. Afterwards . . . The five of us, we basically spent a decade all mixed up with one another. College pranks, first loves, job opportunities. There's nothing that doesn't lead back to all of us and who said what and who did what. After Tim. Losing him. Losing us. I wanted something that was just mine."

"Not property of Dudeville?"

"Not part of the fucked-up twenty-something I'd been. The kid who failed his best friend."

"Awfully hard on yourself."

"Don't worry, I think Scott, Miggy, and Josh suck, too." But there's no heat in his voice.

"After this, do you think you might introduce her to them?"

"She wants to get married."

"And you?"

"Actually, I can't think of anything I'd like more. She's the one. I knew it almost as soon as I met her."

"But you haven't proposed?"

"I couldn't. I can't imagine getting married because I can't imagine . . ." There's a hitch in Neil's voice. "I can't imagine standing at an altar and not having Tim there. I can't stomach attending the wedding he never got. It's the real reason Miggy, Josh, and I didn't go to Scott's wedding. Jesus, just the sight of a tux. One of the last things we did was the final fitting. Five us, laughing so damn hard and sticking each other with those pins . . ." Neil's voice trails off. "I always thought PTSD was triggered by big things like the clap of thunder. But for me, it's the sight of grown men dressed like penguins."

"I'm sorry," I tell him honestly, finally twisting off a lower branch.

"Yeah, well, now I feel like the world's biggest idiot," Neil is saying. "Anna's been waiting five years for me to come to my senses. I sure as hell had better get off this mountain so I can make things right."

"Then why do you keep volunteering for suicide duty?"

Neil shrugs. "Because in case you haven't noticed, we've entered survival-of-the-fittest territory. And I'm already wounded prey. I've watched enough wildlife documentaries to know what happens next. Given that . . . if I'm going down, I want my death to matter, to be on my terms, not some asshole's."

"That's the spirit." I wiggle the next branch farther away from the trunk. Neil drags it the rest of the way out. One more, I think. It's about all I have left in me. Then we'll head back.

I have an itch between my shoulder blades, but I can't decide if that's survival instinct or basic paranoia.

"What about Miguel?" I ask, selecting the next branch.

"Have to ask him. Was in a long-term relationship that ended last year, but I've never heard him talk marriage. Not sure it's on his radar."

"And Josh?"

"Josh doesn't discuss his personal life. Never did before. Certainly isn't now."

There's an edge to Neil's voice that makes me look at him again. "But?" I prod.

Neil stacks up the cut boughs. "If I had to guess? Josh is gay. And Tim was most likely his first crush. Back in college, the way I'd sometimes catch Josh looking at Tim. Nothing ever happened, and

Josh has never said, one way or another. Though I can tell you there's nothing we would've cared less about. But I think that's the other reason Josh was so caught off guard by Tim's night of true confessions. Not just that Tim had gone behind his back and slept with his sister. But that Tim had chosen his sister and not . . . well, Josh."

"Whoa. You think that's also why Josh started drinking so hard?"

"Don't know. Josh worked, played, and studied with us. But he never talked to us. Just wasn't his style. He was closest to Tim anyway."

"Do you hear anything?" I ask abruptly, crawling back out from under the pine tree. I straighten slowly, swiping at my brow.

"No. What?"

"Shhh . . ." I drop my voice to a whisper. "Listen. What do you hear?"

"Nothing," Neil murmurs back.

"Exactly. And when in the woods, do you hear total silence?"

Neil's eyes widen in understanding.

A preternatural hush has fallen all around us. As if every life-form has hunkered down and buttoned up. Keeping out of sight of big bad heading their way.

We don't have to see him to know.

The hunter has arrived.

CHAPTER 35

NEIL AND I REMAIN FROZEN in place beside the pines. The clump of spruce, with their wide-spreading, low-hanging branches, had been an excellent place for concealment. Here, however, we are more exposed as we hold our breaths, listen to our thundering heartbeats.

I do my best to scan the forest around me, looking for signs of human presence. Maybe the shape of a head or the whites of someone's eyes or the reflective glint off a rifle scope. I come up with nothing, but then, I'm not sure where to look. Down low, up high? I can't get a bead on the danger, just the overwhelming sense that it is very close.

Neil tugs on my hand. His already wan features have gone a shade paler. He points to the spruce trees. I nod my understanding.

He takes the first tentative step. No crack of gunfire. A second step, then a third. I follow shakily behind him.

He's still dragging the cut branches. I grab two of them as well, though I'm not sure why.

We hit the thick-needled spruce, duck beneath. Now I'm grateful for the sticky pitch and prickly needles. Evergreens are my new best friends.

We wait again. I count off the seconds in my head, if only to give myself something to do. We still don't hear anything.

Then, from the distance: a trill, like from a happy bird.

Neil and I exchange desperate glances. It's too early. We haven't finished constructing our hideouts. Neil and I aren't even in the right position. Let alone Scott and Miguel . . .

This is not the plan!

Neil rallies first. He reaches behind himself to twist his unbuckled pack sideways. He draws out a can of bear spray, stares at me resolutely.

I can't help but think of his words. He's already the wounded prey. Might as well go out on his terms.

As I watch, he takes a few of our cut branches and twists their ends into the straps on his pack. I don't completely understand it. His own homemade ghillie suit? But then I notice how it obscures his form, changes his silhouette, making it harder to target the human buried beneath. Works for me. I quickly follow suit.

I have my knife but take out my can of pepper spray as well.

NEIL CRAWLS OUT from beneath the trees. The noise of pine cones crunching and branches dragging sounds incredibly loud in the hushed stillness. We both wince but keep on moving.

The happy-bird trill again. Bob, letting us know the hunter approaches.

We should be running away, I think wildly, not creeping toward. We should be disintegrating into every man for himself.

But our group that was not a group has turned solid as a rock.

Death approaches.

Neil and I head out to meet it.

WE PAUSE IN sight of Daisy's snagged red vest. I don't see any sign of Scott or Miguel. Were they able to take cover behind the bushes? Nothing moves. I don't hear so much as the rustle of a leaf.

Once more I scan the horizon. Once more I come up with nothing. Sweat trickles down my brow, stings my eyes. I can hear insects now, droning in my ear. Look. Listen. Breathe.

Then the snap of a dead twig.

Straight ahead, the clump of bushes trembles in response. Scott or Miguel—has to be. But still, my gaze can't pick out another person moving through the trees around us.

Neil is squeezing my arm very hard. Comfort for himself? Comfort for me? It doesn't matter. I read once that soldiers hold the line for the sake of the buddy beside them. I get it now. I can fail myself, *have* failed myself. But I don't want to leave Neil to face whatever's out there alone.

The bitey bugs tangle in my hair, dive-bomb my ears. I'm incredibly thirsty, and simultaneously I really need to pee. The woods are too still, my pulse too fast. I taste salt and bug repellent and pine sap.

Then—

A huge form bursts from the trees. With an animal-like roar, it charges straight toward Neil and myself.

I register so many things at once.

The whites of Bob's eyes as he barrels at us, red canister raised.

A high-pitched battle cry as the bushes behind him explode and Scott and Miguel come stumbling out.

While a form appears just eight feet from where Neil and I are standing. A single tree splitting into two—and the second tree raising a rifle.

It makes no sense, and yet is exactly as Bob predicted.

He hits the spray nozzle on the bear repellent just as the rifle cracks.

Bob goes down like an oak. There's no time to react before a second crack brings a second scream. Scott, Miguel—I don't know which.

Neil and I throw ourselves forward. I trip over one of my dangling pine boughs and careen wildly just as more gunfire explodes. I want to lash out with my knife, viscerally attack this evil tree figure who hurt Bob, attacked precious, oversized, lovable Bob, but mostly I'm pinwheeling my arms while trying to find my footing. In the next instant, I hit a wall of pepper spray, the burst from Bob's canister. Immediately, my eyes well up and my nose streams. I drop my own can and claw at my throat.

It burns, it burns, it burns.

Through my swollen eyes I watch the tree figure move again. Neil has thrown himself onto the hunter's back. I need to raise my knife. I need to help.

Except then Neil is on the ground. And the tree man is raising his rifle.

Gunshot. Single crack. Not from the tree man, but from somewhere behind him. The hunter recoils. Turns back around.

A frozen moment of time. Through my tearing eyes, I can see Miguel square off in front of the hunter. There's a look on his face I've never seen before. Wild. Fierce.

The hunter has his rifle.

Miguel a puny handgun.

I'm raising my knife. Must attack—now—while he's distracted. Go for the hamstrings, Achilles, anything.

Then he's gone. Just like that. The hunter fades back into the forest as if he never was.

Birds resume chirping. Gun smoke and pepper spray clear from the air.

Miggy stands in front of me, still clutching his handgun, his brown skin nearly bone white.

Then the moaning begins. And I am almost undone by the carnage around us.

I WANT TO squeeze my red-rimmed eyes shut. I don't want to look. I don't want to know. If Neil is triggered by men in tuxes, then gunshot wounds are my kryptonite. They take me spiraling back to memories I don't want to have, final moments I still can't bear to witness.

"Frankie," Miggy states urgently.

I shake my head. I can't. I can't see more, I can't lose more. I'm a collection of jagged scars, my own, other people's. My skin has already been flayed away inch by inch. I don't have enough left to cover this.

"Frankie," Miguel snaps again.

But it's the moaning that does it. Forces me to focus, to stand up, dump a bottle of water over my still-streaming eyes and nose. I'm covered in tears and snot. It feels appropriate.

I spy Bob first, mostly because he's the largest of the fallen forms, and the red blood stands out brightly against his pale khaki shirt. He's the one moaning. Neil, closer to me, is crumpled facedown. He makes no sound at all.

"I have Scott. You get Bob," Miggy orders. He's not swaying on his feet, or collapsing at the sight of so much blood. He's moved to someplace beyond himself, where his normal squeamish sensibilities no longer apply.

I follow his example. This is not me, ripping the last of the stupid branches from my pack so I can walk without tripping toward Bob's collapsed body. This is not me, leaning beside my oversized friend's prone form. This is not me, peering into Bob's face as he opens his blue eyes and smiles at me.

"Oops," he whispers.

"Don't talk," I whisper.

"Tell Rob . . . I love him." I shake my head. I'm not me. I don't have to scream and wail and cry. I am someone else, the kind of person who can fix this.

I rip open Bob's shirt. Survey the damage to his red-furred torso. Blood gurgles from a hole in his left side.

"Pays to be a big guy," Bob gasps out. "He was aiming . . . for the heart."

"Joke's on him," I agree, trying to think. We've just done this. Martin. Bob took the lead, but I remember the steps. First aid kit, alcohol wipes, maxi pads. Okay, I got this. I set down my pack and start tearing it apart.

I had a first aid kit. Where the hell is the first aid kit? And tampons? Dammit, we used them on Martin. I need more feminine hygiene products. I got a really giant man here and he demands more feminine hygiene products. Hysteria bubbles up. I squash it back down. I'm not me. I don't need to feel hysterical. I'm the kind of person who can fix things.

Bob's fingers curl around my wrist.

"Stop."

"I just have to get more supplies," I babble. "Neil's pack. He'll have tampons."

"You . . . need to run."

"It'll be okay. I remember what you did with Martin."

"Martin's dead."

"We don't know—"

"I can feel the blood . . . in my lungs. Nothing . . . you can do. The others?"

"Miggy's okay." I think. "Scott, Neil . . ." I don't know, but I can't admit to that level of helplessness. Hopelessness.

"You. Miguel. Go. He'll . . . be back."

"Miggy wounded him."

"He'll . . . be back."

"No. Goddammit!" And now I've had enough. Of blood and bullet wounds and men dying on me. Bob is going to live because I will it to be so.

Bob is going to live, because three times later, the fucking universe owes me one.

"How's it going?" Miggy calls out.

"Alive. Side wound. Need more supplies." I go crawling over to Neil. Feel his neck. "Has a pulse," I announce, "but out cold."

With that, I rip the pack off Neil's back. Supplies are supplies. We're all scavengers now. "Scott?" I ask.

"Shoulder wound." I hear the sound of tearing, Miggy performing his own first aid duties.

"Go," Bob tells me again when I reappear.

"Shut up."

"Terrible . . . bedside . . . manner."

"Rob needs you. Bigfoot needs you. I'm going to patch you up. You're going to live."

"Tell Rob I love him."

"*Shut up!*" I'm beyond furious. I'm livid. I'm enraged. I ransack Neil's pack, discovering a small first aid kit and yes, two tampons and two maxi pads, which I will never look at the same way again.

"Now, you listen to me, big man. This is gonna hurt like a mother. I don't have time to be gentle."

Bob stares at me through glassy blue eyes. "Find it."

"Find what?"

"Whatever it is . . . you're really searching for."

"Shut up! Look at Miggy. Right now. Look."

Bob turns his head. I jam in the first cotton plug. His entire body bows. But he doesn't scream. Doesn't so much as whimper. He doesn't want to call attention, I realize. He's afraid of summoning the hunter back.

Now I am sobbing. I can't help myself as I tear open more packets, and I curse him and clutch at him and just plain beg him to live as I pile gauze on his wound and tape it savagely in place.

Only then do I remember the exit wound.

Finally, I get it. Except I don't want to get it. What Bob had been telling me.

I stop studying the pale hairy torso in front of me; I inspect the ground beneath.

The earth has turned black with blood. Pints of it. Gallons of it. Too much of it.

"Please," I try. To Bob. To the universe.

"Tell Rob . . . I love him."

And then. Then . . .

EVENTUALLY, MIGGY IS there. Miggy tugs at me. Miggy slaps my face.

"Frankie," he says. "Let him go."

Then: "Frankie, Scott and Neil still need us."

Then: "Frankie, *get the fuck up and move.* Time to run."

So I do.

CHAPTER 36

WE'RE SPRINTING. NO, WE'RE SLIPPING and sliding, slamming into pine boughs and scraping off our skin on tree bark and smashing our shins against rocks. But we don't stop. We crash and careen, swallowing our screams and ignoring our pain as we race on.

I trip. Stumble down several feet, whack my shoulder against a boulder. I might be sobbing in terror. There's so much snot and sweat on my face it's impossible to tell.

I can't think. I can't process. I can only move, so I stagger up, stumble on, Miggy right in front of me.

We're not on any trail. Just somewhere in the middle of the woods. We turn in any direction that leads down, the steeper the better. We're probably lost. We're probably about to be shot in the back. We can't worry about such things.

The hunter won. Our brilliant plan failed. And now we're the deer, fleeing before the predator's advance.

I have my pack. Miggy has his. But we have so few supplies left it hardly matters. Help, Miggy said. We must get help for Scott and Neil.

But not Bob. No longer for Bob.

I take a tree branch to the face. My eyes well again, needles adhering to my cheeks, lodging in my mouth.

"Sorry," Miggy gasps. He's faster than me, taking the crazy-steep sections with a rapid-fire sidestep I try to emulate but can't.

We hit a narrow gurgling stream. I fall to my hands and knees. I think of Neil, his head resting in the water as he laughed with his friends. I remember Scott, instructing me to slice open his own chest with a good-natured smile.

I don't want to get up again.

"Frankie," Miggy gasps.

"A tree killed them. A tree killed our friends."

Miggy splashes back to me. He scoops up a handful of water and uses it to scrub the needles and mucus from my face. His dark eyes are so large, so intent, as he peers into mine.

"I saw him," he says.

"The tree man?"

"Full army camo. Short branches stuck into his hat. Textured shooting gloves. He had a black bandana over the lower part of his face and some kind of high-tech goggles over his eyes. That's why the bear spray didn't help. He was prepared, Frankie. Outfitted, geared up for anything and everything."

"We've been outclassed since the very beginning."

Miggy nods. "In my worst nightmares, I never imagined something like this. This guy, he's hard-core. He's ready."

"At least you shot him."

"I winged him. At best."

"Scott and Neil?" I can barely say their names.

"I hid them. Tucked them away behind the bushes. Neil's head took a second hit. He regained consciousness long enough to vomit. He and Scott. They can't make it out of these woods, Frankie."

"We're not going to make it out of these woods."

Miggy doesn't deny it.

"This is how Tim died," Miguel states at last. "All these years, I've wondered. Now I know."

He pulls me to standing. I let him. We're both soaked. And yet I can still feel the blood caked beneath my nails, embedded in the palms of my hands.

"I have five bullets left," he says.

I understand. "It's a race now. Can we make it out of these woods before he finds us again." I start smiling then, I just can't help myself.

"What's so funny?"

"You and me. We're the weakest links. Remember? First day hiking up. Of everyone, we're the ones who struggled the most. And now, of everyone, we're the only two left."

"Ironic, I know."

He doesn't get it yet. I smile again, and now I scoop up a handful of water to rub the dirt and blood from *his* face. My fingers are gentle. I feather them across his brow, the planes of his cheeks, the underside of his jaw. It will not make my next words any easier to take.

"Strategy for taking down a group," I murmur softly. "You start by eliminating the strongest members first. Nemeth. Luciana. Martin. Bob. We are the weakest links. And for our reward, he is saving us for last."

Miggy places his hands over mine. He replies, very somberly, "I wanted to go golfing that weekend. I would've been happy to just fucking whack a little white ball around eighteen holes."

He offers me his own twisted grin.

Then we start running again.

WE PINWHEEL MADLY down steep slopes for what feels like forever. I expect at any moment to feel a bullet in my back. Sliding down rough terrain, we are leaving a trail even an amateur could follow. We're crashing through bushes, breaking small branches, crushing waves of grasses, churning up the earth.

I'm shivering despite our efforts. Going down kills my legs and knees. But it's not as cardio intensive as hiking up, meaning we're not generating enough heat to counter our wet clothes. And now the sky is clouding up, the sun disappearing.

The ritual afternoon rain shower is due to happen at any time. Which will make us even colder and wetter.

Luciana had said eight to ten hours at a fast pace to reach bottom. But she meant hiking down the winding trail versus sledding at breakneck speeds down hillsides of pine needles. Surely we're close. Of course, we're also lost. But if we can just get near enough to civilization, maybe our cell phones will work. Maybe we'll encounter some random person living in a cabin in the woods.

And get them killed, too?

My spinning brain is not my friend right now.

In front of me, Miggy comes to an abrupt, skidding halt. I have to grab a tree branch to keep from crashing into him.

"What?"

He doesn't speak, just points. I follow his finger straight ahead, then straight down. We've come to a ravine. A massive, incredibly deep green furrow that goes on for as far as I can see. Like a giant decided to gouge an enormous slice out of the mountain.

I stare at Miggy. He stares at me. We can't cross that, no way.

Meaning we need to pick a direction, left or right, except I've lost all sense of direction. Down is on the other side of the ravine. But how the hell do we get there?

"Okay," Miggy says at last. "Let's just take a moment. We'll drink some water. Study the map."

I look behind us uneasily. At any moment, the tree man could emerge from those woods. Raise his rifle. When the bullets hit us, we will fall backward, just like Bob did. Except we'll go tumbling down the steep drop-off. Will that give us the last laugh? Steal from the hunter his trophy? Neil wanted his death to matter. I would settle for my death pissing someone off.

"We can move over here," Miguel says. He gestures to a small huddle of straggly pines that form a screen of sorts. We tuck ourselves inside the group, our packs scraping against the sharp branches as we wrest them from our backs.

My stomach growls. I press my hand against it self-consciously. I hate to ask the question. "Do we still have the protein bars? Granola? Anything?"

Miguel doesn't look at me. Finally, "I gave the remaining food to Neil and Scott. They said no, they said we should take it. But I couldn't leave them alone and injured with nothing at all."

His voice hitches. Immediately, I place my hand on his.

"I understand." I feel guilty. I was so lost in my rage and grief over Bob, I imploded, leaving Miggy to deal with the rest. I can't imagine what it must've been like for him. Patching up a bullet hole on one wounded friend, then having to rouse his second, concussed friend long enough to get them behind the cover of the bushes.

They would've been stoic about it. They have been from the very beginning. For five years these woods have been their enemy. They already know nothing good happens here.

But Miguel, having to leave them, after refusing again and again to make that choice. Of repeating the same mistake.

Scott bleeding out. Neil vomiting.

Moments like that take a piece of your soul. Leave the kind of wounds that never heal. You just learn to live with the pain.

A boom of thunder in the distance. Because we're not already wet and miserable enough.

Miggy sees me watching the approaching wave of dark clouds. "Maybe it will slow him down."

The guy who's been outfitted by Survivalists "R" Us? No, he probably has some waterproof supersuit that repels lightning. I hate him so much.

Miggy unfolds his map to reveal the same topographical overview Martin had. He fingers a twisting line of dashes.

"Our original trail," he states. He follows it to its end, which comes up short of a light green patch labeled Devil's Canyon. He moves his finger into the lower part of the shaded area, taps it. "Base camp, where we initially headed out from yesterday afternoon."

"Wait, there's a gap between the end of the dashed trail line and the beginning of the green canyon. What's in there?"

"We were in there. That's the backcountry part of our trek. Remember what Nemeth said on our first day? Not all the trails around here are marked or maintained. That's why Martin always planned these expeditions with Nemeth. You need either an experienced guide or compass skills. See?" He backtracks a short distance on the mountain guide to a tight cluster of black gradient lines. "These elevation marks indicate the steep one-mile descent to the flat area where we spent last night. That path isn't an officially marked byway, but one Nemeth and many of the locals know. Probably an animal trail that got co-opted by humans. So this morning we started out from here. I think we've been heading southwest, but I'm not sure."

"I don't suppose you have compass skills?" Because he's not an experienced guide, and I possess neither of those attributes.

"Once upon a time. Boy Scout training. But I'll be the first to admit, I haven't been practicing all these years. Hell, I liked Nemeth doing the heavy lifting. I didn't want to think any more than I had to about where we were going and what we were doing." Miggy grimaces. "Okay, forget direction for a second and let's consider elevation. Since we started, we've been picking the quickest, sharpest drop-offs. So, considering the gradient lines on our map . . ."

"We're looking for the tightest grouping." I get it now. "Shortest path that drops the most elevation at a time."

"Exactly."

We both study the map. A fresh rumble of thunder, much closer now, then the first fat raindrop hits the map dead center.

Miguel tucks the unfolded paper between us, where we can best shield it with our bodies.

"Not an exact science, but following the gradient lines, it looks like we've been coming down this section." He fingers a new route cutting across the mountain chart. "If that's true, then we're dropping like mad, but drifting too far south. We need to be heading more to the west to hit Ramsey. This is actually leading us deeper into the wilderness area. Lower elevation, but still smack-dab in the middle of the Popo Agie."

He taps the paper, where a huge sea of dark green is marked *Popo Agie Wilderness*. It looks like a long, crooked island, and we're nowhere near the shores. I can't form words as I take in the magnitude of our lostness. If I open my mouth now, I will cry.

Miguel is breathing heavily, struggling with his own emotions. As the sky once again opens up. With a crack of lightning followed shortly by a roar of thunder, the afternoon deluge finds us.

I don't care about the wild beauty anymore. The awesome power of nature feels like nothing more than a kick in the teeth. Mother Nature is already whupping our asses. She doesn't need to show off about it.

Miggy is still studying the map. "I can't find the ravine. Just, the fucking lines, where are the lines? Goddammit, I know this. Why can't I think? Come on, come on, come on. Now is not the time to be stupid."

He's losing it. Once more, I place my hand on his. It feels as cold and clammy as mine.

"It's okay. We've made it this far. You've gotten us this far."

He looks up at me. His features are beyond haggard. He is exhausted and demoralized, weighted down by the guilt of leaving his friends, haunted by the horrors we've witnessed. I wish I could wrap him in my arms and tell him it'll be okay. But lying won't help us.

The rain drips down his face. He blinks his eyes several times. "I heard Bob talking to you. He told you to tell Rob he loves him."

"Rob is his husband."

"I don't have a special someone. But . . . my parents. If I don't make it, and you do, tell my parents I love them, and it was an honor to be their son. Tell them . . . tell them I went down fighting. My dad, he'll like that."

"We're going to get out—"

"You?" he interrupts me fiercely. It seems very important for him to know. But I have no one. I'm not that kind of person. I haven't lived that kind of life.

"There's this bar in Boston," I say at last. "Owned by this guy Stoney who's not much for words. But if you could let him know . . ."

He'd pass it along to Viv, Angelique. Detective Dan Lotham. They will be sorry to hear the news, I'm sure. But my passing won't leave much of a hole in their lives. How could it, when I was never really there to begin with?

I wonder about Amy, Paul's widow. Will she wonder when my periodic phone calls stop? Think about me, miss our strange little ritual? Or will she simply think I've finally moved on, and be grateful to be rid of me at last?

I have no idea.

"When the storm eases," Miguel says at last, pulling himself together, "we should head that way."

He points through the trees. I nod. He's shivering. I am, too. Given the conditions, now is not the time for pulling on additional layers. We'll need them dry for later, when the temperatures truly start to plummet.

Assuming we make it that long.

Miguel folds up the damp map. We both take sips of water, willing our stomachs to believe it's sustenance.

Then we stand together, in the circle of twisted little pines. We turn our faces up to the sky and watch the bruised clouds roil and spears of lightning crack.

One final light show, I think. A last moment of staggering beauty.

Then the storm races on. And so do we.

CHAPTER 37

DREAM OF A HOT shower, cascading down my body as the dirt sluices from my skin. Followed by a feast of food. Steaming bowls of macaroni and cheese, a fresh grilled burger, piles of spicy Haitian meat patties. Then a bed. A massive, king-sized, incredibly soft, piled-high-in-down-comforters bed with twenty-nine pillows.

Then I dream of a particular Boston detective climbing onto that bed with me.

And I'm forced to confront reality once more.

We're trying so hard. Traversing the lip of a gulley that seems to go on forever. We are stumbling over tree roots, trudging through thick grasses, marching up small crests, sliding down modest slopes. Forward, forward, forward.

But still no sense of progress.

We're cold, wet, and twitchy. The storm has passed, but the sun hasn't fully emerged. Hiking up, this kind of shade would feel good. Headed down, we're rapidly losing body temperature.

My footsteps have become sluggish, ungainly. I can't even blame a steep grade or scary descent. I'm exhausted, starving, and freezing. I'm also limping, having twisted my ankle one too many times with all my careening about.

Ahead of me, Miggy is faring little better. From time to time, I catch him wincing. He's favoring his left leg; his knee seems to be troubling him. Like mine, his body has taken a beating.

We can't stop, though. The ravine isn't just keeping us from our target. It's hemming us in. Making us sitting ducks for the next time the shooter appears. Geology has us trapped.

A crack behind us. We both flinch, startle, leap for the cover of nearby trees.

But the gunshot fades out behind us. We watch a flock of birds take flight in the distance, then we exchange glances.

It has to be our hunter. What are the odds of two different people firing off rifles in such a remote area? Miguel is right: tree man does enjoy the chase. And now he's taunting us.

Miggy stares at me miserably. "My knee," he murmurs.

"I know. My ankle."

"We can't stop."

"Neil and Scott," I agree. They're depending on us. Assuming they're still alive. How alone they must've felt—the two of them, unable to move, unable to fight, huddled together, waiting for the end to come.

Not so unlike Miggy and me, right now.

Miguel is still rubbing his knee.

"Would taping it help?" I ask. "Bracing it somehow?"

"I could try. But we'd have to be quick." He hesitates. "Your ankle is bothering you?"

"I could go for an ice pack and an easy chair right about now."

"Best option, given the distance we have left to cover: walking sticks. Maybe, with your knife, you could cut us each a branch, about five feet high. That would help alleviate some of the stress on our joints."

"Okay." I'm happy to do anything to help. I'm happy to do anything that allows a short break from walking.

Miggy pulls off his pack, starts searching for his medical kit. I take my knife and shuffle a short distance away.

I'm tired of pine trees. I want oaks or maples, anything that doesn't cover me in sticky resin while jabbing a thousand tiny needles into my skin. I'm pretty sure these trees are the mean girls from high school.

I gird my loins one more time for battle.

I pick a half-dead subject. Then I pull out my cool, double-edged blade, only to realize it's now a filthy, gummed-up shadow of its formerly wicked self.

"I'm sorry," I tell it. "Help me now, and if I get out of here, I promise you a good bath. Though pretty please tell me it doesn't have to be in human blood."

The knife doesn't speak back, but I have a clear image of it sinking into tree man's chest. Apparently, we want the same thing after all.

I go to work. Either the pine bough is that thick, or I'm that tired, because it takes forever. I'm so stressed about time that when I finally wrench it free, I don't bother cutting a second, but grab one of the dead branches from off the ground.

I hustle back to Miguel, who looks as anxious as I feel.

"How's the knee?"

"It'll do. I took some ibuprofen as well. Here, for you."

He deposits two white pills into my blood-, dirt-, pitch-encrusted hand. I don't think twice as I pop both pills into my mouth and down them with a swill of water. Quickly, I slice the smaller twigs from the main bough, then pare down any remaining needles.

"For you." I hand it over to Miggy, then inspect the dead branch I grabbed for myself. I trim it up as well, feeling like quite the blade professional as I hack away.

My walking stick feels brittle. Too much load and it'll snap, unlike its freshly cut counterpart. But I'm not that heavy and we don't have time for better choices.

We both rise to standing, slinging on our packs.

Second rifle crack. More birds flocking to the sky. Much closer now.

We have no choice but to flee.

WE DON'T GET far before it's clear Miggy's bandaging job and my walking sticks aren't enough. Miguel hobbles like a lame racehorse and I'm skipping more than running.

He pulls up abruptly. I halt beside him. We're both breathing heavily.

"I have five bullets," he says.

I understand what he means. When you're done running, the only option left is to take a stand. Of course, our last stand didn't go so well, but given we're never going to win this footrace . . .

I glance around us. The clouds have cast this side of the mountains in shadow. I don't know much about gunfights, but I'm pretty sure high ground is a good thing. Especially when the other guy is much better prepared.

I point to a small slope to our right, covered in needles and a dense line of evergreens.

"Too many trees," Miguel murmurs, glancing nervously behind us. "Provides cover for us, but so much so that I'll never be able to get off a clean shot." He points to a short rise ahead of us, topped with a mix of rocks and brush, but terribly exposed. "We can lie down flat, like they do in the old Westerns."

"I think you're insane."

He gives me his crooked grin, then heads toward the target. I follow in his wake; we don't have time to argue.

I trail him to the top of the stubby rise. Miguel takes out his handgun, which looks not nearly powerful enough. I know nothing about firearms and I like to keep it that way, so I merely watch as he checks the clip for his five remaining bullets. Loads one into the chamber.

He hands me his pack. I tuck them both away in a slight hollow behind the rocks, then rip out handfuls of tall grass to layer on top of the fabric.

Miguel is already on his stomach, moving side to side to find the best position. I don't know what to do with myself. Bear spray doesn't work against our attacker. That leaves me with my knife. Do I have the courage to stab another person? I think of Bob dying, and the thought gets easier to imagine.

I tap Miguel on the shoulder, then gesture to the patch of scraggly pines. I'm headed there, I pantomime to him. Because me lying on the ground beside him accomplishes nothing. We might as well take advantage of our superior numbers.

Miggy nods. "I don't have his range," he whispers to me. "I'm going to have to let him get very close."

Which gives me another idea. I pick up my walking stick and, after creeping back down, I resume our initial path and now continue on, helter-skelter, past Miggy's perch. With any luck, our hunter friend, deep in tracking mode, will continue moving forward, intent on our trail, and never notice the exhausted, hypothermic dude with the puny handgun right above him.

I crash into the woods. It's not hard given that I can barely walk. When I'm deep enough into the next cover of pines to have hopefully established my ruse, I stop the mad dash and limp much more carefully in a long loop back to my original destination. The closer I get, the faster my heartbeat, the stronger my fear.

He should be here. Any time now. Or is he already here, one tree about to split into two? Or working some kind of strategy of his own, flanking us from the side, or clambering up to a preestablished sniper's perch?

There are too many things I don't know.

I tuck myself into the screen of pines.

The first pine cone crunches to my left.

A silhouette appears.

And Miguel opens fire.

CHAPTER 38

MIGUEL'S FIRST SHOT MISSES ITS mark. He follows it quickly with two more, trying to correct for his mistake. But tree man is already on the move. He spins sideways, nearly crashing into my hideout. With lightning speed, he has his rifle up, positioning the butt against his shoulder.

I spring forward, double-edged Rambo knife in hand, signal whistle pursed between my lips. I blow, as loud and hard as I can, right in tree man's ear.

He recoils, slapping his right hand reflexively over his ear and partially dropping the rifle. He whirls toward me, but for once my slight build is an attribute. I dart in low and quick. Then I squeeze my eyes shut and stab at another human being.

I feel the thud of contact before my knife skitters sideways. I open my eyes, encountering tree man's camouflaged thigh. I thrust with my blade a second time, harder. My pitch-dulled blade is deflected once again.

The fabric is reinforced. Some kind of heavyweight patching.

I'm still processing that detail when tree man shoves me away. I stumble backward, landing on my ass. I look up to see a mythical beast out of every horror movie ever made. Bugged-out eyes. A distorted head. A mouthless face.

Then I watch the butt of a rifle descend straight toward my head.

At the last second, I roll away, then scamper up long enough to throw myself behind a tree.

With a roar, tree man charges after me.

I whirl behind another pine, then another, working a crazy zigzag pattern with no strategy other than dodge and duck, duck and dodge.

Miggy. Where is he? Please let him and his bullets arrive shortly.

I zig left. Bad choice. Tree man slams me in the shoulder with the rifle. My right arm immediately goes numb, knife dropping to the ground. I blow the whistle again. It's no longer a shrill sound, but a whispery, panicked hiccup as I start to hyperventilate from sheer terror.

Then fresh gunfire. The tree next to us explodes. The hunter flinches, takes cover, and so do I.

Miguel. I think I can just see him, advancing through the trees and shadows. Had to get close, he said. I hope he's about to be near enough.

Tree man slams me in the face with his rifle. I go down seeing stars.

Fresh gunfire. Tree man grunting, turning away from me, toward the new threat.

Get up, get up, get up, I will myself. I've spent my whole life in motion. Now is not the time to stop.

A yelp of pain. Miguel. He's outclassed. We both are. Gotta do this together because we'll never make it separately.

I manage to grab a nearby branch and pull myself to standing. My eyes are watering from the blow. It feels like my left cheekbone has exploded. It makes it hard to see, but at this stage, that hardly matters.

Miguel needs me.

I wade forward, pulling myself together as I go.

I'm a small, slightly built female. I can't win battles of strength or brute force. But I've had enough experience by now to know my best options for success. Go for eyes, throat, groin, knees. If you can't hit hard, then strike where it counts.

Tree man is wielding his rifle as a club. Now he smacks Miguel in the arm, causing Miggy to drop his gun. Then in one fluid motion, the rifle is across his back and tree man now has a gleaming blade in hand, a near twin for mine except it's not gummed up with wood fibers.

Miguel pales. He has his arms held wide, his feet drumming, like a football player at the ready. No begging, no pleading. He's gonna go down fighting, just as he said.

That gives me the rage I need to duck low and charge forward. I hit tree man mid leg, wrapping my arms around his knees and heaving for all I'm worth. I don't care how big you are. Knee joints still aren't designed for side impact.

Tree man crashes to the left, slashing down with his blade as he falls.

I scream. A wounded animal. A feral beast.

Then Miggy is there, jumping upon the hunter's fallen form, going after the knife.

We are fueled by adrenaline and sheer terror.

Unfortunately for us, the hunter is powered by sleep, a solid meal, and a lifetime of experience. In a matter of minutes, he shakes us off as no more than bothersome flies. He rises to standing.

I go once more for his knees. He lashes out with his leg and kicks me solidly in the chest. I reel back, the wind knocked out of me.

Miggy lunges for the knife. Tree man slashes him across the face, then the chest, several times.

Miggy stumbles and falls. He scrambles backward like a crab.

The tree man advances, gleaming blade in hand.

Gun. Miggy dropped the gun. If I can just find it. I scrabble around in the dirt. I gasp and heave and search. I'm a seeker, this is what I do. Please, please, please . . .

The hunter stands above Miggy. He raises the knife high, and behind the mask, the goggles, the camo clothes and twiggy hat, I swear he is smiling.

Miggy looks up at him. He declares loudly, "Fuck you."

The blade comes down.

And once more, the woods explode.

I NEVER SAW him coming.

He rams straight into the hunter, who doesn't have a chance to defend himself before being slammed into the ground.

The two shapes roll free of the pines, into the open. I try to pull myself up but my right arm doesn't work and a warm, salty fluid has coated my eyes. Finally, I manage to heave to standing. I have to wipe my face several times.

Even then what I'm looking at doesn't make much sense.

Two men, on the ground, locked in a battle to the death. Tree man and . . .

The tree man gains the upper hand, smashes the other person across the face with a vicious right hook. The new intruder stumbles back. His face appears as obscured as the hunter's. I just make out human eyes peering out from a mask of caked dirt and dried blood.

Martin.

Still alive. Kind of. And really, really pissed off.

The hunter slugs him again. Then again and again. Belatedly, I resume my search for Miguel's dropped handgun.

"You . . . shot . . . my . . . son," Martin is gasping. "Kill you . . . kill you . . . kill you . . ."

The hunter abandons control and starts slugging away. Martin doesn't dodge. Bent in half and clearly grievously injured, he just keeps taking the blows, his lips peeled back into an unnerving grin. "Kill you . . . kill you . . . kill you . . ."

Now the hunter is fumbling with his pockets. No doubt searching for another knife, gun, bear spray of his own.

"Frankie," Miguel croaks.

I turn to see him pointing. The handgun. Just five feet away. I lurch toward it.

"*Shut . . . up!*" the tree man yells at Martin.

He stabs Martin in the chest, his hand coming back to reveal a short, bloody utility knife. Then he stabs again and again.

Martin, standing there, taking it. "Kill you . . . kill you . . . kill you."

I grab the gun. One shot to get this right.

Suddenly Martin howls. A father's rage. A father's pain. Then, even as the knife comes down in another debilitating blow, Martin charges.

He doesn't go low. He doesn't try for finesse. He collides, hard and square against his opponent.

A moment of hush.

Quiet shock.

The hunter, no doubt confused by how his prey can still be standing, still be fighting back.

Then a second of pure disbelief.

As Martin's momentum carries them backward. As Martin's sheer indomitable will shoves them to the edge of the ravine.

The hunter, twisting now, trying to get his footing.

Martin's feral smile, a flash of white against his blood-encrusted face. *"Kill you kill you kill you."*

Martin pushes them both over the edge.

I hear the hunter scream. I swear I hear Martin laugh.

Then there's nothing at all.

CHAPTER 39

Somehow, I crawl my way back to Miguel. The adrenaline is still coursing through my veins. Fight or flight, fight or flight, fight or flight. But I've already exercised both options. I've got nothing left.

Miguel has managed to push himself to sitting, his back against a tree trunk. The light is failing now, the temperature dropping quickly. It's hard for me to tell how much of him is covered in dirt versus blood. I suppose he'd say the same.

"Water?" he gasps.

Our packs are still up on the short rise, tucked beneath their cover of grass. It feels like a million miles away, but of the two of us, I'm in the better shape. I stagger my way in that direction. It takes several tries, then I'm on top of the mound, looping my left arm through both sets of straps. My right arm still isn't working. And I can feel half my face swelling to twice its natural size.

I get the packs back to Miggy. Take out water bottles for each of us.

He manages to work his. I require his assistance to pop the top off my own.

I do some digging till I find the small first aid pouch packed eons ago by Josh.

I don't have the energy for more bandages. We're out of feminine hygiene products and probably beyond help anyway. In the end, I pluck out the ibuprofen tablets. There are eight. I dole out four to each of us. We're living the dream.

"Can you walk?" Miguel asks.

"Not well."

"Me either. My knee. My chest."

I can hear it now, when he breathes. An ominous hiss.

I don't want to know, but now is not the time to be squeamish. I fumble with my pencil flashlight, finally pointing it at him.

"Oh," I say at last. I turn off the light. I was right the first time. I didn't want to know.

"That . . . bad?"

"I'm sorry," I whisper.

"Well . . . if it helps, you look pretty awful yourself."

We share exhausted smiles, the kind seen in foxholes and on front lines.

"That was Marty, wasn't it?" Miggy says at last.

"Apparently, he was still alive."

"Who . . . knew?"

"Stubborn has its advantages."

"Don't have to . . . convince me. You think . . . other guy. Dead?"

"God I hope so."

"We should get going. Put some distance."

Neither of us moves.

"Scott and Neil," he murmurs finally.

He might be crying. I'm about to. We tried. We tried very hard. But now, this injured, in the middle of nowhere, no cell signal for help. I'm out of ideas. I'm out of strength. I'm out of will.

We're both shivering.

I open up Miguel's backpack, fumble around for some dry shirts, and set them on his lap. Then do the same for myself. In the end, I can't lift my right arm. I don't know how to get the wet clothes off, let alone put the dry clothes on.

Beside me, Miguel hasn't even tried to move.

"I could help . . ." I venture. My words come out thick. The rule of threes. Only three hours without shelter in adverse conditions. We are wet and rapidly losing body heat and the temperatures are only going to plummet further. We need to move; we can't even manage a change of clothes.

"A fire," he sighs at last. "Maybe . . . maybe some heat would help."

"I have cotton balls dipped in Vaseline."

His smile is a flash of white in the gathering dark. "Party on."

I keep my efforts simple. Dead twigs and pine cones I can scrounge in the immediate vicinity. I find my knife where I dropped it in the tussle, and use it to hack out a small section of clean dirt. The ground is dry and fairly easy to clear.

Miguel oversees my efforts with his ragged breathing. Finally, I touch a greasy fire starter with my butane lighter, and puff, we end up with a very modest burst of flames. My first ever campfire.

I think of my father, and that night, and the scent of Jack Daniel's. Everything I love and hate so tightly woven together as a single bittersweet memory.

Miggy manages to pull himself closer, moaning slightly. He looks even worse by the light of the fire. He has a savage slash across his face, but the true damage is to his chest. Tree man turned Miggy's torso into something out of a zombie flick.

My issues are my arm, shoulder, and ankle. Interestingly enough, neither of them would normally be life-threatening. Except, of course, when you're stranded in the middle of the wilderness with no access to the civilized world.

We're both still shaking with the cold. I lean over the fire better to warm my hands. Miguel's movements are more feeble. He's fading fast and knows it.

"Tell me a story," he says at last.

"About a princess and a frog?"

"Maybe about a band of brothers. Who set out in the woods."

I play along. "A wild beast emerges. He roars and attacks."

"One brother is separated from the others."

"But he doesn't give up. He journeys the forest looking for a way out. He's determined to survive."

"The other four search for him. But the beast comes back. They fight. One by one. They fall."

"But the first brother is still watching over them," I counter. "He wants his brothers to live."

"They were lousy brothers. They never should've separated in the first place."

"He understands. He still wants them to live."

"But the forest is the forest." Miggy sighs. "It wants the brothers to be together again. For all of eternity."

"The first brother fights the forest."

Miguel looks at me. "The first brother is already dead."

"You are not very good at stories, Miggy."

"What did you expect? I'm an engineer."

"More water?" I offer. Because Miggy's not wrong. In terms of happily ever afters, we're shit out of luck.

"Tell my father I went down fighting."

"Nope. You want him to know, show up and show off your battle scars yourself."

"You shouldn't have joined our mad little party."

"It's what I do."

"Die with strangers?"

"Honestly? I always figured I'd die alone. So all in all, this is progress."

"Did you do something terrible?" he asks me curiously. "Or did someone do something terrible to you? Is that why you now drift from place to place?"

"No. Though once there was a man who loved me more than I could love him. And he ended up dying because of that love, but it wasn't really my fault, or even his fault. Just one of those things. But I'd started wandering even before that. It hurt him that I didn't love him enough to stay. And hurt me that he didn't understand my need to leave."

"I haven't cared about someone that much yet."

"Maybe your new face will do the trick."

"Chicks dig scars?"

"Exactly."

"Frankie, in the bottom of my pack. There's a flask. Get it."

I assume he means another stainless steel water bottle, so it takes my fingers a moment to register the shape. A real flask. The old-fashioned, thin, rectangular kind with a screw-off cap. I free it from the backpack and find myself staring. I talked to Neil about being an alcoholic. But I've never mentioned it to Miggy.

"I brought it," Miguel murmurs, the whistle building in his chest. "For when we found Tim. One last toast. A fitting farewell, I don't know."

My fingers are trembling as I hand it over. I inhale deeply as he loosens the cap.

"Maker's Mark," he supplies. "Our final drink together as friends."

I can only nod.

I'm suddenly so thirsty. Ravenously thirsty. I'm in my parents' backyard, watching my father bob and weave his way back to our ramshackle tent. I'm a little girl, licking bourbon from my fingers in the privacy of my bedroom. Trying to know. Trying to understand.

Trying to discern the flavor of love.

"No more rainy days," Miggy exhales. "No more hellos. No more goodbyes."

"No more pain, no more sorrow," I contribute.

"A drink for the brave."

"A drink for the fallen."

"Goodbye to the past."

"Goodbye to tomorrow."

Toast complete, he tips back the flask and swallows deep. I watch his Adam's apple bob. I imagine the smooth whiskey burning down his throat, warming him from the inside. Even with our little fire, it's so cold, we are so cold.

Soon enough, we will each fall unconscious. The fire will fail. The cold will take over. And our shivering will cease altogether.

Miggy coughs harshly. Spits up blood. Studies the fresh red drops on the palm of his hand.

"Goodbye to tomorrow," he repeats.

He extends the flask toward me. I inhale once more the beguiling scent of whiskey. My greatest desire, my deepest fear.

I take it.

CHAPTER 40

Have you ever pictured your own death?

Are you old and frail, tucked in a sea of plump pillows, surrounded by the ones you love? Spouse, children, grandchildren?

Or do you prefer a blaze of glory? Young and stupid as you plummet down a cliff, crash into a barricade, slip under a bull's thundering hooves?

Do you imagine a clinical hospital room or the comfort of your own home?

Are you alone and desperate?

Or holding the hand of that one person who made your entire life worth living?

Do you pray?

Do you beg?

Do you think, This is nothing like I ever imagined?

I don't have the answer to any of these questions. Maybe I am loved, maybe I'm alone. Maybe I made it to old age, maybe my questionable decisions have finally caught up with me. But I have one single desire:

To die sober.

I think, as I return the flask to Miguel to finish alone, at least I got that part right.

The fire dies down. The cold digs deeper. We curl into each other. I stroke Miggy's dark hair till his eyes close and his shivering ceases. I kiss his temple. I assure him he went down fighting.

Then I close my own eyes, and let the freezing night have its way.

KISSES. SLOBBERY. WET. Panting in my face. The world's worst breath.

A voice. "Shhh, don't move, don't speak. We got you."

I try to say Miguel's name. I struggle for Scott, Neil, Bob. I think my lips move.

More kisses across my cheeks, sloppy wet.

"Daisy, stop that!"

Then I fling out my arms and discover a warm, furry form. A fresh tongue bath. I don't mind one bit.

"It's okay, Frankie. Just relax."

Luciana is here, too. I clutch her hand.

Miggy, Neil, Scott, Bob. I try so hard to speak the names. Maybe I succeed. It's hard to know.

I'm moving. Lifted from the ground, carried through space. My shoulder screams; my entire body aches. But I grab onto the pain, hold it close, relish the sensation of still being alive.

"How is he?" Another voice.

"We need immediate evac."

A sound overhead. The thunder of rotor blades. Chopper.

Our rescue. At last.

———

LIGHTS. TOO BRIGHT. I open my eyes, then shut them.

Surroundings. Too white. I glance, then look away.

Sounds. Too loud. I hear, then burrow down.

Miggy. Neil, Scott, Bob.

Miggy. Neil, Scott, Bob.

Names I keep thinking. Names I keep saying.

Names I'll never forget.

WHEN I NEXT open my eyes, I find myself in a narrow space, surrounded by white curtains. I'm clearly in a hospital bed and attached to a variety of beeping objects. I have a dim memory of my last medical emergency and instinctively try to rub my shoulder. My hand has too many lines sprouting from it to move.

"You're awake."

I blink my eyes a few more times and discover Luciana standing in front of me.

I try to croak out my litany of names, but my throat is too dry.

She seems to understand, pouring me a cup of water, then bringing the straw to my lips. I have to take several long sips before I feel the moisture return to my mouth.

"Miguel?"

"Made it out of surgery. They think they got most of the internal bleeding. He's listed in critical. Another day or two and hopefully we'll know more."

I almost can't say the next two names. "Neil? Scott?"

"A second canine team found them. The sheriff has every available SAR team working those woods right now. Neil is going to be okay. Just needs to rest and recuperate from a pretty severe concussion. Scott." She hesitates. "They got the bullet out, but he's lost a lot of blood. His wife is on her way. Best we can do is pray."

I can't look at Luciana anymore. I suffer a debilitating sense of failure. I never should've suggested my stupid plan. We never should've left Scott and Neil. Coulda, woulda, shoulda. The terrible trio that haunts all survivors.

"You?" I ask at last.

Luciana smiles, brings the straw back to my lips. She looks close to her usual gorgeous self, just bruised and battered around the edges. And tired. Very tired.

"I was attacked," she provides. "Nemeth and I had just completed the steepest portion of the descent. He and Daisy were both ahead of me. And something snagged my ankle. I was upright, then in the next instant went down hard. I thought I'd tripped, tried to get my hands beneath me, when something hard nailed me from behind. I don't really know what happened after that. When I regained consciousness, I was tied to a tree. No idea where I was or what had happened.

"I was still trying to figure out how to break free, when Daisy appeared. She was missing her vest and covered in mud and twigs, but she'd found me. My pockets had been emptied out. I still had my paracord bracelet, however. I managed to unclasp it and use the razor part to cut through the cords. Then, basically, I followed Daisy back down to civilization. Once I reached Sheriff Kelley, he started planning the rescue. Daisy and I joined the chopper crew, arriving at the top of Devil's Canyon. A separate group launched from the base. It's . . . it's been really busy since then."

Another hesitation. "They found Bob," she says softly. "They're bringing down his body today." Then her own question: "Marty?"

"There was a man hunting us. Probably who attacked you. He's the one who killed Bob and hurt Scott and Neil. Miguel and I were trying to get help when he caught up with us. Martin, he came out of nowhere, tackled the man. They both went over the edge of the ravine. Nemeth?" I ask. The fact that she hasn't mentioned him already has me worried.

Luciana takes a deep breath. "He, uh . . . he's in pretty bad shape. Looks like he must've run back to help me—they found his pack near where I was attacked. But it didn't go so well for him. Either the hunter left him for dead or he somehow escaped, but he managed to stagger a fair way down the mountain before collapsing near the trail. Marge Santi found him, first thing. Good thing, too, because I don't think he would've made it much longer."

I wince, being able to picture it too well.

Luciana continues quietly, "Chances are, he saved my life. By the time the attacker finished with Nemeth, he didn't have the energy left to deal with me immediately."

Or the time, I think, knowing that ambushing Luciana and Nemeth had been only the opening act for the hunter's busy day.

"But it cost him," she finishes at last. "Gunshot wound, broken bones, pulverized face. It's not . . . it's not looking good."

I want to squeeze her hand, but I'm attached to too many lines. I understand how she feels, though. I need Miguel, Scott, and Neil to pull through, because the thought of them dying while I get to live is too terrible to contemplate. Both a burden and a grave injustice.

"Bodies," I manage at last. "In Devil's Canyon. There's a chamber, filled with eight mummified remains."

Luciana nods. "One of the teams discovered it this morning. I don't know if you remember, but you were talking about it as you drifted in and out of consciousness. The mummies needed you, the mummies were coming to get you, hunted humans, human hunter. We didn't understand it all, but it was enough to know something else was going on near the cliff face. I remembered the area where Daisy had first picked up a scent trail before becoming confused, and provided a rough direction. If we'd had more time on our expedition, I'm sure Daisy would've made the discovery herself. Of course, our party had things going wrong from the very beginning."

The hunter had been outplaying us from the start, no doubt about it. And yet still hadn't truly appreciated the depth of a father's love, or the power of a father's rage. Neil would approve: Martin had made his death count.

"How long?" I ask—as in, how long have I been in the hospital?

"Thirty-six hours."

I'm startled by this, mostly because it feels like I could easily sleep another year. Beneath the hospital sheets, I can feel the nearly concave shape of my hollowed-out stomach.

"They have you on fluids and glucose," Luciana provides. "Now that you're awake, I'm sure a doctor will be in to see you shortly. This is a small hospital, so having five major trauma cases at once is straining their resources, hence your 'room'"—she gestures to my curtained-off space—"which is actually a temporary bed in the ER. The way I understand things, your injuries aren't that serious, so you don't need to stay. Mostly, you need a week's worth of sleep and probably a month's worth of food. Your body will take care of the rest."

I nod, because I don't know what to say. In all honesty, I have no idea where to go or what to do next. Luciana once told me a week in the woods would change me. She had no idea.

Now Luciana places a gentle hand on my shoulder: "I have a room for Daisy and me back at the original motel in Ramsey. You're welcome to crash with us again. When you're ready to be discharged from here, let me know and I can give you a ride."

"Thank you."

There's a rustle from the curtains behind us. Some kind of signal Luciana must understand.

"Sheriff Kelley would like to speak to you now," she states.

I nod. The debrief. I have done such things before. I'm tired and hungry, and yet still in better shape than my companions.

And someone has to tell the story.

SHERIFF KELLEY HAS the same trim, wiry build I associate with Martin and Nemeth. He's full-on cowboy: boots, jeans, impressive silver belt buckle, and cream-colored Stetson. It really works for him. He strides into my curtained-off space and I already feel slightly safer. Penetrating blue eyes, weathered face, hard lined features. I'm convinced—you want a good-looking man, come to Wyoming.

He positions himself on my right-hand side, shoulders square, feet spread for balance.

"How ya feeling?"

"Okay."

"Docs'll fill you in more. I understand your shoulder was dislocated. Fixed now. Sprained ankle will take a bit longer. Rest is mostly bruises and lacerations, though your face won't look so pretty for a bit." He pauses, as if to see if that news bothers me. I think it's charming he assumed I was pretty to begin with. He continues bluntly: "Your friends weren't so lucky."

"My friends weren't so lucky," I agree.

Sheriff Kelley rocks back on his heels, peers at me intently. "What the hell happened up there?"

I start laughing. I just can't help myself. Except maybe I'm crying. I can't tell anymore.

My silly impulse just three, four days ago. Join a search party, head into the mountains, enjoy the great outdoors.

I laugh/cry harder.

Then, finally, I start to speak.

CHAPTER 41

FILL IN SHERIFF KELLEY as best I can. The threats and sabotage Martin experienced months before the expedition even launched. His hiring of Bob, who in addition to being a Bigfoot hunter was also a licensed PI. The issues we encountered almost immediately—our stolen food, Scott's midnight race through the woods. I wonder now whether it hadn't been triggered by our stalker playing some kind of trick.

Neil being smashed over the head with a rock. The last of our food being snatched. Our party's pivotal decision to break up—Luciana and Nemeth going for help while the rest of us remained behind.

Bob and me returning with Martin to the cave he was convinced had once been occupied by his son. Followed by my terrible discovery behind a fake-rock foam door. Returning to Martin, only to have the hunter open fire.

I deliver the tale in a clipped, steady voice. Even as I discuss our disastrous plan to lure the hunter into the open using Daisy's torn vest as bait, resulting in Bob's death and Scott's and Neil's injuries. Then my and Miguel's desperate flight down the mountain. The hunter catching up with us. Martin appearing and plunging both of them to their doom.

"You're sure you saw Marty O'Day and this fellow fall over the edge of the ravine?"

"Yes. Have you found the bodies?"

"Not yet. But accessing that area will take some time. Now, can you describe this so-called tree man?"

I give the sheriff a look at his dubious tone. "Don't make me climb out of my hospital bed to hurt you."

"Good to know you're feeling better."

Which makes me smile feebly. The sheriff is testing me. Maybe I'm passing, maybe I'm not, but it's nice to feel like my normal, contrarian self again.

"He wore full facial coverings," I relate now. "A black mask over his nose and mouth, some kind of goggles protecting his eyes. I'd say he's around your height and build. He was extremely well equipped. Someone who frequents gun shops and/or army surplus stores."

"That's half my county," the sheriff informs me.

"Which is the point. He's a local. Has to be to know the area so well. And longtime roots. Timothy O'Day was five years ago, but I saw remains that had to be older than that."

"We got a top forensic anthropologist team working the site now. Not to mention whatever other PhDs the feds feel like throwing at it. Crime scene doesn't lack for resources."

Common sense, seems to be the implied insult, but that doesn't surprise me coming from a county sheriff. "Have any good ol' boys been reported missing lately?" I ask him, as local knowledge still applies.

"I got eyes on the lookout for any new reports. Been only two days, though. Not so long in these parts to worry about a loved one who set out on a backcountry trek. Might take a few more days. We'll hear something."

"Or find the body."

"Or find the body," he agrees.

"I want to see it," I hear myself say. "When you, whoever, brings that dead bastard in, I want to personally inspect his body. I want to know he's dead. I want him to know we won."

"You'd like an opportunity to identify the remains as belonging to your attacker?" the sheriff asks, speaking as a man who knows how to navigate multijurisdictional investigations.

I'm becoming a big fan of the sheriff. I follow his lead. "Yes. As a witness, I'm in a position to state unequivocally the dead man is the same one who killed Bob, shot Scott, and attacked Neil, Miguel, and myself."

More nodding. The sheriff takes a step back, his most immediate concerns addressed. "When we find Martin O'Day's remains, do you know who I contact?"

"His wife, Patrice."

"You understand she's not doing so great. Relaying the news of Marty's passing was difficult enough. Burdening that poor woman with the logistics of body transport feels just plain cruel."

I understand the sheriff's point.

"Neil," I murmur at last. Of the friends' group, it sounds like his injuries are the least severe, putting him in the best position to step up to assist. Not to mention, once Tim had planned Neil's sister's funeral, making it even more fitting for Neil to handle Martin's remains. Soon enough, after proper identification, Tim's body would be released for burial as well. And inevitably, given Patrice's diagnosis, three tombstones in a single line. Mother. Father. Son.

I want to find romance in the notion that they will be together forever. I don't. Tim should've lived. Any parents will tell you that. Their child should not lie in the cemetery plot next to them.

I have a question of my own for the sheriff. "There's another friend, Josh . . ." I didn't have enough time to learn everyone's last names, making this awkward. "He was admitted to a hospital to detox. I'm guessing this hospital?"

Sheriff Kelley nods. "He's here. Docs were about to ship him to rehab when the reports came in of injured hikers. He's been bouncing from room to room ever since, checking on buddies. In the beginning, the nurses tried to get him to stay put. No one pays him no mind anymore. You see a guy wandering the halls with his ass hanging out of a hospital johnny, that's your man Josh."

"Okay." I think I'll go looking for him. Though why, I can't really say. Maybe I just want to talk to someone who's also begging the universe to let Scott and Miguel pull through. It's presumptuous of me. I knew them a matter of days. Josh was their best friend for more than a decade. But in a weird way, I also feel I know him, having heard all the stories. The final member of Dudeville. The quiet one, whose tendency toward silence has clearly taken its toll.

"Any new word," I ask now, "on Miguel and Scott?"

"Miguel Santos just got upgraded to stable, I'm told. Scott Riemann . . . I'm not gonna lie. He's in bad shape. Wife should be here shortly."

I nod, feeling each word like a punch to my gut. "Luciana said Nemeth is also seriously injured."

"By rights, Nemeth should already be dead," the sheriff states bluntly. "But that man . . . he isn't a legend around these parts for nothing. He's got a community pulling for him. And I don't bet against any man whose been through everything he's been through.

If anyone can shake this off, it's him." I hope what the sheriff says is true. Losing Martin was hard enough. For both him and Nemeth to be gone would create a hole in the universe—this is where the tough bastards used to be. The world would be an emptier place.

"Stay close," the sheriff informs me. "Still some unraveling to be done."

He wants contact information. All I can offer him is my Tracfone number and a vague reference to the motel across from the diner in Ramsey, room registered in Luciana's name. Sheriff Kelley nods as if this all makes perfect sense. Maybe around here it does.

Then the sheriff is gone. A doctor appears. True to Luciana's assessment, I can leave anytime I want. My right shoulder, recently dislocated, will hurt like a son of a bitch for the next couple of days. Same with my sprained ankle, not to mention my swollen and discolored face. But all in all, my injuries are superficial and time is on my side.

Just let them know when I'm ready to be discharged, says the doctor, who appears to be approximately twelve. I get the hint they need my bed sooner versus later.

The doctor departs. I'm left struggling with basic questions, such as where are my clothes? Or the rest of my worldly possessions, most of which were in my backpack, because I'm that kind of girl?

I last an entire thirty minutes before I just can't take it anymore. Screw lying around, waiting for a nurse to assist me. I pull out the IV needle myself. A little bloody, but compared to the past few days . . . I disconnect the pulse monitor on my index finger. Then, when machines start screeching, I unplug them, one by one.

I pull back the first curtain and, feeling the wind beneath my johnny, venture forth.

———

I HURT. I knew I would, but the first few minutes still take my breath away. I'm pretty sure my heavily bandaged ankle spews fire every time I take a step. But so much of me erupts in excruciating pain, it's hard to be sure. Muscles, joints, limbs, torso, face.

I haven't had the courage to look in a mirror yet. I already trust I won't like what I see.

For now, I shuffle. Out of the curtained area, down a corridor where actual rooms exist. Some doors are open, some closed. I spot a variety of people in various stages of sleep, socialization, and distress, but none are the persons I'm seeking.

Finally, I come upon a room with a johnny-garbed male sitting in the spare chair. Bingo. I stride—limp—through the doorway.

I immediately recognize the unconscious form lying in the hospital bed: Miguel. His eyes are closed, his face half covered by an oxygen mask. But those features, that dark hair . . . I instantly want to touch his forehead, caress his cheek, hold his hand. Not lover to lover. More like mom to pup, except I've never been a mother in my life.

The dude in the pale-blue johnny is watching me, clearly taking in my look-alike apparel. I recognize his lighter blond hair from the diner. He looks less sweaty now than he did then. That's all I got.

"Josh," I say.

"Frankie Elkin?" he ventures.

That out of the way, we stare at each other. Finally, I cross to stand beside him. He's already resumed his vigil, so I do, too, as if together we can will Miggy back to life.

"I fucked up," Josh says at last.

I don't say anything. All the guys said Josh didn't like to talk. Best strategy, make him come to me.

Josh lapses back into silence. We regard Miggy's unconscious form.

"It should've been me. On the trek. Not you."

He's apologizing to me? This catches me off guard. I'd think I'd be the least of his concerns.

"So you could be hunted instead?"

"Is that what happened to Tim?" he asks quietly.

"Most likely."

He shakes his head. Against the brutal truth? The unimaginable horror? Once again, he falls silent.

The rise and fall of Miguel's chest appears peaceful and steady. Forget for a minute that a machine is doing the work for him, and it's easy to believe that at any moment his eyes will open and he'll regard us with a crooked grin.

We survived together. I feel a deeper connection to him than I even felt with Paul. It's probably fleeting—the result of adrenaline and cortisol and lots of other chemicals I don't understand. I just know I need him to be okay. Anything less would be another blow to my already fragile psyche.

"I know the truth," I say at last, in the hushed room. I don't look at Josh, but continue to take in Miguel's unconscious form. "The others told us what really happened that night."

Josh doesn't say anything.

"Do you still hate him?" I ask curiously. "Tim? Or do you hate that fate intervened before you could finish giving him the beating he deserved, or the closure you desired?"

"I keep drinking to figure that out."

"You loved him."

Josh doesn't dispute that.

"According to Scott, Miggy, and Neil, he loved you, too. The bond you two had was special, even by Dudeville standards."

Josh's expression falters.

"I'm sorry for your loss," I say quietly.

Josh looks like he's going to cry.

We sit in silence again, listening to the machines pump and whoosh, watching Miguel remain with the land of the living.

"I don't know your friends well," I say at last. "But I know that when things got tough, they had my back. Neil offered to sacrifice himself for us. Scott agreed to bleed out lost and alone so that Miguel and I could live. Miggy took on an armed gunman so that I might have a chance to escape. They share your guilt. They have their own regrets.

"But in the end, it's not the fault of any of you that Tim's gone. The blame rests with one psychopathic asshole who decided hunting human beings made for good sport. We'll never know everything, but from what I saw, Tim died trying to live. He was determined to get back to his friends. Because you were his people. He loved you. He wanted to make things right."

Josh finally glances up at me. "He impregnated my sister. He betrayed our friendship. And I wished him dead while trying to kill him with my bare hands. Then he was gone, and I can't take my final wish back."

Josh has a point. "What do you want most in the world?" I ask him.

"Peace."

"And how do you usually find peace?"

"Tequila."

I have to smile. "That's forgetfulness. Not the same as peace at all."

Josh's turn to smile. He returns his gaze to Miguel's still form. "I miss the days," he murmurs, "when all could be resolved with a case of beer, a game of hoops."

"Then go back to it. Sober up. Reconnect with your friends. And maybe, in honor of Tim, you hit the basketball court one final time. What's the worst that could happen?"

Josh doesn't have an immediate answer to that. Eventually, he nods.

"AA will turn you into a regular chatty Cathy," I inform him.

He appears mildly alarmed.

"Hey, don't knock it till you try it." I pat him on the shoulder. "Thank you for the use of your hiking gear. I can already tell you, most of your supplies were rode hard and put away wet. I'm sorry, by the end . . ." I shrug. "That's one helluva tactical knife. I learned to love that blade. It's just as fierce as it looks."

"Keep it. It's yours."

"Thank you, but I'm not really a vicious-blade sort of gal. Though you should know, it's dull, filthy, and may or may not be expecting a bath in human blood. What can I say? When things went to shit, they really went to shit."

Josh's eyes widen.

I give him one last smile. Then I clutch my drafty gown close behind me and head back out into the corridor.

I WALK BY the ICU purely by chance. The nurse in charge informs me no visitors are allowed. But then, between my pathetic face and obvious connection to the tragic hiking party who are now monopolizing the hospital's resources, she relents. Grants me ten whole minutes.

I find Nemeth first. Marge Santi occupies the chair next to his bed, holding his hand. Of course. It was clear to me even from our brief interactions earlier that Marge was Nemeth's other half. Like calls to like, and these two seemed not just a logical pairing, but a natural fit.

I don't want to intrude. Marge is totally, completely fixated on Nemeth, as if she can single-handedly fix his wounds, will him to survive. I don't want to interrupt that kind of magical thinking and I'm not sure what to say anyway. Half of Nemeth seems to be covered in bandages, the other half hooked to machines. Luciana is right—it doesn't look good.

In the end, I offer up a mental salute. I'm not sure Nemeth ever liked me, but by the end he respected me. And if I was little more than a grunt on our expedition, well, he was one helluva general.

I discover Scott next. Compared to Nemeth, he's the picture of health. Except, of course, for the deathly pallor and the look on Neil's face as he sits curled up in a chair at the foot of the bed.

"Shouldn't you be resting?" I ask Neil sharply.

"Shhh." He turns his face toward me, his eyes scrunched tightly shut. Against the glaring light and nearly glowing white walls, I assume. I can barely handle it, and I haven't had my brains scrambled twice in twenty-four hours.

"How is he?" I ask more quietly.

"He kept me warm," Neil murmurs solemnly, his eyes still closed. "When night came, he folded himself around me. He said I could make it. Just wait, help would come. He didn't say the same about himself."

"But he did make it. You, too."

"Frankie? I never want to go into those mountains ever again."

"Okay."

"I want Scott to be better and Miguel to regain his health and Nemeth to recover. Then I want to go home to Anna, slip a ring on her finger, and never look back."

"Okay."

"Would you come to my wedding?"

"I will think of you on your wedding day," I promise him.

"I've decided not to wear a tux."

"Excellent."

"And there will be no groomsmen or bridesmaids. We'll do it our way."

"Perfect."

"That man, Martin really killed him?"

"I saw it with my own eyes."

"Good," Neil says fiercely. "Really fucking good."

I smile. "The police are going to need your help," I inform him gently. "With Martin's body and, eventually, with Tim's."

"Okay." No hesitation at all, just as I thought.

"Do you need anything more?" I ask him.

"For Scott to open his eyes. For Miguel to breathe on his own."

"From your lips to God's ears."

I stay with him a bit longer. Then I find a nurse who assures me I can sign out, but I definitely don't want my old clothes back, not to mention the police seized them all as evidence.

An hour later, I'm sitting in a rental car with Luciana at the wheel and Daisy grinning from the back seat. Luciana has brought me a clean pair of jeans, a T-shirt, and tennis shoes, items from my suitcase, which she must have commandeered. I had no idea I could be so grateful to be reunited with my meager belongings.

It's bright and sunny outside. I find that disorienting. It should be nighttime, but maybe that's just my mood. And so many people, milling about the parking lot, climbing into their vehicles. The world, still turning, as if nothing happened. As if eight people hadn't gone into the woods, but not all eight of them made it out again.

Luciana takes me straight to a hamburger joint. We order everything. Cheeseburgers, fries, milkshakes. Even Daisy has her own meal. I find myself nearly in tears over the concept of pulling up to a window and being handed hot food. If I ever do settle down, pick a residence, I'm gonna install one of these. Definitely.

After stuffing our faces—we eat at the same speed as Daisy, and I take pride in finishing first—we drive the hour back to Ramsey in near silence. The food resolved the first issue, leading to the second—bone-deep exhaustion.

Luciana leads me to the motel room. Same as before. Two double beds and simple adjoining bathroom that features hot water and indoor plumbing. Paradise.

Against the far wall sits an entire pile of backpacks.

"The search teams have been bringing them in," she tells me, following my line of sight. "No one was sure what to do with them, so I took over. When Miguel, Scott, Neil, and Nemeth get discharged from the hospital, I'll reunite them with their gear."

I nod, spying my own, or really Josh's. There's blood streaked on the outside. I don't look at the backpacks anymore.

"Shower," Luciana informs me. "Sleep. Drink tons and tons of water. Daisy and I have a SAR team debriefing. We'll be back shortly."

She hands me a key, stifling a yawn. Then she and Daisy backtrack to their car, leaving me alone.

I step into the bathroom. I shed my clothes and turn the shower on as hot as it can possibly get.

Then I climb feebly over the lip of the tub. I turn my face straight up into the needling spray. It stings my bruised and battered cheek but I don't care. I will the water to cleanse my body. Erase my mind. Free my soul.

But I won't forget. I never do. I just head for the next town.

I start to tremble then. I shake and I shake. I think of too many things. Past and present. Dreams and terrors. The things I still want. The things I can never have.

The water goes from hot to lukewarm to cold, and I never want to feel like I'm freezing again. It gives me the incentive to pull myself together and turn off the nozzle.

Towel dry. My own threadbare T-shirt, feeling like a long-lost lover against my skin.

I am okay.

I can handle this.

I will make it to the other side.

I finish drying my hair and go to bed.

CHAPTER 42

MY BODY IS DESPERATE FOR sleep. My brain will have nothing to do with it. I sink into the broken-down motel mattress. I pull the covers up tight and close my eyes.

And the kaleidoscope begins. Too many images. Blood and bullets. Pine trees and flashing knives. From an urban liquor store where Paul has died in my arms for the past ten years, to the deep woods where Bob perished just days ago. Location doesn't matter. Time doesn't matter.

My psyche has had enough. Each death is a loss. Each trauma a toll. Is there really a way to measure such things? The death of the man who loved me but I left is two times worse than a gregarious Bigfoot hunter getting cut down before my eyes? While watching a tree man slice into Miggy's chest is half as awful, and cradling a dying Boston gangster I never really knew is a quarter?

It's all macabre math. At a certain point, the spirit rebels against such horrors.

I give up on rest after an hour. Fucking squirrel brain, I think bitterly. Goddamn fate. Stupid life choices.

But mostly, I hurt.

And I can't bear to sleep in this kind of pain.

I pull my jeans and tennis shoes back on. I turn my back on the free room Luciana has graciously granted me and the bottled water she left next to my bed. People are kind. People are terrible. People hurt my head.

I grab the motel room key and walk out the door.

I wander down the sidewalk toward the picturesque part of Ramsey. Sun is starting to set. Tourists are out en masse. Happy couples, distracted families, laughing friends. So much energy. So much life.

I could stand in the middle of it forever and none of it would touch me.

This is my gift, this is my curse. I joined seven people I never knew, and within a matter of days, I learned, loved, and lost. And yet I'm a loner, belonging to no one.

I'm like a schizophrenic introvert. Does such a thing exist?

I find myself standing outside the steak house where Luciana, Bob, and I first shared dinner. There's a line of people out the door, in various stages of staring at their phones as they wait for their tables.

I want to scream at them to look up. I want to grab them by their shoulders and demand they not take a ridiculously huge and scrumptious plate of food for granted. I want to fall to my knees and beg them to remember this moment, when nothing in their body ached and their biggest worry was what to order for dinner.

I want a drink.

It comes out of nowhere. It comes from deep inside.

I stand on the sidewalk, hands fisted at my sides, and fight the impulse.

This is the irony of the disease—to pass on a drink at death's door, only to succumb once I'm still breathing. But this is the nature of me. I don't need a drink to die. But it often feels like I need a drink to live.

Mostly, I need a drink to escape being me.

I turn away from the steak house. I shuffle down Main Street, each footstep more painful than the last. It takes me a while to realize people are staring at me. That my black eye and limping gait aren't exactly subtle. When the fifth family veers wide and tucks their children closer to them, I give up and head back to the motel. Screw happy, well-adjusted people. I can wallow on my own.

I can't. The motel room is too empty, the bed too daunting. I need to settle. I still don't know how.

I pay a visit to the registration desk. It's manned by a pimply-faced young man whom I'm already guessing graduated from the local high school and is very sorry to still be living here.

"Hey," I manage.

"Hey," he repeats, though his eyes are wide at my straight-out-of-hell appearance.

"I'm looking for a laundromat."

"Okay."

"Walking distance. Well, short walking distance." I glance down at my throbbing ankle.

"You're one of them."

"Who them?"

"The group. You went into the mountains looking for the dead dude. Except then more dead dudes happened." Pimply Face's eyes widen further. "I shouldn'ta said that."

"You're not wrong. Yeah, I'm a member of that party. And I inherited everyone's packs, which is to say, a shitload of dirty clothes. We're talking sweat-soaked, dirt-covered, and blood-spattered."

My instincts are correct. Gore is totally this guy's vibe.

"Well, you know, given the circumstances, I could make an exception . . ."

I nod encouragingly.

"We don't normally let guests use the motel's machines. But we got a coupla commercial-grade washer and dryers in the basement."

I nod again.

"You wanna, you know, gather up what you need to wash? Then I could personally show you the machines, get you set up."

And this kid could get an inside scoop on what has to be the hottest story in town.

I'm not opposed. Everyone likes to have the social 411 and this is pure gold. The motel clerk didn't make the system; he's just trying to survive it. I respect that.

"I'll be back in thirty," I propose.

The dude practically levitates. "Good deal!"

I have to smile. At least one of us is happy. Then I limp painfully back to Luciana's room, and the pile of backpacks that started out days ago as fresh equipment, and are now a tribute to the injured, the dying, and the dead.

MY IDEA IS to launder the dirty clothes. It's not a well-thought-out or detailed plan. I know simply that most of us destroyed many wardrobe items. Given my agitated, restless state, cleaning those articles of clothing is something to do. I will whip each pack into some semblance of order, so when it's finally reunited with its rightful owner, it's not a complete horror show.

I start with my own pack—which is to say Josh's—pulling out the sweat- and dirt-saturated clothing that I borrowed from Luciana. Some items I stuffed into my abandoned sleeping bag as we staged the base camp before leaving. But I destroyed several more items after that. And what isn't specifically dirty doesn't exactly pass the sniff test.

In the end, I determine every clothing article in every pack will need to be washed. This approach is going to lead to one helluva laundry pile, but it's not like I have anything better to do.

I settle in on the floor of the motel room. Grab a pack. Empty out the clothes. Peruse the rest of the contents. I discover empty granola wrappers, plundered first aid kits, used water bottles.

I create piles. Laundry. Garbage. Dishwashing. It's work, and work is good. More time doing, less time thinking.

I tire quickly but, being the obsessive sort, can't stop. I recognize most packs by color. I subscribe to no kind of order. I grab whichever pack is closest.

Realistically speaking, I'll never get each pack reassembled with the correct items. I discover I don't care. This project isn't really about gear, laundry, or proper ownership. It's about saving me from me.

I reach the bottom of the final pack. I remove a glass jar partially filled with white tubes. I don't understand it. It's definitely not food and clearly not first aid. There's a label covered in incredibly tiny print.

It takes me a moment to read it all.

Then I have to sit back.

I think I might vomit.

I know, but I don't want to know. Memories go flying through my head. Things I thought were one thing, but now I realize were another. It all makes sense, and yet it defies understanding.

I stare at the backpack for a very long time, as if it's the one who betrayed me.

Then I slowly rise to standing.

A calm has settled over me.

I have work to do.

CHAPTER 43

ANY CHILD OF AN ADDICT knows what it feels like to be lied to. "I swear I'll never do it again." "I promise this is my last drink." "Of course I won't make a scene." From backyard camping that never happened to a million missed events. You learn to ride the ride.

But that doesn't make it any easier to take.

Night has fallen. At the first contact with the chilly air, I physically recoil, my heartbeat accelerating, a sense of panic building in my chest. What had Neil said about his PTSD being triggered by men in tuxes? I guess mine is now the cold.

I return to the room for my beloved army coat. While I'm at it, I find myself tucking a small flashlight in one pocket, a butane lighter in another. Then helping myself to someone else's rigged-out paracord bracelet for my wrist. I have access to my own emergency whistle, which feels like a long-lost friend. I hesitate over one last item. Then I just have to do it.

I grab the scary serious tactical blade I told Josh I didn't want and strap it to my waist, beneath the cover of my jacket.

The weight of it is instantly reassuring. My breathing eases, my panic recedes. I feel complete.

Maybe I'm a deadly-knife kind of gal after all.

I need information. I usually meticulously research my target destinations. I never did that for Ramsey, and now look at me, covered in giant splotches of violent purple while hobbling around like a hundred-year-old woman. I might be impulsive, obsessive, and a tad self-destructive, but normally I try to be smart about it.

This time of night, no public libraries or internet cafés will be open. Which leaves me with one option. Wrapping my arms around my torso for warmth, I limp back to the front office.

Pimply Face looks up immediately from the counter. His face brightens when he spots me, then falls when he realizes I'm not carrying the promised blood-spattered laundry.

"I decided it was too late to start now," I offer by way of explanation. "Can I still use the machines in the morning?"

"I don't know." He's definitely disappointed. "My shift ends at midnight. Can't promise what the next person will be willing to do."

"What's your name?"

"Seth."

"Hi, Seth. I'm Frankie Elkin. Pleased to officially meet you."

This cheers him up. I continue. "I totally understand what you're saying about permission to use the washers and dryers. I guess I'll just have to hope the next desk clerk is as helpful as you have been."

Seth's expression says, Don't bet on it.

"If it's not too much, I do have another favor to ask. I need access to a computer. Like, right now. I don't suppose there's one in the back office I could use?"

"Why do you need a computer?"

"Well, you know, to let family and friends know I'm all right. Figure out my next steps. That sort of thing."

"Why don't you just use your phone?"

I produce my cheap flip phone and hold it up for his inspection. He nearly recoils in horror.

"Seriously? I didn't know they made those anymore."

"I could use an upgrade."

I remain standing there patiently. This time of night, there's no real activity, meaning it's just him and me, and he's clearly anxious to be part of something bigger.

He takes a full minute. I count the seconds in my mind. It's a fair shot at trying to make the management-approved decision. My respect for him ratchets up another notch. Then he caves.

"I guess I could set you up on the office computer with my password. But you can't tell, okay? No ratting me out to my boss."

"Wouldn't dream of it, Seth."

I walk around the raised counter to the area behind, where sure enough, there's a door leading to a small office. Admin space. The computer sits smack in the middle of a sea of paper. Forget my research project. My biggest challenge will be not knocking anything to the floor.

Seth leans over the keyboard, taps a number of keys. Then he launches the computer's browser, and just like that, I'm ready to roll.

"You're not going to visit porn sites, are you?"

"Can I at least watch one adorably cute cat video?"

He rolls his eyes, then after an awkward moment, when it becomes clear the only way for him to leave and for me to enter is for him to squeeze by me, he does the world's most nervous sidestep.

"Thank you," I tell him honestly.

He blushes, ducks his head. "Just, uh, just yell if you need anything."

He returns to his post at the reception desk.

I start typing.

LIKE ANY COLD case investigator, I specialize in digging up information, especially old and seemingly irrelevant details. Local papers, with their archives of years past, are a gold mine, though fewer and fewer exist.

I'm lucky this area still has one. It enables me to start out smoking hot and downright cocky. Then I hit the first dead end. Then another and another.

But I'm obsessive, and it's not like I'm going to sleep anyway. Pass out cold, maybe, but rest?

It's not possible anymore.

Shortly after ten, I find a record of what I'm looking for.

"Is it okay to print?" I call out to Seth.

He's only too happy to be of assistance again, especially as now both of us are wedged into the tiny space and he gets to rub against me several times as he revs the printer to life and feeds it additional paper.

I hit "print." Seconds later, I snatch up the documents before he has a chance to see them.

More thank-yous, more goodbyes, then I'm on my way.

I can barely walk, my muscles having stiffened up while I was sitting, and my feet, at first enthusiastic to rediscover tennis shoes, now scream in agony. Which pisses me off, because forget walking, I should be running right now.

Instead, I hobble along, teeth gritted against the pain.

It's time to ask for my next favor.

———

LUCIANA AND DAISY are back in the room when I enter. Daisy is sprawled on the bed nearest to me. She lifts her head at my entrance, thumping her tail and yawning impressively.

"Good to see you, too," I assure her. Then, because the dog did save my life, I give her a good scratching behind the ears.

"I see you've been busy," Luciana comments, gesturing to the formal lineup of gutted backpacks, each with its contents spewed out in front of it. Then, of course, there's the pile of sweaty, dirty clothes, which isn't doing wonders for the air in the room.

"I thought I'd get everyone's gear sorted. Do something useful."

"Is that the burn pile?" She points to the laundry heap.

"Exactly."

"Frankie, you need to rest. Your body is nowhere near recovered. Hell, Daisy and I are nowhere near recovered and all we did was sprint down a mountain after a brief interval of captivity."

"Are you two headed back to Devil's Canyon tomorrow?"

"No. There's more than enough cooks in the kitchen now. And Daisy and I need to recuperate, both physically and mentally. That first day, when we finally emerged from the woods, knowing the rest of you remained stranded and vulnerable at base camp . . . we had to go back. Till each and every one of you was rescued. We weren't stopping before then."

"But still no Martin," I venture, with just enough question in my voice. I'm very curious about her answer but don't want to show it.

"A party has been assembled to start scouring the ravine tomorrow. But from what I saw on the map, that's gonna be a total bitch. Hard to access and almost impossible to navigate given the heavily wooded terrain. Better them than me."

I nod. "So we'll return to the hospital in the morning?"

"Exactly. I'll tell you a secret—Daisy isn't allowed in, not being a service dog. But I put her in her black work vest, then waltz in like we have every right to be there, and no one bats an eye. The fact she's adorable and well behaved helps, too."

"Thank you for coming back," I murmur. "Thank you for not giving up, for returning to Devil's Canyon even though you had to be exhausted. Thank you for saving Miguel and me."

The words come out thicker than I intended. I can feel my eyes welling up. I'm exhausted. I do need to recover. Luciana's right— we're all going to need time to process. But not yet. Not for me.

Luciana regards me with her rich brown eyes. They hold a sheen of moisture as well. "Anytime, my friend," she says quietly. "Anytime."

Then, while the mood is still warm and fuzzy, I hit her with the question I really wanted to ask from the very beginning.

"Can I borrow your car?"

LUCIANA TRIES TO refuse. I shouldn't be going out, there's no kind of errand that can't wait till morning. But in the end, my unwavering patience wears her down. She slams the keys into my hand. Orders me to be careful, then watches me with genuine concern as I leave the comfort of the motel.

I feel like I'm aging exponentially, gaining more aches and pains by the minute as my body speeds up breaking down.

After this, I will need to sleep forever.

But not right now.

It takes me several tries to find what I'm looking for. I have to pull over, regard the printed map by flashlight, set out again. Then, shortly after midnight, I'm there. It takes me another nerve-racking, horrifying hour to confirm what I suspected.

Back to the motel, where the room is now pitch-black and silent, broken only by the rumbling sounds of Daisy's snoring, I remove my coat, fumble with the tactical blade at my waist. Then, the trickiest part, bending over and slowly easing my sneakers off my feet.

When I finally manage to straighten, I'm done. There's not another ounce of energy left in me. I collapse back fully clothed.

I close my eyes and will myself to sleep.

Tomorrow will be hard enough.

CHAPTER 44

IN THE MORNING, I WAIT till we arrive at the hospital before making my next request.

"Sheriff Kelley will be arriving in about thirty minutes. Can you and Daisy meet him when he gets here?"

"Why? What are you up to, Frankie?"

I ignore Luciana's question. I made two calls while she was in the shower: one to the hospital, one to the sheriff's department. Both were useful.

"Text me when you and he are together in the lobby. My Tracfone doesn't make these things easy, so my reply will be short. But it'll matter."

"What's going on? Talk to me, Frankie. I'll help."

"You will," I assure her. "Just not yet."

She huffs out a breath but relents. We hit the diner first thing in the morning, ordering two of everything. But my appetite gave out long before the food did. I'm like that when I'm nervous.

Daisy trots happily between us as we cross the parking lot. Just the sight of her search uniform has her energized and ready to go. Luciana is right: The dog loves her work. Daisy also recovers much more quickly than her human counterparts.

We stop at the main desk, signing in as guests. True to Luciana's prediction, no one questions Daisy's presence. Of course, Daisy looks especially charming today as she tilts her head to the side and offers an enormous doggy grin.

I head straight to Miguel's room, shuffling along as fast as I can. I spy Neil still folded into the guest chair, his short brown hair sticking straight up. Somewhere along the way he gained a blanket as well as wraparound sunglasses.

But the real surprise is when I walk into the room and Miguel is sitting up in bed.

"Hey," he says.

The wash of emotion that floods through me . . . I can't speak, can't move, can't breathe. I stare at him, mesmerized by the sight of his patched-up face.

"I thought you died," I hear myself say.

"I thought I did, too."

"You were shaking so hard with the cold. Then you weren't anymore."

"I remember you touching my hair. I remember being grateful that at least we were together."

Now I am going to cry. I suck in the tears, finally moving bedside so I can touch his hand, his cheek, his hair. I repeat the process twice.

"I think I'm all here," Miggy assures me, "but only because every inch of me hurts."

"Me, too!" Then we laugh and it feels good again. Nearly normal, and after such an intense experience, normal is exactly what everyone needs.

"I'm feeling better, too." Neil speaks up from the chair.

"Nice shades."

"Nurse brought them for me. I will treasure them always."

"Your families?" I ask, being careful not to divulge Neil's secret by mentioning Anna's name.

"My parents are arriving later this morning," Miguel offers up. "Funny—they ran into a woman in the airport who also mentioned having to make an emergency trip to Wyoming to assist with an injured friend. Apparently, she's dating this dude named Neil. Been together for years. She's madly in love with him and beside herself with worry. At least that's what my mom said."

Neil, from behind me: "Oh, about that . . ."

I give Miggy's hand a final squeeze, then leave him and Neil to sort through the mess.

When I phoned earlier, I was given another piece of good news: Scott had been upgraded to stable and moved out of intensive care. Now I ease open the door of his room. He's sound asleep, tucked in tightly in the middle of the bed. His color looks better, the rise and fall of his chest steady. A huge bandage obscures most of his right shoulder, but he's still with us. Against the odds, he survived those damn mountains after all.

Latisha didn't have to go through that phone call again.

I tiptoe back out and turn around just in time to collide with Josh, who's dressed in street clothes.

"You got bored with bare-assed life?" I ask him.

"Not nearly as comfortable as I thought." He nods toward Scott. "How is he?"

"Sound asleep. Definitely looks better than yesterday."

Josh nods.

"How are you?"

He doesn't answer right away, the silent one being asked to

speak up. Finally: "Managed to start the day with a cup of coffee instead of a shot of tequila."

"That's excellent, Josh. One day at a time."

"Yeah. Got that."

The polite thing to do now would be to inform him I'm also an alcoholic and tell him he can call me anytime. But I don't. One of the first things you learn in recovery is to set boundaries. I'm in no position to prop up Josh during a weak moment. I can barely prop up myself.

My Tracfone chimes. My cue to depart.

"I'll try to visit later when Scott's awake," I assure him, then turn back down the long glaring-white corridor. I pull out my phone. Sure enough, on the tiny screen:

We're ready.

I take a steadying breath, then pat my coat pocket to make sure I still have what I need.

I pause just long enough to text back, *Fredericka.*

Then I push through the ICU doors.

CHAPTER 45

NEMETH LOOKS MUCH THE SAME when I ease myself into the room. I'd heard he'd regained consciousness briefly in the middle of the night, which was a positive sign. Now, however, he appears like a human mummy, most parts of his body bandaged or casted, while machines beep and whir around him.

Marge Santi still occupies the chair next to him. Like Neil, she seems to have slept there overnight. Probably a violation of most ICU rules, but things seem looser here.

She is why I called this morning.

Marge is who I'm truly coming to see.

"How is he?" I murmur as I creep into the space. The wall behind her contains a giant window, allowing the staff to monitor their fragile charges. Standing on the other side of Nemeth's bed, I can see Marge and anyone who enters the ICU. I slip my right hand into my coat pocket. My tender shoulder squawks, but I ignore it.

"He made it through the night," Marge allows quietly. She looks terrible. Drawn features, bruised eyes. She must really, truly love him.

"How long have the two of you been together?"

She smiles wanly at my acknowledgment of their relationship. "Twenty years. But we've known each other most our lives. Grew up here. Some of the last few true locals in these parts."

I nod, edging closer to the bed. I can't see what I'm doing, having to go by feel to slip the small tube out of my pocket and tuck it under the section of top sheet closest to me. I'd removed the cap since first exiting the lobby, letting the open vial trail with me through the hospital.

"You a hiker, too?"

"When I can. Though running the diner and all . . ."

"Hunter?" I ask casually.

Marge nods absently. "Sure. Grew up hunting with my dad. Still tag a buck from time to time."

The main doors of the ICU are thrust open. The charge nurse is just opening her mouth to object when Daisy comes barreling through, Sheriff Kelley and Luciana hot on her heels. The sheriff is frowning; Luciana is confused. The nurse throws up a hand as if to stop them. One look at the sheriff's face and she backs off quickly.

A second later, paws scrabble urgently at the door of Nemeth's room. The low whine of a dog.

I don't move. I just watch Marge's face as Luciana quickly pushes open the barrier and Daisy darts in, head moving, moving, moving. She sniffs at me, then zeroes in on the bed.

Then she sits.

Holds up a paw.

Stares at Nemeth intently.

Luciana draws up short. It's crowded with both her and the

sheriff trying to squeeze into the space. The nurse is now in the hallway, clearly at a loss for what to do.

Luciana focuses on me. "I don't understand."

"Daisy is a good dog. She found her target. You can reward her now."

Sheriff Kelley is more succinct. "That man is not dead."

"No, but his mattress is."

I withdraw the tiny tube, hold it up. Daisy whines, her gaze never leaving it as I hand it over to Luciana.

"What is this?" Then, as she reads the label: "Pseudo-Corpse Scent. This is synthetic decomp for cadaver dog training. Why the hell do you have synthetic decomp?"

"The real question is, why did Nemeth have synthetic decomp? I found that in his pack. Survival gear I get. But eau de decomp?"

My gaze is still on Marge. Her weathered face has gone blank. She is sitting perfectly still.

Luciana eyes the two of us, the tension now clear in the room. "Okay." Luciana murmurs the release command to Daisy, who reluctantly slinks back to her. Daisy should be getting her reward toy and heaps of praise right now. But even the canine seems to understand there's something else going on here.

I address my comments to Marge: "Your sister is the first one who went missing. Nearly twenty years ago, in fact."

The diner owner doesn't say anything. The sheriff doesn't interrupt, letting me play it out.

"I'm not an expert in murder," I comment casually. "I'm about missing persons because, God help me, I really can't stand gore. But I've watched enough crime shows to know that when it comes to serial killers, the first victim is always the most important."

"I don't know what you're talking about," Marge manages.

"You need to leave, all of you. Nemeth is already at death's door. Hiding the smell of a cadaver in his bed? Is this your idea of a joke?"

"Now," I continue as if she'd never spoken, "we don't know the identities of the bodies in Devil's Canyon yet. That will take some time, right, Sheriff?"

He nods.

"But, from the moment I arrived in Ramsey, I've been hearing about at least six people who've disappeared around here. Old missing persons cases, new discovery of human remains. This is an equation I understand. Last night I looked up articles on the various persons who'd vanished. Which brought me to a local case. Jessica Santi. Your sister."

"That was a terrible tragedy. No need to bring it up—"

"Was it an accident the first time? Maybe you and your sister were hunting together in the woods and your gun went off? Or you two got into a fight and in the heat of the moment you pulled the trigger?"

"Stop it—"

"You got your parents' log cabin out of it, you becoming the sole heir and all. Is such a thing worth killing over? I wasn't sure. So I went to check it out last night."

Marge goes pale. She opens her mouth; nothing comes out.

"My car," Luciana mutters.

The sheriff is watching us all intently. I notice he has his hands close to his gun. If Marge has killed as many people as I think she has, that's a good call.

"Did you call your longtime friend Nemeth, guru of all things wilderness, to help you out? Was it his idea to hide your sister's body in Devil's Canyon, a place few visit and where even fewer probably know about the hidden spaces beneath the rocks?"

Marge doesn't speak.

"Is that how the two of you became lovers?" I venture further, genuinely curious. "You bonded over your sister's dead body? Nothing like a shared secret to bring a couple close. But you didn't stop there. The two of you . . . the need to protect your sister's grave from discovery, frustration with the tourists taking over your town. You did it again. And again. And again.

"That morning, when Timothy O'Day's friends ran into your diner looking for help, they had no idea what they were handing you and your lover. Not your next mountain rescue, but your next victim."

I can hear a slight change in the machine behind me. Nemeth regaining consciousness? I think he should. I think he owes us that much.

"Marge," Sheriff Kelley interjects now, voice stern. "Is this true? You know we have forensic experts crawling all over the damn place. They're gonna figure it out. Better to speak up now, when I'm still in a position to help you out. Because once the FBI arrives . . ."

"I have no idea what she's talking about," Marge delivers in clipped tones. "I think the poor girl's still suffering from the trauma of her experience. Which is why novices have no business hiking through backcountry."

"Your parents' hunting cabin, Marge. I visited it, remember? I also possibly broke into it. But you didn't hear that from me, Sheriff," I add quickly. "Another thing everyone knows from crime novels: Serial killers always take trophies. Those bodies. All of them missing their clothes, backpacks, possibly jewelry. Had to go somewhere."

A single tremor runs down Marge's spine.

I turn my attention to the sheriff. "Send your deputies, notify the feds—hell, send in the marshals. But on that property, you'll find everything you're looking for. Doesn't Wyoming have the death penalty? Feds do. Trust me, Marge, this novice will happily return just to watch you fry."

"Damn you," Marge says, staring straight at me. I can see it then, the coldness of her gaze, the pure predator's gaze.

"I don't understand." Luciana speaks up. "How did you get from synthetic decomp to all this?"

"Why would Nemeth have such a thing in his pack?" I shrug. "The only reason I could come up with was to throw off Daisy. Remember how all this started—with fairly innocuous acts of sabotage. Basically, trying to get Martin to call off the expedition to Devil's Canyon, then when that failed, trying to force us to turn back. I think the synthetic scent was plan C. If we did start searching that area, Nemeth would use it to distract Daisy, confuse the issue. You said Daisy did catch scent at the boulder field but became disoriented. When I finally discovered the chamber, I couldn't imagine why Daisy wouldn't have found it—her specialty is rubble piles.

"Which meant Nemeth had to be part of what was going on. Except he was at the other end of the canyon when Neil got hurt. And you talked about feeling like someone was watching you that day, but Nemeth was right beside you. Plus, all the various incidents, the scope of the terrain covered . . . One person couldn't do all that.

"Once I accepted Nemeth's involvement, Marge became his logical partner in crime. Then, when I discovered the first missing hiker was Marge's sister—no way that's a coincidence."

I turn to Luciana. "I'm guessing she's the one who attacked you. Her job was to eliminate you while Nemeth returned to the cliff face. He must've had a second bag stashed away with his hunter's garb, rifle, other weapons. Hence he left his hiking pack behind. But it didn't go quite as they planned. Daisy escaped, forcing Marge to chase her—a fruitless enterprise. Then Marge had the second task of booby-trapping base camp with the stolen food. By the time she returned to where she'd left you tied up, you'd managed to escape. Which put their plan in immediate jeopardy."

I return to Marge, monitoring the expression on her face. I'm guessing about a lot of this, filling in the gaps with what makes the most sense. Given her rigid spine and hostile gaze, I'm doing a pretty good job of it.

"At that point, you hightailed it back to town," I provide. "You had to reestablish yourself as diner owner Marge while monitoring what Luciana and the sheriff did next. Did you worry about Nemeth?" I ask her. "Taking on seven people all by himself? Or like him, did you assume we were easy prey? Martin got him in the end. I don't know how Nemeth managed to survive the fall or crawl out of the ravine. I'm assuming you must've helped him? Maybe he had one of those fancy coats with built-in GPS. You used it to locate him, then assist him to the trail, where you could call for the other searchers while pretending to have just found him. I'm guessing you hid his crazy face coverings and other gear. It won't matter. The police have his clothes, which will be incriminating enough. His reinforced military pants will bear the marks from my knife. His shirt will have a bullet hole from Miggy's gun. Between what's in your log cabin and his own wardrobe, there's more than enough evidence."

"Nemeth is the one always in the woods. I have a diner to run," Marge clips out. "Like you said, we're a couple. Of course he has access to my parents' hunting cabin. What he does while he's there and I'm at work, how am I supposed to know of such things?"

"Throwing him under the bus, Marge? You love him, but not enough to save his ass? Or is this just what you two do—survival of the fittest?"

A sound. I look to the side and Nemeth's eyes are open. Those piercing blue eyes that reminded me of glaciers and open sky. Not from the wilderness but of the wilderness. More so than anyone knew.

"How could you do it?" I can't help myself. "Killing strangers is awful enough. But you knew Martin. You spent years with him, and still you lined up the rifle sights and pulled the trigger. Planning the ambush of Luciana—would you have killed Daisy, too, if she hadn't run off?"

Luciana flinches, reaches for Daisy reflexively.

"Bob. You murdered one of the nicest guys on the planet. Who'd worked alongside you to keep our party safe. Then Neil, Scott, Miguel, myself. You're no wild predator. You're a snake."

Nemeth blinks his eyes. I see no remorse. I see no emotion at all. He did what he did. What happened, happened.

It breaks something inside me. That he could do so much damage and feel nothing at all.

I don't stop to think. I recognized the morphine pump next to his bed immediately. Now it gives me great pleasure to rip the drug-delivering IV port right out of his arm.

Blood sprays. IV fluid pours out of the severed line. Marge bolts upright as a machine starts blaring.

"Hey now," the sheriff says, but doesn't wave in a nurse or take a step forward.

I keep staring at Nemeth. I want to see it. The moment the tidal wave of pain slams into him. I want him to cry and beg. I want him to know I did this to him. The pathetic woman who could barely hike and had zero wilderness experience.

Survival of the fittest, my ass.

It's adaptability that's key.

Outside in the corridor, medical personnel have started gathering and demanding entrance. Luciana doesn't move aside any more than the sheriff does. While before me, Nemeth twitches. Writhes. His teeth peel back with the effort not to scream.

"Stop it! Stop it stop it stop it!"

I ignore Marge, leaning over close. "Miguel and I beat you. Scott, Neil, Bob, Luciana. We all beat you. And Martin. In the clash of the titans, he took you out. You're no legend anymore. You're just a gutless, pathetic loser who had to shoot at his targets from far away to get the job done."

Nemeth groans. It's a deep, rumbling sound torn from his chest. I don't think it's pain. I think it's rage. It still makes me happy.

"I did it!" Marge, desperate now. "Blame me, arrest me. I shot everyone, did everything. My sister and I had a fight. I just couldn't take her whining anymore so I pulled the trigger. And yes, at first I was horrified; I called Nemeth for help. He knew about the underground chambers in Devil's Canyon and suggested we hide her body there, given its remoteness. But then the location became more popular, hikers not just passing through, but starting to hang out. The second woman, she was a geologist, curious about the rock piles and how they were formed. Nemeth had no choice. And then a few years after that, and eight years after that . . ." Marge's voice drifts off.

"When Tim was first reported missing, his starting location was far enough away, we weren't worried. But once it became clear he'd made it beyond that area and Nemeth started theorizing other routes the man might've taken . . . We waited two weeks, then hiked into Devil's Canyon overnight, when no one would know. Sure enough. The kid was camping out in one of the caves. And come morning, he started exploring the rock piles, checking out some of the underground chambers. We made our decision. What had to happen, had to happen."

My stomach roils. Nemeth moans in distress.

"Please. I confessed. Now help him!"

"Oh, I think there's plenty of confessing still to come," the sheriff says, taking Marge by the arm and snapping on handcuffs.

Luciana finally moves to the side, Daisy tucked beside her. The first nurse rushes in, two other staff members right behind her. They take inventory of the blood-spattered wall and fluid-soaked sheets, then shove me back.

"What did you do?" the nurse demands.

"Just sent him a little love from Timothy O'Day."

"Get the hell out!" the nurse orders.

"But Bob has some love to deliver, too."

I am forcefully pushed out of the room, where I join Luciana and Daisy in the corridor. The sheriff is holding Marge by one shackled arm, already on his radio issuing orders. Her gaze remains fixed on the viewing window, staring at her lover, who is now thrashing wildly as more alarms begin to shriek.

I recognize the look on her face. She is willing him to live. I know, because I did the same thing just a few days ago with Bob. I should say I want her to suffer the same result, but I'm actually crueler than that. I want Nemeth to make it. I want the wilderness legend to spend the rest of his life locked in a tiny cell with only one hour of fresh air a day.

The nights my restless brain takes over, I plan on picturing him there, then sleeping like a baby.

"I can't believe it," Luciana murmurs beside me. "I liked Nemeth, respected him. I thought we were friends." She is stroking the top of Daisy's head. The subdued Lab leans into her.

"We both need a new hobby," I agree.

Luciana regards me earnestly. "Remain in Ramsey for a bit. Stay with me and Daisy, my treat. We could use the company."

I don't answer as we follow Sheriff Kelley and his new prisoner out of the ICU. Marge doesn't turn around, but walks with her head held high, gaze straight ahead. I'm tempted to go to prison just to watch the other inmates break her.

"The feds are going to want to grill both of us," I acknowledge finally. "And I would like to see Miguel and Scott released from the hospital. Not to mention we should meet Latisha. Have you seen her? I'm expecting full-on goddess to have captured so many hearts."

"Exactly. And afterwards we can eat our way through Ramsey and take naps three times a day and use up all the hot water."

"You drive a hard bargain."

"That's it. I'm booking a room for a week, and someplace way swankier than a budget motel. We deserve room service, a soaking tub, and a big-ass TV. I'll even insist on extra dog treats for Daisy. She's worth it."

Luciana's enthusiasm makes me smile. She paints such a pretty picture, everything I fantasized about just two days ago.

She's only missing one thing: a certain detective I once knew in Boston and have never spoken to since.

If I dialed his number right now, would he answer? If he did, would I stay on the phone?

Luciana is happy. She already has her cell out, looking up hotels. I lag behind till I come to a small alcove where I can duck out of sight.

I tell myself I'm not exhausted or heartsick or world-weary.

I instruct myself that there's still a missing eight-year-old boy waiting for me to take up his case.

I remind myself I need to track down Bob's husband. I have to tell him how Bob died saving the rest of us. I must deliver Bob's dying words of love.

I feel a break then. Something deep inside, tearing away. I don't think I'll get it back again.

I push away from the wall. I resume shuffling forward.

Miguel ordered me to run.

But I'm not sure I have many more steps left in me after all.

EPILOGUE

LUCIANA FINDS A TOP-FLOOR SUITE of a gorgeous B&B where the owners love dogs and are so appreciative of her and Daisy's work that they comp the room half price. The bathroom features a claw-foot tub. We fill it to the brim multiple times a day. And eat every crumb of food they graciously send up to the room. The wife is a baker, allowing for a steady stream of muffins, scones, and fancy breads. Even Daisy exists in a state of bliss.

Neil is discharged two days later. We join him and Anna for their first meal together out of the hospital. Halfway through our enchiladas, Neil gets down on one knee, pulls out a makeshift ring he fashioned from his hospital bracelet, and pops the question. She squeals yes. They both jump to their feet. The entire restaurant applauds and another table sends over a pitcher of margaritas to celebrate the happy event. I drink my ice water and dab moisture from the corner of my eye.

Miguel gets to leave the hospital next. It's a regular festival in the parking lot. I meet his parents and tell his father how hard he fought to save his friends' lives. Then we hug and we cry and when they're finally ready to depart, they beg me to visit. *Mi casa, su casa*, and all that.

I smile and nod. Miguel leans over long enough to whisper in my ear, "I know you won't, but just remember, someone in Oregon loves you."

Which makes me cry a little more, though I'm terribly weepy these days.

Luciana and I meet Latisha. And she is gorgeous, a six-foot-tall former college volleyball player who radiates energy and health even seven months pregnant. From her curly black hair to her sculpted cheekbones, she rivals Luciana for jaw-dropping beauty. Latisha starts by clutching our hands in gratitude, then gives up and pulls us both in for a tight, teary embrace.

Scott, still pale and weak, but doing better each day, smiles in near embarrassment. Later, out in the hall, Latisha grows more somber. She thanks us for finding Tim as well. She blesses us for finally bringing her first love home.

Scott and Latisha don't go with the big exit, but instead, one week later, quietly slip away. I don't blame them. I imagine they need time together as a family to heal, reconnect, and relish their new life, about to begin.

I get to talk to the feds a lot. And Sheriff Kelley. Plus even more stern-looking people in suits. They mostly seem suspicious as to how I became part of the expedition. I think that's beside the point. It's not the beginning that mattered. It was the end.

It will take months to identify all eight mummified corpses, but the ME's department releases Bob's remains by the end of the week.

Luciana and I drive out to meet his husband, Rob, who turns out to be an elegantly garbed Italian with neatly trimmed dark hair and striking wire-rim glasses. He is both smaller than I would've thought and very serious. His hand shakes so badly while trying to sign the paperwork accepting his husband's body, I have to steady his arm. Together, we escort the plain pine casket to a local mortuary, where Rob has arranged for the body to be cremated. Later, Rob will scatter Bob's ashes somewhere on the Olympic Peninsula, a fitting resting place for a man who spent his life chasing Bigfoot.

I deliver as best I can the story of Bob. How in his final moments, he took on a man carrying a rifle with nothing more than bear spray, so that the rest of us might have a chance. I tell him Bob died thinking of his husband and how much he loved him. Rob doesn't cry. His deep brown eyes are wells of sorrow that just go on and on.

When Rob finally accepts the plain urn containing the ashes of the largest, bravest man I've ever met, I can barely stand up. Luciana has to help me back to the car. We drive to our B&B in silence. There I wrap my arms around Daisy and bury my face in her fur while Luciana goes to fill the tub.

I think too much of Bob and his final moments. Not just his words for his husband, but his advice to me. To go find what I'm really looking for.

Is it a shot at a different sort of life?

Is it a chance at a real relationship with a cop I can't get out of my head?

Or is it me that I have lost along the way?

I have no idea.

The police raid Marge's hunting cabin. They find the various colored backpacks, hung up in two rows of four in the back room. Nothing too conspicuous, given her and Nemeth's outdoor hobbies. Except the packs don't belong to them, of course.

Most of the contents have been removed, probably pillaged as supplies. But in a separate lockbox, the investigators recover personal mementos belonging to the eight victims. Pieces of jewelry. Driver's licenses.

And in the case of Timothy O'Day, a note. The one he'd been working on that night, sitting by the fire. It's not a draft of his wedding vows, as his friends suspected. It's a letter to them. Telling them how much he valued their friendship. And how he could not have become the man he was today, the man his future bride deserved, without their help along the way.

There are additional scratchings that must've been made later. Stating he got lost. Referring to arriving in a canyon and having taken shelter in a cave.

Telling his parents he loved them.

Telling Latisha not to worry, he'd be home shortly.

Telling his friends he was sorry, nothing had gone the way he planned and he hoped to make it up to them.

Second to the last line: *Tomorrow I'm going to try to climb out of here.*

Final line: *I love you all. Hope to see you soon.*

The police can't release the letter, as the original will be used at trial. But I convince Sheriff Kelley to make six copies. One for each of the college friends, plus one for Latisha, and then a final one, which Neil promises to hand deliver to Patrice.

Martin's body is eventually recovered from the ravine. The number of bullet wounds he sustained . . . How the man ever stalked Nemeth through the woods, let alone found the strength for that final attack, defies imagination.

Upon receiving the news, Luciana and I somberly tend to our final and most difficult chore. We call Patrice via FaceTime and in between bouts of tears we tell her how Martin never gave up. That despite increasingly difficult circumstances, he forged on, determined to bring their son home to her. That he told us she was the great love of his life while remembering Tim with such pride and devotion. That Martin considered himself a lucky man for having such an amazing family.

Martin died honoring the memory of their son, but he also died knowing they would all be together soon.

On the screen, Patrice's face is impossibly pale, her bald head wrapped in a flowered scarf. She dabs at her blue eyes, thanks us for our report. Then she smiles, so bittersweet, I feel my heart break in my chest all over again.

She says she knew Martin wouldn't fail. He promised her he'd find Tim, and Martin never lied. She thanks us for delivering these final memories of her husband and her son. She apologizes that we came to harm, as that's the last thing she and Martin ever wanted or expected.

I tell her Martin saved my life.

She smiles and says that makes perfect sense, as Martin saved her life, too. And made all of it worth living.

She means it, I realize. And despite the awfulness of the conversation, she appears at peace in a way that's difficult to explain. She's a woman nearing the end and knows it. But she's also a woman with no more unfinished business. Her son and her husband are coming home to her. And soon enough, they will be a family again.

Searchers recover more evidence as they scour the mountains. Bolt-holes previously established by Marge and Nemeth containing duffel bags filled with everything from hunting gear to boxes of ammo to additional MREs. No wonder they always seemed one step ahead. They had planned for their strategy well, two lifelong outdoorspeople, putting their knowledge and experience to a much darker use.

The police were able to examine the clothing Nemeth had been wearing when he was first brought to the hospital. Sure enough, the military pants bore Kevlar patches bearing nick marks from my blade, while the shirtsleeve had a bullet hole from Miggy's wild shooting.

Nemeth doesn't leave the hospital. He ends up going into cardiac arrest and that's that. Martin's final victory is complete, though I feel robbed on the subject. At least I can still picture Marge locked up in a cinder-block cell for the rest of her life. She hasn't spoken again since her morning of true confession in Nemeth's room. There are rumors she's on suicide watch. There are more rumors she'll never make it to trial. Plenty of ways to get to someone in prison, and plenty of locals who'd like to see that done.

Luciana and I end up reserving the suite for two weeks. There are that many questions we must answer. Or maybe that many bubble baths and naps that must be taken, as both Luciana and I work our way back to feeling human.

She and Daisy start going for longer and longer walks.

I find myself roaming the streets of Ramsey, getting closer and closer to the edge of town. One day I spy Lisa Rowell driving by and wave at her as she waves back. It feels weird to have been in a place long enough to be recognized by the locals.

It feels disorienting.

When I return that afternoon, I find Luciana sitting quietly at the end of her bed, Daisy sprawled beside her. She looks so serious, I feel my chest tighten with dread.

"We have a gift for you," she says abruptly.

"'We'?"

"Myself, Miguel, Scott, Neil, Josh, and Rob."

"Bob's husband?" Now I'm very confused.

"In the beginning, we all doubted you. Most didn't even want you to come. But none of us would've survived without your perseverance and quick thinking."

Luciana sticks out her hand. It contains a fat envelope. I eye it warily.

"What is it?"

"We respect your lifestyle. This is what you do, and how you choose to live. We also know the pay really sucks."

Now I'm totally flummoxed. "You're . . . you're paying me?"

"Frankie, you've been wearing the same pair of jeans for over a week."

"They're all I have left."

"I know. *We* know. We're not trying to change you. We're just trying to lighten your load. Maybe this makes it easier for you to take up your next case or maybe this enables you to do something else entirely, something you haven't considered before. The future is a gift. You gave it to us. We want to give a piece back to you."

I accept the envelope. No one's ever offered me a wad of money before. And not because some of the other families weren't grateful, but because you can't give what you don't have.

The envelope is very thick. It takes me a few minutes to work it all out. "Oh my God, this is like five thousand bucks."

Luciana smiles. "And yet surviving the three most terrifying days of our lives . . . priceless."

I don't know what to say. My hands are shaking. "Can I at least buy you dinner?"

"You really don't understand this gift thing, do you?"

"It hasn't come up before."

"How about we both do some clothes shopping tomorrow?"

"Okay." Shopping with a friend. I've heard of such things. Maybe Sophie and I did it once upon a time. But it's been so long.

"Oh, and I want you to have this."

"Another gift?"

Luciana smiles, holds out a paracord bracelet. It's in shades of brown and dark green, and the clasp contains a sawtooth edge, similar to the one she lent me at the beginning of our wild adventure. "In case your emergency whistle isn't enough," she tells me.

I snap it around my wrist, genuinely touched. "I didn't get you anything. I didn't think. I'm sorry." Now I'm mortified. She's been so thoughtful; here I am, the selfish one.

"Frankie, stop it." She grabs my hand. "Whatever you're thinking, stop it. This makes us happy. That's gift enough."

I'm going to cry. Except I'm tired of crying. So I hug her instead. Then Daisy wants in on the action, and it quickly becomes a silly, laughing affair that shifts something in my chest. Ever so slightly, but enough. I find that I can breathe for the first time in weeks.

Later, after another huge dinner, I lie in bed, fingering the bracelet around my wrist. I think of what she said. That maybe I could do something different, something I haven't even thought of yet.

What would that be?

What am I really searching for?

We shop. Luciana looks amazing in everything. She decides she needs real cowboy boots, and then while she's at it, ends up with a hat as well. I contain myself till we get to the giant outdoor gear store. Then I can't help myself. I go a little nuts picking out wicking fabrics and pants bulging with pockets that can also be turned into shorts. Multipurpose clothing for the minimalist on the go. I also purchase new boots and a ton of socks.

I have a pang when I genuinely miss my old boots. I console myself that they led a good life and served me well to the end.

What is it I'm really trying to find?

More food. Many of the local establishments know us by now. We return to the steak house from that very first night, where we're immediately told not to worry about the bill. We chatter nonstop and try not to stare at the place where Bob should be sitting or at the half of the table that should be loaded down with platters just for him.

What am I truly looking for?

Final evening before our morning checkout. We both pack, me organizing my new wardrobe into my reliable old suitcase. We indulge in a midnight snack of homemade brownies, then turn in for the night. I lie in the middle of the soft, decadent bed. I listen to the comforting sound of Daisy snoring, the small rustlings of Luciana shifting in her sleep.

Tomorrow, Luciana and Daisy will drive me to Jackson, which has many more transit options. They will then continue on for home.

And me?

On to the case of a missing eight-year-old boy the world has forgotten?

Or something else?

What am I searching for?

Paul accused me of using my cold case obsession to run away from everything. I argued I was running toward. Ten years later, I'm still not sure which one of us was right. The life I lead—my presence matters; my absence never leaves a mark. I keep telling myself I'm okay with that. But maybe, lately . . . Someone in Oregon loves me. A teenage girl in Boston still thinks of me. And Luciana and Daisy, they will always remember me.

It's something, each little pinprick of connection like a distant star. Till maybe someday, I'll no longer be just a shadow passing through, but a constellation of lives touched, people healed, differences made.

Maybe someday, I will return to Boston. Except this time, I'll be ready for it. No longer a woman floating along the edges of life, but a woman who's learned how to seize it with both hands. No longer a work in progress, but a complete soul who understands her worth.

Then, just like that, I have the clarity I need. Who I am now. But also, who I want to one day be.

And then . . . I'm ready to go. The switch has been thrown. It's time to depart.

I climb out of bed in the darkened room. I slip on my new pants, old sneakers. Retrieve my jacket, zip up my bag. I can feel Daisy's eyes upon me as I draw out the thick envelope of bills and count out enough to cover my half of the room. Luciana will squawk when she sees it. But their gift is too much, and a woman with my lifestyle shouldn't be carrying around that much cash anyway.

I cross lightly to Luciana's bed. She's still sleeping. I kiss two of my fingertips and press them lightly against her temple. Then I hug Daisy's boxy head. I tell her, "Never forget, somewhere in this big ole country, there's a drifter who loves you."

I carry my bags to the door.

I could wait till morning, a proper goodbye, a ride to the next town. But this feels right. This . . . feels like me.

One last moment to look around. To feel sad, to feel optimistic. To acknowledge what I've lost, to recognize what I still hope to gain.

Then I step out the door.

My name is Frankie Elkin.

There's a missing eight-year-old boy who deserves to come home again.

And I'm going to find him.

AUTHOR'S NOTE AND ACKNOWLEDGMENTS

People familiar with Wyoming and the Shoshone National Forest are probably reading this going, Devil's Canyon? Where the hell is Devil's Canyon? That's because I made it all up. For this particular story I needed a location with some distinct geographic features. While I'm an avid hiker, and now a big fan of Wyoming, nothing in the real world fits all the requirements I had. So being a fiction writer, I decided to write fiction. It happens.

Writing this book during the pandemic also clipped my research wings. I generally like to personally visit any location I use in a novel. Travel restrictions, however, made a trip to Wyoming infeasible. Instead, I had to rely on my experiences as a hiker plus previous trips west to fill in the gaps. On the other hand, by the end of this novel, I convinced myself I now need to spend some quality time playing in Wyoming. Can't wait!

For information on wilderness searches, I'm deeply indebted to retired New Hampshire Fish and Game conservation officer Rick Estes for sharing his stories and walking me through best practices.

For survival tips and tools, I'm also appreciative of Steve Sanborn from New Hampshire Outdoor Learning Center for his daylong survival course. Most fun playing with fire I've ever had. And like Frankie, I'm now obsessed with the rule of threes.

For readers interested in learning more about the number of people who have disappeared on national public lands, I highly recommend the novel *The Cold Vanish*, by Jon Billman. I also loved discovering the real-life role Bigfoot hunters have played in searching for missing hikers. For more information, check out North America Bigfoot Search as well as the Olympic Project. Please understand my novel is a work of fiction and all mistakes are mine and mine alone.

As a dog lover, I've always been amazed by the incredible skills of working canines. I've had the pleasure of visiting various dog teams over the years. Fictional Daisy came from a real-life story I heard from one of the handlers—how she rescued a pup during one of her deployments and brought it home to be a pet, only to have the goofy mutt surpass all her purebred charges and become her all-time best searcher. To all the Daisys out there, and the humans who fall madly in love with them, this story is for you.

Speaking of rescued animals, congratulations to Lisa Rowell and Laurie Banks, who won character-naming rights after a ferocious bidding war in honor of the Conway Area Humane Society. Lisa chose to have her own name immortalized, while Laurie Banks requested a part in honor of her late birth father, Jim Kelley. My deepest appreciation for your generous donations on behalf of the shelter, and I hope you both enjoy the finished result.

In other good news, there were two lucky winners of the annual Kill a Friend, Maim a Buddy/Mate sweepstakes at www.Lisa Gardner.com. Joanne Cobb won the right for Bobby Monfort to meet a grand end, while Anna Hajlasz nominated herself for fictional fun. Anyone wishing you could also die in one of my novels, the contest is once again open for business. Dream big!

My love to my family and friends, many of whom heard about the making of this book way too much and too often. To Michelle and Larissa, my favorite hiking partners in crime, who also thought spending a day playing with fire in a wilderness survival course was a good idea. To my neighbors Pam and Glenda, who've taught me most of what I know about hiking and, given their nearly encyclopedic memory for trails, continue to recommend new challenges. To Bob, for sharing his own memories of hiking days past while beating me at cribbage, and to Carol, for support and general cheerleading along the way

To my daughter, fellow booklover, and preferred brainstorming partner, who is now launching an exciting new chapter of her life. I am so incredibly proud of you, and miss you already. Can't wait to see where your story goes next.

Finally, in a year and a half that's been like nothing any of us could've expected, my deepest gratitude to my publishing team for hanging in there for all the highs and lows, including my brilliant editors Mark Tarvani and Selina Walker, and my crack agent, Meg Ruley. I'm also so impressed by local bookstores and libraries, who truly went above and beyond to keep us bibliophiles well supplied. Finally, my love to my readers, for sharing the ride and never forgetting the best way to deal with anything is to get lost in a good book.

Looking forward to seeing you all in person someday soon.

ABOUT THE AUTHOR

Lisa Gardner is the #1 *New York Times* bestselling author of twenty-three suspense novels, including *The Neighbor*, which won Thriller of the Year from the International Thriller Writers. An avid hiker, traveler, and cribbage player, she lives in the mountains of New Hampshire with her family.